"*Eyes of the River* is a vivid, captivating and thought-provoking mystery/thriller with a social conscience that grabbed my heart and refused to let it go. It kept me on the edge of my chair from start to finish with a plot that twists and turns and with traumatized and wounded characters who reveal deeper social and political realities and whose compassion and inner strength inspire hope. I LOVED it! A must read!"

— Dorothy Van Soest, author of *Until It's Over, Nuclear Options*, and other Sylvia Jensen mysteries

"Lovers of the storied Mid-Atlantic coast and the region's rich maritime culture will devour Dave Strang's gripping debut novel, a taut political thriller that introduces characters as nuanced and complex as the brackish estuaries of this story's artfully drawn setting."

— Ellie Storck

"In Dave Strang's beautiful debut novel, *Eyes of the River*, a rundown marina on a neglected riverfront holds so much more than the ancient bits of nautical life collected in an old shed and curated by Tre, a gentle, homeless Vietnam veteran. Rick, also a vet, is a sentry, keeping Tre safe from the outer world while trying to navigate it, haunted by his own demons. These two men are the heart of this political caper about a young girl's disappearance. Dave Strang juxtaposes the resilient human hearts of these two veterans upon the soulless power elite of Washington as the search for Allie intensifies. This novel sensitively reveals triumph over that which can break us, with language that asks the reader to pay full attention to the observable and to ponder what lies beneath. Beautiful!"

— Nancy Burke, author of *Only The Women Are Burning*

"A haunting and deeply moving tale of friendship, redemption, and the enduring bonds forged in war's crucible. *Eyes of the River* is a masterful exploration of how three Marines—Rick Larson, Tremaine Wilson, and Adrian Dumars—navigate the long shadows of Vietnam while building an unlikely sanctuary along Washington D.C.'s forgotten Anacostia River. Dave Strang has crafted a gripping thriller that transcends genre boundaries, weaving together elements of political suspense, family drama, and profound meditation on trauma and healing. At its heart lies the extraordinary friendship between Rick and Tre—an honoring and heartbreaking portrayal of PTSD and veteran brotherhood. The novel's vivid setting along the

Anacostia transforms a forgotten corner of the nation's capital into a character unto itself, while the author's unflinching examination of power, corruption, and the price of survival resonate with startling relevance. Both intimate and sweeping, *Eyes of the River* is a testament to the possibility of redemption and the healing power of human connection. Dave Strang writes with the heart of a true storyteller, delivering a novel that will stay with readers long after the final page."

— Sarah Corley

"In *Eyes of the River* Dave Strang weaves an intricate narrative which, as the title would suggest, flows steadily with interest as the reader discovers hidden tributaries that appear along the stream. There is steady and ever increasing current in the writing to keep things moving along when unexpected eddies and rapids envelop the characters along the journey. The reader is in for a detailed and thoroughly enjoyable voyage through the literary waters."

— Major John G. Soule, USMC/USAF, Retired

"*Eyes of the River* is a story that will keep you turning pages, reluctant to put it down. A novel layered with rich detail, as each character's past unfolds and weaves together. Dave Strang is a master storyteller, crafting scenes that evolve with both subtlety and emotional depth, immersing you in a world that feels vivid, textured, and alive on the page."

— Delia Sullivan, contributing author, *Deserts to Mountaintops: Choosing Healing Through Radical Self-Acceptance, Vol. 2*

"Much like the Anacostia River it depicts, this beautifully written novel is a haunting portrait of two veterans suffering from the psychological scars of combat, trying to survive in a world that has passed them by. Dave Strang crafts a richly atmospheric and intricately layered setting that mirrors the characters' inner lives and circumstances, building steadily toward an intense and character driven finale."

— Rob Wood, SSGT, USAF, Retired

"*In Eyes of the River*, Dave Strang delivers a gripping story of loyalty, sacrifice, and the enduring bonds of military brotherhood. As past and present collide, long-buried truths surface, revealing the unseen cost of war carried quietly by those who served. Blending emotional depth with the tension of a compelling mystery, this powerful novel pulls the reader into a world where honor, memory, and redemption flow beneath every page."

— Adora Winquist Soule, Co-Founder, MilSpec Formulas

"I loved this story! What an adventure, from DC to Maine and back to the eerie marina setting, which was such a wonderful and safe sanctuary until it wasn't. Dave Strang has told a wonderful story about friendship, companionship, trust, connectedness and devotion, which results in redemption for some and justice for all."

— Howard Snyder

"*Eyes of the River* has all the hallmarks of great fiction: memorable characters, a unique setting, authentic dialogue, and a thrilling storyline. Dave Strang compassionately captures the shared anguish and enduring friendship of three Vietnam veterans ravaged by the lasting trauma of war. As a mysterious disappearance unfolds, the tumultuous search hooks you early on, keeps you on the line as it twists and turns, and reels you in completely with a dramatic climax. My only regret is that the exciting adventure had to come to an end, but what a wonderful ending!"

— Jeff May

"What an incredible read! A powerful, character driven novel with emotional urgency that pulls you in slowly and then doesn't let go, moving you to the edge of your seat. Underneath the story, it's about connection, atonement, and how people carry, and sometimes overcome, the weight of their past. An impressive and engaging debut work with a strong sense of place and purpose. It's a great story and definitely worth the read!"

— Dolan Sullivan

EYES
OF THE
RIVER

EYES
OF THE
RIVER

Dave Strang

First Edition

Library of Congress Control Number: 2025948873

Casebound ISBN: 978-1-62720-674-7
Paperback ISBN: 978-1-62720-675-4
Ebook ISBN: 978-1-62720-676-1

Cover by Leo Arcelay-Christiano
Internal Design by Leo Arcelay-Christiano and Cecelia Durborow
Editorial Development by Chase Lawson
Promotional Development by Chase Lawson

Published by Apprentice House Press

Loyola University Maryland
4501 N. Charles Street, Baltimore, MD 21210
410.617.5265
www.ApprenticeHouse.com
info@ApprenticeHouse.com

Dedication

With Gratitude for all Courage and Heart
Shared in Service and Kindness to Others

Chapter 1

A short, muffled crack carried downriver on the brisk March wind. Richard Larson froze, fearing it was a rifle round. His back to the marina's cavernous storage shed, he stood motionless beneath the towering overhead door's suspended bottom rail. Silence had returned instantly to the dimly lit structure, but the sound echoed in Rick's mind. He peered toward the river, only two hundred feet away, his eyes narrowed on obscure reflections across the water's surface as unwanted memories from a long-ago war rushed him. Pressure gripped Rick's chest. *How could it be a shot?* The isolated property's oppressive quiet lay heavy around him as it did each day. Long seconds of uncertainty passed before he stepped tentatively across the concrete floor's crumbling edge, emerging from shadow into the late afternoon sunlight. Instantly, he caught the windshield glare from Allie's green Jeep parked across the lot next to his truck. Rick crossed to the center of the entrance drive and spun, hurriedly scanning the empty access road, the abandoned boats on stands, the piers, and stretches of desolate waterfront, growing anxious in search of his friend. *Another muffled crack.* He strained to listen a brief moment, then scrambled down the drive to the small office, throwing open the door and calling out. The sole occupant, his old Lab, Schooner, raised a weary glance and struggled from his bed as Rick turned away.

Rick rounded the office corner and hurried along the eroded gravel path leading toward the water and docks. Pier D was the longest, extending out into the Anacostia past a small cove along the river's west bank. Rick stumbled to a halt on its badly cupped first board and squinted over the pier's length. Beads of sweat drifted down his temples. He rotated nervously, looking north and south along the riverbank, fearful of hearing the sound again.

His scan followed along the shoreline's mix of deteriorated bulkhead and stone rip rap, finally coming to rest on the towering cherry tree; the river's 'Old Man'. A green backpack leaned against the base of the twisted trunk. Rick's eyes darted along each branch as he started across the feeble grass buffer toward the tree. One hundred feet away, he came to a halt, finally spotting Allie sitting safely in the cradle of the lowest branch. He stumbled back a step and leaned over, lowering both hands to his knees and forcing slower breaths as relief gradually filled him. He straightened and wiped the sweat from his neck, trying to calm the hammering in his chest and allowing time for the demons to fade.

Just feet from the river's eroded bank, the scraggly but noble tree had survived eighty years precariously clinging to life, with thick roots extended out from the ground before bending down into the water in search of the river's bottom. With only the rough bark to reach for on that lowest branch, Allie had steadied herself against the cool March wind. The first limb offered the best seat, having grown strangely flat on top and long enough for a visitor to stretch out, a comfortable perch from which to relax and feel alone with the river. The tree's majestic canopy revealed its long and troublesome life. The few hearty branches around her swayed playfully, already budding, appearing eager to welcome the new season. The many more dead ones creaked and groaned in the weather, hanging on without the promise of leaves as they had for years, bending and dancing with confidence though, knowing the old tree would never let them go no matter how hard the elements punished. Lower on the trunk, the scars and carvings, too numerous to count, had sealed; forever to age with the old tree's skin, stories across the weathered bark in testimony to this stoic keeper's enduring purpose.

Rick steadied and started again for the Old Man. Schooner ambled up alongside, staying close, nuzzling his hand.

Allie watched intently as they drew near. "Hey, old man."

Rick managed a half wave before turning away, his watchful gaze fixed in one last survey of the piers, the marina lot, the shoreline, the river. Eyeing the sagging third pier, he mumbled, "You talking to me, Schooner or the tree?"

"The tree of course! Morning Rick." Her smile faded. "You look worried. Are you okay?"

"I always worry about you!" he said sharply. Rick's watch followed upriver again, examining the dance of dark patches of water where the brisk wind pushed across. His jaw tensed, attentive to every noise.

"Rick?"

"Yeah," he faltered. "I was worried. You okay?" He inhaled deeply. "I heard something—I think. Just a minute ago."

"Not me," Allie beamed, showing her ear buds before pocketing them.

"Good," he said quietly. "Guess I'm getting old, too." He rubbed the back of his neck; thankful the dark flashbacks had been carried away.

He turned to her, forcing a faint smile. "Don't often see you without a book in hand."

"Too cold out here," she said. "Audios on the way over."

"It's Saturday. I didn't think you'd be coming. Thought the senator had a big fundraiser tonight."

"The *senator*!" Allie leaned her head back against the trunk. A small brightly colored wool cap provided some cushion. She pulled the remaining length of blowing hair aside and looked toward the higher branches. Rick watched her expression change as both hands raised dramatically to her face.

"My God, I had to get out of there," She shook her head. "You wouldn't believe the way that bitch talks to people around her. Me included."

"Easy. Yes, I would. You've told me many stories. And I believe them all. Still sorry, too."

"The woman's always been on me and it's getting worse. I can't wait for Stanford."

"A couple more months and then the world's your oyster. Hang in there."

"I don't know," she started in a mumble. "What will you do when I'm gone? Gonna miss me?"

"And your words of wisdom. I already do."

A sudden gust rustled the branches. Allie leaned forward, grabbing her hair in frustration, and tightening the band. Soon, she focused across the murky water.

"How's he doing?" she asked. "Have you seen him lately?"

"Tremaine?" Rick paused. "Just this morning. I think he's okay. Still coughing. Still tells me to mind my own business."

"I like it when you call him Tre." Tilting her head, she peeked at the old Lab. "Schooner go?"

"Always."

"You two are a cute couple." Allie pulled her legs around, faded jeans, colorful, thick socks and well-worn canvas high tops hanging close above Rick's head. Resting both hands on the branch, her eyebrows lifted. "Did you give him the flowers?" she asked, letting her feet swing back and forth.

"I did. He loved them. He gave them a place of prominence."

Rick took a step back.

She nodded and let herself drop. "Good," she said mid-flight. As was their pattern, she fist bumped him and grinned. "So, I'm helping him with the decorations. When do I get to go see Tre's digs?"

"Soon," Rick said.

"That's what you always say."

"Only when you ask."

She focused across the water again toward the small island almost a mile north. "Sometimes if I look hard, I think I can see him."

"Well, he can see you. He cares about you."

She spun. "Really? After meeting just a couple of times? That's so nice."

"A handful of hours together is a lifetime in his mind. And, well, he's a great judge of character."

"He always acts like we're best friends."

"That's what happens when he lets you in."

"You both do. And I don't get that a lot. It feels good." Allie paused, seeming lost in thought. "I'd just like to see him again, spend some more time getting to know him, and his stories; *he* should write a book."

"He's a person worth knowing."

Rick watched her expression soften with a gentle nod as she refocused across the water. A brisk gust suddenly swirled, and Allie hunched her shoulders up against the cold, pushing both hands deep into her coat pockets.

"Hey," Rick said. "Tre gave me this. Something he made specially for you." Reaching into his large pocket, he pulled out a tattered, brown lunch bag, stained and wrinkled, with a red heart drawn on one side. Old twine cinched it tightly at the top, hiding something small, with corners and a firm surface.

Allie reached with gentle hands, her eyes widening as she rotated it. She held it to her ear with an emerging grin. "Do you know what it is?"

"He wouldn't tell me, thought I might ruin the surprise. Said it would be best to open it when you get home."

"That's no fun."

"Here," Rick said. "Take this, too." He pulled a sealed envelope from his coat pocket and handed it to her, the crooked stamp applied upside down.

She lifted an eyebrow. "Still no mailbox?"

"It's on the list." He winced. "Do you mind?"

Allie teased him with a wink. "Hmm, not sure. Is this her birthday card?"

Rick crossed his arms.

"You know, you could always just deliver it," she added. "We could go together. I could meet her!" Allie's hopeful voice trailed off, hearing a sudden rumble from tires crossing the gravel lot.

Rick turned toward the office. He took a step, then hesitated, listening for the sound of a turnaround and exit. He knew of no reason for anyone to pay a visit to his marina. It wouldn't be one of the slip holders this time of year; each of them wintered elsewhere, all seven of them. All were older and never found motivation for boat puttering until the weather warmed up. It was unlikely to be a delivery vehicle; there hadn't been one in eight months. His marina wasn't on anyone's beaten path and the location presented as too isolated for a lost soul to wander in by mistake. Any wrong turn would have been evident a mile up the road, where opportunities existed to backtrack. No explanation came to mind. The scrunch of worn stone waned to silence, out of sight behind the office. Rick frowned and headed down the pier, Allie's voice trailing after him.

"Hey, maybe it's some business," she quipped.

The comment received a half stop from Rick and a glance over his shoulder. To her grin, he returned a brief scowl, then continued down the boards toward the lot.

~

"Okay, tell me again how I was volunteered for this outing? In the middle of a Saturday?" Sarah Cromwell glanced across the car toward her daughter.

Lou's hands gripped around the wheel. She lowered her head to peer under the visor. "The gate was open, but my God, Mom, look at this place. Should we have called first?"

Their car idled behind a half dozen engine blocks lined up end to end as wheel stops in front of the marina's small, fatigued office. Left of the door, peeling paint hung across the letters, 'Welcome'. Every window showed caked layers of gravel dust. An old truck sat parked in front of the last discarded engine, a green Jeep next to it.

"I don't know, this is your adventure, dear."

They scanned the property for signs of life.

"See any old, rabid dogs?"

Sarah sighed and twisted in the seat. "Listen, I'm Noah's biggest fan and you know I love everything about this gesture, but do you still think you're going to find it *here*?"

"Beginning to have my doubts."

Sarah quickly surveyed the property once more, then reached a hand to Lou's shoulder. "C'mon, no backing out now. I see no dogs, and the coast appears to be clear. This is the only building that could pass for an office; let's try it."

"The article in the Post mentioned a Mr. Larson. God, I hope he doesn't have an eye patch."

The car alarm beeped loudly as both doors closed.

~

Seconds later, Rick appeared from around the corner and plodded toward them, his forehead creased. He stalled three feet away, taking his time to assess the strangers. Similar in height, close in size. Same eyes and high cheeks, same curl in the corner of their smiles. Both wore quality clothes. The complete picture, decidedly out of place amid the surroundings. Thirtyish for the younger woman, harder to tell for the older one. Streaks of gray showed in her hair but well cared for skin could suggest she was an older sister, if not the mother. Rick picked up on the perfume and shook his head, waiting. Schooner caught up and strolled past to welcome the guests.

"He's friendly," Rick assured. "You both look lost. Like you took a wrong turn." He crossed his arms, watching the two trade stares.

Lou tilted her head, raising her brows toward her mother.

Sarah's lips flattened briefly while she drew a breath. Finally, she directed a poised expression to Rick, stepped forward, and extended her hand. "I'm Sarah Cromwell, and this is my daughter, Lou. We're looking for a Mr. Larson. The owner, I believe?"

"You found him. So, not lost. What do you need?"

Sarah brought her hands together in a soft clap. "Well, it's kind of an interesting story, Mr. Larson. Lou was intrigued with an article in the Washington Post last week about this marina. Your marina. You see, my daughter's soon-to-be fiancé is very fond of boats. You might say he's obsessed with anything that floats—"

"So, you're here for the parts." Rick's hands went to his hips.

"Well, yes. Boat stuff, right? The article—it was wonderful by the way. Describing the history of your place here, and a mysterious shed overflowing with rare collectibles; boat parts of all kinds, scavenged from old vessels. Over decades! Always the romantic, my daughter imagined finding a unique birthday present in your shed for Noah, the man she loves." Sarah paused to insert a smile.

"We were wondering if any of the things might be for sale, and if so, if we could possibly poke around to see what we could find."

Rick nodded. "You're thinking flea market."

Lou chimed in. "A treasure hunt?"

He held his gaze on Sarah. "And you're the consultant?"

"Just a spectator, and a loving mother."

Rick drew a hand across his beard stubble. "You come a long way to get here?"

"No, actually, we could almost be neighbors. We're not far at all."

"You say so." Rick eyed their clothes and shoes again. "Shouldn't be too hard then, to come back next weekend. Today's no good. Sorry. Not ready to let folks stroll through that old shed. If you do decide to come back, though, I'd suggest you both pick out something else from the closet. Lots to trip on in that old building, and probably a few things livin' under the shelves you'll wanna be able to kick if you have to."

"Oh," Lou bit her lip. "Maybe we could borrow your dog? As a guide?"

Rick chuckled. "Schooner knows 'em all by name in there, but he wouldn't be any help. Not much of a bark left."

"Too bad," Lou mumbled. "So, next week?"

"Saturday. Rain or shine. And be early if you want the first look. Lots of calls from people wanting to come by and root through all of it." He twisted, pointing. "It's that big blue shed at the end of the property, right across from the travel lift. Doors will be open. Don't go climbing on the racks I have in there. Pull out what you want and put it in a pile and let me know when you're done. And one more thing, there's a boat in the shed. A 43' Constellation. Chris Craft. Don't bother me with questions about how it got in there or why. She's mine, it's home, and not for sale. Good luck, ladies. Come early. Snakes like to sleep late."

Allie emerged from behind the office and strolled up casually behind Rick. Schooner's tail wagged.

Rick turned. "Allie, meet Sarah and Lou Cromwell. Mother-daughter scavenger team. Trying to be the first to pick through Tre's treasure."

"Hmm." Allie leaned forward. "Watch out for all the snakes."

"Okay then!" Lou clapped her hands together. "That sounds like our cue, Mr. Larson. It was, umm, so nice to meet you. And you, Allie. Thank you for the words of caution. Next Saturday it is."

Sarah held steady eye contact as her expression softened. She extended a hand to Rick's and winked. "You're a good storyteller, Mr. Larson. We'll be sure to bring our boots."

Lou hurried them to the car, and Allie waved as they drove off. She turned instantly and tugged on Rick's sleeve.

"Hey, that Sarah, she's pretty, huh?"

Rick frowned, catching her grin.

"And she's about your age. A little company would be nice. You noticed, didn't you?"

"Too old to notice."

"Bullshit. You're not dead."

"Thanks for confirming that. Besides, I have company."

"An old dog and me? There may be something in between."

Rick's frown held. He intended it as a flag; time for the banter to end.

"Don't you have a fancy party to get ready for?" he asked.

Allie checked her phone. "Ouch! Yes! I gotta go."

"Try to enjoy it."

"Politicians and rich people. What's not to like?"

"Maybe you'll meet someone interesting."

She turned for a hug. "I already did." Pulling back, she held up the gift. "And by the way, you know I'm going to need to thank Tre in person for this."

"We'll see."

"Soon, right?"

"Soon. Careful with it."

Allie held it in both hands, pulling it to her chest.

"Bye, Mr. Larson."

"Bye, Ms. Sheridan. Be safe."

Stones shuffled as Allie backed out. Rick watched her accelerate too fast through the gate, shaking his head and waiting for the gravel dust to settle. He called for Schooner and trudged across the lot past derelict support buildings toward the old storage shed. The dominating structure had served its purpose well for decades, providing shelter for boats undergoing whatever surgery and repair might be needed. Now though, boats no longer sought care or refuge at Rick's, and the building's patina showed mostly as rust, invited by neglect and old age. Across the metal wall and roof panels, the consuming distress signaled the approaching end of life. But not just yet, Rick hoped. The building had one last story in this marina's life to share, and some TLC was needed to ready it.

Rick moved to the large overhead door. His gaze rose to the three worn flags, none of which had been lowered in years. He saluted and moved to the lift chain. He needed the door to cooperate just a while longer; to raise and lower with only moderate effort required. Each time he considered its dimension, though, doubt made him pause. Rick inhaled and started to pull. Loose rust immediately turned his hands a deep orange. A stiff gust of wind swirled around the corner of the shed and swept across the door's face. Rick halted, clutching the chain, and eyeing the groaning panels above him, debating whether he needed the full twenty-foot-high opening for light. He nodded to the dancing flags and started again, more slowly. The door's guides creaked as each panel rose higher along the loose rails. The door hung up, then freed. Rick cursed and encouraged in the same words. When the last panel cleared, he hooked the links and stepped back. Schooner stood close, panting, and patiently waiting for the 'okay' to enter into the warmth. The late afternoon's shadows had begun their stretch across the property, but determined remnants of sunlight crept into the shed, drifting into dark corners, exploring the incredible space as if for the first time. Rick sighed, surveying the task. He would be happy to do the strenuous work for his friend this week. Tre would struggle to say goodbye to this haven.

Chapter 2

East of Washington, DC, the narrow Anacostia curved off the Potomac River at Buzzard Point and meandered north for eight miles. For much of his life, Rick Larson had lived along the tributary's western edge and had shared in its struggle amid the discord across two very different worlds. The waters and adjoining land south of the Pennsylvania Avenue bridge crossing had experienced a rebirth, fueled by responsibility and hope: restoration efforts, new development, and community green spaces. A vision for renewed life seemingly far removed from Rick's setting along the same shoreline just two miles north of the bridge, where the sluggish branch offered little welcome across it's sickly waters and neglected banks.

Historic monuments, graceful landscapes and the United States Capitol, remarkably, were not far—a doable walk away—but the oppressive isolation along this section of riverfront had held inspiration at bay for decades and no new dreams of change appeared. Rick's operation and one other abandoned working marina remained as the solitary residents along this slender stretch of land between the waters' edge and the inadequate, shadowing road; M Street, SE. A winding, constricted paved section in disrepair, barely wide enough in places for two vehicles to pass, and providing the only access to both. Rick's two-acre marina had sustained a simple life for him, but little work entered the gates anymore. It was a forgotten place whose time was passing away, much like its neighbor, the forgotten river. Rick Larson had come to this isolated refuge thirty-five years ago, embracing the waters' eternal loneliness, and hoping to forget as well. But could a river have two souls, as he occasionally considered true for himself? He believed so and often pondered the contradiction; his river would never be postcard worthy—never adorned of majestic breadth—but to Rick, a residing serenity would always lay across her forsaken waters.

~

The weather deteriorated through the rest of the weekend and refused to abate. Tuesday late afternoon found Rick with both hands planted against the cold wall paneling, peering through a cracked window from his small office. With termite-infested walls void of insulation, siding in disrepair and a sagging roof, the old building struggled to shelter its occupants when the cold wind blustered. Rough work accommodations squeezed around a closet-sized bathroom and an occasionally used bed in one corner.

The fire was fading in the undersized wood stove. Rick added the last small log, nursing the only source of heat and trying for patience. He rubbed his hands close to the pot, staring blankly at the flame. Today required a delivery, a task he would never search for reason to postpone. But here he stood again, stalling in front of the warmth, after finding new ways to wander the small, tired space and repeatedly glancing outside for any sign of a break in the weather. A broken branch landed suddenly and scraped across the metal roof. Rick shook his head; the Old Man was testing him. He straightened and roamed again, busying himself rinsing dishes, organizing papers on the desk, leveling the framed photographs sprinkled across the front wall. Soon restless again, he circled back to his desk and reassessed the weather radar and hourly forecast.

Schooner sat patiently at the door, watching each of his movements. Rick frowned at his watch, hesitated, then pushed back from the screen and crossed to the bed for his coat, gloves, and hat. He grabbed both bags of supplies and opened the door to an immediate greeting from the raw March blast and heavy snow, both extending a challenge to their decision to walk out on the pier. Rick slammed the door behind them and pulled his collar closed. Clutching the bags to his chest, he dropped his head to watch the footing.

The northwesterly should have been diminishing by 5:00 p.m., but it persisted, relentless in strength and still cold across the water. Mercifully, the shoreline provided some wind shadow, and the gusts seeking to torment the river's surface held a ways offshore. Rick took note of the conditions but didn't pause. At the end of the pier, he managed a slow, careful step down onto the small skiff's gunwale and settled in at the stern. He primed the gas line ball and pulled several times on the old outboard's cord, calling it to life. The engine reluctantly sputtered before settling into a smoky, loud two-cylinder chorus. He brushed the flakes from his sleeves and checked his watch again, regretting the earlier procrastination, as a push of heavier snow swirled around them. He glanced at the sky and shook his head, uncertain whether enough daylight remained for the trip. He inhaled the cold and leaned down to confirm the gas level in the small tank.

The old Lab stood nobly on the pier, panting slowly, wagging his tail, attention locked on each deliberate move Rick made and waiting for the invitation. As Rick pulled a tarp over the bags sitting at the bow, he called over his shoulder.

"You know, you'd be a lot more comfortable if you went back inside. You're not a pup anymore, and it's damn cold out here." He eyed Schooner, the tail still in motion. Arthritis aside, Rick knew the dog wouldn't budge from the pier until he returned. In his younger days, Schooner would likely have jumped off and tried to swim after him if left behind. They stared at each other for a moment, the familiar pose played out hundreds of times before. Schooner's tail moved faster as they both anticipated the negotiation's inevitable outcome. Rick scowled and reached up to lift his loyal companion off the pier.

"We're getting too old for this, you know." Both groaned for their own reasons as Rick carefully situated Schooner on the blanket, already prepared and lying across the floorboards. Content, he curled up quickly and shared an appreciative sigh.

⁓

Allie shook the wrapped heavy chain in disbelief, never having encountered a locked gate at the marina. Her eyes darted across the lot. She grabbed the fencing and shook it frantically.

"Rick! No!" she cried out. "Let me in, please be here!"

The wind shrieked at her. Snow circled chaotically. She searched the length of fence for a break. Twenty feet away, behind the ivy-covered trunk of an old walnut tree, a section hung loosely off the post. The opening seemed too small, but Allie ran to it and pulled on the free edge. The hole opened slowly. She fell backwards, still clutching at the chain-link, straining against the rusty diamond mesh. A wire tie gave way, and the fencing loosened more. Allie lowered to hands and knees and forced her way into the gap. Her left leg was last to squeeze through the opening, but the baggy sweatpants snagged. She reached back, clutching at the material until it pulled free. As she rolled away, the back of her wrist caught a jagged edge of wire. She tried to stand quickly but stumbled. Catching herself, she saw the blood—a shallow cut, but substantial bleeding spread immediately across her hand. Shocked, she felt a rush of nausea, then dizziness, but she managed plodding steps to the center of the marina lot. She screamed for Rick, trembling as she rotated slowly past the office, the shed, and the rows of old boats.

⁓

Schooner slept curled, head buried, hiding from the weather. The gusts found them occasionally, sending snow sideways against the port side of the skiff and screaming through loose rigging of the few sailboats still slipped at the marina. Rick took a few seconds for a resolved look upriver; intending to stay near shore, in the lee, as close as the bottom would allow. He pushed away from the pier and turned the throttle grip for more speed. The old engine grudgingly complied. He leaned forward, laying the blanket over Schooner, adding an affectionate hand on the greying nose. He settled back and pulled his thick hood tight, masking the first scream from behind struggling vainly to reach him against the storm.

Allie ran down the pier, waving her arms, crying out for Rick to come back, her torn sweats, tennis shoes, and dark tee shirt all dusted with snow. The tireless wind blew hard across her face, tangling her long hair. She fought it back with frantic motions, still pleading after him. Quivering, she fell to her knees and wrapped both arms around her ribs, holding herself against the cold. She wiped the tears from her cheeks and yelled hopelessly one last time for Rick, searching the gray water as the skiff disappeared around a bend in the shoreline.

An ominous shiver swept over Allie's body, and she forced herself to stand. Her steps wavered along the length of slippery pier as she struggled toward the gravel lot. Her tearing eyes blurred the fading sky and darkening shadows growing behind overgrown buildings and equipment in ruins. Across the rutted drive, a metal door into the large storage shed creaked and flailed helplessly against the building's metal siding. Above the frame, a rusty fixture's weak, yellow light flickered.

Allie lifted her backpack. She wiped the snow from her brow and peered upriver, a last hope Rick had heard, but the skiff did not appear. She shuddered, braced against the wind, and staggered toward the shed.

Chapter 3

Two days later, the snow was melting, but more was forecast. Roads were clear and Rick crawled past the parking lot a second time. No empty spots. He grumbled at the need to walk but accepted it as a good sign; lots of help for Thursday night's cooking. He parked a block away and negotiated the elevated sections of wavy concrete sidewalk where the largest roots had not been denied their journey. The kitchen door stood open, as it did on most nights when both ovens were in use, regardless of the temperature outside. The space held no operable windows. Trinity Cathedral's adjoining Parish Hall, however, revealed many; large and vertical, each one featuring a unique collage of stained glass. All the lights were on inside and the tall openings glowed in radiant welcome.

Rick stopped on the concrete landing and looked in with anticipation, hoping to see Allie. He could count on her attending every third week or so. He surveyed the bustling kitchen: four men, two women, one teenager, and Fay Wilson, Trinity's tireless senior warden. Each worked at different stations, some moving quickly and efficiently, others more deliberately. All efforts toward the goal were valued, though; package one hundred quarts of soup for delivery to other shelters across the city and to make the same number of sandwiches for those on the street who would never go inside again. Rick nodded his approval at the exuberance; loud conversation, people talking over each other, instructions, stories, and some laughter. Fay was singing her hymns. Rick sighed. It was a good turnout for prep night, but no Allie.

~

Rick inspected the large soup pan and dropped it back into the sink. His hand swirled, searching the soapy water again for the brush.

The young man working alongside finished drying the last plate and turned to him. "Fay told me you started all of this."

Rick's head tilted. "Not alone." He paused in thought. "Years ago, there was a January storm; we lost an old friend from the war." Rick fixated on the water, his forearm flexing with each push against the pan.

Fay came up behind and rested her hand on Rick's shoulder. "The poor soul was out on the street alone in need of everything, wasn't he, Rick? Wasn't any good shelter from the wind and cold *that* night!" Her lips pressed together as she examined the sink. "Sorry, my friend. Looks like someone left us with their clean up, huh?"

Rick cast a frown.

"Thanks for getting this out of the way," she said, patting his back. "See you've met Kyle, our newest high school recruit. Friend of Allie's."

Rick's hands slowed in the sink. He eyed Kyle, then lifted the pan to inspect again. "Kyle was asking about the start," he said over his shoulder.

Fay shook her head. "Humbling night, to say the least, young man. The snow and the blowing; loud and tireless for a full day and into the early morning hours." Fay's brows closed as she pointed a finger at Kyle. "The fury of it was warning us what was coming. Storm took two of our dear ones overnight."

Rick glanced at Kyle. "Dehydration," he said quietly. "And our friend was starving," Rick sprayed warm water across the pan. "He fell asleep and didn't wake up. The cold likely didn't make a difference."

"So avoidable." Fay rubbed Rick's back and sighed. "Two weeks later, though, Mr. Larson here and one Tremaine Wilson discovered the same purpose." Fay rotated, extending her arms to the bustling group. "And here we are," she said with a satisfied smile. "First thought was to stage out of Delia's diner down the street, but she sent 'em here; their dreams were too big. Trinity had the facilities—"

"And Trinity had Fay Wilson," Rick chimed in, as he pulled the strainer open to a noisy rush of water.

Fay turned to Kyle, gesturing with her hand again. "And what Fay Wilson had was the Holy Spirit!" she blared. "And no better co-pilot when you need to get something done! And he was fine giving Richard some space, 'cause back then, there wasn't any pattern in this man's life or love for organized religion, so the idea of teaming with a church made him pause. But I kept plenty of just that in reserve to cover him. And Tremaine, he and I found good common ground around the meaning of spirituality." Fay winked. "Mine's usually spoken. His is always silent. But it was all meant to work out."

Rick leaned against the sink, folding his arms.

Fay went on, shaking her head. "And all of it about that sad night, Kyle. Was a tragedy what happened in that storm, and Lord knows Rick and Tremaine suffered enough tragedy in that war. Feels like the same overwhelming struggles, though; unachievable objectives, unrelenting loss. All seems the same to me at times."

Fay held a hand to her heart briefly with a solemn nod to Rick. Then she twisted the corner of her mouth and tugged on Kyle's shirt. "Now, go on, and you be sure and keep all that in mind while you peel those bags of potatoes."

~

The soup had been cooling in the refrigerators for fifteen minutes and the energy across the kitchen had shifted to clean up. Rick kept his back to the room, head down again at the three-compartment sink, finishing up the last of the deep pans.

Fay looked up from scrubbing the iron stove top and called across the room. "So, where was your partner tonight, Rick?"

"Allie, or Tre?" he asked over his shoulder.

"The cute one."

"Thought so. I don't know, Fay. I was hoping she would be here."

"We missed her. She's always good with a knife and the veggies. Had a good teacher."

"Tre was that."

"Tell her we said hello. Maybe next week, huh?"

Rick focused on rinsing. "Hope so, Fay."

Forty-five minutes later, all was ready for the drivers to pick up early the next morning. The guests had eaten, and the night team arrived. Fay hit the last light switch. Rick shut down the exhaust fan. One emergency light remained on all night. Fay waited at the exterior door holding a box.

Rick didn't try to hide his tired limp as he approached. "Thank you, dear."

She patted his shoulder and handed it to him. "Tell our friend it's a good delivery this week. Nice flavors, and we made it go farther than usual. He's going to enjoy that chicken salad."

"He always does."

"I know. Give him a hug, and Allie, too. I put enough in there for her; in case she surprises you tomorrow and your fridge is empty."

"I hope she does, Fay. I would like that."

Fay eyed Rick and said, "My friend, you seem exhausted and worried, and I can tell you're ready to be done for the night." She leaned in for her weekly kiss on his cheek, as he held the door. "Allie's fine." She reassured him with a quick hug. "Now, go home."

Rick chewed on his lip and scanned the kitchen, then ambled across the space to check the double doors into the parish hall. A separate door across from the pantry entered into a narrow corridor. Rick stepped quietly along its length coming to a stop at the entry into a smaller gathering space. He peered in through the half-glass panel. Fewer windows, high ceilings, calming lighting. The sleeping area for this cold March evening. Essential refuge. Fifteen cots lined both long walls. A few unclaimed beds remained. Many of the guests though, were already asleep. With daylight ended, others who held part time work would begin to arrive soon, leaving no beds empty before lights out. The small television sat on a corner table with low volume on the college basketball game, but only for another twenty minutes; the shelter required all to be quiet at 10:00 p.m. The offer of a safe, warm place, for one night of life at a time.

A loud buzzer sounded at the exterior door down the hall. Rick noticed the overnight assistant greet a middle-aged man and his young daughter. The assistant signed them in. Rick took a few steps closer to listen. The man asked about food, hope in his voice for a couple of unclaimed reserve meals. The assistant shook his head but offered to check the kitchen. Rick approached as Tony started out of his chair.

"Rick," he said. "Hey brother. Didn't hear ya. Late night for you guys, huh?"

"We're never finished 'til Fay says we are."

Tony grinned. "I hear that."

Rick faced the man and offered the bag. "Chicken salad," he said. "And the soup should still be warm. Please take it, I can get more."

"Hey, thanks, Rick." Tony turned to the man and his daughter. "There's a small table just inside the room there. If you're quiet, it should be okay. I'll get you some water and spoons."

The man hesitated, then reached out a shaking hand to accept the gift. He pulled out a sandwich for the young girl. "You're Rick?" he asked.

Rick nodded.

"Just a minute ago . . ." The man shot a nervous look to Tony. "There was a guy outside. Parked across Pennsylvania. He saw we were coming in and caught up with us. Said he was looking for a girl. High school girl. He said she might be working here this evening, maybe even staying here." The man took an anxious bite of sandwich. "Mentioned a guy named, Rick. Big guy. So, that's you?"

Rick stepped closer, studying his exhausted expression. "What kind of car?"

The man chewed as he spoke. "Black, expensive, quiet. He handed me a hundred dollars and asked me to let him know if she was in here. Maybe a Tesla. He said he'd wait."

The impulse hit and Rick stepped brusquely past him, uninterested in hearing any last words. He pushed hard through the door, but his hip twisted on the first step. He started to stumble but grabbed hold of the handrail in time. He limped to the corner of 19th and Pennsylvania and scanned in both directions. The thoroughfare had quieted for the night: only a few cars and some delivery trucks, only a handful of late-night dog walkers. Three customers congregated outside the convenience store a half block to the west. Rick crossed 19th to see farther along Pennsylvania, but no cars were parked along either curb. The ache buried deeper across his leg, but he pressed ahead up the street. Hearing the sudden acceleration seconds later, he spun, catching just a glimpse of a dark car's taillights exiting 19th and speeding away down Pennsylvania.

Rick halted his search and struggled to lower onto the steps in front of a laundromat. He rubbed the soreness and peered down the sidewalk toward Trinity Cathedral, replaying the last few minutes and the curious urgency that overcame him.

Chapter 4

The unsettling dream woke Rick at 2:30 that night, after three hours of sleep. He pushed up instantly, desperate to preserve the intense images, but each one he tried to cling to escaped. In moments, all were gone. The disquiet left him unable to sleep again. He stared along the dark ceiling, his mind still searching for any piece of the dream: a fading scream echoed, with no vision of the person, though. Rick rose slowly and shuffled to the window, disheartened to see the snowfall coming again in larger flakes. He scowled and braced against the window jambs. The complaining voice in his head intruded, frustration and disbelief aimed at the relentless winter weather.

Across the dimly illuminated lot, a line of scraggly yews sagged, the spindly boughs yielding to the accumulating wet snow. Lightly covered and weighted, the lowest branches hung ominously over the old Lyman runabout resting on blocks in the corner of his property. Rick often considered moving it to a safer place, but an endless list of other tasks always seemed more important. His mind came back to the dream, and an image of Allie strangely appeared, leaving Rick to question why she hadn't called. Being a teenager in her senior year, few things resembled a pattern with her. Long ago, though, she had proclaimed her trust in Rick's confidence, and from that instant, one thing he could rely on was a day-after report; a replay of the suffering she had endured attending any of her step-mother's political functions. Allie told Rick she hated them, but then always found some comfort in the aftermath venting to her older friend.

Rick peered through the swirling flakes. It had been five days since he last saw or heard from her. He lowered his head, and closed his eyes, hoping the meaning of the scream would find him. Minutes later he dressed and moved quietly out the door, leaving Schooner sleeping peacefully.

The late night cold found its way instantly under Rick's collar, and he regretted his choice of coat. As he lumbered across the lot and approached M Street, SE, the chill was settling into his chest and arms. He considered returning to see if the truck would start, or at the very least to grab a heavier layer; the mile plus walk from the marina's gate to Delia's diner on Pennsylvania Avenue would take much longer than usual in the conditions. Neither option to backtrack brought motivation, though. Rick buttoned the collar and quickened his pace, electing to take the shortest route, a well-worn path through the steep hill's dense overgrowth. The snow-covered trail slowed his progress. Ascending the hill, he struggled on the slippery footing and needed to stop for several breaks. Coming out of the brush and vines at the top, he lingered to catch his breath. Ward 6's Hill East neighborhood spread out before him; residences and small businesses filling each block and all still quiet in these early hours. Historic Congressional Cemetery stood dark and silent across an expansive fifteen-acre parcel to the north. The entire area elevated high above the Anacostia, offering sweeping views of the river, but little testimony to the marina's lonely existence below. Only a few lights illuminated Pennsylvania Avenue a half block away, and Rick took comfort in the solitude. He jammed his bare hands deep into both pockets, and pushing through his fatigue, trudged along the few short blocks to Delia's.

The corner diner stood dark when he arrived, but the

storefront Delia maintained offered greeting at all hours. A bright red awning extended the length of the facade with bare vines and strings of lights meandering along the edges. A shelter for the diner's entrance and occasional sidewalk tables, it also served as refuge from weather for anyone waiting at the corner bus stop. Hardy pansies brightened the window boxes. The community notice board in the window overflowed with announcements and opportunities.

Rick turned the corner on 17th Street and made his way to the side entry. He moved tentatively through the door, relieved not to hear complaints from the old hinges. The side door remained unlocked twenty-four seven. Delia's choice. Everyone knew it. Having called the neighborhood home for so many decades, it was how she chose to live. Rick respected the sentiment but oftentimes questioned the decision. She defended it as being less about living in denial or casting off concerns and more about insisting on a gesture of welcome. Rick accepted that painful struggles along the life journey had left her without irrational fear. Reassuring him, though, they had not caused her to abandon wisdom; everyone also knew Delia was more than capable when handling her gun.

Across the narrow hallway, the swing doors into the generous kitchen stood open. Steps away down the hall, a warm light glowed from the lone table lamp on the corner of the bar. Rick pulled off his boots and tiptoed through the kitchen doorway. The coffee maker sat next to the pass-through window, prepared as always for the busy morning shifts. Rick switched it on and leaned back against the counter, staring at the water in the pot as pieces of the dream flashed.

Sudden creaking followed slow steps across the wood floors above. Rick flinched and his eyes darted to the ceiling. Seconds later, Delia's voice boomed from the darkened stairway.

"If your name isn't Richard Larson and you're here for anything other than food, you're gonna have a problem shortly."

Rick focused on the doorway. The gun appeared first around the corner. Delia's close cropped, graying hair came next, then the glasses and her full cheeks as she peeked through the opening. Seeing him, she relaxed instantly, but chose to maintain the unwelcome glower, chewing on her bottom lip and pulling the colorful robe closed. Rick stood crookedly against the counter, bracing with one hand, tilting to his left to unweight the complaining hip.

Delia assessed, presenting no concern to the evidence of his exhaustion and discomfort. "You look awful," she said flatly, shaking her head. "Tough walk up the hill?"

Rick shrugged.

Her scowl deepened. "You blew that hip up forty-five years ago. Maybe it's time to see a doctor."

"No sympathy?" Rick asked.

Delia snorted. "Not this morning."

Rick lifted his hand from the counter and pulled his shoulders back. When he wasn't compensating for the pain and could stand straight, Delia needed to tilt her head or stand on something to find his eyes. Rick had reported to basic training camp at 6' 3", two twenty-five. He lost fifteen during the war and never put the pounds back on. His body and mind had encountered destructive forces that should have taken their toll by now via another significant injury or disease. Maybe both were lurking, but he wasn't aware of either and didn't want to know. The last doctor he saw was the one who saved his leg in the war. His habit was to ignore the hip.

Delia glared. "You're a strong man, Richard, but I think arthritis and scar tissue are winning this one."

Foreseeing more, Rick twisted to avoid eye contact. His friend never intended to disrespect his courageous time in service to their country, but she had wondered lovingly aloud to him, on more than one occasion, why he wasn't dead, all things considered. Rick remembered only two times when he had angered her enough to have the question posed with an association of hope. Delia set the gun on a counter and folded her arms. Rick caught the expression and deflected with a forced smile, concerned this could be another one of those occasions.

"It is too damn early," Delia grumbled. "What are you thinking, Richard? You trying to get shot? Again?"

"We both know that weapon's never been loaded."

"So, what! I could still hit you over the head with it!"

Raising an eyebrow, he glanced along her 5' 4" frame. "Guess you're right. I never considered that."

Delia shook her head and checked her watch. "Just 'cause you can't sleep doesn't mean I'll open up early and make your breakfast! It's no hour to wake an old woman. I had more good sleep left in me, and you know that. Don't you? And besides, it's too slippery for your old bones to be out there walking around in the dark."

Rick offered another shrug. "When *is* this weather gonna break anyway?"

Delia ignored the dodge. "Sleep's important!" She scowled. "What do you want?"

"Sorry. Allie—just needed to ask if you've seen her lately. It's been almost a week since she's been by. Just wondering. For some reason, I was thinking about her last night; a strange dream kept me awake."

"And that's why you woke me up? We both know that when I cross paths with young Allison, she's most likely on her way over to see you and those old boats. If you haven't seen her, I haven't seen her."

Rick slid away from the coffee maker, offering her space. Delia stared from the doorway, set her jaw, then shuffled across to start the morning ritual. Her gait and expression sold the crankiness. She filled two mugs and held the face on Rick as she handed him the smaller one. After a sigh and a long, slow sip, she looked down at his leg.

"Thanks for taking the boots off," she mumbled. "How's the hip?"

Rick exhaled, relieved to hear a tone of forgiveness. He straightened, poised to answer, but unexpectedly lost the words. He tried to focus on Delia's face, sensing her urgent movements toward him. His vision blurred the familiar features though, and her suddenly strange voice faded into deep and slow words. Rick reached back to balance against the counter but lost his grip. As he struggled to recover, Delia grabbed him, her strong hands taking hold of his right arm.

He murmured "This doesn't feel right."

Delia helped him lie on the cold tile floor. His arms collapsed to his side. He lay there motionless, his chest straining to rise through each slow breath. His gaze drifted from light to light, squinting at the too bright wash of white across the ceiling, all of it appearing to steadily swirl and descend on top of him. He closed his eyes to shut it out, hoping darkness would end the spinning.

~

EMS arrived minutes after Delia's 911 call describing an older man possibly in cardiac arrest. Loud siren bursts accompanied flashing red lights as the ambulance pulled up to the side entrance on 17th Street. An EMT and paramedic team hurried inside and quickly assessed Rick's vitals. He blinked slowly, surrendering to the aid. Delia stood to the side, both hands lifted to her face, peering between Rick's blank gaze and the team's efficient, urgent motions. Monotone dialogue fired between them, frequently engaging Rick in conversation about what they were doing; skin color good, blood pressure acceptable for his age, pulse high but not alarming, pulse oximetry checked out, penlight on the pupils got a thumbs up. Clear speech and no numbness.

Delia eased closer.

"I'm dizzy," Rick mumbled. "Feel sick."

The young paramedic spoke comforting words, encouraging Rick to inhale as she opened his shirt to attach the ECG leads. Silence fell as she concentrated on the small screen. After a long moment, they nodded to each other and removed the wires.

~

The assessment showed no signs of a heart attack or stroke, and Delia finally exhaled. The paramedic put her hand on Rick's shoulder and conveyed the good news. He managed a faint smile, as she calmly proceeded to talk with him about stress, dehydration, and caffeine. Rick shook his head slowly at the alcohol question. She offered a recommendation; he should be fine, but considering his age, they advised a trip to the ER for a robust intravenous cocktail of vitamins and electrolytes, and a few more tests. Rick tensed. The paramedic talked it up; it was early, and the emergency room wouldn't be crowded. Rick didn't bite. She delivered a compassionate frown and reiterated that he was in fact dehydrated: not dangerously so, but when associated with older age and stress, enough to complicate things.

Rick tilted to Delia with a grimace. She shrugged at the two of them and answered for him, "*Thank you, no.*"

The paramedic confessed to hoping for a different answer; it was possible Rick had A-Fib, not unusual for someone his age, but again, if the condition existed, stress and dehydration could be triggers. She emphasized that if the prudent tests weren't going to happen this morning, they should be done soon. His symptoms were common, but they could also lead down several different paths, some more challenging than others. She made him promise to see his doctor this week. Rick offered a thumbs up. Delia chimed in saying she would see to it.

After helping him to a table and observing his color a while longer, they left with reassurances and instructions for him to take it easy for a day or so. In a weak voice, Rick assured them he was feeling better and offered his thanks.

Delia leaned back against the closed door and held a hand to her mouth. She shook her head slowly, eyeing the unfamiliar concern across his face. Rick shifted in his seat and finally caught her look.

"You gave me a scare, friend." Delia moved over to sit.

"Surprised both of us," he said in a weak voice. "That was new."

She reached for his hand.

Rick winced. "A-Fib; that sounds official."

"I wouldn't spend too much time on that one, you could push Tre's old truck if you needed to."

"Just quoting the cute doctor."

Delia frowned. "There's more here, Richard."

"Besides getting old?"

She pushed the water bottle closer to him. "The cute doc also said to drink this mixture every ten minutes. So, get started. Bottom's up."

Rick shook the bottle, watching the bubbles. "What do you suppose is in this?"

"Good stuff." Delia leaned back while he drank. "So, I'm not buying the old age and steep, slippery path through the woods line. You didn't walk to the diner without a real coat this early just to wake me up, expecting breakfast; you came in to talk about Allie. You mentioned a dream. What's going on? Something got you worried?"

"Not so much worried, just wondering."

"I don't believe you. You passed out in my kitchen."

"Like you said, it was tough sledding on the path."

"Richard, you said you haven't heard from her, but it's only been a couple of days. Why so troubled?"

"That dream, Delia—it felt so real. There was a scream. It's been a long time since I heard a scream like that."

"I'm sure it did, honey. You're all alone down that dark hill. No one around."

"You saying old age has me afraid of the dark now?"

"It's a dreary, lonely place where you live and it's all closing in on you. Makes everything feel darker. It's no way to grow old; alone in all that."

"It's home."

"It was, but there's not much life left around there anymore. Allie gave it some, and to you, too, but she may be the last of it. She's something special, and you don't want to lose that, or your home. She filled a place in your heart, and your heart got afraid. But she's a young, smart girl who's going to be moving on with her life."

Delia took his hand. "She's leaving, Richard; college next fall. It's all just starting for her, and she'll do great things. You're helping her take that next step, and you're helping her get through some challenges here, too. She's lucky to have you care. That's a happy thing, not a worry thing."

Rick tapped his fingers against the bottle, contemplating another drink. "I don't know, Delia, just not sure I'm ready for all that's coming."

"What's coming for you is going to be good. Believe that." She squeezed his hands, tilting her head. "Maybe that scream was yours? Could be your time at that old place has run its course."

Rick's lips flattened as he offered a resigned nod. "Yeah, maybe. Guess it's going to be fun thinking about what's next, right?"

"A new door to open." Delia leaned across, pressing a palm to her heart. "How are you feeling now?"

"Better."

"Good. I have to get started." She rose slowly.

"I know. Sorry about all this."

"Don't be silly. I'm glad you're okay, and you stay here all day, upstairs in a bed if you want. Or I can run you back when Billy gets here." She tightened the robe and drew a deep breath. "Thinking I should cancel my trip plans. You need somebody close by, to be here for you."

"No way."

"You heard the conversation, I just promised to get you to a doctor this week."

"A few more days won't matter. You can give me a ride when you get back."

Delia resisted. "We'll see how things go today." She plodded to the bar and returned with a stack of mail. "Present for you. Guess what this is? Some reading material for your day of rest. Teddy was mad again yesterday. He's definitely not loving this weather. He said if you don't get the mailbox fixed, you don't get the mail. Not anymore."

Ricked looked away. "It's on the list."

"He told me to stop feeding you 'til you do. What do you think of that?"

Rick struggled to stand and reached for the letters. "Think I'd lose some more weight." He leaned over to give her a hug. "Thanks, dear. I think I'm good. I'll walk and take it slow."

"Not my first choice. You sure?" Delia frowned and shook her head. "If I can't convince you to stay a while, you at least want something warm to put on? A real coat maybe? Warms the bones, old man."

"Not today. Maybe when it's cold outside. Let me get out of your way. We'll talk later."

Delia handed him the water bottle and the extra packets at the door.

"Slow," she grumbled. "No path."

Rick nodded his response and moved out into the cold air, hunching forward against the persistent remnants of snowfall.

~

Rick endured the next half hour, adhering to cautious, slow steps. He halted at the entrance to the path, weakened and sore. He sensed a sudden, rapid beating in his chest, believing he heard his heart's plea for a pause. Feeling lightheaded, he rushed a drink from the bottle. He lowered slowly, intending to rest for just a few minutes. He breathed deeply, seeing a brighter sky to the east and sensing a warmer day's approach. Settling into the soft covering of snow, Rick leaned back against a lamppost and cast a vacant gaze down the hill across his perishing world and home.

Chapter 5

All of the snow across the deck had melted. Rick sat on the drying boards at the end of Pier D, his legs hanging over the calm water. The full sun had appeared slow in rising, but now shone squarely on his face, heralding a long-awaited warmth for the coming day. Rick raised his coffee mug in full appreciation for the river's broadening reflections. He had been missing this connection with the sun, which could begin for him some years in early March, and in others, much later. March weather in the nation's capital could be fickle, leaving forecasts more closely resembling guesses. Rick no longer listened, for good reason; as stubborn as the lingering winter had been over the last week, this morning offered a welcome twenty-degree temperature swing and blue skies.

The new day heartened Rick. The disruption twenty-four hours ago was too much for him, physically and emotionally. The very slow walk home from Delia's after the EMTs left provided time for unwanted reflection on the meaning of something he'd rarely given thought to; being alone. The isolated steps he followed yesterday along M Street, SE, once so familiar, had not held the same resigned comfort: each one experienced by him more as a visitor might. Lonely steps leading him to a forlorn setting inside the marina's decaying office. Offering no pretense of comfort, the environment did little to speed his recovery through the afternoon and evening. The packets helped though; his lightheadedness faded, and two small, uninspiring meals stayed down. An atypical late afternoon nap extended overnight into the early morning hours, with Schooner, his ever-present empath, curled up close beside him on the office bed.

The words Delia planted awoke with him, opening his eyes wide as he stared above into emptiness. She and the paramedic had held nothing back; each speaking their truth to his reality; different versions of the same story. A failing life lived alone. Allie stood at the center of the turmoil, but Rick tentatively accepted Delia's description of life with a teenager. She encouraged him to temper any expectations regarding Allie and to trust her. At 5:00 a.m., the recalled admonition, accompanied by Schooner's wet nose on his cheek, inspired Rick's early morning walk across the property's melting snow, to the end of Pier D, to the river, and into the sunshine, where he could clear his thoughts and believe Allie was fine.

Rick held the Nikon with both hands, steadying the camera on a partially sunken tugboat farther north. The boat rested in solitude, laid over on its side, its large cabin and foredeck all that remained above the water's surface. Motionless, without an anchor or lines to pilings, there appeared no indications of how its journey had come to an end, only the evidence of a very long repose in that same spot. Rick surveyed through the lens, searching for the perfect angle to capture the soft rays of light streaming through the tug's clouded cabin windows.

Schooner lifted his head, hearing Sarah and Lou's cautious steps along the deteriorated pier. His tail thumped loudly in greeting. Rick rotated and stood as they approached, appreciative of their full concentration on the largest gaps in the deck boards. A sudden puff of wind lifted Lou's hat. She clutched at it, reaching her other hand to the nearest piling for balance. She yelped instantly and pulled back, dropping her surprised eyes to examine the substantial splinter.

Rick stepped closer, handing Sarah the camera. He reached out to Lou. "Ouch. Sorry about the hazards. You haven't even met the snakes, yet. Can I take a look?" As Lou deliberated, he took her wrist gently and pulled out his army knife. "That's a good one," he mumbled, opening the smallest blade.

Lou squeaked, "Wait! Is that clean?"

Rick swiped the blade across his jacket sleeve. "Clean enough." He focused, delicately jabbed the sliver, and eased it back out.

Lou winced for only a second.

"There you go," he said, rubbing her hand carefully. "Anything left?"

Sarah offered a sympathetic smile to her daughter. "You're very brave, sweetheart."

Lou faltered, inspecting the small puncture. "No, umm, you seem to have gotten it all. Thank you for that."

"My pleasure. I've had more than I could ever count." Rick leaned down and picked up her hat, regarding it. The war had left him with an appreciation for the necessity of shade on his face. Relentless sun, blinding glare. Hats proved vital in southeast Asia. They preserved vision, which could be lifesaving. The lesson was not lost; Rick wore them more than shoes. He brushed off the wide brim and returned it to Lou. "This is a nice one. It was worth saving."

"So—" Sarah started, extending her hand to Rick. "Perhaps we could begin again, with a new greeting? Good morning, Mr. Larson. How are you today?"

Rick stalled at the question, instantly rushed by a replay of yesterday's scare; the clear subject of one possible response. He deliberated, as a stirring breeze out of the south wrapped them in a milder puff. Briefly uplifted by Sarah's determined kindness, the relief of still being alive lightened him. He cleared his throat and let the prompted memory swirl away with the gentle wind.

"Just great," he finally said, raising the brim across his forehead. "You came back."

"What can I say? My daughter is in love and following some strange steps."

"And early ones."

Sarah winked. "We embraced your words of wisdom. Anything to avoid your pets in there."

Lou scowled at the reminder, then turned to Rick. "Thanks for this, Mr. Larson. I know it may sound silly, but—"

"Not at all." He took a few seconds assessing their outfits. "Much better. I think you're ready."

"It did take some shopping." Sarah grinned and handed back the camera. "So, another medium for your storytelling?"

"The best kind," he said. "No words necessary. This was for slip fees. Debt installment. The boat owner offered it first and then ended up just giving me the boat."

Sarah folded her arms. "Hmm, and the boat you bartered for?"

"Sittin' on stands over in that back corner of the lot. Bad habit of mine; taking in stray old boats."

Sarah glanced across the marina lot. "So, it would appear. And stray dogs?"

"Mostly just boats; Schooner's part of the family."

Sarah inched her way closer as they talked, positioning for eye contact. Lou folded her arms, and Rick spotted the frown intended for her mother.

Sarah turned abruptly. "Lou, why don't you go ahead and get started? I'll be right behind you."

Lou tugged on her mother's jacket and grumbled under her breath, "You're kidding!"

Sarah rubbed her shoulder. "It will make the gift so much

more meaningful. I'll be right there, honey. Promise."

Lou peered anxiously back and forth between them.

Rick said, "The shed is open. Snow's mostly gone. Plenty of light in there. Probably have about an hour before others start to show up." He leaned closer. "Little secret; the good stuff is in the far-right corner. First three shelves."

Lou looked back toward the looming structure, biting her lip.

Rick had to clear his throat to get her attention. "You want some company?"

"Schooner?"

"Sure. You've had a rough start."

Lou accepted with a quick nod and spun away. Several steps down the pier, she twisted and patted her leg, imploring, "C'mon Schooner."

The old dog watched for Rick's okay, then rose quickly to hurry after her.

"Thanks," Sarah said. "That was kind of you." Her eyes came to rest on the wooden yacht looming behind him. "This is gorgeous." Her eyebrows scrunched. "But you mentioned a boat in the shed?"

"Different boat, and not as gorgeous. We take care of this one for a friend. *MORNING STAR*, 1965 Trumpy. Sixty-five feet. Amazing lineage. The young girl you met last week—"

"Allie?"

"It's her dad's." Rick cast an affectionate look along the glistening hull and varnished cabin. "Not sure which one of them cherishes this old girl more. Allie's grandmother christened her with the name; Allie says it's all about timelessness. She calls *MORNING STAR* a work of art with a soul. Says the smell of wood brings back memories of her grandfather. Probably the real reason she's back here as often as she is. We talk, we putter, we baby this beautiful craft."

"And you two are friends?"

"Almost two years now. Strangely, she took a liking to our spot. Claims she can escape and talk here."

"Well, she's lucky to have a place for both." Sarah turned casually to examine the shoreline. "And you have a neighbor."

"*Sea Keepers*," Rick said. "Just another marina squeezed into the last few feet of land where the trestle bends east and crosses. Rough spot, but they made it work for a long time. Everything's overgrown and boarded up now, though. Piers are gone. It's all just dark and silent."

Sarah gestured, "And the old tugboat? Speaking of dark and silent."

"She caught fire and sank in that very spot twenty-two years ago. Tugs are hardworking boats, rain or shine." Rick showed the camera. "A favorite subject."

"A compelling image and more storytelling." Sarah rotated slowly, taking in all of the unexpected view again. "Twenty-two years. That's a long time to live anywhere. There must be a lot of stories."

"Thirty-five years. Being here served a purpose."

Sarah's eyes casually came back to him. "Allie has quite an adventurous spirit, doesn't she? This isn't a setting I would typically picture for a high school girl, but it does offer some interesting contrasts, don't you agree? The Trumpy, the tug?" Sarah's smile grew. "The owner? That must be intriguing to her."

Rick's concern about Allie suddenly flashed and he lowered his head. "She says I'm a good listener."

Sarah nodded. "More caretaking. That seems to suit you, Mr. Larson. I would say Allie is *very* lucky to have met you."

They shared a brief regarding look.

Sarah finally peeked behind him, drifting her gaze along the yacht's graceful lines. "You and *MORNING STAR* make a good pair," she said. "Both nicely preserved classics."

Lou's whoop from the end of the pier startled them. "Mr. Larson!" She grinned and hoisted a small canvas bag above her shoulders. "Success! I think!"

"Well, that was fast." Rick crossed his arms. "Looks like the scavenger hunt paid off."

"And she survived."

Lou waved and pointed toward the lot. "You have some other people arriving."

Chapter 6

Rick and Sarah caught up with Lou at the car. Their trunk stood open. A blue sedan was parked two spaces away, the engine still running, the driver holding a phone to his ear. Rick glanced in the direction, then turned to Lou. She offered the bag to him, brimming with pride. "Just two small things!" Rick delayed before looking. He held it gently, weighing the found treasure in his mind.

"How's your hand?" he asked.

"Good as new."

"Snakes?"

"Not a one. Schooner was my hero."

Rick chewed his lip, still deliberating. "Feels like—five bucks."

The sedan's door opened and a man got out.

Rick watched him spin slowly and scan the property, guessing him to be early fifties. Maybe six feet tall and carrying some unnecessary weight around the middle. The man pulled his sunglasses off, revealing serious eyes, but shadowy bags underneath. Rick noticed his shoes. The choice didn't fit the task if he had come to rummage, and the clothes said office, even for a Saturday.

The man proceeded toward them, stopping a couple of feet away. He pulled out his badge by way of introduction. "Mr. Larson? I'm Detective Ward. Sorry to interrupt your morning. Could you take a minute for some questions?"

Rick studied him, hiding any concern. The last visit from

Metro Police was fifteen years ago. A slow response to a call about an armed intruder. Rick had waited as long as he could, then decided to deal with it. The decision landed him in jail overnight.

Rick paused, giving the detective time to appraise Sarah and Lou. "Sure. Gimme a minute."

The detective nodded.

Rick put Lou's bag in the trunk and closed it. "I'm sure he's going to love it," he said to her. "I'll collect the five another time. Good luck." He moved around the car to hold Sarah's door, a courtesy gesture disguising his anxiousness for them to leave.

"It was a nice sunrise," he said in a low voice. "Thanks for the company."

She leaned closer with a hopeful look, "Do you text?"

"Not well."

"Perfect." She winked. "Two of us then." She peeked around his shoulder at the detective. "Hope everything's okay."

"Yeah, it will be. Thanks again." Rick stepped back as they pulled away.

The detective displayed no interest or concern in Sarah and Lou's departure. "Didn't mean to chase off customers," he said, as Rick approached.

"What can I do for you, Detective?"

Ward eyed Rick briefly and said, "I'm here about a missing girl. Allison Sheridan."

Rick signaled nothing.

"Forty-eight hours, or so. No one's sure. Her dad was traveling on business, so day one didn't register with the parents, which is its own flag. It's day two now, and all the wheels are starting to turn. Mr. Sheridan is making it official." Ward took a casual step forward. "You know her, don't you?"

Rick's blank expression masked an encroaching fear. He met the detective's stare, silently counting the number of days since hearing from Allie.

"Her parents say she spends a lot of time here." Ward said flatly. "Helluva long way from Georgetown."

Rick took a moment. "The place grows on you, and she seems to enjoy the old boats."

Ward looked past him to the long pier. The Trumpy rested peacefully.

"Like that one?" he asked, gesturing.

"Yeah."

"Well, she's nice. Maybe too nice?" He glanced around. "Why the *hell* does Ben Sheridan keep that beauty here? No offense."

"None taken. You aren't the first to ask. But if you know she belongs to the Sheridans, you probably know the answer."

"Maybe. Help me out anyway, though. If you would."

Rick sighed. "Closest travel lift is eighty miles down the Potomac to the Bay, then take your pick, another thirty or so either north or south. You could try Colonial Beach, but—"

"Sounds inconvenient."

"There's not so much work anymore, but we had our run. Doing the jobs nobody else could figure out. We were the scruffy guys up the river. Troubleshooters, and good at it. And we only charged what we promised. That's valuable to the right people. All of it got us a reputation—for a while. Then it slowed down. Mostly because we slowed down."

Detective Ward locked on Rick's expression. "So, Allie Sheridan comes over to watch you work on her dad's boat?"

"And helps."

Ward tilted his head.

Rick added, "Says she likes it around here."

Ward's head jerked back. "Really?"

"You sound surprised, Detective."

"Mostly curious; why in the world would she be here? Why would her parents let her? You can imagine lots of questions come to mind when a high school girl chooses to spend time with a—"

"68-year-old recluse?"

"Yeah, and around this place. Just seems like, let's call it a unique relationship? Didn't all this ever seem strange to you, Mr. Larson?" Ward held out his arms. "I mean, a seventeen-year-old girl who could be absolutely *anywhere* she wanted to. And she comes here? Because she likes old boats? Kinda difficult for me to understand."

Rick drew a deep breath. "The first couple of visits surprised me, too. Mr. Sheridan brought her along, then after a while she started coming alone. He kept track of her, though—"

"Every time?"

Rick heard sarcasm and chose silence.

"Never mind," Ward said. "I know that answer."

Rick added, "It would have been disappointing to me if he hadn't."

"That's good to hear. When was the last time?"

"A week ago."

"How often would she come by?"

"She's a senior in high school, Detective. Wasn't really a pattern."

Ward rubbed the back of his neck, his eyes locked on Rick.

"There are times I'll see her a couple days a week," Rick went on. "Other times, like now," Rick faltered. "As I said, she's living the life of a teenager, and I don't see her much at all."

Ward shook his head, his gaze wandering again. "You know

her mother's a senator, right?"

"Stepmother."

Ward smirked. "Yeah, well, the stepdaughter of a senator is missing, and we don't have much. Nothing from any of her friends. Strangely, there aren't many to reach out to. Seems that you may be close to the top of that list: the friends list. The top? Some friendship, don't you think?"

Rick shrugged.

"So, would you say Allison Sheridan considered you to be a friend?"

Rick offered nothing.

Ward frowned. "Like I said, we don't have much. Last contact with her was an Uber driver; said she was picked up here." He raised his hand to his chin. "Picked up but not dropped off. How's that work?"

Rick's mind raced. Allie's dad had purchased the Jeep for her eight months ago: her only mode of transportation to the marina since. "She has a car," he said. "Can't remember the last time she used an Uber."

"Well, I'll help you with that. It was four days ago, Tuesday, around 5:00 p.m. Not a long ride, though. Allie hopped out two miles away. Crappy weather that evening. Maybe you weren't here?"

The question jarred Rick. His eyes drifted past the detective, out across the river toward the island. Finally, he said, "No, I wasn't. Probably running an errand."

Ward waited.

"For a buddy," Rick added.

"Another friend? Good for you." Ward worked his jaw, glancing to the river. "How's the fishing?"

Rick folded his arms. "Good, most days. Some cast a line to

relax, some need the catch for dinner. That always comes with a question mark, though. The water's still struggling, in spite of all the city's efforts. So are some of the fish."

"I can smell what you mean," Ward said. "Kind of a pleasant mix of trash and bones."

Rick let the comment pass.

"Did Allison like to fish?"

"Not too much." Rick dropped his arms. "Anything else, Detective?"

Ward released a deep breath and scanned the shoreline. "Know what the city's missing person stats were last year, Larson? Close to eighteen hundred; that's just the juvenile cases. If you add in the adults, and Allison could be either at this point, it's closer to twenty-six hundred. And that's sad. All of it; too many lost people, and children. The good news is, we're fortunate to close most of them." He turned to face Rick. "That usually comes with some help, though. From families and any friends. You'd be surprised; anything can be a lead." His stare held. "But it's a dangerous time for every one of them, especially for girls Allie's age. It's a hard decision to run. A lot of times that leads to bad decisions to survive."

"Allie's smarter than that."

"Everyone's smarter than that. Until you get cold, tired and hungry. It doesn't take long. It's why these first couple of days are so critical."

"I believe that."

"Good. So, here's the next step, Mr. Larson. Since you were, according to Ms. Sheridan, one of her closest friends, but you're old enough to be her grandfather, the senator and the girl's father are asking if you would meet with them. Nothing official, just turning over all the stones. They asked for a conversation, and we'd appreciate your being available for that: just a brief talk with the parents.

A senator and a wealthy businessman, you can understand; they're trying to control the media."

"Sounds like it's my choice, but not really."

Ward's faint smile faded quickly. "We'd appreciate the cooperation. Ben Sheridan says he's known you for a while. Like I said, anything can become a lead. You can imagine how concerned they are."

Rick's eyes narrowed across the water. "Where?"

"They live in Georgetown, asking if you would come to their place. It's not far from—"

"I know where it is. I've heard all about it." Rick looked back. "Are you going to be there?"

"The invitation wasn't extended to me. I'm okay with that. I'll still get every word." Detective Ward stepped closer. "You know, I came here expecting to hear that you saw Allison last Tuesday. Maybe even held the Uber door for her. That's what I was hoping for. That would've been of some value. Would have made you the last person to see her before she disappeared. It might have proved to be very helpful. Or just very interesting. But she was here unnoticed, as you say. So now there's a gap. A conflict. The last time the senator saw her was at the fundraiser, at their home."

"I never said she was here," Rick affirmed bluntly, his attention escaping to the old tug. "If she did come by though, we must have missed each other. And that's never happened." He turned back. "Last time I saw her was a week ago, Detective."

Ward's lips flattened as he rubbed the back of his neck again. "So, Vietnam, huh? How long were you in?"

"Sixteen months too long is my typical answer."

"I had an uncle, did a tour in '70."

Rick's hands landed on his hips. An audible exhale followed.

"And fate landed you here," Ward added.

"A friend actually played more of a role."

"More friends." Ward lifted an eyebrow. "Got it. Thanks for your time, Mr. Larson." He handed Rick a card. "If you hear anything from her, there are ways to help. Other people to talk with if she needs that. Oh, and, you won't keep the senator waiting tomorrow, will you?

Rick held silent.

Ward turned toward his car, calling back over his shoulder, "And Larson, you can always call me, too."

~

Tre stood close to the water's edge along the island's southern shore, binoculars held in both hands and trained downriver across calm reflections toward the marina. He twisted slowly, letting the objective lenses follow M Street's meander south from the trestle landing only yards from *Sea Keepers*, railroad tracks shadowing just thirty feet off the neglected road's untended shoulder.

Tre's shaky hands gripped the old field glasses, struggling to steady his adrift view across the marina property, his slow surveil of the battered chain link fence line, the sparse, early budding walnuts and maples defiantly clinging to life, and the meager, barren patches of ground. Pieces of Tre's life briefly coming into focus, then departing. The stoic black cherry slowly appeared, strong roots holding it fast to the river's eroded bank. Tre halted his turn, peering along the Old Man's suspended arms: offered perches for quiet contemplation of the river's enduring loneliness and shame. Lookouts from where you could see the defacing trash along the shore; you could see the habitat's death and life across the water's surface; and from where on a clear sky day, you could see his home. The island. Tre's hands steadied as he spied a bit longer, searching for Allie in the old tree's embrace.

Sensing company, Tre lowered the binoculars and lifted his gaze to a young hawk slowly circling the shore's perimeter. Not quite an acre in size, the small island lay south of the railroad trestle crossing, favoring the river's western shore. Two small stands of trees somehow flourished in the sandy, clay terrain, with pockets of low brush filled in around. Tre's shelter stood fifty feet from the island's southern edge, the ground inside channeled into an embankment to shield against the north and west winds. The covering low walls and lean-to roof stood as a weaving of tarps, driftwood and long ago, lost pieces of lumber and plywood; bountiful offerings carried upriver from the Potomac to this final resting place, where the shallow river's current lost its motivation to carry them further. All was scavenged; all had become useful parts of the puzzle. The encampment had survived for years.

The hawk dipped sharply, rose again, then glided off toward the eastern shore. Tre's vigilance returned to the marina, as gentle rolls of water lapped, sneaking up the sandy bank to kiss the worn toes of his boots before retreating into the river. Gripping the binoculars' casing tighter, Tre's hands shook again. Cracked skin across his knuckles wrinkled as the trembling fingers rolled the focus wheel. Tre's breathing slowed as he finally found Rick in the sight. For a long moment, he fixated on his friend's expression. Assured then, Tre angled his view slightly toward the lot, centering on Detective Ward's slow steps to the unmarked cruiser. With tired eyes narrowing against the bright sun, Sgt. Tremaine Wilson renewed his grasp on the worn casing, and held his gaze steadfastly on the detective's car until it exited slowly through the gate and onto M Street, SE.

Chapter 7

Rick rubbed his neck and glanced a third time at the dark direction arrows. Waiting for the lobby elevator in Adrian Dumar's building always proved the hardest part of his visits. He arrived early, believing he had beaten the Monday morning rush. Twenty seconds ago, standing happily alone, he pushed the button. The doors still hadn't opened though, and now some of Adrian's attorneys, five men and three women, stood impatiently queued behind him. Rick scrutinized his wrinkled jeans and worn boots in the mirrored doors, against a backdrop of tailored suits and snug skirts. Never clear on the protocols, he debated holding the door for just the women or the entire group. The bell rang, the doors opened, the decision made itself; all eight moved forward at once, etiquette nowhere to be found. Rick squeezed in last, as various arms reached in front of him in simultaneous urgency, hitting buttons for half a dozen different floors. Adrian's office was on twelve, the top floor. Rick stared at the panel board. Seven lit numbers glared back. He squeezed his arm through the bodies to add the one last stop, sharing an audible sigh with the group. Too early in the morning for a delayed trip in a small box. He propped against the side wall, pulled his hat brim lower and rested his eyes, shutting out the silent tension swirling around the cab as all heads dropped to fix attention on phone screens.

~

As the doors pulled back on twelve, the floor receptionist greeted Rick warmly.

"Good to see you again, Mr. Larson," Mary said. "Mr. Dumars is expecting you. Shall I walk with you?"

"Thanks, no, Mary. Good to see you, too."

She picked up the phone and dialed as Rick started down the wide hall to the smaller reception area. Adrian's personal assistant rose from her desk as he approached and opened the door to Adrian's corner office.

"Your timing is perfect, Mr. Larson."

"Thanks, Nancy."

Adrian Dumars stood as Nancy ushered Rick through the double doors. He moved around the large desk and beamed. Age had not diminished him; a strong posture still managed his substantial frame, an immediate and broad grin showed, bright eyes, graying temples distinguishing strong features. He approached Rick and landed both very large hands on his shoulders: the prelude to an imminent, extended hug. Adrian's enduring habit accompanied any greeting, regardless of the grease often observable on his friend's clothes. In deference, Rick offered his customary reaction; he recoiled slightly and extended his hand, not wanting their opposing outfits to meet. The gesture drew a laugh, and Adrian pulled him in.

"Good to see you, brother. I'm glad you called. Grab a seat, and gimme a minute." He turned and followed Nancy through the doors.

Rick drifted across the large office to the expansive glass wall, appreciating the interlude. The view opened to the east; a hazy sun suspended above the Capitol dome beyond. His friend's reputation, success and influence touched every corner of the world spread out below: Adrian's world, but not his, and not Tre's. From here, theirs always seemed so distant to Rick.

He reached for the framed photo on the round side table, staring at the three of them arm in arm at basic training. Adrian stood in the middle, towering over Tre, holding tight to his two new companions. He had embraced them from that first day and never let go once in the fifty years since. They were fortunate to have met but arriving at Parris Island held a different meaning for each of them. Tre and Rick shared a necessary personal journey, committed in their hearts, but weighted with apprehension. Adrian enlisted as well. The decision for him held no fear, though. He entered with positivity, enthusiasm, and a strong commitment to his country, and he returned home with the same. Rick and Tre came home broken, immediately facing collateral hostilities with trauma and self-destructive addictions and rage. Their three lives followed incompatible paths, with memories of the two horrifying tours always looming. Adrian would never let go of them though, or question what had mysteriously held their very different journeys together. For him, they had become family on the bus to boot camp, and their lives would remain inseparable.

The door swung open. Adrian reentered and strode toward Rick. Nancy leaned in.

"Can I get you anything, Mr. Larson?"

Adrian answered. "Iced tea for Rick, water for me. Thanks, Nancy."

They moved to opposing leather couches arranged in the office's glass corner. Adrian leaned forward, elbows on his knees. His gaze softened with a knowing nod to his friend.

"Your eyes are sad, man." He waited for Rick to look up. "I know it's about Allie. Talk to me."

"How much time do you have?"

"Say the word, and my day is yours."

"You know she's officially missing."

Adrian sighed and leaned back. "I know, I know. Just this morning. Wasn't sure you did. Sorry I didn't reach out. Can't. Senator Baxter has the lid shut tight. Family only. I understand that."

"I do, too." Rick shifted in the soft cushion. "I'm meeting with her and—"

"Baxter?"

"And Ben Sheridan, tomorrow. Their request. And the urging of Detective Ward."

"Tomorrow? Damn, that was fast. Chris said the invite was coming, but—"

"Chris who?"

"Evans. Chris Evans. Junior partner here."

"Ward didn't mention him."

"He handles the senator's affairs. Everything."

"Think he's on the invitation?"

"I'm sure he is."

Rick focused vacantly toward the glass, following the small white clouds floating past. "Anyone else?"

"Probably not. Chris is her guy, and she only wants one. No team effort. One point of contact. It's a privacy thing. Discretion when needed, and not negotiable. The senator can be a handful on occasion; demanding, entitled, aggressive. She's not an easy gig, I know. I've been first dial on her call list for too many stretches. But no more; things are on cruise control now with Evans. He's ambitious and intent on keeping her happy. He wanted the door key into our wonderful world of politics, and he got it. Assured me it would represent well for the firm in the future. It's been a good match. We'll see. So far, he's not wrong."

"So, he may be doing the talking tomorrow? What do I need

to know, D?"

"About Chris? How much do you want?"

"You tell me. Never met another lawyer."

"Lucky for you." Adrian smiled and let his big arm rest across the back of the couch. "Both parents were damn good trial lawyers. Neither had time for a kid, though. Got divorced when Chris was eight. He got all the DNA; the good and the bad. The senator has groomed him well, and that's meant success, but the home life is a struggle. Seems ambivalent about it, though."

Nancy knocked and came through the door with drinks. She set them on the table. Rick stood, scrunched his shoulders, and stretched his neck.

Adrian took a long drink. "Rick, don't worry about Chris. I'll get him on the same page. And don't give Bobby Ward another thought, either. That man is straight as they come, my friend. Fair and sharp. Be glad he's on this; could be worse. Hopefully it doesn't get there."

Rick shook his head. "What the hell's going on, D? First a detective, and now I'm holding court with a senator? I don't need this. Not sure why people would think I know where Allie went. There have been times when I wouldn't hear from her for weeks. Not a surprise. Why would I? She's a teenager with a life." He swallowed hard, trying to check his frustration. "It's March and she's tired of winter, like everyone else. Maybe take a look under her bed."

Adrian frowned. "Damn! Where the hell'd my Rick Larson go? Known the man for fifty years, and that's sure not him."

Rick waved him off. "Allie's fine. She's somewhere safe, cooling off about something the stepmother did." He sensed Adrian's skepticism and searched the room for distraction. "I wasn't thinking it could be anything else," he went on. "But then Ward showed up."

"You don't need a lawyer," Adrian said quickly. "If that's where you're going. Are you?"

"Needing an attorney is low on my list," Rick mumbled.

"Well, that's good."

"Can't afford them." Rick cocked his head, fixated on a new painting on the wall.

"That's true. Now listen, Bobby came to talk to me earlier. Mostly about you, but—" Adrian scowled and shouted, "Hey!"

Rick peered over his shoulder.

"I promise. I've got you."

"Thanks, D. You've always had us."

"I know you, Richard Larson. You're concerned about what's important, and you and Allie are close. Any ideas where she might go?"

"The only time she and I shared was at the marina." Rick crossed to the window. "I think about her being in trouble. Scared. Gone."

"I get it. All of it. Gone is too close to home. Am I reading you?"

Rick stood motionless. "Don't know if I can go through this again, D."

"I'm sorry, brother. But, I said I got you. Tre and me, we're here. And I have some people out there looking, too. We'll find her."

Rick studied the busy street below. "You haven't lost a beat my friend."

"Good for the blood pressure. Does Tre know yet?"

Rick turned, shaking his head. "No. I waited. Probably a day too long. Thought Allie would show up back home, or at her dad's boat. Somewhere. It's going to be tough on him."

"Give it a couple more days. Your instincts may be right on."

Rick winced.

"You need to trust me on this one," Adrian said. "She's gonna be okay."

Adrian loosened his tie and undid the collar button, waiting for Rick to join him again on the couch. "Funny thing. Did I ever mention our so-called grass there at the marina reminds me a lot of your rundown playground up in Jersey?"

Rick smiled. "Many times."

"Rough place to begin. You and Tre were lucky to have each other." Adrian shook his head. "Not sure why that just came out of nowhere." He glanced away. "Missing Tre, I guess. Tell me how he's doing."

"Some days I'm not sure how he makes it through. Breathing is harder for him—every day. He needs to see a doctor."

"Good luck with that. It's only gonna get worse, you know."

"Yeah, it is."

Adrian faltered. "I have some news we need to share with him soon. About the offer. With Allie's situation, though—"

"Don't think it's the best timing."

"Might never be good timing." Adrian hesitated. "The sale is going through, Rick. The numbers are good. We can live with the rest."

He pulled forward as Rick lowered his head.

"Don't you go there, Rickie. This is good. And I told you, remember? When I handed you both the keys, remember what I said?"

"The day would come." Rick's voice faded. "I know."

"That's right. The day would come. And everything will be good. I said that, too." Adrian pulled a hand across his chin. "The challenge is, they want it fast. And the city's in the mix now. Permit expediting in exchange for an acre. They want some community space with their name on it. The heat is cranking up to get the environmental analysis done. It's remote land now, always has been, but the master plan for that western frontage shows a different future. It all hinges on the clean-up, though. A lot of shit's soaked into the little piece of ground over the years. The majority of it before we got there, but the city doesn't care whose shit it was. Now it's ours. Long and short of it is, they want it free and clear, empty in four months. I can probably get us five. Or they'll just wait for the city to condemn it and take their chances on a deal behind the curtain."

Rick leaned back, crossing his arms. "That's fast. Guess it's happening, isn't it?"

"For all the right reasons. It's time."

"This is gonna rock Tre, too."

"You both are going to have some money out of this. There's more life out there to find."

"Yeah." Rick pushed up slowly and retreated to the windows, casting his empty gaze across the brilliant sky. "Tre's lost too much, D. Over too many years. I know he holds onto that. And now Allie . . . it's a lot to leave behind."

Adrian moved close. "We have to help him try."

They stared across the city, both seeing different meanings in the change Adrian had shared.

"I'll talk to him, captain," Rick said. A slow, thoughtful nod followed. "Thanks for everything, D. You're a good man."

Chapter 8

After leaving Adrian's office, Rick drove aimlessly through the city. He had an hour to spare and took every minute of it debating whether or not to follow through on the unexpected invitation from Sarah. The visit with his friend had unsettled him, which contributed to lingering indecision about sharing his afternoon.

At 2:00 p.m. though, he parked the truck and started a slow walk around the Tidal Basin. As was typical, pockets of water remained along depressed areas of the basin's path from the previous night's high tide. A lone seagull stood perched on the damp edging a few yards ahead. Rick veered to join him and stepped close to the stone lip, stopping with the toes of his boots extended out over the water. The afternoon's sunlight lay across the surface, sharing mirrorlike reflections of the monuments and cherry trees gracing the perimeter. Early budding would start soon, and droves of tourists would follow, crowding the bordering walks all hours of the day. Rick enjoyed the spot and spent time here occasionally, but never in March so close to the blossoms. Off-season months suited him, when he could be assured of finding his valued moments of solitude.

"Hi there!" Sarah's cheerful voice from behind stunned him.

Rick tensed, unable to turn. He contemplated the murky water, curious how he had been entrapped by indecision.

Sarah moved close to the edge beside him. "Thanks for meeting me." She beamed, catching her breath. "Apologies if you've been waiting long. Traffic. Yikes!"

He glanced at the growing smile as she pulled off her sunglasses. Soon, he sighed and relented. "No worries. Just got here."

"See, we did it! Successful texting even at our age. Did I surprise you? I wasn't sure if you would—"

"I wasn't either. I probably shouldn't have."

She faced him. "Is everything okay?"

Rick rubbed the back of his neck, then adjusted his hat. "It's not the best day for this."

"For what? Meeting new people?"

"Yeah. A lot on my mind."

"Just a walk," she said with understanding. "Some company on a pretty day. Maybe a new friend."

"I'm okay on friends," he mumbled, drifting his focus across the basin.

Sarah's brow wrinkled, "Are you sure about that?" She tilted her head, trying for eye contact. "Would walking help?"

Rick answered by starting slow steps along the path. Sarah joined him in silence.

After rounding the first curve in the basin, she said, "You seem worried. Was everything alright with the detective?"

Rick cleared his throat and clenched his hands together.

Sarah faltered, looking away. "Oh, forgive me. That's none of my business."

He continued the sluggish pace; focused on the walkway ahead. "It's okay," he said finally. "It's heading for the news anyway." He breathed deeply. "Allison Sheridan is missing."

She stopped abruptly. "As in Baxter-Sheridan?" Her mouth fell open. "Wait, is that Allie from your—"

"That's her."

"Did the detective say anything?"

"He did. Be available and go meet with her parents."

"They must be worried sick."

"The dad is. Her mom passed away. Not so sure about the senator."

"And no one knows where she might have gone?"

Rick took a few seconds. "Teenagers, I hear they can be unpredictable."

"That's terrible, Rick." Sarah extended a hand to his arm. "I'm sure she'll be okay, though."

"Yeah, I'm sure she's fine. A boyfriend I don't know about, or a cousin is helping her hide out in the basement. Allie's an only child. She's a good kid who needs a break on occasion. The home front she describes with the stepmom sounds pretty rough sometimes."

"Her mom dying, it's so hard to recover."

"Sounded horrible. It was very fast."

"And she found refuge with you. Something she needed."

"I tried. Her dad uprooted them to DC to get away from the pain, but I don't think Allie ever will."

Silence fell as they rounded a bend in the trail, turning their backs to the retreating sun. Rick sensed Sarah peering.

"Ever married?" she asked tentatively. "Any kids of your own? You seem to be good with them, if Allie's any indication."

He registered no reaction to the question, holding his lowered gaze a few feet ahead.

It was a while before Sarah said, "Man of few words, I see."

"I'm not used to conversation, Sarah. If you don't practice, this is what you offer. And I don't practice."

"I didn't mean to—"

Joggers surprised them, calling out from behind on their left. A leisurely stride, the three older women gestured a quick 'thanks' as Sarah and Rick gave them room.

Rick bit his lip and slowed, veering away gradually, He came to a stop on the stone edge and studied the reflections. "I did have a family, Sarah."

She moved next to him.

"We married young. When I came back from 'Nam. We had a child. A girl. Then they needed to leave." Rick muttered, "It was the right thing for them to do."

"Oh, I'm so sorry." She wavered. "Do you ever get to see them?"

Rick lowered his head, deciding. He squeezed his hands intently, considering the dark scars across the backs as if for the first time. "Beth is in her forties now, somewhere. No . . . I never see her. Allie is somewhere, too. I hope it's for different reasons."

Sarah's eyes held on him.

He eventually faced her. "Tough day. I told you I shouldn't have come." He met her stare, once more restless with the presence of compassion and her expression's curious readiness to smile. He had dismissed these unfamiliar offerings and the imagined ease between the two of them in the wake of Detective Ward's visit two days ago. *Too close to home,* were the words Adrian had probed. Rick sensed a rising need for retreat.

Abruptly, he jammed both hands into his coat pockets and looked away. "I'm alone most of the time, Sarah, and that's okay. But thank you for today." He spun. "I should go."

Sarah didn't call after him. Rick couldn't look back. Several steps along, he fell captive to a painful vision of Tre: they would both be homeless soon. Again. Rick plodded, gradually able to draw deep breaths and quiet the panic; Adrian had them; he always would. Rick's head fell back. Thin clouds were sneaking in from the west, slowly fading the last hours of daylight. March had offered him its long awaited comfort this day: late afternoon stillness, the sun's low path on the horizon, soft south light flickering across the tree's bare branches. Thankful, Rick exhaled and continued slowly down the walk, his mind far from Adrian's piercing wisdom and the pain of Sarah's innocent curiosity.

Chapter 9

The following afternoon, Rick needed forty-five minutes to make the trip across DC. Endless idling for long minutes at more than one traffic light left him reconsidering the decision to attend, believing also the impending discussion could easily become an inquisition. Rick's fingers tapped the wheel. The red light caught him. The rear half of the truck extended far into the intersection. Horns, loud and incessant, sounded from multiple directions. Rick hated Georgetown. He couldn't recall the last time he had reason to be there. He avoided the M street corridor. Too many historic buildings preserved only in service to a single purpose: one for which he no longer had use. Too much alcohol on the streets.

The truck's temperature gauge crept toward red as Rick managed to inch forward clear of the bottleneck. Before he left, Delia had offered use of her Accord, but Rick remained a creature of some habits, and fiercely, though inexplicably, loyal to Tre's old Chevy. It had never made him walk. The frustration of the drive brought him full appreciation for Allie's commitment to their visits and the effort she expended in coming to see him. She said the Uber ride gave her time to read, and when her dad bought the Jeep, driving in and of itself served to restore her spirit.

Fifteen minutes later, Rick parked along the circular drive in front of the largest estate on Laverock Place. He meandered along the winding brick walk to the front door, recalling Allie's descriptive reference. He paused at the first step to assess what 'rich as shit' gets you in the Georgetown world: big house, old brick, stone and slate, manicured bluff a mile and a half west of Key Bridge. With possessions in life having lost any meaning for him long ago, Rick examined the hulking residence with little outward expression and less feeling, quickly coming to understand why Allie hated it. He delayed at the soaring entrance portico and contemplated walking away, but the door opened unexpectedly. An energetic assistant in his mid-twenties sporting a conservative jacket and tie, welcomed him and anxiously ushered him down a hall, through a family room and out to a sun porch facing south across the Potomac River. The dramatic view to the west offered rushing water over the rocky riverbed. To the east, the Georgetown waterfront and Kennedy Center beyond.

Never a fan of crowded gatherings, Rick released an audible exhale as he surveyed the room of eight people, most returning his stare. Ben Sheridan rose to greet him. Senator Baxter did not, choosing to remain seated on the settee under the windows. She nodded at the young man and her two staffers, who each quickly exited, closing the French doors behind them.

"Let me introduce you, Rick," Ben said. "My wife, Senator Baxter."

Michelle held her eyes lowered to the laptop.

Ben bit his lip and continued, "This is our family attorney, Chris Evans, and his associate, Leah Benning." Ben raised a hand to Rick's shoulder. "Leah, a little context for this meeting. I had a mishap with our boat a couple of years ago; a mechanical issue that left me no choice but to introduce myself to Rick here, who ran the only working marina for a hundred miles. He took care of us, and we got to know each other a little, and I still keep *MORNING STAR* there through the winters. Allie was with me when we limped into his place that first day." Ben smiled at Rick. "If my daughter likes someone, she's all in. She and Rick became friends and—"

Michelle slammed her laptop shut and pulled her glasses off. "Don't you mean *our* daughter?" She folded her arms. "So, are we finished with story time, Ben?"

Ben eyed her and lowered his hand. "Anyway, Leah, their friendship is why we asked Rick to join us. We're all just trying to figure this out."

He sighed, turning to Rick. "Thanks for coming. Grab a seat. Can we get you something to drink?"

Michelle cast her laptop aside, staring intently at the visitor. "Mr. Larson won't be staying that long," she said bluntly. "I have a meeting." She held her assessing gaze on him. "Mr. Larson, do you know where our daughter is?"

Ben's generous words had lulled Rick into a relieved sense of welcome. The senator's veiled remark and accompanying glare jarred him. She sat poised—a snug suit over her slight frame, straight, dark hair above the shoulders, a slender nose and high cheeks, thin eyebrows, almost disappearing. Heavy make-up hiding some work. Rick imagined the obsessive preparation needed each day. Allie's stories had not prepared him for this contrast, though—a polish masking the chill behind her piercing eyes.

He took a second to recover, finally managing a wary voice. "I'm sorry for the concern you're both going through, Senator. This is very difficult. I know how you're feeling. I've—"

"I'm sure you don't. Please answer the question. Do you know where she is?"

Rick's jaw tensed. "Of course not. I have no idea. I wish I did."

Her eyes narrowed on him. After a moment she turned aside, nodding to the attorney. Chris stood and buttoned his suit coat, prepared to approach the stand.

Ben extended his arm to intervene. "Rick, what *can* you tell us? Details you can remember? When did you see her last?"

"The police asked me the same question, but I'm sure you already know that. I saw her two weeks ago. She helped me with *MORNING STAR.* That's what we do mostly when she's there, we work on your boat."

"She likes you," Ben said. "She talks about you a lot. And yes, I know you've had a discussion with Detective Ward, but we wanted to speak with you in person. The detective understood. He was fine with this."

Rick deliberated, scanning the expressions around the room. "So, speaking of the detective—I have to ask. Did Ward mention the possibility of a ransom request?"

Michelle stared at him. "Interesting for you to mention," she said quickly. "That very possibility is why I approved this meeting with you. I was curious as to whether you would show."

"Michelle!" Ben spun toward her. "Dammit!"

"Money always plays a part, doesn't it, Mr. Larson. Is it the reward for information that brought you here?"

Rick glanced at Ben. "I guess I'm not surprised," he said, turning back to Senator Baxter. "But how did you get from letting your daughter cross the city for two years to hang out with a stranger, to now considering that he might be a kidnapper? She's seventeen and crosses town by herself, from here to there. I know it's not across the country, but it's not around the block either. You let her come; I assumed it was because you trusted me with her."

Michelle returned a cynical smile. "Trust or not, Mr. Larson, the play dates are over."

"Apparently they are. But just so you know, when Allie was there with me, and Tre, she was safe. I offered to drive her home. I listened to her." Rick grabbed a breath. "And I haven't always been good at that. But it seemed important to her. I didn't hear or see any flags. But then, we don't always."

"Sounding like quite the expert, Mr. Larson. Do *you* have a daughter?"

Rick's shoulders slumped.

Chris Evans closed on him, breaking the silence. "Mr. Larson, as you describe them, all your efforts with Allison are noble. Understand though, that the circumstances surrounding your acquaintance with the senator's daughter leave much room for concern. Anything that could have precipitated the situation we currently face and placed Allison in danger, all of it will be scrutinized. That includes you, Mr. Larson. Ben's testimony on your behalf is why you're here, and not in jail. But that testimony is only worth so much. He actually knows very little about you."

"Chris!" Ben snapped.

Chris went on, dismissing the censure. "And Ben knows even less about your older African American friend."

Rick's hand went to his chin, observing what Adrian had signaled. Senator Baxter's grooming on full display. Chris Evans had learned well; timing, expressions, when to listen, and when to turn up the volume. Rick followed his eyes. All of it seemed intuitive, even the walk, more of a swagger. A man overdosed on the importance of image and power.

"That's enough!" Ben stepped closer.

Chris' chest pushed forward with a deep breath. "Tell me something, Mr. Larson, have the police spoken with him as well?"

"Nobody talks to him," Rick said bluntly.

Chris smirked. "I knew the answer. They haven't. But that may change, and possibly soon."

Rick's prompt look to Ben and the senator forecast the

conversation's end. "Maybe you should be more worried about your friends than hers. Just a thought." He backed away and crossed toward the French doors.

Ben shook his head and hurried after him, knocking into a chair. He shoved it out of the way and seconds later the doors slammed behind them.

⁓

Michelle stared through the patterned glass, mumbling as she watched her husband walk away down the hall. "Jesus, Ben." Lifting her chin, she turned to Chris. "Okay, first thing. All of this stays with us." She shot a glance at Leah. "Chris, as of this moment, managing Allie's situation is your life. Do you understand me?"

"Of course."

"Nothing else matters to you. If you don't preside over this for me, my first call will not be to you. It will be to Adrian. And those political aspirations of yours will be a non-starter. Do you understand that?" She didn't wait for an answer. "Mid-terms are seven months away. Up until last week, I was assured of holding my seat. But that was yesterday's confidence. Something like this can change everything, and very quickly. And I won't accept that. Ben's selfish little shit of a daughter can blow it all up. I've had to answer too many questions about her these past few years, and I'm done."

Michelle stood and approached Chris. "Ben's putting this out there, everywhere."

"I know he is."

"His special little girl is missing. Well, what a surprise. He's a weak man whose daughter is beyond entitled. And she's destructively impulsive, thus the situation. We don't know how that's going to play."

"The media pump feels chaotic to me, Senator. From Ben's

perspective, it's an understandable effort to extend, but not a good one for you."

"I don't disagree. So let me make this clear; I've held this seat for six terms. I will not lose it. So, find the girl, or don't find her. I'm not sure if I give a damn *or* have a preference. If we find her, we have to manage whatever fucked up story comes back with her. If we don't find her, all we have to do is appear sad and wait for the story to get run over. News cycles are fast."

"Senator—"

Michelle raised her hand instantly. "Don't screw this up, Chris. Adrian believes in you. We both do. Time to live up to that. You need to push on this Larson guy. And find that other old man."

"They're both Vets." Leah's strong voice surprised them, quieting the room. "There's history."

Michelle tilted a look to her. "*And*?"

Leah stepped closer. "Vietnam. Fall of '68 into '69. Combat. Basic training camp at Parris Island. Both reported the same day. Arrived together. They grew up friends in New Jersey." She hesitated to glance at Chris. "Adrian Dumars was on the same bus."

Michelle's hand went to her chin. "Really?"

"Marines. All three enlisted."

Michelle turned intently to Chris. "Did you know?"

"Not that I'm—"

Michelle scowled, waving him off again. "Never mind! Not that important. Brave patriots, but too long ago to matter. We've endured three wars since. They get no points for that one. Ancient history. So, you heard me, push on them a little. Let's be sure they aren't our story; latent sociopaths or God knows what else. One or both of them. That would suck, reeking of irresponsible parenting. The old guy was right about that, and I don't want my name in any such headline. Ben is on his own."

Chris folded his arms. "What about the kidnapping ask? Against your wise objections, we let Ben have this discussion with his boat buddy. It was worthless, we knew it would be. But the fact is, Larson shows as a tired old man, maybe desperate. Maybe looking for a payday. Hell, there are half a dozen buildings at that marina. Allie could be tied up in any one of them right now. Larson knows Ben and how he could play it."

"The possibility has not escaped me. And Ben is an idiot for making it easy on him if that's what's happening here."

"Is the first call to Ward then? I think we need the search warrant."

"I'll handle that with the detective. Adrian and Larson are friends. And Adrian knows all the detectives in DC. He would slow things down."

"Let us check first," Leah said. "It will be faster, quieter. Easier to control the noise if she happens to be there."

Michelle assessed her, finally nodding. "Agreed. Do it." She moved back to the couch and picked up her laptop. "I want to be clear of this by June." She returned her attention to the screen. "Heaven forbid Allie turns up dead."

The French doors slammed back, and Ben entered with directed anger at Michelle. "I couldn't catch him! Rick's gone. Thanks to you both!"

Michelle didn't look up, gesturing for Chris to leave. "June, or sooner, Chris," she called to him. "Do what you have to."

Chris led Leah out, both avoiding eye contact with Ben as he strode past. The doors closed loudly behind them. They moved into the den across from the foyer and Chris held the door as the staffers hustled through. Leah stood by the windows attending to her phone as he approached.

"Did I really just hear her say those words?"

"Forget it," he said sharply. "She's under a lot of pressure with this re-election. Of course, she doesn't want any harm to come to Allison. The important takeaway there was stay on Larson, as in right now."

"I did hear that, as well, and I already sent a message to an acquaintance: he can be trusted. Larson just pulled out. Ron's got him."

"Ron?"

Leah nodded.

"You sure?"

"Of course."

"Okay, good. That's why you and I click."

"Because I can read your mind?" She lifted an eyebrow. "Or because I make my own decisions on your behalf?"

"All the above."

Leah's phone buzzed.

"For now, he's just following. Right?"

Leah looked up. "Whatever you want. Ron can be direct if we ask him to. Money, or something else off script?"

Chris backed away and paced the room. "Nothing else. Not yet. Let's just see what his pattern is. We need to know why Larson is in her life. Fuck if I have any clues on that one."

"He seems harmless, but who knows?"

"Like I said, he looks desperate to me."

Chapter 10

Endless lines of brake lights along Wisconsin spread out in front of Rick. Inching up to the fifth red light in a row, he brought his fist down in frustration on the truck's cracking dashboard. Twenty-five minutes of inhaling exhaust fumes while also trying to breathe away the vision of Michelle Baxter's smug smile was enough. Rick had no more energy reserves to process the infuriating encounter. He needed distraction and the fastest route home. He imposed his way over into the next lane and chose the parkway along the Potomac. Views across the river would help: no buildings, clear sky, and green grass along the shore's edge. The noisy old truck puffed out smoke in each gear as he accelerated down the ramp. Traffic thinned out quickly, and he worked his shoulders, trying to relax his clenched grip on the wheel and erase Chris Evans' jutting chin and absurd posture. Rick stole glimpses of the calm water, feeling the needed serenity taking hold. The vain image of Evans was fading.

Rick glanced at his side mirror to change lanes and picked up on a white BMW several cars back, blinker on and moving into the left lane as well. Recall of the white BMW in the circular driveway at Laverock Lane distracted him for only a second and his gaze returned to the river. Five minutes later he entered the C Street tunnel under the Capitol, loud echoes from the truck's exhaust trailing behind. Rick glanced in the mirror again, wondering. Three cars shared the tunnel with him; none drew a second look. He didn't use his mirrors again until turning off 12th onto M Street, SE. The open area between the narrow road and railroad tracks hid nothing and Rick easily spotted a similar white car at the same light on 11th Street behind him. Rick had the street to himself, and he slowed to a crawl, focused on the intersection. With the light change, the car swerved onto M Street. Instantly, Rick shifted gears and accelerated to the overpass. He came to a stop in the middle of the pavement, shadowed from the bright sun by the low structure. After several tries, he found reverse and backed the truck across the deep shoulder. He was out quickly and moved to the front grille to open the hood.

Across the street, beyond the few trees and underbrush, a half dozen elderly men congregated around two distressed wooden picnic tables, laughing, lifting beers, and gesturing. Four lines were in the water; poles wedged into the remains of old stumps. No fish in the buckets yet. Rick peered down M Street, SE, and crossed the road to warm greetings from the group of fishermen.

"How's your day, Timmy?" Rick said.

"Almost as good as yesterday was." Timmy's broad grin showed instantly. "Good to see you, Richard. How's my man Tre doin'? He good?"

"Always." Rick casually took up position behind the largest tree, his back to the road. Hearing the approaching car accelerate, he inched closer to Timmy and sneaked a look over his shoulder.

Two hundred feet from the overpass, the driver slowed suddenly. The group watched the car creep into the shadows shrouding the truck. Rick fixated on the passenger side window, but the heavy tint offered nothing about the occupants. Coasting off down M Street, SE, the car soon disappeared around the next bend. Rick stared unblinking down the empty road.

"Hey, Richard, maybe have a buyer there." The others joined

in with Timmy's laugh.

"Tre's never lettin' that ol' girl go," came another voice.

Rick turned, managing a smile as Timmy slapped him on the shoulder.

Timmy cocked his head, squinting past him. "You keepin' some new company, aren't ya, Richard? Look' it there. Your ride's back."

Rick spun as the white car approached at speed. The driver eased off to a crawl passing the truck again, then pulled onto the shoulder.

After a moment, a man slipped out through the driver's door. He glanced across the street and moved toward the truck, inspecting the open hood and leaning in to regard the engine. He straightened after a few seconds, checked over both shoulders and stepped to the passenger door, peeking in through the open window.

Timmy said, "I tell ya that man is *lost,* Richard. And now I believe he's just fuckin' 'round with Tre's truck."

Rick pulled his brim lower. "Yeah, he is," He moved past Timmy and marched across the road.

The man reached for the rusty door handle, unaware of Rick's nearing steps. He shook it roughly. As the door finally creaked open, Rick came up behind, extended his right arm and slammed it shut.

"Can I help you?"

The man pulled back several steps, tilted his head slightly, and surveyed Rick.

Rick picked up on the tensed jawline. He was solid and decades younger. Rick had at least five inches on him, but he also knew size didn't always guarantee advantage.

The man fixed on Rick and slowly pulled a hand across his chin. "My dad had an old Chevy like this. Same model. Probably the same year. Just remembering. That's all."

"Not for sale."

He looked past Rick's shoulder. Four of the fishermen were walking across the street toward them. He pivoted and moved alertly back to the BMW. Opening the driver's door, he said, "I work for a developer here in town. Trying to find *River View Marina.* Didn't mind being lost when I saw the truck, but—am I close by any chance?"

Rick studied the stranger. Sunglasses didn't hide the hard features. Hair was too black for his age. There was nothing to discern from the casual clothes, only that they didn't fit the car.

"Marina's not for sale either," Rick said.

The man appraised each of the fishermen again as they filled in behind Rick. Two of them stood taller and thicker. "My mistake." The half smile came quickly then faded as he slipped into the driver's seat and slammed the door closed. Instantly, the engine raced and the tires scattered gravel as he backed onto the shoulder. The window lowered, and he accelerated south on M Street, SE.

Timmy stepped close to Rick, shaking his head. He extended a hand to Rick's shoulder. "Told ya that man was lost, Richard. Now c'mon with us and sit a while. Maybe bring us some luck." Laughs and commentary started quickly as the four strolled back across the street to the tables.

Rick moved to the middle of M Street, SE, his eyes still fixed on the car speeding away.

Chapter 11

The overhead door was open early the next morning, but dark, lowering clouds offered little chance of daylight finding the far reaches of Tre's shed. Shelving along the back wall extended high into shadow. Tre teetered on a ladder, eight feet up. He wasn't supposed to be: Rick's orders from last year, when Tre fell off the fifth rung and landed awkwardly, his shoulder hitting first on the concrete slab too close to a rusty anchor fluke. A long discussion ensued, and Rick believed he had persuaded his friend to stay on the ground. Whatever gems were stored above reach could remain there, until a younger buyer came in with an offer and a willingness to climb the ladder for them. At the time, Tre bowed, indulging his friend. Rick chained the ladders to the boat stand under the Constellation. Subject closed. But Tre had later insisted a customer would only buy what he or she could see and reminded Rick that there were many ways to cut a chain.

Tre reached to the back of the shelf and slid a large bronze ship's bell out to the front edge. That's where it should be. He dusted it off. The bell would bring a hundred dollars.

~

Sarah pulled into the marina lot and parked in front of the office. Schooner greeted her first as she got out. Everything about his hello conveyed acceptance. Happy eyes, excited panting, wagging tail. He leaned in to nuzzle her, then, with his work done, he ambled off toward the shed. Rick's truck sat parked in front of the open overhead door, windows down, loud music confirming him to be an early riser. Reassured, Sarah balanced the small box of doughnuts on top of two filled coffee cups and followed her furry guide.

Stepping through the door opening, her gaze landed on the old man balanced atop a wooden ladder along the back wall. Instantly concerned, she hurried to the bench seat and lowered the coffee, ready now with free hands to help if needed. From behind, Sarah observed him as frail. Well-worn army fatigues and a baggy long-sleeved sweatshirt hung loosely across his upper body: all of it wrinkled but surprisingly clean. Each of his movements showed slow, deliberate intention. Sarah watched him pause to focus on both hands, tilting his head, appearing uncertain about whether the fingers were doing as instructed by the mind.

Sarah tested his hearing with a weak cough. Tre cocked his head to listen. In an instant, he backed down the ladder, only becoming aware of Sarah's presence upon turning. His round eyes narrowed immediately in their deep sockets. He bit his lip and shuffled to the bench seat.

Rick's brief discussion with Sarah about his friend had come with little description, only that he was too thin. Rick conveyed this with concern; eating had become less and less important to Tre. From the few details, Sarah had created a much different image in her mind, of someone seemingly much younger. The weariness showed instantly across Tre's expression, though. His eyes shifted often, with deep furrows pushing out from the corners. A short gray stubble rose high on his cheeks. The same gray followed down his neck and disappeared into the vee of his sweatshirt. The green fatigues faded to light brown in the thighs. Sarah caught herself staring at his boots; canvas green and brown high tops, dusty with observable holes, not many miles left on them.

She smiled. "Good morning."

Tre creased his brow without answering.

"Forgive me for wandering in, I was looking for Rick." She flattened her lips, hoping for a response. "I'm Sarah Cromwell."

"I know who you are." Tre's gentle words stunned her. "Good morning, Sarah."

Her mouth fell open. "You know my name?"

"I've seen you. You're Rick's friend."

She balked, collecting herself. "As are you."

Tre bowed his head, then leaned over the ship's wheel table to pick up a half-smoked joint. He lit it and closed his eyes, his head falling back with the deep inhale. Seconds later, he extended his hand, tentatively offering it to Sarah.

She reached for the two cups. "Thanks, I'll umm, just start with coffee this morning. Would you like some?"

Tre declined with a gesture and nursed the joint again.

Sarah's cast darted around the space. "My daughter was here in your shed a couple of days ago; she found a gift for a friend." Sarah swept her arms out. "This is amazing what you have here! Rick shared a little, but I had no idea. It's a bit of a lost world. So many pieces! Like treasure. It's a museum, really. Lots of old stories, I'm sure."

Tre twisted, surveying all of it with a slow nod. "Just a lot of stuff now. Used to have more meaning. Not so much anymore. Time to move it on."

She turned to the large cruiser occupying the entire left side of the shed. "I can't imagine how that boat got in here—"

"Rick fell in love with her; not too hard to understand. When he attaches, he takes care of you. Wanted to be able to work on her year-round. Calls it home, too. He and Schooner sleep aboard, sometimes."

"Really?" Sarah cleared her throat, fumbling for more words. "You and Rick, you both wear hats."

Tre glanced her way, then raised an unsteady hand to intently adjust his. "Good hat can save your life. Was a time that was important to know. War teaches you that—about taking care of yourself and your friends. Some of it takes hold."

Tre reached gently to secure the strap. "My brother's. From the war. His boonie." Tre sighed. "My honor to wear it."

Sarah's head tilted. "Boonie?"

"There's a story goes with that name, but . . ."

Without notice, Tre turned away, shuffling back and forth slowly behind the bench seat. He rambled in a soft, cracking voice, his vacant gaze wandering the walls. "Jon was a good man. But Quang Tri Province took its toll in '68. Bad time." Tre's hands pressed to his temples. "Too many Marines. I should have been there for you, brother."

He stopped abruptly, bracing motionless against the seat. "Should've taken care of you, like always." Absently, his trembling hands lifted the joint, and he tried hard for a last draw.

Sarah looked away, needing to take a deep breath, wanting to understand. "I'm sure you—" She fidgeted with the top of her coffee cup, finally glancing back at Tre. Meeting his moist eyes, she stalled and took a long drink. "I'm sorry about Allie," she blurted.

Tre tossed the joint instantly with a glare. Both hands went to his thighs, intently rubbing the worn cotton fatigues. "What'd Rick say about Allie?"

"Just that," Sarah faltered, watching his somber expression harden. "Oh, that she's missing? I thought you knew."

Tre's deep eyes widened.

Sarah froze. "I—I'm sure she'll be okay."

Without warning, his hands slammed hard against the bench seat, "You need to leave!" Tre's eyes danced nervously as he started toward the Constellation. He stopped instantly and spun back. "Go!" he thundered. "You don't know that! Allie could be dead. Like all the others!"

"Tre!" Rick's loud call from behind echoed through the shelves. He stood centered in the door opening. "It's okay, Tre. This is Sarah. I asked her to come by to help us."

Tre's lost expression found his friend. "Where's Allie, Rick?"

"Tre—" Rick twisted, hearing a vehicle approach through the gate. A silver Land Rover accelerated across the lot. Gravel dust settled as it stopped feet behind the truck. He pulled a hand through his hair and checked over his shoulder. "Allie's fine, Tre. You keep going on the shelves. And stay off the ladder!"

Rick stepped closer to Sarah and extended a hand, encouraging her to follow. He dismissed her urgent apology as they approached the car.

The driver's side rear window lowered and Ben Sheridan leaned his head out.

"Morning." Ben loosened his tie and showed a distracted smile to Sarah. "I was hoping to catch you, Rick."

"Tell me you have news."

Ben's gaze fell as he shook his head. "None. Have you eaten?"

Rick nodded and moved closer.

"Just as well," Ben said. "I don't have much time anyway. Strange request: can you and I take a ride together and talk?"

Rick folded his arms. "Thought we did that yesterday."

"That felt more like an interrogation." Ben frowned. "I'd like to try again. Can you ride with me to Reagan? I need to be in New York for a conference in four hours."

"Gotta be tough to keep the wheels spinning with all that's

going on."

"Yeah, it is. And I could use your help. Can you take a ride? Kate will drop you at the station—I know you have an appointment."

Rick studied Ben's face, then turned to Sarah. "I should do this," he said. "But you had a nice idea. Thanks." Rick rushed a sigh. "And I'm sorry about our walk. I just . . ."

"Don't give it a thought. I was being nosy; I should be the one apologizing. It sounded like a tough day. Raincheck?"

Kate tapped the horn.

"Sure. And Sarah, don't worry about Tre. He's forgotten already."

⁓

Rick's door had just closed as Kate pulled away. The dividing window rose as he struggled with the seat belt.

Kate's calm voice came through the small speakers. "Traffic looks good, and the plane's ready, Ben. We'll be fine on time."

"Thanks, Kate."

Rick smiled. "That's what I like about you; always first names."

"Formalities get in the way. And speaking of formalities, damn, my apologies again about that bullshit yesterday."

"Wasn't worth much." Rick said. "I know you're worried about Allie. She'll be okay, though. I was hoping when you pulled up this morning that you were coming to tell me that."

"I wish that was the reason." Ben wavered. "Listen, about yesterday, I don't know if Allie has ever shared anything with you—" He twisted in the seat. "I hope not, but it wouldn't surprise me. I don't think there are a lot of other people she trusts. Things have not been easy between her and the senator. A lot is missing for my daughter right now. I'm not sure I know all of it: obviously, I don't."

"Ben, that's none of my business."

The Rover swerved into the next lane to pass a Metro bus, then sped through the intersection at 16th and R Street as the light turned red. A soft *'sorry'* whispered through the speakers.

"It *is* your business, Rick. You understand my daughter better than I do at this point. I mean that. And you should know, we've been in contact with everyone: relatives, friends, school." He shook his head. "Coffee shops. Her co-work space. No one's seen her." Ben's jaw tensed. "I don't have anyone to blame for this but myself."

Rick sensed the panic growing. "Ben, I care about Allie, and your family. She befriended a lonely old man. And you said okay with it."

Ben snapped, "Can't you think of *anything* else?"

Rick's mouth fell open as he pulled back against the door. "No, Ben. I wish I had—"

"There must be something, dammit! Anything!"

Rick caught Kate's glance in the rear-view mirror. He gave Ben some time, shifting in his seat to face him. The etched lines in Ben's forehead seemed deeper. The close cut beard wasn't perfect as usual. The same straight features he shared with Allie had tightened. Ben pulled both hands straight back through his wavy hair.

Rick said, "She's gonna be okay, Ben."

Ben sat motionless, staring out the window. "Shit," he finally muttered. "So much for trying again. You don't deserve that, Rick. I'm just not so sure she is."

Rick hesitated. "Ben, you asked. All I know is, Allie's worried. She's afraid of the senator and she thinks that you're, well, too *decent* at times. She doesn't see you stand up to her."

"Decent?" Ben's jaw tightened. "What the hell is that about?"

"I thought you would know."

Ben clenched both hands into fists. "Damn. She must love that contrast: her stepmother is anything but."

"The stepmom reference, I don't think Allie ever warmed up to that." Rick watched him, waiting for permission.

"Tell me," Ben said.

"Allie sees the cracks. Between you and the senator."

"Not surprising. I haven't warmed up to it either." His head fell back against the seat rest. "We fight. A lot. About most things. Michelle does, anyway. Hell, we fought about which high school to send *my* daughter to. I suggested private. Michelle insisted on DC Public: for the polling boost. Allie didn't care. She studies. She reads everything. She's smart. She was going to achieve in either setting. She's opened her own doors, even knowing we would have opened them for her. And with Michelle, all of it became a brush-fire. She's relentless. She controls and demands." Ben shook his head. "I'm exhausted. I'm sure Allie is, too. What choice did she have but to seek understanding beyond the walls of Michelle's precious 19483 Laverock Place? She wasn't getting any there."

Ben peered over at Rick. "You saved her, my friend. She's told me that more than once. That you always gave her space for whatever she needed. It wasn't easy for a father to hear, but she and I were both lucky that log jumped out in front of *MORNING STAR*. This chance connection with you has done good things. And I can't disagree, you did save her."

"Just a fellow boat lover." Rick reached a hand to his shoulder. "Bottom line, Ben? Allie wants nothing to do with Senator Baxter. She's afraid for her father. I'd like to respect her trust and not share the details. Just know that it's pretty bad."

Ben shook his head. "After all she went through with her mother, I thought this is what she needed: a new place, a new start."

"I know you did."

They rode in silence the last few miles to Reagan and Kate

slipped into an open spot along the departures drop off.

"Thanks for taking the meeting downtown this morning." Ben sighed. "The FBI's involved now. They're building the profile on her. We've given them all we can think of. I've got people looking as well. I thought you might have something important to share, something we didn't get to yesterday. Whatever they need, okay?"

"Anything I can do, Ben."

Chapter 12

Twenty minutes after dropping Ben at Reagan, Kate pulled up to the Metropolitan Police Department entrance on Indiana Ave., NW.

Lowering the window, she said, "Just text me when you're finished, Mr. Larson."

"Kate, thanks. But I'm not far from here."

"I'm happy to wait for you," she said, smiling into the rear-view mirror.

Rick knew Ben would have insisted, and Kate's generosity would not be denied. "Thank you. I hope this doesn't take long."

"Please, take your time."

Rick got out and meandered across the plaza, pausing at the austere building's entrance. He stalled to scan the surroundings. Minutes later, he stood in front of the information desk.

"Hi. Rick Larson. I have an appointment with Detective Ward, at 10:30."

The woman spoke without looking up. "I'll let him know you're here."

The detective came around the corner shortly, phone to his ear, and motioned for Rick to follow him. Halfway down the corridor, Rick entered the small conference room. A forty-eight inch wall mounted screen was anchored at one end. The other three walls held nothing. The blinds were closed. Seven hard chairs were pushed in around a wide, dark wood table; the eighth was taken.

Ward made the introductions. "Richard Larson, this is Special Agent Parsons, FBI." Parsons didn't get up or extend his hand.

The detective pulled out a chair across from him for Rick.

Parsons lowered his chin to assess Rick over the top of his glasses. Abruptly then, he fired, "Okay, Larson, full disclosure. You pissed off the senator yesterday."

Ward paced along the end of the room. "You walked out of a meeting with the senate minority leader," he said. "Not a good first impression."

Parsons continued. "So, she's not happy, and that's why you're here this morning. The discussion you were supposed to have with her and Ben Sheridan, well now, you get to have it with us. And there are more than a couple of ways to approach it, you being one of the last people who isn't family to see Allison Sheridan."

The comment hung. Rick eyed each of them. "And one of those ways might be as a suspect?"

Ward halted and leaned both hands across a chair. "You're reading the senator's mind," he said.

"Can I ask, in what?"

Parsons leaned back, narrowing his eyes on Rick. "A seventeen-year-old girl is missing." He spoke each word with an edge. "The reasons as to why are rarely good. Kidnapping, murder, trafficking?"

Rick shifted in his chair.

Parsons held his stare and continued. "If she's a runaway, just hiding out, strangely, that would be the lesser of all evils. Until it isn't. But that's not the discussion we're having with you. Not today. Not yet. You've got some star power in your corner, so this is all about cooperation. Ben Sheridan said treat you like family. Pretty sure Senator Baxter doesn't agree, though." Parsons shot Ward a look, exchanging irritated expressions. "It's been a shit show of a morning," Parsons grumbled. "All because of your exit yesterday, Larson. Why didn't you just flip her off, too?"

Ward cut in. "But your attorney said you would cooperate, even though there was no evidence of that to Baxter."

"Adrian?"

"Mr. Dumars, yes."

"He's right. About the cooperation."

"He said give him any reason, though, and he would be here, sitting in that chair next to you. But in Adrian's calm way, and I've known him a while, he assured me that would not be necessary. It could mean he's conveying his full and complete trust in you, or it could mean, don't get on his bad side."

"He's right about that, too."

"Yeah, let's hope so. Having him on the other end of the phone saying nice things about you sure moves the needle. That's a helluva bond you two have."

"There's some history."

"Regardless," Ward said. "We want to make sure you—"

Parsons slapped his hand on the table. "Larson!" he barked. "Let me paint the picture for you! When a girl goes missing, when any kid goes missing, it gets a big push right out of the gate. When a senator's daughter goes missing, the goals stay the same: find her and the shitbag, if there is one. But there's always another foot standing on the gas pedal."

"The senator's?" Rick asked.

"And her lead counsel. You've met Chris Evans. He's a badger, and you don't want him coming for you."

Ward said, "But your buddy knows them both. Mr. Evans works for him, as you probably know, and the senator has Adrian's cell in her favorites."

Parsons straightened. "And that's lucky for you, and it's also why you aren't sitting in a different room right now." He shook his head. "Nevertheless, we're going through all of it. Today. You need to walk us through every conversation, every memory. Everything you can recall. Names, places, dreams. Don't edit a thing. One option is that she split. On her own. Family squabble, it happens. Wouldn't be a surprise with that family, but time will tell. For now, we've got video: bus stations, trains. Talked to Uber; you know that already. She wouldn't have gotten through TSA, so air travel is on the list, but not high. If she left town on her own, she was smart about it, which sends its own message. The footage gives us nothing that positively ID's her, nothing we can see. So, it's your turn. You might notice something, and we need the break. We're following up on what we can; the few kids who paid with cash, and the few who were alone. Like I said, the best option is that she's cooling off somewhere. But that's only the best option if we find her. The longer this takes, the less likely that option is real. Then everything comes into play."

Rick rested both hands on the table and looked back and forth between the two of them. Parsons scowled. He was clearly the lead.

"So, we all understand what today is about, right, Larson?"

"Of course."

"You on board with helping us out? It isn't really a request."

Rick slumped back against his chair. "You're wasting time asking if I'm concerned about Allie. I am. So, why not get started?"

Parsons looked quickly to Detective Ward and got a nod.

~

The afternoon crawled. Questions were repeated and challenged. All of it was recorded. Three different people came and went, laptops open, frame-by-frame analysis of endless video on the monitor. Bottled water only, no time for lunch.

At 2:30 p.m., Rick stood on the entrance steps again, relieved to get outside with some afternoon left. Hours in the unpleasant chair had stiffened many of his parts. He balanced against the railing, trying to let his lower back stretch out. The Range Rover pulled up on cue. Kate stepped out and moved around to hold the door.

Rick smiled. "You're going to spoil me, Kate."

"Long day, huh?"

"I hope something comes out of it."

She held a deli bag in her right hand and offered it. "I am certain this is better than what they served you inside. Moe's Deli. Tuna salad, okay?"

"Perfect."

"Courtesy of Mr. Dumar's office."

Rick peeked in. "Kate, you're a keeper. Thank you for dinner."

"Did they work you over?"

Rick inhaled, frowned, and nodded. His gaze drifted south along the plaza toward the National Mall, squinting into the bright sunshine. The break in the weather had enticed some tourists. Groups of people leaving work early hustled along the sidewalks. Traffic on Constitution Avenue inched along.

"Kate," Rick said, holding his tired expression across the scene. "Could I ask a favor?"

"Of course. Anything."

"It's a big ask; about Allie's grandfather. He was very special to her. His name was Ben, too."

She leaned against the hood.

"The elder Ben had a business partner, lifelong friends. Herb something. They were a favorite topic for Allie. She loved to talk about how close they were. When time slowed them both down and the business was sold, Ben stayed in Massachusetts to be near

Allie. Herb and his wife escaped to a small farmhouse on a sizable piece of land just south of Annapolis. It was apparently too far from a city, though, and after just a month, Herb's wife left him there alone on the farm. She moved to New York to live with her sister in Soho. People change, even when you think they might be too old to."

"Are you thinking—"

"It's close enough and remote enough, from the way Allie described it. She loved her grandfather. Maybe today, that extends to his friends as well. Might be worth a try."

"Did you mention Herb to the detectives?"

"Memory failed me," Rick said, shaking his head. "I will, though."

"After we check it out, right?"

"Why waste their time?"

Kate winked and reached into the car for her phone. "Gotta last name?"

Rick needed a second. She stood poised.

"Foreman, I think."

"Foreman," she repeated to herself, searching. A second later, she straightened and looked at Rick. "Okay, says he's still out there. The property is anyway. I'm all yours, Mr. Larson. Ben's exact words. I don't have to meet him at Reagan until 9:15."

"That's a long day. You sure?"

"Doesn't get any more important than this."

Kate displayed a style behind the wheel; keep moving, regardless. Rick approved. She typically exceeded the speed limit, nothing egregious, but fast enough to warrant undistracted diligence. A necessity along this stretch of Branch Avenue, where people, kids, and dogs, all felt they could cross anytime and anyplace they needed to.

Ten miles east of the city, they merged back onto Pennsylvania Avenue, leaving behind the chaos of travel inside the beltway. As the four lanes divided along a wide green median, Kate accelerated. She had achieved what was needed: escaping DC on a spring fever afternoon in twenty minutes, not ninety. The car rode effortlessly. The cabin was expectedly quiet. Kate asked about music earlier; Rick had declined. He leaned back against the seat, his head turned toward the window, scanning the large parcels of undeveloped land racing by. Kate peeked into the rearview mirror, catching his distant expression.

"If I may, Allie is fortunate to know you. Having friends to trust is important at that age. You two must communicate very well."

"Sometimes it's about the company," Rick said. "Not so much the communication. Allie's the talker. She needed a listener. It wasn't so hard."

"Sounds like her dad. I can see why you connected with both of them. Ben saw it, too, the trustworthiness and assurance that his daughter would be safe with you."

Rick caught her eyes in the mirror and offered a weak smile as thanks before turning away. The endless fields spread out again. Winter's brown inviting the faint greens of early spring to join. Rick didn't understand any of it—why Allie wanted to *just hang out*. Time together with her was uncomfortable for him to accept. With anyone. Too many years of grief had left him clinging to solitude for comfort. The image of Allie wanting something he never had the chance to give his daughter overwhelmed him at times. He forced his way through the motions for a while, but Allie saw through it all. She could see things: she saw him.

Rick clenched both hands as the car slowed. The four lanes turned into a winding two and Kate eased off more. Three miles farther, she took a left onto Muddy Creek Lane and followed the meager, worn road to Home Port Farm. The gravel drive pulled off to the right, just beyond a steep rise.

"Here we go, Rick," Kate said with hope. She crept along the washed out ruts slowly and came to a stop at the closed gate a hundred feet down the drive. A rusty chain and two locks wrapped a post below the no trespassing sign. The tall fence line leaned dramatically, choked with overgrown ivy and vines. A large for-sale sign stood prominently on substantial posts inside the gate. The small, wood-sided house sat far off atop a gentle hill, with views east extending to Chesapeake Bay.

Rick opened the door. "I need to stretch my legs," he said quietly, twisting out of the seat. He trudged to the fence and gazed across the winter wheat blanketing the undulating fields. Puffs from a gentle southerly were teasing the soft grasses into dance.

Kate got out and approached. "I'm sorry."

The breeze swirled fragrances of rich dirt and damp, matted grass. Rick filled his lungs and closed his eyes, welcoming the fresh air and smells he rarely found.

"Just a long shot."

Kate spoke softly beside him. "The long shots are the ones to listen to in times like this. Allie's young and possibly very scared, and you know her. You followed your intuitions. It's as good a path as any."

Rick pulled back slowly, unexpectedly rushed by a long-forgotten worry he once knew as a parent. "It's painful to think about Allie being out there on her own," he said finally.

Kate reached for his arm. "We'll find her. It's not easy to disappear in today's world, especially someone like her."

"Yeah, let's hope."

Rick stared across the grasses, images filling his mind of a small three-year-old girl running and laughing through the swaying softness.

~

Kate pulled onto M Street, SE just after 6:00 p.m. She slowed considerably, cautious along the confined section of road with daylight yielding to shadows and darkening overgrowth crowding the shoulders ahead. Approaching the marina gate, the headlights shone brightly across the old wooden sign.

"I love that," she said, turning to look over the seat. "Seems like something you might have made."

Rick nodded. "Thanks Kate. It was a long time ago." He reached for the sandwich bag, got out and moved around the car. She lowered the window, as he leaned a hand on her door. The few lights in the lot flickered weakly. The shadows seemed foreign. Rick sensed unease as he cast a tired gaze across the forlorn property.

"Are you okay?" she asked gently.

"Feels different. Seems lonely here this evening."

"She's going to be home soon."

Rick didn't hide the deep sigh. "Thanks for today, Kate. It was nice to try and do something."

"It was. And I'm sure Ben would appreciate talking to you, to get your perspective on the discussion at the station. Can I tell him it's okay to call later?"

"Sure. Anytime."

Chapter 13

Rick motored around the shoreline curve later that evening and waved. Tre would be watching the water and would see him, even with the last remnants of dusk lying heavily in the western sky. With only the slightest of headwinds on the bow, he and Schooner closed quickly across the last fifty yards to the island. The favorable end of the weather roller coaster had finally found the DC area. Last week's snow was a memory, and the occasionally warm, end-of-March pattern had arrived. Rick welcomed it, savoring the river's awakening earthy smells as he watched the half-moon peek through the low horizon mist. Schooner lifted his nose to the island's greeting, sniffing in the familiar stories adrift along the light breeze.

The skiff slid gently ashore. Schooner jumped out and splashed. Tre didn't appear. Rick rested both hands on his knees and scanned the encampment. Things hadn't changed, though sometimes they would; subtle rearrangements Tre would expend energy on for diversion. The fire pit in the middle of the berm blazed. Tre's rifle lay covered on the stand at the south corner of the shelter's west wall. An M40 with a Redfield scope, the same issue he had relied on in Vietnam. The rifle was a gift from Adrian, a gun show find from western Maryland. Seeming harmless in 1991, Tre had received the offering as the gesture of respect and appreciation intended by his friend. Through the years, though, as Tre withdrew, Rick saw the rifle holding him captive, an ever-present reminder of the one shot Tre wished he had not taken. Rick had delicately suggested on many occasions that he store it in the shed. But Tre had attached to the rifle in a new way; regardless of any other revisions to the encampment, the rifle remained in the same position, facing south downriver toward the marina. With the weapon forever secured in that chosen spot, Tre perceived the faintest control over the two worlds the three of them had forged—the powerful scope always trained on the marina and the only approach strangers could make to the island. To protect and remember. *Always Faithful.* Justifications he shared when pushed.

Rick tilted the outboard and stepped out of the skiff. He pulled his brim lower and reached for the first supply bag, mumbling the count as was his habit. *Three hundred and seventy-two bags*—over the three years Tre had called this home. Prior to that adoption, Tre had managed to function in the marina's setting, tending to the grounds and scavenging for the shed during the day and retreating to shelter in the old Owens cruiser at night. For twenty-two years. The isolation imparted by the boat and shed had signified security and offered some measure of calm for him, but any found peace proved vulnerable to desperate echoes in his mind, panicking him into seeking escape. With greater frequency and for longer periods of time, the quiet, overcoming anxiety would hold its relentless grip. Sadly, the war's significant scarring to Tre's mind and body went untended, as errantly stipulated by him. Each year, Rick saw him drifting farther away. Less contact, distracted conversation, insomnia, swings between anxiety and depression. Tre never received an official diagnosis. Through the 70s, he presented as one of the many experiencing 'Vietnam Stress'. When the Veterans Administration finally recognized the trauma disorder that Veterans confronted, Tre was beyond wanting or accepting help. None of Rick's compassionate insistence or Adrian's demanding optimism would move their friend. Tre's pattern became his mooring and weed assured his reprieve, blurring the darkness that so often overwhelmed him.

Rick rested on the gunwale. The darkening sky blanketed the island. Enjoying calm breaths, he surveyed the solitude—Tre's vision for life on the island. It had appeared to him one distant spring afternoon. The warmth of that day brought Tre to the Old Man's substantial canopy. He rested there comfortably, finishing a joint, transfixed in contemplation. From the office window, Rick observed his friend's gaze across the water; the island's reflection mirrored back. Tre extended a hand to the weary tree's skin and nodded. His decision had been made.

Tre had needed only two months of preparation, never wanting, or asking for help. Rick and Adrian contributed needed purchases and little else. Tre departed for the island late one night, perched in the bow of the skiff, his arm around Schooner. He needed to receive the greeting alone, in the darkness of deep night. Rick dropped him just before midnight. Honoring Tre's wishes, he and Schooner stayed in the boat. Tre pushed them off and marched slowly toward the encampment. The skiff floated silently, feet away from shore. Rick had watched his friend disappear silently into the black, alone as he needed. His last retreat from the demons.

~

Schooner sauntered back from the nearest bush wagging his tail. He sniffed as Rick lifted the last two bags out of the skiff. Rick glanced around again, uncertain of when and whether his friend would welcome him. Though Tre's mind relentlessly relived the past, the trauma at times lay buried below the surface, allowing for intervals of lucidity and occasional conversations and remembrance with his friend. But the insidious consequences of war had defeated his body; chemicals, nerve damage, and disease were all taking him away now faster than his mind.

Tre appeared from behind the lean-to holding a rag. He squatted next to the rifle and pulled away the cover, immediately wiping the barrel, his full attention on the task.

Rick approached slowly with a quiet greeting. "Pretty night. Nice moon coming." He waited as Tre continued his effort in silence. "Did you see me?" Rick asked.

Tre's answer came with a soft nod. "Always watching you, brother. You see me?"

"Schooner did, without fail. He's my eyes."

"Well, I saw you, too—the other day. Had a date on the pier."

Rick shook his head. "Just keep cleaning that scope, Sergeant." He smiled, as Tre found him. "I'll tell you the story in a minute." He moved past the shelter and lowered the bags in front of Tre's bank of coolers, four of the largest ones Adrian could find, aligned, and partially buried on the north side of the berm. Three of them held food, one served as Tre's closet.

Tre cast an approving look at the gun, then attentively repositioned its battered canvas cover. He spotted Rick next to his coolers and hurried to help him unpack. With quick motions and concern across his face, Tre relocated several of Rick's placements. He reached anxiously for the jar of peanut butter and coaxed it out of Rick's hands, disguising any judgment. Rick accepted Tre's obsession with order and recognized the cue. He stepped back and watched for twenty minutes as his friend placed every item with reverence. Rick took note of Tre's focus, relieved he appeared present. It was a good thing and necessary for this evening. The discussion about Allie was overdue. Tre wouldn't retain the information, but it was nevertheless important that his friend hear about her when he could understand and remember the connection.

Tre studied the arrangements, delicately adjusting cans of

beans and containers of soup across a thinning layer of ice.

Rick peered over his shoulder. "Time to restock?"

"Ice?" Tre nodded.

"I should be able to get out again tomorrow."

"No rush. Cold as it's been."

"That soup's good for two days. Not much later than that."

Tre waved a thumbs up. "Everything's got a shelf life, even us."

"Fay was proud of the batch. She said you're gonna love it."

Tre repositioned two bottles of water. "So, who was the date?"

"A customer. For the shed." Rick crossed his arms, intent on closing the topic.

"Told you they would come."

"You were right. Still a few thousand parts left to sell, though."

"Patience."

Rick moved close. "Tre, do you remember Allie?"

Tre's eyes rose. "Of course," he said quietly.

Rick stalled, looking away. "She's gone," he finally began. "Tre—Allie's missing."

Tre paused, his hands instantly lifeless in the cooler.

"We don't know where she is." Rick went on. "Has she been here? I need you to tell me if you've seen her."

Tre returned to his methodical task. Rick's shoulders slumped. He would need to wait.

Minutes later, Tre stood abruptly. Both hands went to his hips as he assessed the coolers. Finally, he closed the lids and pivoted. "Thank you for this, brother."

"Tre. Have you seen Allie?"

Tre pulled a half-smoked joint out of his coat pocket and held it up. Rick caught the probing look. He could only follow where Tre led.

"More is coming tomorrow," Rick said. "I'll run it out. How

are you feeling?"

"Always good."

"Breathing, okay?"

"Only when I have to." Tre turned away and walked to the water's edge, staring at the reflection. "A lot of years that moon's been tryin' to make this old river show nicer than she is." A rough cough intruded.

Rick moved close, sensing the familiar sadness blurring his oldest friend's eyes. Tre recovered quickly and took another drag, fixated on the moonlight resting across the water.

"When was the last time you saw Allie?" Rick asked.

"Haven't seen her." Tre hesitated. "Not since the last time you came out. Does seem like a while ago. There was snow. Allie was on the pier. Sad. That was the last time. Maybe." Tre worked his jaw. "She went in my shed—it's okay. I said she could."

"We don't know where she is. You understand?"

Tre scrunched his eyes. "I do. She's lost? Maybe alone. How could . . . I just saw her."

"Here?"

Tre wandered, "How can that be? On the street, maybe. And hungry? We know what that is. Hoping for food, just one thing for the night . . . to eat. Maybe they drive by and wonder, *How's that help*? Some change?" Tre drew a husky breath. "Then there's tomorrow, brother? What's her plan then?"

Tre shook his head and paced. Three steps to his left, three steps back, looking down, each foot placed carefully in the same sandy depression. "There *is* no plan for tomorrow," he muttered. "Just one thing, in that moment. Sometimes you get it, maybe Allie will. Other times, not so lucky?"

Tre spun to Rick. "Allie's lost? No. No! Got to have someone to run to. Remember? You and D had me. You did. Who's got

Allie?" He tried to pull more out of the joint, then tossed it. Both hands crept to the sides of his legs, and he rubbed anxiously, his vacant stare returning to the river. "Why'd she leave?"

Rick sighed. "I don't know."

"Beth left!" Tre's louder voice cracked. "Why did *she* leave?"

Tre turned back, his weathered face dark in the moon's shadow. "You need to ask Beth," he said excitedly. "It's time. Ask her! She'll know why they left."

"Tre, it's not the same—".

"Allie's gone!" Tre stumbled closer. "You have to find her!"

Rick reached for his shoulder, but Tre jerked away.

"Tell me you'll ask!"

Rick stood motionless, watching it. The desperate expression. All of it beginning again. Sadness bringing the crippling anxiety. Depression would follow and carry him into a cave. The memory rushed to Rick; the dawn of his friend's frightening journey, three and a half years after he flew out of Saigon: the very night Rick's family ran. His friend had gone inside for refuge. It could be for minutes or for days. Rick never knew.

"I'll ask," Rick said quietly.

Silence hung over them a while; each cast distracted looks around the encampment and into the darkness across the river.

Tre said, "Did you check the island?"

Rick balked, lowering his head. "Why don't we do that tomorrow? It's late."

"You have to leave," Tre blurted. "I'm tired, brother."

"I know. I will, soon."

"Go now. Go ask Beth."

Tre turned and plodded to the berm area under the shelter. Green waterproof carpet wrapped tightly and taped around an old futon mattress served well as bedding. Rick had scavenged it from a lost boat a year ago. Tre threw more wood on the fire and disappeared into the layers of blankets. Schooner laid beside him, chin on his front legs, peering back at Rick. Tre's next cough rocked his body. Gradually, his wheezing slowed and he closed his eyes. Escape. His lungs struggled in the position, settling into a raspy, irregular rhythm, with long silent gaps that left Rick anxious.

Rick listened for minutes, then pulled his collar up. Remnants of the day's warmer air were gone. He walked to the bow of the skiff and sat, staring at the fire, searching for the path away from his memories.

Tre's faint voice emerged, reaching Rick above the fire's crackle. The broken words didn't surprise him; nightmares came most nights for his friend, and it never took them long to arrive. Clear calls to Allie though, brought Rick to his feet, pausing his breath to hear. A long silence was followed by Tre's louder plea to Allie. Rick hurried to the berm and knelt. Tre lay motionless. Rick leaned close as his friend rolled to his side. *Sea Keepers* was the last word he mumbled before falling into what peaceful cycle of sleep he could.

Rick reached to his shoulder as goodnight, then rose and wandered to the skiff. He helped Schooner aboard and pushed off. Tre's words repeated, each time compelling more reflection from Rick. Just as quickly though, he dismissed them as images of Tre's injured mind, images conjured in an effort to help any way it could.

~

The trestle ran no more than two hundred feet from the northern edge of the island and came ashore on the western bank of the Anacostia along the northernmost property line at *Sea Keepers*. Surprisingly, Tre never mentioned being disturbed by the occasional rumble from crossing trains. Rick's intention at that late hour had been to call an end to the long day and return straight to the marina, but he found himself steering the skiff toward the looming steel and wood structure, holding a slow speed, and shadowing the intermittent red lights as he angled over to shore. The engine idled roughly, and Rick made cautious headway approaching the remnants of piers and pilings that had once extended out from the untended riverbank. Most of the structures had collapsed long ago, leaving some of the broken pilings still visible above the water and some, Rick knew, lurking just below the surface. If he bumped one in the dark, he wanted to make contact gently. He reached for the small floodlight under Schooner's blanket and shined it across the water. The remaining pilings stood in disarray, leaning at angles, with sections of pier hanging on between a few. Rick reconsidered the decision to approach from the water. He could tie up at his pier and walk the overgrown quarter mile along M Street back to *Sea Keepers*, but Tre's words lingered, and as Rick floated amid the decay, he found himself believing what Tre had described. It became urgent for him to confirm.

Rick crept along, the moonlight offering random help as thick clusters of clouds occasionally opened up gaps in their journey to the east. But the darkness in between fell deep and untouched, seemingly impenetrable by any ambient light emerging from the city just blocks to the west. The river dissolved into the black shoreline, and Rick scanned with the weakening light. As he approached the first line of pilings, the skiff suddenly bumped and groaned. The boat's momentum, slow as it was, still carried its length across the submerged piling, the hull's smooth bottom scraping against jagged wood in the black water below.

Stone riprap along the shoreline met the water, with trash, plastic bottles, and broken limbs resting in the voids between large boulders. The next unforgiving bump came from a submerged rock, and Rick shut off the motor. The grade along the water elevated four feet, and Rick needed to stand. He held the floodlight high, starting at the water's edge and exploring slowly across the property. Desolate shadows and rampant vegetation consumed the boarded buildings and discarded trailers. Only one boat remained, lying on its side near the clubhouse with rusty, collapsed stands punched through the hull. Rick broke the light's sweep as a small reflection appeared from just behind the boat's vine-covered cabin. He let the skiff slip farther south along the shore for a better line and moved the light back and forth across the derelict hull. The reflection appeared again and grew. Rick struggled to steady the flood's beam as his raised arm began to shake. He leaned forward, gaping in disbelief along the light's path, his eyes landing on a bright wash across the Jeep's tailgate window.

Chapter 14

It took twenty minutes for the first two patrol cars to barrel down M Street, SE. Lights flashing. No sirens. Their speed decreased rapidly as they passed the marina and found the remaining length of road leading to *Sea Keepers* narrowed significantly from neglect along the shoulders. Standing by the shed, Rick observed two more units arrive moments later. Both unmarked. He expected Detective Ward would be in one of them.

After returning from the island last night, Rick had struggled to sleep; getting two hours at best. Unsettling thoughts about Allie's car had awakened him with the first brightening of the sky, followed closely by the acceptance that he should not delay his call to the police. Practical questions of *why* plagued him while he waited. Frightening images crept in. What happened to her? His heart raced. Lightheadedness recurred as well, but no nausea. Rick replayed the EMT's advice: fill the lungs and steer clear of the stress. But in that instant, he was frozen with foreboding and indecision. *Should he walk to Sea Keepers or wait for Ward to pull into his lot*? He felt for his pounding heartbeat and finally plodded to the shed. He reached for the overhead door chain and pulled. The door offered mercy that morning, as it sometimes would, rising slowly but smoothly along Rick's steady tugs.

Rick stopped the door halfway up and hooked the link, urgently needing to sit. He tottered toward Tre's bench seat, an uncomfortable relic from a 1957 Chris Craft Capri balanced on old bricks in the middle of the shed. The seat's upholstery was worn, with tears and likely home to several mice. Tre had salvaged it from the classic wooden boat long ago, a sad day when he and Rick decided the old girl was beyond saving. The seats came out first, followed by all of the hardware. The foam was shot, and getting comfortable sometimes proved impossible.

Rick tried but instantly abandoned all hope. He was pacing the cold slab when Detective Ward knocked on a loose metal wall panel left of the door. Ward approached, his gaze instantly distracted with the walls of shelving and the overflowing stockpile. Uninvited, he stepped around Rick and walked deep into the space. His mouth fell open slightly as he scanned each of the walls.

"Damn," he said after a minute of wandering. "What the hell is all this?"

Rick hesitated. "Recycling."

Ward nodded absently, continuing to browse. "Impressive collection." He assessed the Constellation and gestured to Rick, "Home?"

"Sometimes."

"I'm sure it's cozy." Ward made his way over. "You look beat, Larson."

"Long night."

"Finding lost cars?"

"Part of it."

"Thanks for the call," Ward said. He surveyed the yard through the large opening and shook his head. "That car isn't a hundred fifty yards away from where we're standing, if that. First time you noticed it, huh?"

"You would've heard sooner."

"Hope so. Kind of ironic, though. Such an important piece of a complicated puzzle. And it's been there the whole time. So close."

"No one's been down to the end of that road in years. Sometimes there's maintenance along the tracks, cutting back brush, but that's it."

"Probably some kids at times." Ward paused. "Like Allie?" He returned Rick's stare. "And you saw it in the dark? From out on the river? Good vision. What time was that again?"

"Late."

"What were you doing out on the river? Visiting the friend?"

"I saw him, then I was fishing. It was a nice moon."

"Guess it's pretty easy to keep your own schedule out here, isn't it? I bet fishing around those old pilings can be good." Ward worked his jaw. "You sure caught something, right? And lucky for us. Maybe for Allie, too."

A truck's back-up horn suddenly sounded. Rick took the distraction and brushed past the detective. The loaded roll-off backed onto the marina lot, waiting for the other unmarked cruiser to leave.

Ward closed on Rick. "It's hers, Larson."

"I know."

"Any thoughts about why she would have dumped it?"

Rick concentrated on the truck as it barely missed his gate. "Scared," he finally said. "She's running."

"From what?"

"You tell me. It's been a week. I'm sure you've learned a lot about Allie."

"Maybe. Obviously not enough, though. But don't get me wrong, Larson; a kid running is never good. I hope that's all it is."

"None of this is good, Detective."

"No argument. Like I said, the car's important; we'll check it for prints." He eyed Rick. "Will we find any of yours?"

"Likely. I moved it out of the way a couple of times when she was here."

"Anything else you want to get out of there before we pull it away?"

Rick waited for the smile to follow, but Ward's flat expression held.

"Watch out for snakes," Rick said. "They like to find their way into the grilles."

"Will do. Not a fan." Ward turned toward his car, calling back over his shoulder, "Thanks again for the call, Larson. Be in touch."

Chapter 15

The southern edge of Old Town Alexandria's residential waterfront ended at Ford's Landing Park, a three-hundred-foot-wide green buffer between the city's burgeoning townhouse development along the Potomac and the Woodrow Wilson Bridge. Just three miles south of Washington, Colonial Square had been one of the last coveted parcels to be developed, squeezing in forty-eight three-story traditional brick townhomes along the northern boundary of Ford's Landing. All thoughtfully designed and planned to reflect the area's rich history, with wide divided lanes and planted medians meandering through six clusters of eight homes each. Elegant, stately, remote.

Chris stood close to the French doors, tucking in his shirt, gazing across his balcony toward the bridge span's relentless Interstate 95 traffic, a reliable Thursday evening nightmare during rush hour. His five years spent enjoying the terrace view had passed quickly. Five years ago, Chris made partner at Baker, Dumars. In private celebration, he had registered a shell LLC in Delaware and hired a distant, estranged cousin as the nominee director, whose only interest was in being paid substantially to sign as signatory on Chris' discreet transactions. The LLC's first purchase became the model end unit townhome on Wharf Street in the Colonial Square community, one of only ten fronting the Potomac.

Chris sipped his bourbon, inviting back the ambitious memories. He had deemed all of it well-deserved: a fitting business entity to add, one that would, as needed, serve to ensure his privacy. An oasis, far from the lifestyle his wife demanded for their family in the Chevy Chase zip code northwest of DC. The last trimester of their second pregnancy was proving a challenge for Chris. Endless, exhausting, emotion-laden discussions, invariably reaffirming his disdain for any lifelong commitment to one woman. He lived what he had witnessed in childhood and never found cause to dismiss his present-day inclinations or the urgings that would surface after the frequent, irrecoverable exchanges with his wife.

The young woman approached silently on bare feet, wrapping both arms around Chris and kissing his neck. "You had some aggression to work out," she whispered. "Something on your mind?"

Chris turned to her.

She tilted her head buttoning his top button. "You were different this evening. Kind of rough." Her eyebrows raised. "I liked it." She pulled him close for a long kiss.

Chris drew back and leered into Maggie Emerson's equally ambitious eyes; another asset added to his ghost LLC, knowledge of which, along with its holdings, remained solely with himself and his vagabond cousin. Maggie, the firm's newest paralegal, had been told the unit belonged to one of Chris' wealthy college friends, someone who rarely frequented Alexandria. Chris never extended their visits.

He finished his drink. "I have a meeting."

"Too bad." Maggie wet her lips. "See you at the office."

~

Ron crawled down the opposite lane, hidden somewhat from Chris' townhome by the newly budding median, watching as the young woman scurried down the steps and sidewalk toward her car. He parked at the end of the street, adjusted his mirrors, and peered longer than necessary, understanding the attraction. As she pulled away, Ron got out, crossed the street, and took the steps.

Chris opened the door before he could ring the bell. "You've been out here the whole time? I was unaware. Apologies."

"We could've scheduled for another night," Ron said. "Didn't realize you were having company."

"A colleague needed to talk about a case we're working on. An unexpected visit."

Ron extended his hand. "Of course. Ron Temple." They shook, and he followed Chris inside.

"Nice to finally meet you in person," Chris called over his shoulder as he moved to the bar cart in the dining room. "Can I get you a drink?"

"A beer would be great."

Drinks in hand, they moved to a pair of Eames lounge chairs in the corner of the living room, the view beyond extending downriver.

Ron lifted his glass. "Beautiful place."

"A good friend's, who travels all year and generously shares the key. I love it here. Grew up in Alexandria and never doubted I would come back after law school. Secluded, quiet, history-rich, with proximity to the nation's capital."

"Pricey area. Nice friend. You come from a family of lawyers?"

"Leah must have mentioned my parents."

"Only in passing."

Chris lifted his chin. "Important careers; each of them, and not without some small amount of celebrity and influence. DC politics and wealth. Since I was young. Both have always intrigued me. So, my life path brought me home, to be in the midst of it all."

Ron nodded. His gaze floated around the room. "You wanted

to talk?"

Chris took a drink, studying his potential colleague. "First, thank you for helping us with the search for Allison Sheridan. It's a terrible thing: a missing young girl."

Ron's attention returned.

"Leah and I have known each other a while," Chris continued. "We're kind of brother and sister: the ones who never really got to know each other, but with enough history to keep you together. You've known Leah as well, and her specialties; she does things for people. People who insist on discretion and competence."

"Fair assessment."

"But she has her boundaries, and I've always accepted that about her. And that's why she introduced you."

"So, she said my boundaries tend to blur?"

"At times. When necessary. Sometimes that's a good thing."

"Flattering."

"As intended," Chris said. "As for Leah, though, I have only accolades. But let's just say, she's the type who stays in the car."

"Does she know I'm here meeting with you?"

Chris shifted in his chair. "Does it matter?"

"I don't know yet."

"Well, only you can discern personal loyalties. I will say, though, going the extra mile for Senator Baxter always pays returns." Chris smirked. "I just thought it would be good for us to meet. Put a face to the name. I have expectations for people I deal with. It's important that understandings are clear to everyone. Leah and I have that clarity. And I know what I can count on her for."

"And that is?"

"I have a responsibility to the senator and their family to ensure Allison gets home safely. Leah shares that responsibility. We all hope Allison is out of harm's way, collecting herself somewhere.

But things can get complicated, and we always have to be ready to adjust if they do."

Ron leaned forward. "Let me skip ahead if I may. Just so I'm clear on the expectations you referred to. How much information will I get?"

"You'll only get the direction. Nothing more."

Ron took a few seconds. "I do know Leah, and I know what she's comfortable with. I've never known her to be shy, or hesitant. She has a reputation with people who travel in your lane. You don't get that by staying in the car. There's not much she won't do."

"This will take a team effort. If someone has endangered Allison, that will have to be dealt with. Backup is always good."

"Isn't that the police?"

"Sometimes."

Ron shrugged. "Anything for Senator Baxter."

"Good. We hope extraordinary measures won't be necessary—we don't anticipate any, but it's my role to plan for all contingencies. The senator wants this situation with Allison resolved quickly."

"Resolved?"

Chris' eyes narrowed. "The senator wants Ms. Sheridan home, of course, and we'll do whatever is necessary to get her back. As I said, there will be accountability for the person responsible."

"Understood. You're assuming there is such a person."

"I don't assume anything, and you should understand that. However, it's been two weeks: how could I not consider the possibility?" He paused. "They found her car—"

"Leah told me. That's good and bad."

Chris poured back the rest of his bourbon. "Yes, it is." He rose and crossed to the kitchen counter, opening his briefcase as Ron approached.

Chris extended his left hand, holding a burner phone. "Keep

this close. If I call, I expect you to answer."

Ron nodded. "Expectations."

"Teamwork."

Ron offered an assuring smile. "Like I said, anything for the senator."

"I share that loyalty and I'm glad we could meet. Now if you would, I have company arriving soon: expected company." He moved to the door and handed Ron an envelope. "A small gift," he said. "Just to cover your time. The first of many. We'll talk soon."

Ron strolled the sidewalk, in no hurry to depart the secluded setting. Once inside his car, he started to re-adjust the mirrors, then delayed, watching longer than needed as a young woman took the steps up to Chris' open door.

Chapter 16

Sarah scowled across the kitchen at Lou.

"Mom! Twelve days ago! You met this guy twelve days ago! Are you sure about this?" Lou closed the fridge and moved to the island carrying romaine and tomatoes, continuing to ramble. "He's got the rugged good looks; I'll give him that. Hats have definitely saved him. Only a few lines around the eyes, not many wrinkles, his hair could certainly be thinner *and* grayer. It appears that most of the parts have aged well." She took a minute to spray the tomatoes. "Seems polite. Seems to have it together, more so than I might have imagined living in a place like that. Good teeth, too. That's something."

Sarah placed the napkins and plates at the table. "Is that *really* the depth of your observations?" she said. "So very proud of my daughter."

Lou closed the oven and turned, quickly folding her arms. "Okay, tell me then, what is it?"

Sarah shrugged and grinned. "Different world from what I've endured the last forty years. It's intriguing, and his dog is very cute."

"You've spent all of three hours with our Mr. Larson, and *now* he's coming over for a birthday dinner?"

"It's just company. Relax."

"That's what I'm having trouble doing. This is kind of fast with someone you know nothing about. Is it even safe for you to be here alone with him?"

"It's safe, dear. I learned a lot the other day. I believe he has a good heart, and he appears to care about the important things. You saw some of that as well, didn't you?"

"Not enough to invite him for dinner!"

Sarah gestured away the comment. "He's befriended a young girl who is struggling with some tough issues. Isn't that testimony enough?"

"That may not be your best endorsement."

Sarah dropped both hands to the dining room table. "Well, this is a surprise. Are we forgetting our *own* personal missteps at that age? You of all people should appreciate the value of having a friend to trust. And he's concerned about this young woman right now, so how about showing some empathy."

"We are not having the same discussion—"

"Well, I would say we are. If Allison Sheridan and her very accomplished parents trust Mr. Larson, I think we can as well."

"But you don't know this guy! It's too soon for—"

"We're all wiser as we get older, dear. And more intuitive. And some things just move faster."

"Oh, please."

Sarah turned first to the sudden rumbling outside.

Lou's shoulders slumped in resignation. "My God, is that his truck?"

"Nice entrance, huh?" Sarah set candles on the table and started toward the living room.

Lou pleaded after her. "Mom!"

Sarah spun, her eyes bright. "*Yes*?"

"I get it. You're ready to date again. Perfect! You're a great catch; you sold your successful business. Lots of money, more than you'll ever need. You could live anywhere and date anyone—"

"But I choose to live here, close to my daughter in southeast.

The neighborhood has a wonderful energy, and I love that Eastern Market is only two blocks away! Where else would I go?"

Lou frowned, "*And* you could date anyone you wanted to. Look at yourself. You're gorgeous! Please, let me help you with some other options. There are a thousand guys in this city who would love to sweep you off your feet."

"You said he seemed nice at the marina. Remember him coming to your aid with the splinter?"

"Yes, I do, but you weren't asking him out at the marina!"

Sarah's grin appeared. "And how about those blue eyes, huh? The ones he holds on you while you're talking? Eyes tell you a lot. I'm sure that's something you can appreciate." Sarah winked. "He certainly does have nice eyes, doesn't he?" She whirled eagerly toward the foyer.

The old truck creaked as Rick squeezed into the last open curb space on the block. Parallel parking inevitably proved a challenge for them both: no power steering in the truck and limited flexibility in Rick's neck for looking over a shoulder. It was all mirrors for him, and it usually required multiple tries. As he checked the side mirror to assess his aim, a Lexus waiting behind accelerated aggressively past. Rick considered the decision made and left the truck parked eighteen inches off the curb.

He ambled along the sidewalk, intentionally delaying his arrival. The brick townhomes stood as original builds throughout the southeast area of the city, most revealing significant love and attention over recent years. Across the street, Burley Roads Park still held some life for the remaining daylight: dog walkers, older kids with a football, and a few couples on benches. Rick came to a slow stop in front of the fifth unit; three stories, beautifully painted brickwork, rich white in color with brighter accents, a deep front porch unique to the street, and healthy beds of landscaping around the small front yard. Sarah's brief, humble description had not done it justice.

Her overture to Rick had come early that morning, an invitation to a spontaneous birthday dinner. Her first since the divorce. Not to be deterred after the failed coffee delivery, Sarah had reached out with the offer before 8:00 a.m. in a comforting but persuasive voice over the phone. Rick had imagined her uplifting smile on the other end as well. His awkward departure at the Tidal Basin two days ago apparently had been accepted with understanding and forgiveness, and though he couldn't match Sarah's excitement over sharing a home-cooked meal, the thought of declining never occurred to him until he parked the truck and started down the sidewalk. He faltered along each step, his stomach churning. He had anticipated being uncomfortable and warned Sarah in so many words. She promised compassion and Tums.

Rick shuffled in front of the warmly lit house, searching for a reason to walk away. But the door pulled open too soon, and Sarah faced him, beaming across the porch. She ushered him inside warmly with a hug. Rick tensed, processing the contact. He handed her the bundle of flowers and drew both hands across his flushed cheeks. He followed with an audible exhale and scanned the rooms for distraction.

Evidence of Sarah's love for the house appeared in every corner and along each wall; plush furniture, a fire burning, candles lit, photos and paintings perfectly spaced on walls and tables, expensive area rugs across glowing oak wood floors. A beautiful home to see, cozy and inviting, but awkwardly unfamiliar surroundings to Rick. Comfort in life for him awaited at the corner table in Delia's diner. Rick's disquiet persisted. He winced at Sarah then quickly lowered his head. His shoulders slumped as he shoved both hands into his pockets.

She promptly came to his rescue. "Come with me," she said, taking his arm and leading him to the kitchen. "Lou offered to cook the birthday dinner for us. Let's go say hi."

Lou stood, leaning over the large pot on the stove. "I got it," she called to Sarah over her shoulder. "Almost ready." After a moment, she turned and took some time appraising Rick. She flattened her lips to hide the sigh.

"Good to see you again, Mr. Larson," Lou finally said, managing a noncommittal smile. "So, do you prefer Rick or Richard?"

"Rick is what I'm used to."

"Perfect. I hope you're hungry."

"Always."

Sarah handed him an iced tea. "I'm glad you came."

"This is nice. Thanks. It's uh, a beautiful place."

"Thank you," Sarah said. "I've been here two years. Still lots to do."

Rick rubbed his chin, spinning to take in the immaculate kitchen. He saw no loose ends.

"I want to show you something!" Sarah beamed and reached across the counter, pulling back a small carved wooden box. She held it up to Rick and his brow promptly wrinkled. He took his time examining the delicate work.

"Lou just gave me this. My first birthday present as a single woman. Again."

Lou turned down the burner and crossed the kitchen. Indulging her mother's enthusiasm, she added, "Isn't it beautiful? This is what I found in your boat shed. It was a great shopping day for me. Birthday and anniversary covered, but you were a tough negotiator."

Rick looked back and forth between them.

"It's locked though," Sarah said, feigning a pout. "We tried but couldn't open it. We didn't want to break it. Could you give it a try?" She handed the box to Rick.

He pulled glasses out of his shirt pocket and held the gift close in both hands.

Sarah tilted her head, sensing the unease. "You, okay?" She reached a hand to his arm. "You look like you're seeing an old friend. Did we take something we shouldn't have?"

"There were two boxes in there," Lou said. "About the same size. I thought that would be okay."

"No," Rick said, hesitating. "It is, it's fine." He clutched the box with another quick look to both of them. "Tre—he carved several of these."

"Oh no!" Sarah said. "Please then, take it back to him."

"Don't be silly." Rick pulled out a small pocketknife.

"Are you sure?"

"He intends them as gifts." Rick delicately worked the hasp.

"Well, then," Lou said. "Drum roll." She retrieved her phone from the island to take a video. "Your first treasure chest, mom. And we didn't even need to dive for it. Maybe a winning lottery ticket, or gold?"

Rick worked the small lock, coaxing it apart. Lou leaned in close as he handed the box to Sarah to open. She pulled the top back slowly, peering inside.

"Well, it is a treasure," she said. "Not big, but *very* beautiful." She lifted a small ring from a bed of shiny round shells, most of them broken. Lou zoomed in.

Rick pulled back, unable to avert his eyes, unaware of the intensity of his stare. He reached out, and Sarah handed him the box.

"It's a nice piece of work," he said. "The carving takes some care."

"It's gorgeous," Sarah said. "Thank you, honey. That day was a fun adventure. And thank you, Mr. Larson, for inviting us into your undiscovered world."

Lou's phone buzzed, and she checked the text. "Shit. Sorry guys. Ben's flight is apparently landing early. I need to go." She turned to the stove for a last stir and taste test.

"Okay, Mom, everything's ready. Hope you both enjoy it." She rushed to Sarah for a hug. "Happy birthday. Wish I could stay and serve."

"It smells great," Rick said. "Thank you."

"Don't be silly," Sarah said. "You should go. I'll walk you out."

Rick leaned, watching them cross the dining room. When they were out of sight, he lifted the box again. He fixated on the ring, searching for a memory that would explain it being tucked away deep in the shed.

The heavy front door closed.

"Be right there," Sarah called from the foyer.

Rick glanced to the dining room, then fumbled, lowering the top in place. He jammed the lock to secure it again.

Sarah returned through the hall pocket door as Rick spun. He straightened and cleared his throat, holding the box out to her.

"It's a beautiful birthday present," he said.

⁓

Sarah moved her plate aside and leaned back from the table. "So, still have room for cake?"

Rick rested a hand on his stomach. "Maybe in a minute."

"Me, too." She held her smile, hesitating. "It was nice to meet your friend Tremaine the other day. I hope I didn't—"

"You didn't. It's okay. Some days for him are better than others. That wasn't one of them. I'm sorry he growled at you. He doesn't like strangers in the shed. That's his sacred ground where he goes to escape."

"You know him well. Lifelong friends?"

Rick nodded.

"That's nice. You don't see that often these days, friends caring for so long."

"Since we were eight. He's more than a friend. We grew up together, and now we're growing old together." Rick sighed. "The rest of the story doesn't hold much."

"That's hard to believe."

"Rough parts of Jersey, the war, and darkness that followed us home occupied most of the in-between. But we've always leaned on each other, and Tre still loves the river." Rick paused, sipping his tea. "We had enviable draft numbers," he went on in a quiet voice. "Mid-300s, so, maybe it could've been a different life, but Tre was going in for his brother."

They sat in silence. Sarah studied his expression. "I overheard him murmuring something," she finally said. "Being there for Jonathan?"

Rick leaned back and met her eyes. "His brother. Jonathan was killed serving in Khe Sanh. Tre couldn't understand why, and guilt took a big part of him away. They had always watched out for each other. He enlisted two months later, and I followed the next day, with no idea of what was about to open up to us in Vietnam."

Rick shook his head, suddenly entranced with Tre's box. After a moment, he mumbled, "Maybe life wouldn't have been different."

Sarah leaned in and said softly, "You weren't going to let him go alone."

Rick's eyes narrowed on the candle's waving flame. "No way I was letting him go alone."

She reached across the table for his arm, but he tensed back into the chair. Finally, he clenched both hands together and raised a pained gaze to her.

Sarah hesitated. "Rick?"

Long seconds passed before he drew a deep breath and said faintly, "They found Allie's Jeep."

Chapter 17

Lou spent a good part of the following day reflecting on her mother's questionable decisions. At 8:15 that evening, she hopped out of the Uber, holding a brown leather jacket over her head. The rain had steadily increased over the last fifteen minutes. As she rushed down the sidewalk to the bar entrance, she bumped a man walking his dog, stepped in a puddle, and cursed loudly more than once. Under the entrance canopy at Clancy's off the Maine Avenue waterfront, she stopped to pull back her hair, silence her phone, and generally get composed. Once inside, she was instantly relieved to see only a small group of patrons out on a damp Friday. She surveyed the room, finding Chris at a high top across from the bar. He started for a greeting hug as she approached, but Lou extended a hand and gestured to her very damp blouse.

"Nice tie," she said. "Don't you want to keep it dry?"

Chris grinned. "Good to see you, Lou. Been a while."

She pulled some lost wet hair back, trying to return the smile. "You too."

Chris shook his head slowly. "I tell you this every time I see you; Adrian should never have let you leave us."

Trying to straighten her outfit, she caught his leer and scowled. "Why? Because I look good in a wet top?"

"Among other things. But seriously though, how's our wonderful profession treating you these days?"

"Women attorneys. Women ownership. Women on the Board

of Directors. It was a good move for me. Human Resources has meaning again."

"That's a lot of women. Giving up on us men completely?"

"Nope. Not on Noah, and not on you." She winked.

"Good to hear."

"Thanks for meeting me, Chris." She pulled the remaining damp hair off her shoulder. "Wow. Shitty night, huh?"

"Wanna grab a table by the fireplace?"

"Too far from the alcohol. This will dry fast. I hope."

The waiter arrived, and Chris glanced over. "It was chardonnay last time, as I remember?"

"Still is."

"Food?"

Lou shook her head. "At the office."

"Me too." Chris ordered for her and held his glass up for a refill. Turning back, he checked his watch and said, "So, that's a long day for you. Damn."

"Look who's talking. You'll probably go back to the office when we leave."

"You inspired me to take the night off," he said, smiling. "You do look good, Lou. Things must be going well."

"Yeah, right." She adjusted her blouse as the waiter returned.

They held their glasses to toast, and Lou hurried a long drink.

"So, what's up?" Chris said. "Is this work or friends?"

She pulled her phone out and leaned in closer, arms on the table. "Both, I would say. I need some advice. Let me get through this, and you'll understand why I started with you."

"Got it. No small talk. I'm all yours."

Lou's words came quickly. "So, the Sheridan girl—"

"Allison Sheridan?"

Lou nodded and slipped in another sip. "It just hit the news this morning. I'm sure you're aware."

"Of course."

"I spent a good part of the day reading about her disappearance, everything I could find."

Chris' expression registered little. "Okay, any particular reason?"

"So, it's been almost a week, right?"

"Almost."

"And she just disappeared?" Lou shook her head. "I don't think so. How does that happen? She's everywhere, easily recognizable to say the least. Her dad's rich and her mom's a political star in this town. My thoughts went to kidnapping, right out of the gate. But no contact yet."

Chris shook his head. "No, there hasn't been much to go on."

"No leads?"

"No leads. None that are proving to be of any value."

"I might have come across something," she said in a hushed voice. "Just last night."

Chris took a playful scan around the room, then turned back, attempting to mirror her serious expression. "Okay, why are you whispering?" he whispered to her. "What are you talking about, Lou?"

She scrolled her photos and continued. "I went to this old marina last Saturday. With my mom. It's down on the Anacostia. Kind of a shithole. Anyway, this old Black guy has been working there for decades." Lou focused on her screen. "And he apparently likes to collect things. Vintage stuff. Old boat parts. Most people would call it junk. There's a huge shed full of it. You wouldn't believe how much was in there."

"So, what brought you to this shithole? Just curious."

"Birthday gift for Noah."

"Noah. Right. Does sound like a perfect place to shop for him. So, how is he?"

"He's engaged. To me. Well, he will be soon. And probably all because of the amazing birthday gift I found him there at the shed. A solid bronze something, but that's not all I found."

Chris leaned back against his chair. "I'm hooked. Don't stop."

Lou found the photo she'd been searching for, zoomed in on it, and turned the phone. "Look. See this ring? You can just make out the inscription; it says *A.M.S. Always.*"

"Okay. So?"

"Chris," she said, trying to inch closer across the table. "Allie Sheridan's middle name is Marie. That's her mother's maiden name."

Chris studied the image, eventually rubbing his chin as Lou pulled her phone back.

"Allie's rich dad keeps his boat at that marina and—"

"I know."

"And there's an old guy who runs the place."

Chris folded his arms.

Lou grabbed a quick breath. "Well, *apparently* Sheridan's daughter would go there to hang out and help him work on it. God only knows why. But it makes sense, doesn't it?"

"What part of it?"

"Chris! She spent time there. I saw her there! She's a striking young woman and this could be hers. I might have found her ring!" Lou waited as a couple walked behind their table. Her voice lowered. "Do you think he could have done something to her?"

"Lou, slow down. First of all, help me understand; you said this shed is huge. How did you possibly find this tiny ring?"

"Well, I didn't find the ring until later. What I found was a small, very cool carved wooden box. It was mostly buried under all this coiled line, two shelves up. It had a small lock on it. But that wasn't the gift for Noah; that was for my mom. The birthday present. I gave it to her last night. I thought it would make a nice jewelry box. She loved it, but the lock was jammed, and we couldn't get it open at first. When we did, the ring was inside."

"Jesus, Lou." Chris sipped his scotch. "Not sure what to say. So, you're thinking this could be Allie's ring? And that's your lead?"

Lou frowned and leaned back, taking her glass with her. "I'm wasting your time, aren't I?"

"Nothing about the Sheridan girl could be a waste of time." Chris reached for her hand. "The family will be grateful you came to me with this."

Lou's energy returned instantly. Her wide eyes fixed on his. "I think it's hers!" She pulled forward again. "And look at the picture closely; there's something dark on the side of the band. Maybe lipstick? I thought it could be blood," she whispered.

Chris shook his head, reaching for the phone again. "Blood?"

"Maybe the old man who owns the place hurt her. Should we do a DNA test? Maybe the family can identify it." She wavered. "I came to you because you know them, Chris. Or do I go to the police first?"

Chris examined the photo again. "Where's the ring now?"

"At my mom's."

"Have you said anything to her yet?"

"No! Not a word. She's actually spending time with the guy!"

"What guy? Rick Larson?"

"Wait. How do you know his name?"

"We've talked to him about, Allie. As you said, she used to hang out there."

Lou's mouth fell open slightly. "Really? Wow! Damn. So, yeah, my mom had him over last night for her birthday dinner. He's the one who got the lock opened."

"And when he saw the ring?"

"He kind of froze. Not long, but long enough for my mom to notice and ask if we took something we shouldn't have."

Chris nodded. "The Black guy you mentioned; he's a homeless Vet. The two served together."

"I know!"

"Well, keeping company with Mr. Larson may not be the wisest thing for either of you to do right now. I know who the guy is, and so do the police. He's been questioned by the detective handling the case and also by the parents."

"You're kidding! My God, some old dude from a marina. What is she thinking?"

The conversation stalled as she turned to stare absently at the television screen above the bar, processing the cautionary comment about her mother.

Chris tapped a hand on the table. "You, okay?"

"Yeah, fine." Lou looked back. "So, there it is. Advice time. I don't know where to start. Do you think this guy did something to Allie? Do I really need to keep my mom away from him?" She finished her wine and studied the photo again.

"I'm sure it's ok, Lou." Chris hesitated. "But I think I should speak with the Sheridans."

~

Waiting for the rain to let up, they were the last to leave. Chris and Lou walked casually down the broad sidewalk along Washington Channel fronting the re-developed waterfront. New hotels, luxury apartments, restaurants, and music venues; the city wall brought to the water's edge.

"Where'd you park?" he asked.

"Uber."

"Ok, I'm actually back in the garage."

Lou checked her phone. "Almost here. You don't have to wait. I'm good."

"It's nice to be outside."

"Thanks for your help, Chris. I didn't know who to go to."

"Not sure how much help I've been."

"It's probably nothing."

"Probably, but I'll talk to Senator Baxter and Mr. Sheridan. See if they'd like to speak with you or see the ring. Likely, they'll just have the detective contact you. I'll call on my way home, so keep your phone close."

"Will do. I hope she's ok."

"Allie? Yeah, we all do."

Chris tilted a look past Lou as the car approached along the curb. "White Camry?" he asked.

"That's me."

"Great to see you, Lou. Let's not wait so long next time."

"Deal. And a different discussion."

Chris watched her hurry to the car and waited until the Camry disappeared around the corner. He drifted to the guardrail. East Potomac Park across Washington Channel was quiet. Three sailboats rested on moorings. The docks to the south had no empty slips, winter's resting place for many. The buildings behind Chris cast a warm light across the water, inviting him to turn. He leaned back, beholding the grandeur. His long-held dream had become his reality. He loved DC. The world's stage. All he wanted to control lay before him. All could be achieved, and all of it simply waiting here for him to reach out. And he would. Chris pulled out his phone. Leah picked up after two rings.

"We have something we need to follow up on," he said.

"Sheridan?"

"Yeah."

"Tonight?"

"Tomorrow. Mr. Larson's establishment. We're moving up the timeline for our search. I'll text you when."

"Do I get a reason?"

Chris took a few seconds scanning the sidewalks. It was getting late, and the walkway wasn't crowded. His voice quieted, nonetheless. "This evening, I came across something. Something Allie Sheridan may have lost or may have been taken from her. It was found at Larson's marina."

"By whom?"

"Too long a story for the phone. Not sure why it would be there; maybe there's something else of hers there."

"Under the circumstances, that might be a hard thing for the old guy to explain. Bad luck for him."

After a pause, Chris said, "Maybe worse for, Allie. If Larson knows something, he's hiding it pretty well. Let's see if there's some other leverage."

Leah waited for more, finally saying, "Any other details you want to share? I like to be prepared. You know that."

"Don't dress up."

Chapter 18

Rick stepped off the boarding gangway and moved toward the stern to adjust a fender. The old Trumpy rested quietly along the pier. Coiling the line, he heard quick steps on the deck boards approaching from behind and glanced over his shoulder. Chris Evans strode toward him, ignoring the proximate gaps and cupped boards, his head moving back and forth as he surveyed all that occupied the land and water. The same confident walk. Rick took note instantly. Adrian had also mentioned his handshake, both forecasts of the man's resolve. Rick studied the expression as he closed. Chris stopped two feet away, his hand warmly extended as if greeting an old friend. They shook, and Chris squeezed. Adrian had not exaggerated.

"This is a surprise," Rick said. "You on the clock Saturdays?"

Chris smiled. "Always." He rotated, scrutinizing again. "Damn, Larson, the place is a lot rougher than I imagined. Not exactly where I would want to see Allie: old buildings, old piers, abandoned boats. Hell, I walked past a half dozen dead engine blocks and transmissions still seeping oil. You know that?"

"It's on my list," Rick said flatly.

"Well, it should be on DC's Environmental Management list, too. Maybe it will be soon." Chris folded his arms and scanned the waters. He lowered his sunglasses to peer over the frame. "So, looks like four piers? Not much left of one of them, maybe two I'd walk on. And the boats? I count more sunk than floating."

"True, some have found the bottom. Their own peaceful resting place in the shallows."

Chris chuckled. "Yeah, is that today's eulogy for derelicts?" He shook his head, finally taking notice of the Trumpy's gleaming woodwork. "At least you're taking care of her. She seems a little lost, though, in the midst of all this." Chris spread his arms wide. "Let's call it end of life putrescence, shall we?"

"Help yourself. I lost my sense of smell a long time ago."

Chris stepped closer to the yacht and ran his hand along the perfectly varnished toe rail. "Beautiful boat." He leaned down to rub at a water mark. "Wood, though. Sure as hell doesn't leave much time for anything else, does it? Ben held some great parties and all, and I did enjoy being aboard, but damn, that's a lot of work. He must be paying you a fortune to keep it up."

"I lost all sense for money a long time ago, too."

"I can see that." Chris straightened to admire his polishing effort. "And this is what Allie supposedly came all the way across town for, to help you baby sit an antique?" He cocked his head. "Boss's daughter. Guess that's job security, huh?"

Chris stepped back from the edge of the pier, his eyes locked on Rick. "Hope you don't mind me barging in on you, Larson," he said flatly. "I was hoping we could talk." He left no room for response. "Tuesday's meeting could best be described as a shit show. I thought we could try again. Maybe come to an understanding."

"Things were pretty clear to me."

"There's a lot of emotion around all of this. You knew, Allie. I'm sure you understand."

"I still know her."

"Of course you do." Chris raised his chin and brushed past him, sauntering to the end of the pier. "We're all concerned, Mr. Larson," he called over his shoulder.

Rick couldn't read the intent.

Chris spun and took his time approaching again. "Yesterday was an attempt to share notes. Ben's idea. He wants us all working together. Good?"

"I'm okay with that. I have respect for Ben."

"I do as well. I'm close to the family. Professionally, and personally. They rely on me. They trust me. That's important." His jaw flexed. "I just got off track yesterday."

Rick watched his face, hoping intuition would kick in and resolve the debate in his mind, whether to believe Chris' words as genuine or nothing more than a polished performance. He appeared credible to Rick on the surface: holding eye contact, the measured voice, deliberate movements, hand gestures interjected for effect. All of that could be expected though; the man was a trial lawyer. And a damn good one according to Adrian, who had largely been responsible for the grooming. Nevertheless, Chris' reversal from the narrative presented at the senator's residence came off as forced.

"I'm trying to help, Mr. Larson," he went on. "To do whatever I can. I would like to think that would be true for all of us, that we all want to help. You're in the unique position of having seen Allie most recently."

Rick chose to leave the Allie comment alone. "The boat keeps me busy," he said. "And Ben's always fair."

"Well, from what I hear, looks like you'll be slowing down soon. Adrian tells me you're closing up shop. Selling."

Rick flinched, curious how Chris had come across the information. "It's Adrian's to sell," he said.

"You've got a piece of it though, don't you? And the other guy, the Black guy? He does as well, right?"

Rick's face tensed.

Chris glanced down the length of the Trumpy again. "Guess Ben's going to have to find another mechanic."

"He's moving her to Annapolis. She'll be well cared for."

"Hope so. Guess the Allie connection goes with it, though, right?" Chris landed an intense look on Rick. "Are you worried about her at all, Larson? Allie? I'm not so sure you are. I just don't see it, and that makes me curious. I think the police are curious, too."

"I was waiting for some good news about her. I assumed that's why you came all this way."

Chris cocked his head. "No, no good news. I wish I had something to share. She *is* the reason I came all this way to talk, though. About her, and what you know."

"You heard it all Tuesday."

Chris removed his sunglasses. "Did I?"

The direct sun glared back off the brilliant white hull, and Chris' small eyes promptly narrowed to slits locked on Rick: a forecast to the end of his short lived civility. Rick saw the *get to know you* salesman demeanor disappear, and with it the wry smiles and solidarity references. The character flip impressed Rick. Chris' deep stare didn't waver; his greeting was over, no more small talk. The cross-examination would begin now.

"None of this adds up, Larson. You, Ben, his boat. And Allie. She disappears, and you shrug. There are too many rough edges around here, and unfortunately, you're one of them. Too many reasons to believe you know more than you're saying. And without you convincing us otherwise, why wouldn't we?"

Rick recognized the terms of engagement. Adrian called it a technique. Chris was not partaking in a discussion. His statement had a beginning, and it would have an end, and that would be all. Opening and closing statements in the same breath. He had no interest in opinions or comments from Rick.

Chris pushed ahead, "I don't care if Ben trusts you. Understand that I work for the senator, and she does not, so I need to ask this on her behalf. Did you hurt her, Larson? Did you do something to Allie? Is that where she is right now, running from you?"

Rick's jaw tensed. His impulse was to help Chris into the river, but he forced an inhale and continued the staring contest.

Chris assessed the expression only briefly. "Doesn't matter. Whatever your answer, it will tell me what I need to know. Even silence. You see, Larson, I think the answer *is* here, somewhere. Or maybe your old friend on the island has some thoughts. Should I go out and talk to him?"

"That would be a mistake."

Chris nodded, sneering. "Of course it would. War heroes, right? But very old war heroes, so old that everyone's forgotten. It was a good act you put on for the senator and Ben the other day; burned out harmless, decaying relics. Felt like bullshit to me. Maybe I should just have some friends search the place, every building here. It wouldn't take much to set that in motion."

"I have to imagine Detective Ward is already working on that. He's probably going to beat you to the punch. Why don't you hold onto those favors."

Chris squinted upriver. "Maybe the island, too."

"As I said, you don't wanna do that."

Chris inched closer. He stood almost as tall as Rick, and their faces landed just inches apart, eyes fixed on the other. Rick felt the exhales and endured the stale smell.

"What I want to do is find Allison Sheridan," Chris said coldly. "And I'm going to. Do you understand *that*, as well? Whatever it takes. And until I do, you and your friend out there are staying at the top of my list."

Without warning, the silent shot struck the piling inches above Chris' head, exploding chunks of old wood and sending slivers flying around his face. Chris winced for only a second, then blinked into the glare, studying the splintered wood.

The gunshot jarred Rick, but somehow he didn't flinch. His breathing paused, expecting the demons would surely find him. After long seconds though, he was still tracking Chris' poker face, and his lungs had filled. Strangely, the past did not invade, leaving him able to assess the man's composure. The non-existent reaction brought immediate concern. There should have been something in Chris; surprise, question, any hint of startle or fear. But nothing, only the thin, unblinking eyes returning their fix on him.

Chris stepped back. Feigning surrender, he raised both hands, adding a curious smile. "Message?" he asked. "Wait—warning?"

Rick twisted slowly to examine the gaping hole in the piling. "Damn, I'm not sure what that could've been."

"I'm pretty certain I know." Chris' face tensed. "I'd say we came to that understanding I was hoping for."

"Then it wasn't a wasted trip."

Chris straightened and brushed a few small splinters from his shoulders. He peered upriver again, speaking collected words across the water. "You're an old man, Larson, and the rest of your life is right on the edge of getting complicated. I hope you didn't hurt her." His expression flattened as he mocked a salute to Rick. Abruptly then, he strode away down the pier. Reaching the corner of the office, he glared back toward the Trumpy. Rick had vanished inside.

~

Minutes later, Chris found his way to the shed, finding Leah and Ron waiting out of sight by the side door. They traded looks as he approached.

"How'd it go?" Ron asked.

"As expected."

"Anything?"

"Oh, yeah. Plenty. What about both of you?"

"We got a good look around," Leah said. "Something you need to see inside. It's important."

Chris checked his phone and glared down the empty pier. "Sixty seconds," he said. "Lead on."

Ron and Leah hesitated, and Chris brushed past them into the shed. His steps slowed immediately, and his eyes went high across each of the walls, surveying the bewildering space. He stopped and rotated. His forehead creased.

"What the hell is all this?"

Leah stepped closer. "Somebody's idea of treasure."

Chris shook his head. "Fucking old men."

"And I think I know who." She moved to the bench seat and handed Chris a framed photograph of Allie and Tremaine. They stood side by side, both cradling their hands around the small carved box. Allie's expression glowed. Tremaine's look conveyed little.

Chris studied it, then refocused on the obsessive order filling shelves all around them. He nodded to himself, tossed the photograph on the bench seat, and turned toward the door.

"I got what I needed today," he called bluntly over his shoulder. "Take a shot of that. Let's get the hell out of here."

Chapter 19

Monday evening's dinner rush at the diner had Delia busy but smiling, with customers seated in most of the twenty-five chairs. She got Rick's call an hour earlier and saved his table, always the one toward the back of the room, closest to the kitchen doors. For some reason, he liked it, the noise added to the privacy, and the spot offered a large, centered window. Rick and Schooner came in the alley door fifteen minutes later, Delia's preference when they arrived together, less chance of Schooner's bad table manners being on display. Schooner flopped quickly and snuggled into the corner. Delia walked over with Rick's iced tea and gave him a hug. Both settled into chairs.

"Welcome back," he said. "Good trip?"

"It was fine." Delia sighed, leaning forward. She reached across the table, laying her hand on his. "Thank you for letting me know about Allie," she said. "It's terrible."

"I didn't want to bother you while you were gone, but I thought you should know." He paused. "There's nothing new from the police."

"Not what I was hoping to hear. Are you okay?"

"Worried." Rick searched the cozy room for distraction. Finally, he said, "So, some friend I am, huh? Welcoming you home with a dog-sitting favor. You sure?"

"Schooner's low maintenance. Happy to."

"Thanks."

Delia tapped the table with two fingers. "So, what about the heart follow-up?"

Rick exhaled and reached for his napkin. "Yeah, that. I won't be gone long."

Delia frowned, but not for the reason he expected. "You take as much time as you need," she said. "This is not one to rush. Your ticker will be fine, and I won't let you forget."

"Counting on it. Can you cover me at Trinity this Thursday?"

"Of course. Be good to see Fay." Delia studied his face. "You sure you're ready for this trip?"

Rick's phone vibrated and he checked the text. Sliding it away, he lowered his head and reached both hands to his forehead. After a moment, he glanced out the window. "Looks like I'm going to have some company."

"I won't ask."

Rick turned back. "Am I ready?" He pulled in a breath. "Always faithful, Delia. This one's for Tre."

Delia shook her finger. "Nice try," she said quickly. "You know I love Tremaine dearly, but this has to be all about you, Richard. You and Beth."

"And Allie," he said in a quiet voice. "Tre thinks she might be there."

"Well, bless his heart. He's a wise old soul. Maybe he sees something more in this visit."

Rick leaned over to lay his hand on Schooner. "Tre's not good, Delia."

"I imagined him to be struggling. Haven't seen him at all this year."

"He doesn't always want to see me either. He's lost much of the time. The swings are sudden and getting worse, full of fear. The dementia is complicating all of it."

"I've asked you before, and I'll probably keep asking. Ever think about pushing past the resistance? Getting him in to see someone again?"

"I'd be the first to say yes. But the three of us talked a while ago. Adrian was there. Tre asked us to just let it take its course, no matter what. Closest I ever want to come to signing off on a living will." Rick took a slow drink of tea. "Tre asked us to promise, and he had his lawyer there to witness."

Delia shook her head slowly. "That may be a hard one to keep."

"It will be. Trust me."

"Is the rifle still there?"

Rick looked out the window again. "Yeah."

"Probably not a good thing anymore."

"Never was."

Delia heard the door chime and twisted toward the entrance. Detective Ward walked in. "This must be your date," she said. As Rick turned, Delia reached over and put her hand on his again. "I just want to say, Sarah's a trooper for driving you."

He lowered his head. "Yes, she is that."

"This is going to be life changing for you, Richard. And intense. I guess it's time, though. I'll say a prayer."

"I'd appreciate that, my friend."

"In that case, I'll say a couple." She winked at him as the detective approached the table.

Delia rose with a warm welcome and offered him a menu. He settled on coffee, and she left for the small station in the corner of the room.

Ward dropped a hand to the chair. "Can I sit?"

"Long day for you."

"I love my work." He smiled, waited a few seconds, then grew serious. "Before you ask, I have nothing on Allie. The tips are still all over the place. We're trying. The FBI has the big net out, but we didn't get the quick bite. The rest of it will likely take some time. Not what we wanted."

Delia came back with one cup of coffee and another iced tea for Rick. She let her hand brush slowly across his shoulder as she moved away.

Ward spoke as his eyes followed her. "Another friend, it appears." He turned back. "Good friend?"

"The best."

"Long time?" He waited, stirring in cream and sugar. "Just curious."

Rick leaned back. "Thirty-five years. We met at this very table."

Ward nodded and scanned the room. "Business is good. Sure seems that people like her."

"Born and raised here in Ward 6. She could run for mayor. They opened up in 1989. The effort has paid off."

"Yeah, it has." Ward leaned forward on his elbows. "Mind if I ask what brought you two together?"

"Is this part of your investigation, Detective?"

Ward dodged, showing the smile again. "You two seem close. Can't I be happy for you?"

Rick leaned back, crossing his arms. "For a while, Delia and I worked together at the marina. Concessions stand. She can't swim and doesn't like boats and wasn't a huge fan of the dirty river. But she loves hospitality and real work. No grand opportunity, just some food for the fishermen and community."

Ward focused on adding more sugar. "I respect you, Larson," he said out of the blue, stirring again.

Rick's forehead wrinkled. He lowered his glass, catching the detective's curious stare.

"Your service. Your friend, Tremaine. I know about the pieces."

"Not a lot there to know," Rick said.

"Not sure I would agree with that. There are some." Ward took a slow sip. "I know about the shrapnel hit you took in the leg."

"Hard to hide that one."

"I know coming out of a war with decompression time is current protocol. Wasn't the case so much in 1969." Ward deliberated before continuing. "I know Adrian brought you and Tremaine to town and set you up at the marina; labor at first for a while, then a partnership with him after he bought it in '93." Ward shook his head. "1993. The middle of a recession? A marina? Guess he thought there was one more run in it."

Rick's brow wrinkled. "Is this what you came to talk to me about?"

"Seems like more of a gift than a business strategy, but good for you. More friends. Whatever it was, though, Adrian's resources, or your hard work, you apparently got the pulse back for a while."

Rick lowered his head. "Yeah, we did. For a while. Something welcoming for people who didn't have a lot. Picnic area, banana trees." His voice faded. "For a little while."

"Interesting." Ward took a second. "Until the fire? The concessions building, right?"

Rick glared across the table. "Yeah, until the fire . . . and Delia's husband died. Took some wind out of our sails."

"Must have been difficult for Tre—"

"Okay, Detective!" Rick straightened in his chair and dropped a fist on the table.

Ward pulled back, raising both palms. "I meant what I said about the respect. Look, I know it's been some tough steps along the way. That's all." He pinched the bridge of his nose and cleared his throat. "Unfortunately, this is going to be another one." He twisted in his chair, stalling a few seconds. "Senator Baxter's attorney is pushing the D.A., which really means the senator is pushing the D.A. They want a search warrant. Now. The marina. The whole place."

Rick slumped back in his chair, staring blankly as the detective painted the future.

"I've delayed as much as I can, chasing anything we could, any diversion. There was a camera shot at a toll booth in upstate New York that got some attention, but nothing conclusive." Ward averted his eyes for the first time. "Finding the car, though," he went on. "Where it was, the spotlight came right back to you, I'm afraid."

"Why are you telling me this, detective? Sounds like you should be taking me in."

"Does kinda sound like that." He stirred the cup again. "But like I said, I lost an uncle in Vietnam, and well, you just happen to be a war hero. I can't make that jump."

"You had to dig deep for that. Not enough to do?"

"Not so deep, but yeah, sometimes I find a little extra time to fill."

Rick's eyes drifted to the window. "That was a long time ago. A lot of people lost someone."

They let some time go by as a server hurried past their table and into the kitchen.

Rick finally turned back. "I wouldn't be the first one to have come off the rails, Detective."

"True, but we'll see." Ward leaned back. "Besides, your friend Adrian Dumars is still saying hands off, and I trust his reason. But nevertheless, the wagons are circling. The judge will likely sign the warrant in the morning."

"It's a waste of time."

"Too many times they are."

"Watch out for the snakes," Rick said. He finished his tea and pushed the glass away. "Do you really think I would ever hurt that young girl?"

"No, I don't. But on this one, there are only a couple of votes that count."

"The senator."

Ward nodded. "She's not your biggest fan. Claims she never agreed with her husband about letting Allison hang out with you. She's firing at people."

"Do I need to be there?"

"I thought you'd want to, but no, there's no talk of an arrest warrant."

"Not yet."

Ward was silent.

"Do I need to stay close?" Rick asked.

"Is that a problem?"

Rick studied the detective's face. "I'll leave the gate unlocked," he muttered.

Ward finished his coffee, holding the empty cup in both hands. "There's one more thing, Larson. Depending on how things go tomorrow—the next warrant may be for the island. I'm sorry. It's teed up."

The two stared.

"That's good to know," Rick mumbled as Ward rose. "Just do me a favor, Detective, take care with Tre's things. That's all he's got."

Chapter 20

It took a year to blend their patterns and another year to find the home. Michelle had insisted on leading the search; the address required an appropriateness to the merging of their influential lives and careers. The property required separate areas for each of them, isolated completely from the other activities that consume a family's time and space. Solely for their personal use, accommodating the privacy essential to their demanding individual paths. Separate entrances; the opportunity for unannounced guests. Michelle deemed the estate on Laverock Place as the only Georgetown address suited to her needs. The area she claimed stood apart, a separate building occupying the southeast corner of the property.

—

The low lighting faded into shadow in the far corners of the room. Michelle stood inches from the large windows, contemplating the dark Potomac. Unsurpassed views framing the DC skyline to the east served as a reminder of what she had accomplished and what she still saw as achievable in the years to come. The accommodations empowered her. Dark wood paneling, extravagant area rugs, walls of bookshelves flanking the fireplace, expanses of south-facing glass. Comforting elegance familiar to her childhood years. A cultivated ambiance fitting for the intimate gatherings of dignitaries, bipartisan meetings, and occasional dinners with the House Speaker. All of it proper and essential for portraying her professional triumphs and ambitions. Michelle claimed the space not only for her sanctuary but also as her home court, for advantage when engaged in grating discussions with the man she now considered to be her only failure in life.

Michelle crossed the room slowly, eyeing Ben, pitying his fatigued look. The remaining connection between the two of them had so dimmed, the façade of marriage was nothing more. Their patterned positions testified. She settled deeply into the soft leather chair close to the fireplace, poised to escalate and bully if needed. He leaned against the deep windowsill, eighteen feet away, shoulders rolled forward, his arms crossed loosely.

"Can't believe I brought my daughter into this life," Ben mumbled, his eyes fixed on the low flame.

"I know that must be troubling to you. Something to ponder, isn't it? I can see you searching for the very reason as we speak." Michelle tilted her head. "It never materialized, did it, *husband*? The life you promised your precious daughter?"

She studied his slack expression, finally sighing aloud. "It seems I misjudged you terribly. Power was never high on your list, was it, Ben? It's curious: when we first met, I mistakenly believed the very significant wealth you have amassed was a result of a lust for privilege, not unlike my own. I felt we shared a similar passion to live a unique life. Money and power create separation. That's very important to me."

Ben shook his head. "It isn't to me, Michelle. I build things, that's all."

"Ahh, simple ambitions. Quaintly virtuous. I applaud you." Michelle stiffened, her fingers drumming both arms of the chair. "Mine, as you know, are not so simple. Mine require an unwavering commitment in service to our country, a path now compromised by my association with you and your daughter." She held her impassioned stare on him. "You both proved to be a detour I never should have taken."

"We're agreed on that, but Allie deserved more from you."

"On the contrary, I feel you misled me. I perceived her as a placid child, someone who would require little energy and have zero impact on my mission—"

"She was still grieving, for God's sake."

"Understandable. Your wife died, and you were trying to put the puzzle back together. Trying to find a new missing piece for your daughter. The problem, though, I never imagined what that would entail."

"Helping to raise a child is—"

"Helping? Is that your description? You were never here, Ben. You and your ego traveling the world in the name of providing for us? Disappearing. Like Allie."

Ben scowled and abruptly pushed away from the window. "What the hell happened that night?"

Michelle's brows closed. "That night? Is that where you've landed? The latest fundraiser is the culprit? Mystery of the missing daughter solved?"

"I came back, and Allie was gone."

"For me, it was reasonable to believe she was just living her autonomous teenage life. It was certainly not the first time our paths hadn't crossed for days."

"Your aides had to tell you she was missing! You were right here, dammit, and you have zero contact with her for two days?"

"Nor did you! And I feel certain she must have reached out to you several times. Yes? Perhaps your scrutiny should lie there."

Ben snapped. "What the hell happened?"

"Asked and answered!" Michelle promptly rose and stormed across the room to face him. "I cannot speak to what happened that night, Ben. Do you understand? I didn't see Allie or talk with her before or after the gathering. However, I can provide great detail on the fallout of her decisions. Look what she's done to us! To me! Your daughter's actions have compromised my re-election." Michelle tensed and pulled back. "I have more to accomplish, but the issues are being run over by the significant drama your over-indulged little girl has caused. And behind whatever *sympathy* value I can derive, the rest of it is just too much risk and too much focus—"

"On her and not on you."

"Tell me, Ben! Isn't that where the focus belongs?"

He slumped back against the sill. "You tell me you never wanted Allie; why did you even try?"

"Simple. I believed the association would be good for me. You were new and shiny and good in bed. You came with headlines."

Ben feigned a smile. "And you wanted them."

"Of course. Oh, I suppose for a while, it was intriguing. The conversations were different, sometimes interesting. Not what I was used to. You made me consider other possibilities, maybe a fleeting awareness of mortality. I hear that happens. All of it has led to an epiphany for me this evening regarding our connection, our brand. I used to think it was worth it, that it could survive." Michelle crossed her arms. "Well, it isn't worth it anymore, and we aren't going to survive. Sorry to burden you with more details amid this difficult time." Her chin lifted. "*That's* what happened that evening!"

"And our daughter, a seventeen-year-old girl, went missing."

"*Your* daughter. I never wanted her in my life. You brought baggage with you, and I played along. Truth is, I never had space for either of you."

Ben hung his head, staring at his clenched hands. "In spite of it all, I thought this devastation might bring us to common ground. You must feel something."

Michelle rolled her eyes. "Oh, please. It was a mistake for us to believe that staying together until Allie left for college was the best thing for her. What I feel now is, that mistake could not be more glaring."

"That makes it easy. We're agreed on something else." Ben sighed. "I'll be staying in Massachusetts until Allie comes back."

Michelle registered no surprise or objection. The comment landed only as confirmation of their end. Her mourning lasted mere seconds. Relieved, she drew a deep breath to recover. "You're assuming she's coming back?"

Ben swallowed hard, barely managing a response. "Yes, I am. Maybe she'll go there."

"Tell me, if that was her plan, don't you think she would be there by now?"

"I doubt she had a plan. I know now, though, she won't be coming back here."

Michelle nodded thoughtfully. "Ahh, the Sheridan DNA, one misstep after another. Her decision or yours?" She turned and crossed to the bar and filled a large glass with red wine. "I say let her wander. Maybe this will give her some direction."

She turned casually toward Ben, her expression going cold. After a substantial drink, she said, "As for my personal direction, I want you to know something. From this day forward, I will be protecting myself, my career, and my life here. I won't let the bad decisions made by you or your tragically misguided daughter impact my path, not any more than they have. You can't comprehend the importance of the calling before me and—"

"Calling?" Ben howled. He straightened and drew closer. "There is no calling, Michelle! You've accomplished nothing of importance. Yours is a life of privilege. A mere testament to the effectiveness of nepotism. You are simply the embodiment of congressional dead-weight, like so many others."

Her face tightened instantly and she took some time studying him, finally lifting her glass for another sip. "You're upset and lashing out, husband—looking for someone to blame. I understand. You miss your daughter, of course. But inside, what you fear is actually the truth. You know she won't be coming home, and there you've spent all these years on her, only to find you've raised a statistic." Michelle waved a dismissive hand. "Allie's gone, Ben. Like her mother." Her sneer grew, savoring his stunned expression.

"My God, I knew you had a darkness; how deep does it go, Michelle?"

She shrugged and took another drink, her eyes taunting as she stared into his above the rim.

"So, back to the old homestead, huh? And all the comfort of friends and family? What family's left that is." Michelle shook her head. "The Sheridan women certainly have their troubles, don't they?"

The smirk vanished in an instant, and Michelle hurled the glass at Ben's head. He deflected it in time with his arm, but the crystal shattered against his elbow. Michelle strolled closer, staring at the seeping blood.

Jaw clenched, her words came slowly, "Disrespecting my family and my path? You just crossed a dangerous line, Mr. Sheridan. Be careful." She leaned to within inches and whispered. "And trust me, you and your daughter don't want to know how deep."

Chapter 21

Their Tuesday departure time from DC was later than planned, and a construction project on the New Jersey Turnpike approaching New York added an unexpected two-hour delay. Rick and Sarah were several hours behind schedule, and it was late, already 10:30 p.m. by the time they reached Portland, ME. Rockland was still eighty miles away, almost two more hours of driving, maybe longer for them having to navigate the last leg of a long trip at night. Sarah was exhausted and Rick's leg had stiffened from too much time in one position. They wisely agreed to break up the drive with an overnight stay in Portland. With no energy for being choosy, they took the first exit advertising a budget hotel just south of the city. Neither had given much thought to sleeping arrangements on this trip, and surprisingly, with all the topics they covered over the drive, hotel bedrooms was not one of them. The subject was left as an unspoken understanding to include separate beds in separate rooms. But as the desk clerk checked his registry again confirming only one double queen room was available, they had to relent. They traded exhausted looks and returned the same back to the clerk. It sufficed as their answer, and he reached for the key cards as Sarah slid her VISA across the counter.

The room was fine and neither of them was awake long enough to regret the lack of privacy. Rick awoke an hour and a half later, though, his tired eyes lost in the emptiness across the dark ceiling. Minutes later, Sarah started to snore. It was loud enough for

Rick to abandon all hope of falling asleep again. For too long, he struggled with a torrent of anxious thoughts about the coming day, thoughts that would not abate, and now clearly energized by the vibrating tissues in Sarah's throat. At 4:00 a.m., Rick's pacing and third visit to the bathroom awakened her, immediately signaling it would be best for them to finish the last part of the drive now. They threw on clothes and pulled out of the hotel lot minutes later, grateful for the continental breakfast offered to early risers. Thirty miles up State Road 295, they exited onto Route 1 east, driving in silence, both watching a deep redness of morning light creep above the horizon.

"Red sky at morning," Rick mumbled.

Sarah laid her hand on his shoulder. "Sailor's delight?"

"Nice try." Rick held firmly to the wheel with both hands, his intense focus straight ahead.

The last five miles followed a narrow two-lane stretch leading them straight into Rockland. The traffic light at the intersection of Route 1 and Park Street turned green, but Rick didn't pull forward. Two cars passed on Park, but for the moment, Route 1 remained empty behind them. Rick peered left down the town's main street, distracted by the bright sun's wash across the old storefronts.

Sarah reached a hand across to his. "Are you ready for this?"

"Elm Street, right?"

Sarah checked her phone. "On the corner."

"Maybe it's not the best time." Rick rubbed the back of his neck. "She's a baker for God's sake. She's probably been up working since 5:00 a.m. It's probably her busiest time of day."

Sarah nodded. "True. But she was probably up at 4:00, and that would make two of you."

Rick missed her attempt to lighten the mood.

She gave him a minute, then said, "What do you want to do?"

He glanced over to an understanding smile.

"It's going to be a good thing."

Rick winced and shook his head. "You don't know that."

"No, I don't. I *believe* this is going to be a good thing."

"Sorry I dragged you up here."

"No, you aren't. You needed my car." She tapped his arm playfully.

Rick's fingers drummed the gearshift.

"Why don't you take some time and walk around," Sarah said. "Let Beth get through the morning. You don't have to rush this."

A loud car horn sounded behind them, and Rick flinched. "Damn!" He accelerated through the light as it changed to red and took the first space along the curb across the street.

Sarah raised a hand to his shoulder. "Rick, it's going to be okay. But it seems like you could use some time alone to collect your thoughts. Why don't I take the car and explore town a little."

Rick exhaled and twisted in his seat. "I didn't mean to wake you up."

"Yeah, now that's worth an apology, but it sounds like I should be apologizing to you. I snore? Really? Bad habits of the alone, I guess."

"It doesn't matter. Sleep wasn't going to happen for me."

"Well, I'm glad then, the sunrise was worth it. Everything worked out."

Rick turned to her. "Let's hope so."

At 10:45 later that morning, Rick stood alone and unnoticed on the sidewalk in front of Jess' Market at the corner of Tilson Avenue and Carroll Lane. A Hannaford Foods truck lumbered away down the street, leaving a rush of diesel exhaust swirling around him. The sun had started its ascent above the higher roof lines, but remnants of the Maine winter wasted no time in bidding him welcome. Rick's teeth chattered as he scanned the street. He lowered the brim, pulled his jacket tight, and began a slow walk up Tillson Avenue from the waterfront, pausing at the corner of Elm Street.

He watched two men leave *Morning's Buns*. An ornate metal sign cantilevered above the entrance door projected the bakery's name in rich orange and purple letters. The name his daughter chose. He imagined her sharing the meaning behind it, a valuable conversation starter. After waiting another minute for any lingering customers to leave, Rick wandered across the street, unable to take his eyes off the colorful bay windows framing the front door. Approaching his past for the first time, he struggled with the rush of emotion, never envisioning being face-to-face with an important piece of his daughter's life. He stalled on the sidewalk, consumed with a buried regret he inevitably feared and had been unable to face. His mind had always managed to push it aside. As he walked, weakness filled his legs, and his heart pounded faster.

A welcoming patio ran along the side of the bakery with four small wrought iron tables and chairs. Rick labored to make it to the closest one and dropped heavily. Avoiding any glance through the windows, he insisted to himself he could get through this. Over four decades had passed since he last looked into his daughter's eyes. That look so many years ago filled with fear and pain for both of them, neither being able to find an understanding in that instance or since. Rick held no other images of his only child.

Through the last night's restless hours, he had envisioned so many first words to express, but the cold clawed at him, and his mind escaped to the memory of his friend, Tremaine, tenderly holding his precious daughter, Beth, on her first birthday. Rick's shoulders sunk as he dropped his head, in realization that his search for Allie served only part of his reason for being here. Unease overwhelmed him immediately. He dwarfed the frigid metal chair. The cold wind engulfed him. He thought he knew cold, but this was different. This wind swarmed him with a relentless authority as he aimed resentment at his inadequate boots. He lifted his collar and pulled the brim of his hat even lower, then jammed both bare hands deep into his coat pockets. Thoughts of Allie, Tre, and Beth swirled around him like the unforgiving wind. He twisted away from the gusts and waited.

~

Minutes passed before Beth looked out the patio windows again, surprised this time to see someone hunched forward at one of the tables. She frowned, grabbed her coat and gloves, and pushed through the door. Nothing registered with the customer as she approached, not the squeaky door closing behind her or the crackle of her brisk footsteps across the frost-crusted pavers.

"Morning," she greeted. "Cold out here!"

The man jarred, looking up instantly.

"Can I get you some coffee?" Beth said, glancing at his bare hands as they started a slow rub across both thighs. "Or some gloves!" She smiled. "It's warmer inside."

"Beth . . ." The man pulled a card out of his jacket pocket, hesitated, then held it out to her.

"What's this?" Her brow promptly knitted. "Birthday card?" She opened it, squinting to read, and instantly released a hushed gasp. Her gaze rose slowly to study the lonely, unfamiliar face.

"Richard Larson?"

"It's Rick," he said faintly, lowering his head. "I mailed the original a couple of weeks ago. It may have gotten lost." He pulled a shaking hand slowly across his forehead.

Beth stood motionless. Her mouth fell open, waiting for him to turn. Somehow, they held a long stare. She could have been trading looks with anyone, though, having only the faintest of memories to associate with this person. Beth's hands trembled, but she erased the emotion instantly, clasping them together tightly. Her eyes darted all around for escape, up the street, toward the empty planter boxes, and behind her back to the door, until finally she brought her pained expression back to Rick.

"My God," she said, shaking her head. "Why?"

Rick offered nothing.

Beth leaned closer, her voice weak. "Why are you here?"

"Tremaine." Rick turned aside. "He's sick and probably doesn't have long. I thought it was important that you know. I needed to tell you, in case you wanted to say goodbye. He was only a part of your life when you were very young, but there was a connection. Tre still mentions you."

Beth couldn't release her glare. Clouded memories from their few years together tried to pry, but this was an awakening, a meeting for the first time. She had no reason to recognize the man. Late one night thirty-nine years ago, she had been awakened and hurried out of bed by her mother. Beth recalled being four, and life for the family she knew had become frightening. Screaming and rage followed them around the house that night, her mother frantically grabbing what few things of theirs she could. Beth never remembered the hateful words themselves, only her father's threatening shouts and her mother's terrified expressions. She had rushed them to the car in darkness, burying Beth's head beneath the coat's hood, unwilling to let her child's last memory of this man, known briefly as father, be his rageful pain. Rick Larson had become a casualty; lost in the addiction he believed would heal him.

Beth squeezed her eyes shut, envisioning her mother's struggle to start the car, torn, still wanting to help him, but knowing she couldn't. She had tried for years, but the war had broken all of them, and they were no longer a family. Her mother vowed that night to save her daughter from the world Rick brought home after Vietnam.

Beth lowered her head, covering her mouth with both hands. Following that night, she and Rick had never spoken. Not one moment since had she cared if he continued to drink. When she grew old enough to understand the conversation, her mother never allowed her to trust he would stop. As strange as it seemed to her at times, over so many years, only rarely had she ever concerned herself thinking about him; such was the effectiveness of her mother's conviction to leave and forget. Their flight from home offered protection for decades: a fearful parent devoted to immersing her daughter in life's distractions, all in the best interests of burying the past. But the past lay uncovered, and now sat across from her, veiling a tremble and sharing this somber news that so unexpectedly, had filled her with sadness.

Beth peered at the stranger, the old man whose body had carried such heaviness along so many years, his visible scars, and the weary eyes that drifted away. The image held the man's truth, his pain of knowing a dear friend would die soon, and a fear of the crippling loneliness that would follow. Beth pulled her coat closed and dropped into the chair across from him. She held her posture stiff, probing his deflated expression. Her hands dropped under the table, still clasped.

For a long while, they each sought distractions nearby.

"I'm sorry," Beth finally said. "You clearly stayed close."

"We did. He's struggled for a long time, Beth. It all caught up with him years ago. The war destroyed him. You may not remember—"

"All I remember is what my mother told me. She said he saved us from you. More than once." Beth wavered. "She described him as a gentle man, with kind eyes. I still have a photograph."

Rick turned, shielding his face from the bright sun. "That's good. I'm glad you do. He's worth remembering. For all of it."

Beth slumped, curious her anger had not intruded. In recent times, when her mind weakened for various reasons and she slipped into the story of seeing her father again, anger was the first emotion to surface, as she replayed the nightmare her mother insisted she preserve. Thankfully for Beth, the visions of reuniting had dimmed, finding her less frequently and with little effect. Sharing this table in the cold wind, though, Beth was left to face a surreal reality of the returned vision. The villain of her story sat across the table, likely grasping the enormity of his failings as a father and husband at last. So, why hadn't the anger stormed to her voice and thoughts? Was it gone and no longer important? Beth narrowed her eyes on Rick's, a strange contentment perceivable, perhaps in his also having accepted the nearness to an ending of his tired life, and the pain of knowing defeat and regret.

Rick repositioned his hat, then blew into his hands. He glanced at his boots, dragging them across the heavy frost still clinging to random bricks. Beth imagined him forcing movement in his toes. She shook her head, refusing to open the door for pity. The guardian anger finally knocked.

She leaned forward and spoke in a flat voice, "You came very far to tell me your friend is sick. That was a long time ago. So many other ways you could have let me know about Tremaine. Why this?" She watched his struggle. The indifference in her voice would surely hold no surprise for him. Her dispassion was deserved, and she intended it to return a wound. "What are you really doing here, Rick?"

He balked, shifting again in the small chair. "I told you about the young girl," he said in a quieter voice. "The one who spends time at the marina?"

Beth's jaw tensed. "You didn't tell me. You wrote it; in one of your random birthday cards. One every year. Such a cliché; the obligatory gesture." Beth found satisfaction in his need to look away. "Most of them I never read. That one caught my eye, though, for some reason. Was she your do-over?"

"Beth, she's missing."

"Missing?"

"She's the daughter of a very wealthy guy. Her stepmother is a senator. It's been over two weeks, with no word. A lot of people are searching for her and concerned."

"Is that what you're doing in Rockland? Being concerned?"

Rick sighed. "Tre thought she might have come here. Maybe to hide."

"Hide from what?"

Rick had no answer.

"Is that why you came?" Beth leaned back in her chair, shaking her head. "My God, Rick, if it is, Tremaine was wrong to think that. And you were wrong to make the trip." She glowered across the table. "So, you came up here because you lost another kid?"

"Beth—."

"But you're *looking* for *this* one. Interesting."

"Is that fair to—"

"Fair?" Beth's voice raised. "That's interesting as well, coming from you. I think you can answer that one for yourself."

Rick's gaze wandered along the sidewalk following a young couple as they slowed in front of *Morning's Buns* to peek through the window.

"I just thought, maybe I could help get her back." His voice trailed off. "I didn't think that was a possibility with you."

A tear started down Beth's cheek, and she wiped it away instantly, never averting her eyes. "You'll never know what might have been possible," she said. "You only succeed where you try, Rick."

Beth rose and pushed her chair in, waiting for him to look. "Thank you for letting me know about Tre," she said bluntly. Somewhere inside, she knew the words held a different meaning; a tribute to the kind man she knew once. But she refused to share any such truth with Rick.

"If not for your weakness, though, my life with Tremaine could have been so very different. Thank you for that as well." Her faced tensed as she crossed her arms. "I haven't seen the girl," she said coldly. "Sorry."

Rick nodded, then pushed back slowly and stood. He met her eyes, needing to balance against the chair.

"We stay open for lunch on Tuesday and Thursday," Beth said flatly. "I need to get back to work."

"Another time."

She started toward the door.

"Beth," he called after her.

She stopped and lowered her head, waiting.

"There will be something for Tre. I'm not sure what, or when."

Beth pivoted, folding her arms again. "I don't know, Rick. At Arlington?"

"No, Tre never wanted that. A box in the ground; the idea wasn't comfortable to him. Said he'd feel trapped inside with the memories of every shot he took. He always wanted to go to the Keys. Maybe there."

Beth's boot tapped against the bricks.

"He was always there for you . . . I know I wasn't. It would be nice to have you."

She pulled both hands slowly across her temples. "Let me know the details," she finally said. "Is that the appropriate response you hoped for?"

Rick gazed at the clear sky a moment, drawing in salty whiffs along the calming breeze. "I walked around a little bit. It's a beautiful place to make a life, Beth. I'm happy for you." Needing to stall, he fussed with his hat. "But I should go now, of course."

To Beth, the long look they shared was good-bye again.

"I wish I'd done better," Rick said softly. He managed a weak smile, then turned and trudged across the intersection.

Beth watched him hesitate at the corner of Tillson, before disappearing down the street. Wavering, she stared along the empty sidewalk for minutes, following the image of a stranger she might have known long ago.

A rush of cold air followed Beth inside as she pushed through the door. She yanked off her coat and collapsed back against the wall, gazing blankly at the pressed metal ceiling panels.

A soft voice came from the corner. "Hey."

Beth glanced.

Allie sat at a small table, spying out a window across the vacant patio. "Are you okay?" she asked.

Beth blew out a breath. "I don't really know."

"That must have been very hard." Allie shook her head. "I can't imagine."

"I hope you never have to know how hard." Beth wiped away new tears and crossed the room to her table. "So, how about you? You okay?"

Allie was silent as she twisted to peer out the streetside bay window. A man casually crossed Tilson, stopped in front of *Morning's Buns*, and squinted in through the windows. He checked his phone and started toward the steps.

"Customer," she murmured.

"No way." Beth hurried to the front door, and flipped the sign to 'closed', gesturing her apologies to him.

Allie fell back in the chair, trembling. "Beth," she faltered.

"No lunch shift today. You and I should talk, but I need a minute. Shit, I can't believe this!" Scowling, she grabbed a pile of dirty plates from behind the counter and backed through the kitchen swing door.

Allie spotted the man moving toward the window. She recoiled deep into the corner, raising a hand to cover her face. As he lifted his phone to the window, she yanked the curtain closed. In silhouette, she saw him delay and turn down both lengths of sidewalk. Allie peeked as he spun away and crossed the street to his car. The man looked back once more before jerking the door open.

Beth stood in the kitchen, staring across the space, blankly surveying the disorder from the morning's rush. Her partner, Karen, worked at the big sink in the corner, finishing the pans.

The kitchen door burst open, and Allie stumbled through, shaking and clutching her arms to her chest. She teetered back against a table.

"Allie?" Beth moved close and reached for her shoulders. "What is it?"

Allie sobbed, hiding her face in both hands. She went limp, and Beth had to steady her. Breathless, Allie let her head fall to Beth's shoulder.

"He tried to rape me."

Beth turned her stunned look across the kitchen to Karen.

Without warning, Allie pushed away and bolted through the rear kitchen door.

Chapter 22

Allie crossed Tilson at an angle. She walked fast with both hands held to her face, wiping furiously at the streaming tears. She rounded the corner at Carver Lane and stopped to lean against a rusty steel porch railing, lowering the brim of her baseball cap and pulling out sunglasses. She scanned both ways and instinctively broke into a sprint, immediately centering on the empty back street. She side-stepped puddles and launched across potholes, her eyes locked on the blurred image of a track lane showing ahead. Four hundred and forty yards. The same quarter-mile lane for each event through high school. Soon, she would run again for Stanford. Allie would always run. Her mother had, early every morning. It held purpose for her. Strength. Even being young, Allie saw it. Years later, she grew into the inseparable purpose, gripped by the exertion, the exhaustion, and the renewed strength that would then ultimately return to her depleted mind and body.

The grade rose in front of Allie, and she clenched her fists. Strength could save her; a belief she knew her mother had held. But she died so fast there had been no time to be resolute and to fight back. The finality of loss. Allie's eyes teared from the cold. The remembrance brought back a sadness and deep panic; the buried motivation to always be prepared through strength. Allie pushed harder.

The pavement ahead deteriorated, and she veered to the sidewalk. Her shorter, controlled breaths came fast. She focused down the lane, the last twenty yards, unmindful of the broken edge of rain gutter along the curb. She missed her step, and the ankle rolled. Her right leg buckled. She slowed, stumbled, and managed to grasp the light pole to unweight her foot. Wincing, Allie hobbled to the closest stoop and collapsed onto the second step. She rotated to lean against the painted brick wall and let her head fall back. A cold breeze rushed between the low buildings crowding the narrow road. Allie shivered against the swirl. She elevated her leg and tried to flex the ankle; the sting forced a quick, deep inhale. Grimacing, she wiped the sweat from her neck, then peered under the lowered brim of her hat. She shook her head and rested an empty stare on the hidden throbbing inside her boot.

Allie's grandparents' home endured as one of the oldest in Salem, Massachusetts. Nestled in a quiet waterside block, the leisurely walk to town required less than fifteen minutes. The door between the large kitchen and screened porch didn't latch. One hundred-year-old hardware and countless coats of paint forced reliance on a worn brick to secure it in place, either back against the wall or as far as possible into the frame. During summer months, it rarely mattered; the door remained open day and night, an invitation for the cooling wind to sneak its way through each of the rooms. Comfortable rooms with cozy, solid furniture, grand and colorful. Ornamented rooms with endless framed photographs and paintings. And books, everywhere. Her grandparents' livelihood and love. Books filling walls of shelves, occupying side tables, neatly stacked in corners, ever present in most spaces, with rich leather chairs close by to offer escape. A passion, a gift, and a coaxing from Allie's grandmother to her grandchildren to embrace the musing retreat of reading. The quaint house glowed with remembrance of family and friends. Allie had summered there from an early age, often choosing the porch for sleeping over a bedroom, comforted by the goodnights from choruses of crickets and melodies of soft wind and rain. Comfort lost in the spring of 1990, when her mother was diagnosed.

The faint lightening in the eastern sky seemed to arrive early that April morning, awakening the birds. Allie lay still on the generous cushions, half asleep, listening to their far-off calls to the new dawn carry across town. Allie's mother approached with silent steps and squeezed in on the couch. She sat, her expression slack, tears streaming as she extended a hand to her daughter's face. Allie let the book fall away and wrapped an arm around her mother's waist, desperate for her moist eyes to find escape across the peeling bead-board ceiling.

A truck rumbled down the rugged street, startling Allie, honking as it passed the stoop. Immediately, she rotated her ankle to loosen it. After a while, she stood and guardedly crossed Carver Lane. She ducked into a service alley running parallel to Main Street two blocks west, testing her steps, and pushing when she could. Clearing the alley, she moved aimlessly along intersecting backstreets, unaware of the number of times only luck and the randomness in her path had protected her. She pulled off the hat and sunglasses, her eyes filled with new purpose; she had stopped the tears and moved the trauma back to its distant place in her mind. Now, she needed to find Rick. What had pulled him out of his cherished isolation on M Street, SE, to travel here and meet with Beth after their lifetime apart? The thought of herself being the reason never occurred to Allie. But if Rick were in Rockland, he would help her. Holding that possibility and the hope he might be nearby heartened her to take each next, tender step.

⁓

Rockland Harbor Park occupied a half block where Tillson dead-ended at the water. Rick sat alone, slouched against the bench, head back, squinting to the sky. Sarah approached and sat next to him, resting her hand on his arm.

"Found you," she said, smiling. "How did it go?"

He hesitated. "Harder than I thought. There's nothing there." He leaned forward, elbows on knees. His lost gaze lowered to the soft swells rebounding gently off the stone bulkhead.

Sarah sighed. "There is something. It may just be difficult to see."

Rick shook his head.

"Are you ok?" she asked.

"Not sure what that means anymore." He paused. "Allie's made me think a lot about Beth. A lot of worry, feeling helpless. Pissed off about so much wasted time."

"Rick—"

"I lost them both," he mumbled. Rick's anxious hands rubbed along his jeans. He averted his eyes, staring across the water, then down the empty sidewalk.

Sarah inched closer. "What can I do?"

Rick pushed up abruptly from the bench and moved several steps away before turning. "Nothing! You can't fix this for me, Sarah. You can't fix me! Tre and I are both broken! You know that."

Sarah stood and moved close, bowing her head. "I, I know what that can mean—"

"Bullshit! You couldn't." Rick raised both hands in surrender. "I need some time, Sarah. You should go home now."

She stared, motionless. "Aren't those Tre's words to you

sometimes?"

Rick glared.

"You want me to leave?" she asked quietly.

"I want to know where Allie is," he said, his voice cracking. "I want to know my daughter."

"Rick, let me help. You don't have to do this alone. I can wait—"

"Don't do that, Sarah. Don't wait. I told you, I'm okay being alone." Unexpectedly, he spun and plodded away down the walk, quickly disappearing into the first alley.

Chapter 23

Gravelly Point Park sat across Roaches Run, a small tributary off the Potomac, just a couple of hundred feet north of the runways at Reagan National Airport. The eastern edge of the park ran along the river, directly across from East Potomac Park on the DC side. The area offered green space, a boat ramp and dock for access to the Potomac and insufficient parking to accommodate the popular spot's number of visitors. Few empty spaces could be found most days, from late morning through dusk. When the wind blew from the west or northwest, planes took off heading north, passing over the park not more than 200 feet above. You could count the rivets.

The southwest portion of the lot hadn't filled in by noon. Chris' Tesla sat in the corner, angled across two spaces. He leaned against the trunk, his head tilted back watching the American 737 pull up. Minutes later, Leah arrived. She coasted into the adjoining space and finished a call as she got out. She showed a slight smile approaching Chris.

"Maybe some good news," she said, foregoing any greeting. "We followed the old man and his girlfriend."

"We? Ron?"

Leah nodded. "Destination, Rockland, Maine. They arrived early this morning."

"Okay—and?"

"Larson's daughter lives there. Owns a small bakery and lunch spot. The two were face-to-face at her place this morning, outside on the patio. It wasn't a long visit. She stood for most of it, and he sat. Ron said the mood seemed pretty cold. No hugs or kisses."

She paused, gazing to the sky as the next American flight roared overhead.

Chris tapped his foot. "Still listening."

"The reunion didn't last ten minutes. Larson walked off. The daughter stormed inside. Something else, though. We saw a girl run across the street from the daughter's place; she just showed up out of nowhere. Ron said she was about Allie's height. Couldn't tell if she came out of the bakery or not, but he thinks so. She was going north. Larson was heading east. He had to pick one of them and decided to stay with Larson. That hit a dead end when his girlfriend pulled up next to him on a park bench."

Chris shook his head. "A girl about Allie's height, that Ron didn't follow. This is your good news?"

Leah finished, "Ron was going door to door thirty minutes later when he spotted the same girl again. Small town. They got separated, but before that, he was pretty close. Thinks it could be her. Larson's daughter lives south of town with her partner. Ron said he could watch the house for a while if we wanted. Seemed to think it would be worthwhile."

"Watch for what? The girl he thinks might be the same height as Allie Sheridan?"

"He thought it was strange, that's all; the way she ran across the street at that very instant, just after Larson left. The daughter may be a connection."

Chris offered nothing, holding hard eye contact with Leah. Finally, he asked, "How long have you worked for me?"

Leah dismissed the patriarchal overtone. "You and I have worked on special efforts together for five years now," she said. "As

I have with other clients."

"Five years? Really? In what we do, that's considered a long relationship."

"It is."

"Relationships like ours only survive with trust. And they only move forward with trust."

"I'm in this for the long run with you, Chris, if that's where you're heading. Not the senator; she's going to flame out. But your trajectory looks intriguing to me."

"That's good to hear."

Leah continued, lowering to check a text. "So, why are we here? You have something you want to share with me?"

"Perceptive. That always makes it easier." Chris took a quick look around the lot. "It's not big picture, but it could be."

Leah pocketed the phone and folded her arms.

"I've made an error in judgment, and it involves Allison Sheridan." Chris squinted, raising his chin. "If her father, Ben, was talking to her," he faltered. "If the police were talking to her, Miss Sheridan may try to implicate me, involving an unfortunate connection she and I had. She might say that it happened recently." His jaw tensed. "In her bedroom."

Leah gestured to her ear. "Plane noise," she said, raising her voice. She waited for the roar to follow west, then looked back, tilting her head. "Did you say bedroom, Chris?"

He scowled and jammed both hands into his pockets.

"Guess you decided to trust me," she said.

"This would be the time to tell me if that was a mistake."

"Not so far."

"This needs to be dealt with."

"Sounds like it." Leah nodded slowly. "Okay, so wrong place, wrong time with a senator's stepdaughter. Whatever she says means nothing really, without proof. Your reputable word against hers; could be okay. Messy, but okay."

She peered at him under raised eyebrows, sensing concern. "*Is* there proof, Chris?"

"I don't know; there may be a ring. Fuck! Somehow a ring with her initials turned up. In a jewelry box that may be hers—"

"What are you—"

"At Larson's marina! It was found there."

"Really? Assumedly, before our recent search?"

Chris forced a slight nod.

"Intriguing. Well, with what you've told me, that occurrence would seem to work in your favor. But regardless, you aren't certain that it's hers, right?"

Chris shook his head, balking. "There may have been some blood on the ring."

Leah's head jerked back. "Now that's a complication." She leaned in. "And would Miss Sheridan say that could be your blood?"

Chris pushed abruptly from the car and paced a few steps in front of her. "Okay, enough with the fucking word games."

Leah smirked. "Fine. More direct? Did you hurt her, Chris? Physically? Anything that would show?"

"I'm married, dammit!"

"That may not be your biggest concern right now. Was she still seventeen when this happened?"

"Just. It was a mistake."

"Understatement. Yes, it was. Could there be anything else? Other than the ring?"

"I don't remember. Too many drinks. The day after an all-night case prep."

"At their home in Georgetown? You mentioned her

bedroom—"

"The night of the fundraiser." Chris stopped and faced her.

Leah glanced at the next plane and said, "I know your ambitions, Chris. Senate terms not too far off. Takes you into your mid-fifties. Then a run for the White House. It's why I'm here. It's why I've been here. But all of this could certainly change the trajectory I mentioned. Potentially. I'm sure you know that."

"This doesn't change a damn thing! That's what you're paid for."

"To take the trash out? Please tell me, what do you see happening here?"

"I don't know."

"I didn't think so. Well, not to be insensitive, but until she's found, the possibility still exists that Allie Sheridan may become one of the many unfortunate statistics. I hope not. That would be devastating for Mr. Sheridan. Senator Baxter, though, may secretly welcome the news; maybe you would as well, Chris?"

"Fuck you."

"Did you rape her?"

"No!" he growled.

"Did you try to?"

Chris averted his eyes. "It wasn't the first time she looked at me—"

Leah's hand went up instantly. She shook her head. "Please, I would suggest that you abandon that strategy immediately. You screwed up, and as you said, you pay me to help out when needed. But let me offer two things. First, if your involvement with all this surfaces, you will respectfully and with compassion deny it. Believable contrition. At the moment, you work in service to the family, and you'll therefore offer to do anything you can to help. With that response, and only that response, I will stay in your corner, for reasons important to me. Secondly, however, if I ever hear you try to justify what apparently happened at the expense of the Sheridan girl, as you just started to, I will take this conversation to the police, and your future will flatline. And then I may ask Ron to shoot your prick off. These are the conditions in which you can trust me. Are we still good?"

Leah stepped closer, not waiting for a response. "The ring," she said. "Did Allison swing at you? Did she cut you anywhere? You mentioned blood?"

Chris glowered, slowing his deep, audible breaths. "Yeah, my forearm," he mumbled.

"She hit you?" Leah waited. "Did you hit her back?"

Chris turned away.

"Damn." Leah exhaled and leaned against the car.

The next plane seemed lower. She watched it bank and ascend steeply, heading west into the thickening clouds. A park ranger truck approached, coasting through the noon rounds. A female officer pulled alongside and lowered her window. Politely, she directed the Tesla to be moved into a single space. Leah smiled and raised a wave. As the officer pulled away, Leah returned an appraising look to Chris, uncertain of his expression.

He checked the time and folded his arms. "We have two minutes."

Leah tapped a finger to her chin. "Okay then. Next steps. First, we need to confirm if Ms. Sheridan is alive and well in Rockland. I'm texting Ron right now."

"Telling him what?"

Leah frowned. "Find her, of course!" She held the phone to Chris. "See? All caps. It means do whatever you damn well have to, with your permission, of course. And I'll instruct him not to contact us until he's certain." Leah's eyes narrowed on him. "Still good?"

Chris stared blankly.

Leah went on, "While we wait, we need the ring. You seem to know where it is. Can you get it carefully, or should I? I would need some information."

The park ranger's car rounded the lot's northwest corner and crept down the aisle toward them.

Leah said, "Well, that seems to be enough for today. Just one last thing, Chris. The shed, the big one sitting off by itself at the end of the lot? Any chance this box turned up in there?"

"I think so."

"Interesting." Leah paused in thought. "Okay, so don't worry, I'm going to take care of your flight path for you."

A Delta 757 climbed steeply above them, and Leah stepped closer, titling her head slightly. "Like the reference?"

Chris glowered at her. "Don't fuck this up, Leah."

"Any more than it already is? You're one to talk."

Chapter 24

Rockland's only bookstore occupied an envious location at the corner of Granite and Talbot Avenue, just half a block off Main Street. Minutes earlier, Allie had carelessly ventured onto Main. Pausing in front of an insurance office, she stood mesmerized with the charming shop across the way. A small bookstore like her grandmother's, the word 'VINTAGE' prominent in the wooden sign above the entrance. Allie couldn't pull her eyes away from the large corner window, its bright yellow frame inviting welcoming looks to the multi-level display within. Standing out in the open, unmindful of the risk, Allie's mind drifted to memories. Lost in reflection, the importance of staying out of sight faded. Instincts about covering up. Cautions that had become pattern. With sunglasses in her pocket and holding the Red Sox hat in her left hand, Allie crossed the street and entered the store. A loud bronze ship's bell announced her arrival, a hefty, aging gray cat brushed against her leg in greeting.

~

Two blocks down Summer, Ron rotated to survey the street, growing frustrated at not having seen her again. An hour earlier, he had hurried past the streetside patio outside *Morning's Buns* in pursuit of the young girl he imagined to be Allie. At the time, he didn't have the best angle; she was running with a hand held to her face, appearing upset. But the height and weight matched, as did the hair; similarly wavy and very long. It could be her. Larson was here. A plausible connection could be made. By the time Ron got to the corner, though, the alley was deserted. The girl had disappeared. He returned to wandering the streets, probing various businesses and occasionally, innocently, inquiring about a young girl he described as his wife's niece.

Ron pulled the door to the antique store closed behind him. Planting in the middle of the sidewalk, he pivoted slowly, shaking his head. Bright sunlight reflected from the second-floor windows fronting Talbot, forcing him to shield his face as he scanned both sides of the street. A block and a half up, he caught the glimpse he needed: the same blue sweatshirt, the unmistakable long hair. His Allie double had just entered Coldwater Books.

Ron crossed Main Street with long strides, his eyes darting all around. He hurried along the short block to the bookstore, holding close to the building façades. He pushed through the door and flinched as the loud bell sounded. Standing motionless just inside, he settled his breaths and analyzed the setting. A short service counter ran parallel to the left wall. A woman perched on a stool at the far end, engaged with a call and scrolling on her computer. One customer, an elderly man, braced a hand against the discount shelf, perusing a small hardback. Low and tall shelves, free-standing, and wall-attached, all stood tightly grouped across the small floor area. A sense of abundance, selection, and also clutter.

The sightlines did not favor Ron. He leaned against the door, reached behind his back, and flipped the 'Open' sign to 'Closed'. He checked his phone and strolled toward the counter. As he approached, the woman finished her call and welcomed him. Ron smiled and continued to peruse, slowing to examine the back of the store. Two large windows along the rear wall brightened an elevated reading area. Comfortable chairs sat tucked into cozy corner alcoves, carved out around a small bathroom and a smaller closet. The confining stair to the basement hugged the opposite wall.

"There's quite a bit more downstairs," the owner volunteered.

Ron gestured a thanks, and continued to wander. He glanced often, keeping his attention on the old man until he paid for his book and left.

~

Allie huddled in the biggest chair in the darkest corner, directly across from a small writing desk. She had turned off the table lamp. The bookstore's fully buried lower level offered no windows, only a single narrow door exiting to an areaway stair. The stained wood ceiling hung oppressively low over sturdy wood perimeter shelving. Meager floor lamps did little to banish the shadows lurking in the dim surroundings. The air lay heavy and musty. A dehumidifier labored, droning above the soft classical music floating from invisible speakers in the dark ceiling. Allie clutched a book tight against her chest, head down, her long hair covering the side of her face. She sat with eyes squeezed tight, her mind tormented, back and forth between thoughts of Rick and the search for comfort she shared in the Salem house long ago before her mother died. She squeezed her hands. She just needed a place to hide again, like the dark, still reading room of her grandmother's bookshop; the single small octagonal window; the favorite leather chair tucked away in the corner behind towering shelving units. A place where she could hide her pain.

~

The stair treads creaked under heavy footsteps. Allie didn't look up, raising a hand to hide the side of her face. A man's deep cough echoed through the confined space. Allie listened to his sluggish progression between shelves, hoping he would simply browse and return promptly to the first floor. Groans from the loose wood flooring fell silent. Allie froze, imagining a fixed stare across her back. She reasoned quickly; *the customer had merely stalled along a shelf* . A chill rushed through her. If she looked, she might be certain, but hesitation gripped her, and she couldn't turn. Her heart raced. The shrouding silence extended, strangely too long. The plaguing memory she had buried jarred her; the bedroom in Georgetown, trying to fight off the attack. Each passing second trapped in this grim suspicion brought new fears that night's darkness had followed and found her here. Allie pulled her hair up under the hat and put her dark glasses on.

"Excuse me." The deep voice startled her.

Her book dropped to the floor as she scrambled out of the chair and stumbled toward the small door. Grasping at the locked knob, she shook it desperately. The cough came again, closer, and Allie spun. The man stood only feet away, staring at her, showing a slight smile. Allie shuddered. It was not the look of a fellow book lover. The features showed menace. Allie's black lenses hid her panicked eyes. Another threatening stranger had trapped her. She had no capacity to believe anything else.

The man inched closer, his impassive expression fixed on her. "Are you okay?"

Allie recoiled but held her glare, fighting the stirring tremble down her arms. The stairs creaked again, and the man turned. Allie rushed across the room, trying to push past him in the cramped aisle, but he grabbed her arm and yanked her close. Allie's face tensed, and her breaths came fast. He stiffened as she leaned in.

"No!" she cried.

Allie jerked her arm free and lunged at the stranger, pushing hard into his chest until he stumbled backwards into a shelf. Books fell as he tried to recover, but Allie made it to the stairs. An older woman tottered on the last tread, trying to make way. Allie's ankle buckled on the first step, but she grabbed the railing and forced two at a time. She reached the main level, hearing nothing from behind and not looking back. She rushed through the store, tearing off the sweatshirt and pulling the hat's brim lower. Straightening her glasses, she pushed through the door and out onto the sidewalk. Allie didn't pause for decision; instinctively she called to her strength and ran, across Main Street, then down the shadowed alley leading to the marinas. She knew how to hide there.

Chapter 25

Clouds broke the early afternoon sun's wash across the large bay windows. Rick held up at the entrance door, trying to recall the last time he had entered a bar. After minutes, his body moved inside, leaving his reflections lingering alone on the sidewalk to contemplate the regretful memories. Deep into the room, the heavy wooden bar turned back to the wall, dead ending with one last stool against the deep wainscoting. It felt private and safe to Rick, a seat that reminded him of his corner table at Delia's.

He walked slowly past the one couple at a high top in the corner and then along the line of empty bar stools, his eyes drawn to the lonely seat against the wall and its offer of solitude. The choice provided good views out the window to the harbor or an opportunity to lose your thoughts staring down the length of mirrored wall behind the bar. Rick sat tentatively, immediately casting a blank gaze along the three glass shelves filled with everything that had shattered his life so long ago. The nights of rage flashed back to him. What he remembered could not have been real. Where did those demons come from, and why did they take him? Questions asked in reflection on a life lived in the misery of lost control. Rick sat alone at the bar. The man and woman across the room leaned in, contentedly enthralled with each other. Rick fixated on the wall of mirrors, the reflection doubling the count of bottles there for the choosing. Once he would have seen it as a vision of abundance. And deliverance.

"Get you something?" The bartender's voice pulled Rick back.

"Yeah," Rick said. "Iced tea. Shot of Jack."

"Anything to eat?"

Rick exhaled, impatient with the interruption and request for further decision. "Club sandwich," he said without thought. "Everything on it."

"You got it."

The bartender disappeared through the kitchen door and came back quickly with the tea. He set it down, passed a quick check across Rick's expression, then poured a full shot. Rick followed him with a firm stare until he moved away and reached for a towel, wiping down whatever was close and scanning the empty dining room. Occasionally, he glanced back.

Rick avoided eye contact and sipped his tea, but he couldn't evade the rich bourbon's shimmer—the haunting temptation seeking a return. Rick wiped his forehead and lifted his chin, refocusing on diversions down the long bar. All was ready for the four o'clock crowd: glasses stacked, ice machine full, limes cut, napkins neat. A suitable distraction from the shadowing impulse. Unknowingly, the inquisitive young bartender's curious attention to detail and order had aided Rick in escaping the past. But sensing the man had nothing else to do for the next half hour except talk, Rick twisted away to secure his shelter by watching the busy harbor.

Within seconds, the bartender was hovering again. Nonchalantly, he asked, "What brings you to town?"

Rick didn't turn back. He lowered his head and took a moment in silence, deciding if he was in the mood. "Visiting an old friend," he said flatly, rotating in the chair. "I'm not here long."

"Not here long?" The bartender slapped a hand down on the bar and grinned, revealing an array of bad teeth. "That was me, just what I said a long time ago! Came to visit a friend and she convinced me to stay." His mouth closed; a broad smile remained. "Thirty-seven years. Funny how things work out, isn't it? Who's your friend?"

Rick pulled in a breath, then mumbled, "She owns the bakery—"

"*Morning's Buns*? Beth Gilbert?"

Small-town information. Rick tensed at the question, hiding the disheartening surprise rushing him. He dropped his eyes to the gleaming wood surface, face-to-face with a consequence he never gave thought to; of course, Beth would take her mother's name.

"That's her," Rick managed. He sighed and escaped to the waterfront view again as the bartender set silverware and napkins in front of him and headed to the kitchen.

A few minutes later, Rick leaned back and placed both hands on the bar, pondering the overstuffed sandwich.

The bartender pushed in. "How do you know, Beth?"

Rick's shoulders slumped. The guy wasn't going away. "I knew her mom a long time ago," Rick finally said. "Old family friends."

"Well, that Bethy, she's something. Never seen a person work so hard. The way she took on that old building. Used to be Ed Fisher's hardware store. Let's see, probably been seven years now since she opened the doors. Sad to see Ed's place go, but real glad to have Beth's shop in there. She keeps us all a little heavier than we were before."

"I bet it's good."

"Could be the best muffins I've ever had," he said with a nod. "Said she's starting to ship some orders now, too. Good for her. The place fixed up nice. She really put her heart into it and great to see it paying off. So, have you seen her yet?"

"Only a quick talk so far. She's busy in the mornings. We'll catch up later."

"So, just a visit then?"

Rick delayed, realizing the depth of his entrapment, unless he chose to be blunt. He rotated the plate, deliberating on which corner of the sandwich to start with, then decided on a chip instead. And patience. "A family friend is very sick," he forced. "A war buddy I've known a long time. He and Beth were close when she was young."

"Iraq?"

Rick's left hand shook. "Vietnam."

"Really? You sure don't look old enough for that one."

"Guess that's good to hear. I'm old enough."

"That was a long time ago."

Rick reorganized the chips on his plate. "Yes, it was."

The bartender straightened. "Thank you for that," he said sincerely. "My son served in Iraq. After 911, he said he had to go in."

"Lots of different reasons people end up in a war."

"That's sad about your friend."

Rick stared blankly. The etched desire was hovering again, slowly drawing his attention back to the shot glass. With shaking fingers, he moved it in studied, small circles. "Yeah. He said he had to go in, too."

"My son was Army."

"Marines. Both of us. He made it through basic training and qualified for the sniper program—somehow. He had never hunted. Just had the vision. And the will."

"You both made it home, though. Good for you."

Rick didn't look up. "Yeah, we did, but you never knew." He lifted the shot glass to toast, his voice elevated. "Sergeant Tremaine Wilson, United States Marines. The man saved my life more than once."

The bartender leaned in, resting both hands on the rounded

wooden edge. His eyes widened on Rick. "The war?"

The wood floor creaked under slow steps. Rick turned with the bartender as Sarah approached. She pulled up at the corner, eyeing the glass in his hand.

"Two drinks, I see. How'd you know I like bourbon?" She pulled out the barstool and moved next to him.

Rick lowered the full shot and pushed it away. "Tre's favorite, too." For distraction, he centered on the middle shelf again, a fifth of Jim Beam beckoning.

Sarah gestured to the bartender, and he wandered off, needlessly re-positioning some of the condiments in the middle of the bar. She took her time surveying the space. "Wow, quite an abundance of nautical décor in this place, huh? As salty, dark bars with lots of character wood go, this one has to be right up there. What is it about this room? Feels like a different world, doesn't it? Pulls you in. Gives you permission to escape." Her eyes returned to Rick. "You doing okay?"

He took a while before answering. "Not really. Sorry I barked at you."

She rubbed his shoulder. "Hey, considering the circumstances, I think I got off easy."

Rick lifted his tea.

"Must have been difficult for you to walk in," she said.

"I did a lot of damage in places like this."

"Is it a good thing, then? Sitting here?"

His gaze drifted across the room, pausing on the couple's robust display of affection.

Sarah leaned closer. "I overheard your toast to Tre."

"One of many over the years. All deserving."

"He saved your life?" she asked in a low voice.

Rick exhaled, tapping his glass on the bar. "There's a time

when you know you've lost. It can be just an instant, one decision. Just one more drink." He nodded weakly. "But you can see it, and you know your life just changed. Mine was angry, hurtful drinking, Sarah."

Her brow creased.

"It was bad. After two tours in the jungle, I was suddenly scared. Tre knew I'd lost the battle. Meetings, rehab, medications; nothing was going to work. He stayed with me through all of it, but he could still see the monster." Rick's eyes lowered to the shot glass. "Tre saw what I was doing to Beth."

"Rick, you were sick."

"That's true," he said weakly. "That's true." He twisted enough to find her stare. "So, my best friend shot me. June 17, 1978." He tapped his right bicep, watching her eyes grow wide. "Drinking arm. I can show you the scar."

Sarah froze. "You aren't kidding."

Rick shook his head. "Tre's prescription for going cold turkey. Worked for my head right away. The body took a little longer, but no permanent damage. It was a good shot he summoned that last time—to chase away my demons. His evil against mine." Rick swallowed hard. "His stated motivation. So, I forgave my friend for shooting me and pledged my eternal gratitude to him for killing the monster. Forty-two years ago and fifteen days." Rick pulled both hands across his forehead. "Long after I'd lost Beth. And long before I lost Allie."

Sarah's shoulders fell. "My God," she faltered, tears starting. "This is why they had to leave—Beth and your . . ." She shifted on the stool and leaned in close. "Did you ever grieve her, Rick? Your daughter, Tre, all of it? Did you ever talk to anyone?"

Rick's jaw tightened as he refocused on the mirrored reflections and shelves. "I wouldn't know," he mumbled. "That night they left, I knew they were gone for good. Can't tell you what happened after that."

She reached for his hand. "This first time seeing Beth was going to be complicated, Rick. It was. The next one won't be."

Sensing her stare, he looked away. "I don't see it."

"Of course, you don't. You're sitting here with a glass wall of painful memories in front of you. But this was the darkness and it's over. I think you've done your penance."

Rick sighed and they sat in silence for a while. Finally, he rotated on the seat to face her.

"Thank you for coming to find me."

Sarah smiled. "It must have been difficult for you to walk in here. Facing all of this alone." Her eyes softened. "There are other memories, though. Beth brought you a lot of joy when she came into your life, and there is more to come." She quickly wiped away a tear. "I'd love to hear a story about her as a two-year-old." She pulled him close and kissed his cheek. "It's warming up outside. Take me for a walk?"

Rick shook his head slowly. "Where the hell is Allie? I missed something. Not surprising I didn't see it again."

Sarah turned his face with a gentle hand. "Hey, no answers in here. How about that walk?"

Chapter 26

The stately, two-story frame house sat on an elevated bluff along Osprey Lane on the Owl's Head peninsula. The quiet outskirts of Rockland, a long but doable walk to town. Karen's parents always wanted their only child to continue to call it home if she chose. The expansive views across Penobscot Bay provided endless retreat, now embraced by Karen as a bittersweet homecoming, a sanctuary from the past for Beth. The beloved family property sheltered them, peacefully alive on most days, glowing with storybook welcome through the night.

Beth huddled on the lowest porch step early that evening, both arms limp across her lap, a lost gaze fixed across the ocean's serene darkening. Karen approached softly and lowered close behind her. Their big rottweiler settled with a groan next to Beth, his large head landing heavily on her foot. Beth filled her lungs with the crisp sea air as Karen reached both hands to her shoulders and rubbed.

"It's cold this evening," Karen said softly in her ear. "You missing California?"

Beth peered into the stillness suspended across the yard. A while passed before she leaned over close to Gibbs' face and ruffled his big ears. "California?" she said, wiping away a tear. "If it hadn't been for California, you wouldn't be here, Mr. Gibbs."

Beth straightened and reached a hand back to Karen's. "I'm missing a lot of things right now; Cali isn't one of them." She sighed, looking down. "I miss my mom. She tried so hard to protect me from him, never letting me believe Rick was still out there, anywhere."

Karen wrapped her arms around Beth and pulled her close. "I know, honey."

Beth's eyes teared again. "And now he's here." She quivered. "I can't believe he came. Why would he?" Her hands clenched in her lap. "What the hell did Allie mean?"

Karen tightened her embrace. "I don't know. It's been almost two hours. She came in unwilling to talk, sneaking through the kitchen door, trying for the back stair. I intercepted her, but she had nothing to offer. Straight to the bedroom. She's been in the tub, and probably still is." Karen's breathing paused. She stood abruptly, her words trailing off as she turned for the door. "I should go check."

~

At 7:30 p.m., the house remained dark, but for the dimmed lights in the kitchen and dining room. Beth carried plates. Karen balanced a dish of lasagna and salad bowl. Wine glasses had been poured. Beth and Karen traded unsettled looks as Allie stared blankly at the candles' soft glow in the center of the table. Allie's right hand held a fork, moving it in slow broken circles across the rustic wood.

Beth tilted her head slightly, trying for eye contact. "Allie? The last thing we heard from you—it was horrifying."

Allie lowered her head, clutching the fork now in both hands. "He pushed into my bedroom . . ." She shook and forced an inhale. "I remember after it happened, pausing in front of the large hall mirror, just staring at a frightened image of someone else."

"Your bedroom?" Beth said quietly.

"A fundraiser. He was drunk." Allie squeezed her eyes closed. "There was no one to help, and she wouldn't listen."

"Allie, who?"

"Dad's *wife*." Her voice cracked. "She just screamed at me to 'get out'!" Allie's hands trembled. "So, I did. With all the cash I could find, and his gun. Then I ran."

"Gun?" Beth raised a hand to her mouth, unable to blink. "You came here?"

"I had to hide. I had to get away from everything and find someone who would help me. I'm sorry I came here; it was wrong." She wavered before finally looking at Beth. "I know why you had to leave when you were young. I'm sorry about that, too." Her voice faded. "But I had his birthday card for you. He asked me to mail it, but I forgot." Allie pushed back and drew her knees up on the seat, lost again in the candles' flicker.

Beth leaned forward, unable to speak. Several nights ago, she and Karen had opened their door to an exhausted stranger; shivering on the porch, Allie had lowered her head and extended a shaky hand with Rick's card. Stunned, Beth had delayed only seconds before pulling her inside for refuge. The birthday cards meant nothing to her; they were always quickly discarded, along with any memories seeking a return. The association with Rick, however, and Allie's despair, had jarred her.

Allie raised her eyes to them. "Your home seemed so nice that night. And safe."

Beth pushed her plate aside. She reached across to take Allie's hands, shaking her head. "Allie, my God. We were so worried about you today, walking around all alone."

Allie pulled her hands back and looked away.

Beth's face tightened. "Who tried to rape you?" She sat motionless, afraid of the answer. "Rick?" The word barely escaped.

Allie shifted in her chair, clasping her hands. She shook her head faintly. "Rick is my friend," she said in a shaky voice. "Maybe my only friend."

Beth glanced at Karen, seeing her disbelief, then moved around the table and sat on the banquette next to Allie. She reached an arm around, and Allie's head fell to her shoulder. Beth pulled her close, turning to the dark windows and squeezing her eyes shut to hide the tears.

In a quiet voice, Beth said, "Allie, tell us who it was."

Allie pulled back abruptly. Her hand shook as she reached for the full wine glass. She sipped hesitantly and gazed across the soft flames. "This guy," she muttered. "He works for Senator Baxter—my stepmother."

~

Narrow roads void of centerline striping twisted and turned across the Owl's Head peninsula. Large residences with deep front yards stood nestled among an abundance of old-growth trees. Many of the homes remained unoccupied through the winter, with mid-April typically marking the owners' return. Streetlights were not welcome on the peninsula; people came here to escape, and darkness to most equated to peacefulness. Several remote streets dead-ended at the water. Ron shut off his lights at the corner and assessed the dark lane. He preferred having two ways out. After a moment's deliberation, he eased forward down Osprey Lane.

The house across the street from 157 had no fencing along the property line. Ron inched over onto their grass, far enough away from the baker's house not to draw attention but close enough to calculate his approach. A large porch wrapped the front and two sides, with broad sections of windows flanking the main entrance. The living room with its substantial stone fireplace and a large dining room occupied the street-facing corners.

Ron left the car and moved cautiously along the shadowy street. He crossed the driveway and stepped silently up the porch steps, pausing to lean and spy in the windows. Three people, all blurred through the dining room's patterned glass, huddled around the table. Ron pulled off his cap and knocked. Soon, a woman peeked through the sidelight curtain and opened the door with a gracious, 'Hello'.

"Can I help you?" she added.

Ron's expression brightened at the trusting, quaint greeting. "Hi," he responded. "Excuse me. I don't mean to interrupt your evening." Attentive to the woman's stare, he casually stepped to the right, trying for a better angle on the dining room table.

"Beth, who is it?" came a voice from the other room.

Beth folded her arms, and Ron instantly held up both hands with an accompanying forlorn expression. "We've lost our dog," he said. "She's an escape artist. My wife and I are staying over on Cooper's Beach Road for a couple of days. It's nice up here this time of year."

Beth lowered a glance to his clothes. "Well, good for you both. Not everyone likes the cold March wind. You must be a little chilly in that light jacket."

"Yeah, I was in a rush." He continued quickly. "One of your neighbors a few houses around the bend there said she saw a dog heading this way.

"I'm sorry. Wow, she could be anywhere."

He shook his head, inserting a look of concern. "Golden Retrievers. They're notorious explorers." He twisted to survey the yard. "Not sure what to do. It's so quiet up here. Any chance someone else here might have seen her? Her name is Maisey. She's only three."

After a tense pause, Beth said, "Let me see, I'll ask. Come on in."

"Thanks." Ron stepped in and flinched immediately, noticing the large dog lying on the living room Oriental. Gibbs lifted his head to appraise him and started to rise, but a quick hand motion from Beth settled him. He lay there, panting heavily, tracking back and forth between the two of them. As she turned away, Ron immediately scanned the first floor. His attention quickly landed on a worn backpack sitting on the third step up the stairs. He sensed a probing look and spun to find another woman standing, arms crossed, in the arched opening to the dining room.

Beth approached her and spoke softly, "Karen, this guy lost his dog. Have you seen a Golden wandering?"

Karen instantly moved past her. Ron straightened, averting his eyes as she crossed the foyer.

"A lost dog? That's not good around here." Karen's face tightened as she pulled open the front door. "Wish we could help but unfortunately we haven't seen her. If we do, though, we'll try to bring her home."

"That will be easy. She's very friendly. Thanks for any help." Ron browsed the living room again. "You have a beautiful place."

Karen's faint smile disappeared.

"I grew up not far from here," Ron added. "It's nice to be back."

"So did I," Karen said, lifting her chin. "Good luck."

Ron took the cue, turned hastily, and crossed the porch as the door closed forcefully behind him. Taking the first step, he sneered over his shoulder as the deadbolt clicked.

~

Karen exhaled and collapsed back against the door, listening a moment before finally returning to the dining room. She met

Beth's questioning look and lifted her wine glass for a long drink.

Allie sat wedged into the seat corner, staring out the window into darkness. "Who was that?" she mumbled.

"Just a man who lost his dog," Beth said.

Karen pulled up to the table.

"Are you sure?" Allie asked, her voice still weak. "A man followed me today into a store. I'd never seen him before. He grabbed me when I tried to walk past . . . I had to run again."

Karen shot Beth a look, rushed to the wall and slammed the rheostat to darken the room.

Beth crossed to her. "What is it?"

"Allie!" Karen snapped. "Get to the kitchen stairs and go up to the bedroom. Go now! No lights. None!"

Beth didn't hesitate before turning to Allie. "Go!

Karen switched off the foyer light as Allie stumbled around the table and down the short hall to the kitchen. Karen stood motionless in the dark.

Beth's forehead wrinkled. "Karen?"

"This doesn't feel right. That guy, I don't know."

"Who could he be? The same one?"

"Someone who's after Allie. And for the wrong reasons. He would have said otherwise if he was trying to help her." Karen exhaled. "I'm not believing the dog story for some reason."

She waited, glancing to the ceiling as squeaks along the old floors followed Allie's steps down the hall.

Karen went on, "I caught him staring at Allie's backpack, with a strange, serious expression. The '*I lost my dog concern*' was gone."

"Yeah, he was moving around, taking some small steps. It seemed casual, but now that you mention—"

"Like he was trying to see something." Karen's face tensed. "This is not paranoia, but all of this is about Allie. I feel it. That guy's looking for her."

"What? Here in Maine? Somebody found their way to Maine just to knock on our door?"

Karen bit her lips. "Rick did."

Beth turned away and Karen reached for her arm.

"We shouldn't be doing this Beth, letting her stay. Not any longer. She isn't just any runaway. Allie's in trouble and she needs help."

"She's an adult, Karen."

"She's a senator's daughter and she's been assaulted," Karen said bluntly. "And she's been here for days. End of story. You have to think about what you're doing, what *we're* doing. Is it about helping this scared young woman or are you reliving your own nightmare?"

Beth scowled. "My God! That's a shitty thing to say!"

"I know! It is a shitty thing to say. And I'm sorry. But regardless of the answer, you need to take her home. Right now. Leave tonight. You know that people are looking for her. One of them may have just been in our house. It may not be safe to keep Allie here any longer; for her or for us, and we never should have." Karen stepped closer. "She's been assaulted, for God's sake! And she didn't mention any of this! So, it's not our choice anymore, or hers. She needs the police and a hospital."

Beth pulled both hands through her hair and stared out the front window.

Karen reached for her shoulder. "You need to take her home, honey, as soon as possible. Please."

Beth stood motionless. "Tonight," she finally managed in a quiet voice.

"It's the right thing. We both know it. I'll go talk to Allie and help her get her things together."

Beth's voice faded after her, "Throw some clothes in a bag for me."

~

Minutes passed before Beth moved back into the foyer. Her jaw set, she hurriedly pulled open the top drawer in a side table and retrieved her gun. After checking the chamber, she stepped lightly to the front door, peering cautiously through the sidelight.

"Gibbs!" she said in command. The big dog rose quickly and came to her side. Beth turned to find Karen halted on the fourth step, gripping the handrail and fixated on the gun.

"I'm going to walk the yard and check the driveway," Beth said, forcing a controlled voice.

Karen hurried down the stairs. "You don't need to do that!"

"I'm not leaving you here, wondering if he's gone or not."

Gibbs sat close to Beth, waiting. He panted heavily, his focus down the dark hall connecting to the kitchen.

Karen took Beth's hand. "Are you sure?"

The faint noise outside the kitchen door could have been anything. A racoon knocking over a pot, a dead tree branch finally falling, anything. But the sound brought Gibbs to attention. He barked and charged down the hall to the back door, ears up and alert. Karen and Beth started after him and froze. Hidden in the shadows, Allie slumped against the powder room door, trembling and clutching her backpack.

"It's him," Allie said weakly. "The man who chased me this afternoon."

"What?" came the response from both.

"It has to be him. How did he find me?" She dropped her gaze. "I knew he would."

Beth reached for her shoulders. "Allie, tell me exactly what happened! Why would someone be following you?"

"That night, I tried to hit him," she said feebly. "I begged him. Then I scratched at him and screamed, but he covered my mouth. I tried to hit him again, then I couldn't breathe." Allie lowered her head. "I'm so tired."

Gibbs' aggressive bark shook them.

Karen's wide eyes darted to Beth. "What the fuck is going on?"

Beth leaned close to Allie, cradling her face. "It's going to be okay, Allie. Don't go there. He's not going to find you. But I'm sure as hell gonna find him. You're safe. Do you understand?"

Allie could barely nod.

Beth said, "Did you hear us talking? You and I have to leave. Tonight, and now. Karen will get you in the car. I'll be right back."

Beth hurried into the kitchen and found Gibbs on guard by the door. She hooked his leash and switched on the porch light. Gibbs moved ahead of her through the screen door and pulled insistently. Beth gave him most of the leash. Nothing appeared out of place on the deck. She rushed down the steps, searching with the light, holding her gun ready. They moved around the corner of the garage. Gibbs' ears went up, and he took an urgent step against the lead. Beth released him, and he bolted toward the driveway. Beth followed, scattering the strong beam across the property. A car halfway down the block started as she rounded the corner. It jerked in reverse across the lawn and crushed a low hedge, then sped away, lights coming on at the turn. Gibbs growled, holding at the end of the drive. Beth rushed to him and connected the leash, flashing the light in all directions. She scanned the street as their garage door crept open. Karen stood in the opening in front of the car.

Beth rushed up the driveway. "They're gone," she said, breathing hard.

Karen reached for her hand.

"You need to go. Break up the trip, honey. Get to Portland this evening and rest. Drive at night as much as you can. Allie's in the car. I'll be fine here. I have Gibbs."

Chapter 27

At 12:15 a.m., as they crossed the Interstate 95 bridge over the Susquehanna River in Harford County, Sarah broached the subject. She and Rick had made their final caffeine pit stop minutes before, a necessity for the grueling last two hours down 95 into DC. They were resolved to complete the twelve-hour drive back from Maine that night. The hotel stay in Portland had been comfortable enough; separate queen beds, exhaustion, and Rick's anxiety about connecting with Beth had overshadowed any hesitations about sharing a bedroom. Fatigue had left them no choice. But hotels were no longer an option; both were ready to be home.

The topic Sarah introduced—an invitation for Rick to stay at her place for what was left of the night—was instantly met by silence. Rick evaded the exchange with a glance out the side window, uncomfortable with her promises of good coffee, a hearty breakfast, and as much privacy as he needed in a California King. She justified it by conveying her worry about him; the connection with Beth, and the lack of news about Allie. Other than a brief mention of the search warrant that had been scheduled for his marina the day before, he displayed no interest in talking throughout the monotonous turnpike hours. She had tried to pull him out on several occasions with different topics, but after an hour and a half, Sarah was resigned to his need for boundaries. She came back to the overture only once, as they entered the Fort McHenry tunnel east of Baltimore. In her most convincing, unassuming voice, she again described the bed, the towels, the tub, the heat.

They arrived in Southeast at 2:45 a.m.. Sarah believed she had cajoled a silent yes from Rick, but when they pulled to the curb in front of her place, his hands remained on the wheel. He fixated on the windshield and wearily expressed his discomfort and unfamiliarity with something that should come so naturally; with the exception of Schooner, he had not shared a bed with anyone since destroying his marriage long ago.

Exhausted, Sarah offered a sympathetic smile and pressed a quick finger to his lips. "You're too tired to take my car," she said. "And I'm not driving you home. I'm going in and falling asleep. It's a big bed. I'll stay on my side. You should join me." She caught herself instantly, regretting the transactional soundbites. She reached a hand to Rick's face, gently turning him. In a softer voice she said, "I would like it if you did."

~

There had been no end-of-trip, adrenaline-fueled glass of wine or bowl of ice cream; they both had carried bags straight upstairs, and within minutes, crawled beneath the thick comforter. The bed was as Sarah advertised, very big and immediately comfortable. Rick lay still, wide eyes surveying the unfamiliar surroundings, his breathing heavy, raspy from exhaustion. Sarah rolled over and rested her head against his shoulder, her hand tentatively exploring the rough skin across his arms and chest. Her fingers stopped on an unusual depression, and she lifted her head to look.

"You've certainly had your fair share of scars, haven't you?"

Rick stared at the ceiling; his voice quiet. "More than you can see."

She gently touched a rough area on his right arm. "Would this one be Tre's gift?"

"My favorite."

"He must love you very much." Sarah's hand came to rest over his heart. "Tell me something," she said softly. "The boat parts, what does it all mean to Tre?"

Rick nestled his head into the pillow and inhaled deeply. "Homeless pieces of lives."

Sarah nodded, her eyes glistening. "Of course." She let her head fall gently back to his shoulder as her arm found a comfortable position across his chest. "I know who you are, Mr. Larson." Her voice faded. "You care for lost souls. That's an incredibly noble way to live a life, and very sexy, too." She paused. "I do like you."

Rick sighed and moved his hand to hers. "Thank you for taking me to Maine."

She squeezed him. "No way I was going to let you go alone."

~

Rick blinked the sleep from his eyes, finding only the dark, disappointed to be awake at 7:15 the next morning. It wasn't the room's fault. Not a crack of light showed around any of the blackout curtains. He managed to ease himself out of bed and through the door without waking Sarah. The window at the top of the stairs washed the second-floor hallway in bright light. He navigated each step tentatively, giving his stiff joints time to wake up. He padded quietly across the dining room's wood floor and into the kitchen.

The potted fern on the corner of the counter drew his attention immediately. The small birthday box sat in the same place, now obscured by drying fronds. Fixated as he crossed the tile floor, Rick bumped into one of the island stools. He stopped instantly, watching the ceiling and listening. The sound of footsteps never came and after a moment he carefully hurried to the counter. He lifted the box and turned each side to the bright light streaming through the window. The intricacies of its delicate work recalled a similar one Tre had carved for his brother long ago, intended as a gift when Jonathan came home from the war. Months earlier, Tre mentioned in passing that he was carving one for Allie as well. Having never seen it, though, the gesture had escaped Rick, but he knew this was Tre's. Gently manipulating the lock, he opened the top. The small ring lay on the bed of shells as before. He held the box closer but was unable to bring the engraved initials into focus without glasses. The blurry outline of letters offered nothing.

The diamond was small and brilliant, but Rick noticed a dark redness covering the left side of the stone. He squinted at the discoloration as questions stirred; *Why would Allie have put it in Tre's box? How did it end up in his shed?* Rick's brow wrinkled. If he thought it might be blood, Allie's or anyone else's, he wouldn't admit it to himself. Still, he chose not to touch it. The question of why it was in Tre's shed persisted, however any explanation remained unclear. Not enough sleep, and nothing firing well yet.

Rick sighed and set the box next to Sarah's laptop on the island. His focus drifted across the kitchen in search of a coffee maker. An espresso machine sat on display in one corner, but the perfect shine dissuaded him. He settled on a glass of water and pulled up a stool in front of the computer. Moving a pile of mail aside, he opened the screen, anticipating a password prompt. When the field of icons appeared, he nodded, appreciating Sarah's evident faith in simplicity and her fellow man. Rick typed 'Allison Sheridan' into the search bar and his eyes widened, as a long list of articles and photos filled the left margin. A pop-up appeared in the upper right corner; the hotline site posted by the family. Rick focused on the accompanying picture of Allie and slowly scrolled through the details of her life—age, birth date, height, hair and eye color when she disappeared, hobbies, interests, anything identifiable. Rick leaned against the stool back and folded his arms, peering helplessly across this invasion of her privacy. Detective Ward's words drummed faintly; *Everything is important, anything can become a lead.*

Rick hadn't seen Allie in over two weeks. Not a long time in the context of their pattern for visits, but this morning, the fifteen days overwhelmed him. He lifted the box, holding it close to the screen, and focused between the two. He let all of the scenarios swirl, the good ones and the ones that closed his eyes.

Sarah's slow footsteps sounded on the stairs. Rick clutched the box and looked quickly down the hallway. He spun back, nervously considering each cabinet. He moved hurriedly around the kitchen, quietly opening and closing drawers. He found the plastic baggies next to the sink and opened the box, emptying the broken shells and ring into one. He stuffed the bag into his pocket and crossed back to the fern to reposition the box, then pivoted and made it back to the laptop by the time Sarah entered.

"Good morning," she said, visibly exhausted but still able to greet him with a warm smile. "Good thing we're young, right?" She set his phone down on the island and moved over behind him. "You've been buzzing" she said. "Someone's desperate to find you."

"Schooner probably ate the doughnuts."

Sarah wrapped both arms around his waist and peeked over his shoulder, noticing Allie's happy face on the screen. Rick didn't resist. She pulled back gently, her eyes starting to water.

"So many kids," she said, shaking her head. "Allie's lucky to have you in her life." She moved beside him and leaned close. "Beth will be, too—soon I believe."

The phone buzzed loudly, vibrating on the granite counter. Absorbed with the images, Rick ignored it. "Can you check that?" he mumbled.

Sarah read the message.

"Delia?" he asked, still engrossed.

"Detective Ward," she said hesitantly, laying a hand on his arm. "He needs you at the station by 10:00 this morning."

Rick leaned forward, zooming in on the image of Allie, a Thursday group photo taken last November at Trinity.

Sarah said, "Rick, the detective's message is all caps. It ends with *URGENT*."

Rick pulled back and shook his head. He took a last brief, look at Allie, then closed the laptop. "I need my truck."

Sarah rose instantly and started for the counter. "Get dressed. I'll make us some coffee."

They were out the door in ten minutes.

Chapter 28

"Do you think this is news to me?" Senator Baxter glared. Chris averted his eyes. After a moment, she turned away, briefly surveying the line of customers queued up at the counter across the room. Her security team occupied a distant table, ensuring the separation and privacy she demanded for this simple, enduring morning ritual; the same chair at the same corner table in the same café. A quiet, peaceful way she had chosen years ago to start each Thursday. Peace and quiet Chris Evans just shattered.

"I have security footage," she finally went on. "The entire house, of course. Allie's bedroom as well. That may seem like an invasion of privacy, but the girl came into my life as a stranger. I don't take chances with my career, Chris, and I don't overlook things. Not surprisingly, my intuitions proved correct about Ben's daughter. And about you."

"Michelle—"

"Your actions were beyond deplorable, but it wasn't a complete surprise. I know the things in your past you've tried to forget." Michelle flashed a cold smile. "Not to worry though, I have too much invested in you."

Chris wavered; his jaw clenched. "There's blood. On a ring," he said quietly.

Michelle looked down to her cup, her finger circling the rim. She nodded slowly in thought. "Really? Whose ring? Allie's?"

Chris shifted in his seat.

"And whose blood?" Michelle glanced up. "Yours, I assume?"

Restless, Chris loosened his tie and twisted to check the entrance door.

"Where is it now?" Michelle's index fingers tapped against the mug. "The ring."

"We thought we knew. Sarah Cromwell's."

"Larson's friend?"

"It's not there. Leah did the search."

Michelle took a last slow sip of coffee. "Your searches have not proven very effective. Is that really Leah's specialty?"

Chris reached for his phone and scrolled the photos. He turned it, offering Michelle the image of Allie and Tremaine. "The ring was in a box," he said. "Like the ones they're holding. It was a gift to Cromwell from her daughter. Leah found nothing. No box. No ring."

Michelle lifted her glasses to study it. "That would obviously be Mr. Tremaine Wilson standing next to our Allie, yes? And shall I assume this is the *mysterious shed* I've heard so much about?" She lowered her chin, observing him above the lenses. "Seems it's time to connect some dots, isn't it? You inform me of damning evidence of your indiscretion, missing evidence which at one point was unfortunately in the possession of Ms. Cromwell, but apparently no longer is. So, if not there . . ." Michelle examined the photo again briefly, then gestured the phone away. "Telling," she quipped. "The ring could be anywhere. If not at Ms. Cromwell's, perhaps Mr. Wilson and his lost world within those walls can shed some light. And perhaps *you* should be more thorough, Chris. More effective? As of this point in time, I would suggest your personal involvement is required. Take some help if needed, just not Leah."

Michelle clasped both hands loosely on the table, holding firm eye contact, her voice composed. "You can feel it slipping away, can't you? All of it—the dream, the power. I can see your panic, Chris. You need to use that, though. Don't let it be the undoing of all you've worked for. Let it fuel your commitment to resolve this." She studied his narrowing eyes. "You know, it has occurred to me that you and Allie are not so different."

Chris leaned back, folding his arms.

"Both of you, lone children, abandoned really, in those critical developmental years. She, a victim of tragedy, and you, a victim of disinterest and obsession. Both left to survive on your own by parents who held other pursuits more important. But you've let a hatred for that time in your life intrude on the path, when all you really need to do, Chris, is to achieve. Achieve what we both want for you, and then whatever pain that memory still inflicts will be gone forever. I promise you."

Michelle remained patient while Chris searched for diversion around the café, but only briefly. She finally snapped her fingers in his face and said, "Allie's lifeline is more vexing, though: she is proving to be quite formidable, wouldn't you say? The girl always sought to shy away from attention, keeping to herself and avoiding distractions. Her looks, though—" Michelle shook her head. "Her looks and stature make that so very challenging. I never wanted her in my life, but from a distance, I have an odd appreciation for her person. She is truly a natural beauty, physically confident and unadorned. Intimidating in the way she carries herself as a young woman in her late twenties might. All of it proves quite a hindrance to sheltering one's privacy, though. Ahh, the curse of beauty that haunts young women with either fortune or misfortune." Michelle leaned back. "Months ago, in a rare moment when Allison displayed a tolerance, I cautioned her with those words. I had hoped she would accept the admonition as the challenge it was intended to impart. Because for women like us, it is so very burdensome to avoid attention." Michelle's head tilted. "And yet, here she is, Chris, doing just that. Isn't she?"

Michelle exhaled and gathered her things to leave, motioning to her security lead. "Chris," she said quietly. "I believed this was under control, your control. I'm only willing to forgive so much, though."

"Nothing's changed," he said sharply.

"We'll see."

Chris met her glower as she rose from the table.

She leaned slightly, closer to his face. "You need to find that ring, Mr. Evans. There is a great deal at stake. And I would suggest that happen before Allie surfaces; if she ever does."

Chapter 29

The sun peeked through low, broken clouds hanging over the eastern horizon. Sarah and Rick didn't acknowledge the dramatic sky as they turned onto M Street, SE, twenty minutes later. Sarah checked the time and accelerated. Rick leaned forward, squinting through the windshield. Two hundred feet away, the marina entrance drive appeared open. Sarah slowed pulling through. Both sections of the gate stood ajar: one lay wedged between two large stones, the other forced back on its hinges and lodged against a tree trunk. The chain and lock hung from the bent hasp. Rick scanned the yard as Sarah pulled in next to his truck. He got out quickly and scrambled to the shed. The single side door stood open, the light breeze causing it to swing back and forth against the rusty frame. Rick rested both hands on the jambs and leaned inside. Instantly, he pulled back and slammed it shut. He hurried around the corner to the shed's overhead door and yanked on the chain. The old door resisted. Sarah started toward him but stopped. Rick's face contorted, and he grunted against each pull; his arms trembled, and his hands slipped. He tilted his head, and clutched at the rusty links, fixated on the next panel to rise. Sarah stepped hesitantly again as the door began to run easier along the tracks. Sunlight rushed to fill the space, and Rick ducked under the bottom edge. She hurried to the opening to follow and froze, her eyes wide. Rick rested a shaking hand against the bench seat. Sarah's shoulders slumped, staring with him across the ravaged scene spread before them.

~

Rick walked into the station at 10:25 a.m.. The condition of the shed had eroded any willingness in him to be on time or cooperate. He gave his name at the desk, and Ward appeared instantly, offering no eye contact, only a blunt hand gesture signaling for Rick to follow him down the hall to his office.

"You're late," Ward snarled, pulling up behind his desk. "You just missed Dumars."

Rick took one of the less comfortable chairs across from him.

Ward went on, "I wanted you both here so I could say it only once. Just once! At 10:00 a.m. dammit!"

Rick waited, hoping his indifference was being read as intended. The understanding and collaborative spirit Ward had expressed in their last meeting were gone. This morning, Rick was okay with that.

Ward shifted in his seat. His face tightened. He fussed with his phone, then set it down with emphasis. He leaned back, his focus finally settling on Rick. "The search did not go well," he grumbled. "Not for you!"

Rick stared impassively.

"We found blood on the doorknob—the side door into that shed of yours. We found more blood on the boat seat inside."

"It's not always the safest place to work—"

"It's a DNA match for Allison Sheridan!"

Rick hesitated at the comment. "She wasn't afraid of getting her hands dirty, Detective. Comes with bumps and bruises sometimes."

"Bullshit!" Ward pulled forward, his arms landing on the desk. "Talking around evidence is not the best strategy right now,

Larson!"

"Evidence of what?"

"The chief stopped by when Adrian was here. And the chief wants to take this to the DA. He wants to move the needle. He says we have enough. The car, the blood. You understand what I'm saying? He wanted you picked up this morning, not invited to stop by."

Rick nodded slowly, accepting the inevitable. "Well, guess I'll ask you the same question I asked Adrian two weeks ago. Do I need a lawyer?"

Ward waved off the comment. "It's the exception these days if anyone can get through life without needing one at some point—damn attorneys. And that's why people will pay and pay. Apparently though, you've got one, speak of the devil. And he's tough, and it doesn't matter who's in the room with him. Adrian's old and he's smart and I'm sure he's not cheap and he advised us not to waste our time, or yours, or his. He also reminded us again that you're a decorated veteran and that you're cooperating fully and that you're old and harmless. His words."

"He always speaks the truth."

"I hope that's what it is. He also said that blood found in a place like yours should be no surprise. He wrapped up this morning by convincing us all to leave you alone."

"I did Adrian a favor a long time ago. He never forgets, and he says there's nothing he could do that would ever even the score. So, he keeps trying. I always appreciate our friendship."

"I'm happy for you both," Ward snapped. "Even so, my boss is trying to put the pieces together—"

"What are the other pieces, Detective? You probably found fingerprints all over the seat, too. No one's denying Allie spent time there."

Ward dodged and glanced at his phone again. "Let's just say Adrian was persuasive on your behalf," he said. "On this one piece. But you aren't going anywhere Larson, not for a while. Not until Allison Sheridan is home safe and sound. That trip you just took. Bad idea! Thought we had an understanding."

"Guess I misunderstood. I was looking for her."

"Allie?"

"Following a hunch."

"Next time you have a hunch, you bring it to me. You're staying put." Ward leaned back in his chair, pulling in a deep breath before he went on. "Okay, first things first. Today isn't just about you; nothing else turned up in the search—"

"Except the blood."

"Yeah, except the blood. But like I said, Adrian calmed the room and bought you some more time."

"That's good. I'll need it, after what your search did to my shed. And to Tre's property."

Ward shook his head. "Nope, don't go there. I heard you at the diner. Loud and clear. Believe me, it could've been worse. You can imagine; with us finding the blood, things got intense fast and—"

"Intense?" Rick leaned forward. "You guys did some damage! That typical protocol for a search warrant?"

"Easy. We were there to search, and that's what we were doing. We didn't go for housekeeping. And tell me something, did you know Adrian was gonna show up?"

"Doesn't surprise me, he owns the place."

"Goddamn, that man's a powerful force!"

"Should have seen him fifty years ago in a uniform with a rifle. Just be glad our other partner wasn't there."

Ward's lips flattened. "Yeah, your other partner. Your friend, the one on the island."

"His name is Tremaine."

"I know his name, dammit, and he's the other piece." Ward hesitated. "Listen, I wanted you and Adrian to hear this together; we had a boat out on the water during the search. We didn't go ashore, just circled the island a couple of times, which wasn't easy in that part of the river. Sgt. Wilson wasn't crazy about us being as close as we were."

Rick crossed his arms. "That's his place."

"No, it's not his place! The city owns the island, Larson! He can't stay."

"It's where he lives, and it could just as easily be any sidewalk in the city where there's a ventilation grate."

"It's a tough situation wherever it is, but it's not the same. We got a good look at things from the boat. I saw the photos. He's set up out there. He should be paying property taxes for God's sake!"

They locked stares until Ward finally averted his eyes.

Rick leaned back. "Tre would say, 'Soldier's lessons. Gotta take care of yourself'. The man always took care of his teeth, Detective—"

"What?" Ward's brows pinched together. "You two helped him with all of it! Am I right?"

Rick's attention drifted past the detective to the window. In a distant voice, he said, "If we didn't help, Tre would have died on the street." Rick turned an unapologetic glare to Ward. "Do you really think we would let that happen? Just leave him out there? He spent a long time in the jungle and a year wandering alone. That was enough. That old marina, the island, all of it gave him a chance to live a little more of life; life that war tries to take away from him every damn day."

Ward stalled at the comment's truth. With restraint, he finally said, "I'll take that as a yes. Adrian's answer was yes, too. Problem is, as I mentioned, the city owns it."

"He's not hurting a soul out on that island."

"Well, maybe. And it's true, he has no record. And he does have some very honoring medals from the war. But here's the other problem: he's also got a gun out there. But you knew that, right? The rifle? With a scope for God's sake. On the stand and covered, but not very well and not hard to spot." Ward shook his head. "That's not happening anymore, Larson. We've got a missing girl who was a regular visitor at your marina and a sniper's rifle less than a mile away. Throw in the PTSD, and on the surface, that's always going to be seen as a threatening situation."

Rick set his jaw. "Or protective."

Ward glowered instantly. He pulled forward again, chewing his lip. "Adrian told me it won't fire, and it never did. He also said it was a rare find, a gift for his friend. He assured me the firing pin was ground away. Said it was mostly a lawn ornament and harmless. Bullshit! Gun laws exist, Larson!"

"D always plays by the rules."

Ward's eyes narrowed. "You sure? I've known Adrian Dumars a while, and I like him most of the time. But I don't trust attorneys. At all! So I'm asking you, dammit, is that gun live?"

"Why would it be?" Rick swallowed hard, letting Ward's impatience settle. "That war was over fifty years ago."

Ward blurted, "Yes it was, and not our finest hour."

The cynicism echoed in Rick's ears. He tensed, eyeing the detective across the desk. "We did our best."

Ward pinched his lips and looked away. "Not what I meant—"

"Doesn't matter. I've heard it too many times in my life." Rick rested both elbows on his knees. "Tremaine?"

Ward pulled forward and slapped a hand on the desk. "If it wasn't for Tremaine Wilson, you'd be alone in jail right now. He is repeatedly mentioned in the search report, and that's why I'm talking to you two first. It's not on anyone's desk yet, except mine. But it will be, and soon, and then that will be it. There's no way he's staying. Clear? You and Adrian are going to have to figure it out."

"He's sick, Detective."

Ward drew a breath. "I understand. But find a solution. Move him onto your property and pray we find the Sheridan girl soon."

Rick muttered, "No, I don't think you do understand." He lowered his head, shaking it slowly. "How long?"

"A lot of people are trying to connect you and Tremaine to this, but it's all circumstantial at this point. That can change quickly. I can give you a week. That's as long as I hold it. Adrian heard the same, so rally some of his resources. And if you need to talk with someone—"

"I've got all the contacts I need." Rick exhaled and pushed up from the chair, looking down on the detective. "If the rifle disappeared?"

Ward stood and met his eyes. "Maybe if it was never there . . . but it's too late."

Rick nodded. "Anything else?"

"The timing with Sergeant Wilson sucks, Larson. I do appreciate that." He moved around the desk to face Rick. "But we've got a missing girl. And with who she is, there's going to be some collateral damage." Ward extended his hand. "I'm sorry."

He said it believably and Rick returned the gesture.

"Allie?" Rick said.

"I wish I had something. It takes time."

"Thought the first couple of days were critical."

"They are," Ward said quickly. He looked away. "They were."

~

Rick's decision to visit the island had come after hours of slow, reflective wandering along the length of M Street, SE. A brief conversation with the fishermen at the overpass and a quick, favorite story about Tre brought smiles, motivating Rick's brisk pace back to the marina in the late afternoon hours. As dusk settled in, he and Schooner landed the skiff on the island's sandy shoreline. The flags drifted casually in the light breeze; the fire pit held a soft, retreating flame. Tre slept in the lean-to under three heavy blankets. Schooner hurried to him, sniffed, and promptly curled up alongside. Rick watched his friend; a deepening sorrow seized him with each of Tre's labored breaths. He knelt to adjust the blankets over his feet, then moved to the bank of coolers. He opened the red one, 'the closet', and pulled back sweaters that hadn't been worn in many months and likely never would be again. Rick eased the plastic bag from his pocket, held it up to the sky's fading light, and studied the broken shells and ring. Finally, he laid the bag gently into the corner of the cooler and repositioned the sweaters for cover. He moved across the encampment and took a seat on the log next to the fire. More branches would be needed. Maybe in an hour. He cast his eyes across the peacefulness of the river, content to be settling in for the overnight watch.

Chapter 30

Beth seethed. Eighteen hours out of Rockland, but only four hundred miles away. "Fuck this!" she muttered through clenched teeth. She shook her head. "I can't do this."

She checked both side mirrors and veered across two lanes. Her paranoia about being tailed had heightened as they followed Interstate 95 south past the Newark Liberty International Airport. Beyond exhausted, her head filled with anxious thoughts. She made the decision to get off onto 278 heading east, not knowing how far they would take it. Once across the Goethals Bridge, Beth continued the route for miles, watching in her rear-view mirror often, still uncertain but weighing all possible scenarios. Allie slept in the passenger seat.

Her suspicions were confirmed at the Verrazzano Bridge as they approached the lane divides for the upper and lower decks. Beth swerved at the last minute to cross a lane and take the lower level. In the mirror, a black Forerunner two cars back, cut off a tractor-trailer to pick up the same level. Allie stirred from the sudden road noise along the bridge and shifted her position. Beth kept watch, testing the driver repeatedly. She slowed, she braked without warning, she cut around a camper to change lanes. At the mid-span, the Forerunner veered around a pick-up truck that had moved in between them. Beth witnessed the car accelerate, swerve back into the right lane, and close on them. Disbelief and panic crept in. She shook off a sudden tremble.

"What is it?" Allie asked, glancing across Lower New York Bay. "Where are we going?"

"We need a rental."

Allie peered toward the approaching skyline. "Why? In New York?"

Beth released a deep sigh. "I could just be tired, but I think we're being followed."

Allie instinctively checked over her shoulder through the rear window as they descended. Each bump over the old deck's expansion joints jarred them, returning Beth's edgy, prolonged focus on the mirrors. She waited as long as she could, then broke desperately again, forcing a Mercedes to brake hard as she crossed two lanes to stay on Interstate 278 toward Brooklyn.

Allie reached for the dashboard to balance. "New York? Isn't that a little out of the way?"

"Yes! New York! And yes, it is!" Beth's forearms tightened against the crush of responsibility sitting next to her; the lost girl who walked into her home only days ago. As they had traveled south, the heaviness grew; the heartache she felt for Allie, the pain of seeing Rick, all of it consuming her as she accelerated erratically through the congested streets of Brooklyn. She maintained an incessant focus on the rear view and side mirrors, holding her troubled looks too long and receiving loud, close horns demanding her attention.

Beth reached a quick hand to her shoulder. "I'm sorry, Allie. I'm sorry for snapping at you."

A delivery cyclist pulled out between two parked cars, and Beth slammed on the brakes. She looked back. "I can't see it now! It was a black Forerunner. It's too dark."

Through Williamsburg, Beth took random turns in different directions, rarely using her turn signals. She pulled into the Trader

Joe's underground garage at Metropolitan and Kent Streets and parked two levels down. They rushed to grab backpacks and disappeared into the stairway, exiting onto 3rd Street. Side by side they stepped quickly, veering into shadows where they could along the sidewalk. Their Uber sat idling at Wythe and 6th. At Beth's urging, the driver promptly accelerated away from the curb and turned immediately onto 7th, happy to comply for a trip fare to the airport.

Allie slouched low in the back.

Beth twisted in the passenger seat for a quick check behind them, then said bluntly. "Change of plans, driver. No airport. I want a twenty-minute tour of Greenpoint. Dark streets, lots of turns. We'll end up back on Wythe, down by the water."

The approaching signal changed from a quick yellow and the driver slammed the brakes. He scowled at Beth. "What? You being followed?"

Allie pulled forward in the back seat. "Beth, what are we—"

Beth glared at the driver. "You get the difference plus more in cash. Go!"

He assessed a moment watching the light turn green, then accelerated through the intersection.

The Forerunner crept down Wythe Street four cars back. Ron punched in Leah's number, and she picked up immediately.

"It's her," Ron said. "Confirmed. She's in Brooklyn, with Larson's daughter. Have to believe they're on their way back. I'll stay close."

"Good," Leah said impassively.

"Are you going to reach out to—"

"No." Leah ended the call.

The Uber driver ended the tour abruptly after only twelve minutes, screeching to a stop in front of the TJ's garage. Beth and Allie were out quickly and back into their car. The trip to La Guardia proved painfully slow. Beth finally pulled into the long-term lot at 8:45 p.m. and deliberated for long minutes until she found a remote spot. She handed Allie the keys.

"I'll get us a car," Beth said. "You're waiting here. We're not taking any chances with you being seen. Do not get out of this car. Understand?"

Allie shook her head. "Just put me on a plane or a bus," she said in a weak voice. "You've done too much already. I shouldn't have brought this into your life."

Exhausted, Beth had nothing. She turned to Allie. "I won't be gone long, hopefully." She got out and hurried toward the bus stop, casting fearful looks down each row.

~

Parking lot 8A had 2,446 spaces across twenty-six rows. The black Forerunner crept along the first one in section C. Thirty minutes ago, Ron had gotten trapped behind a UPS truck and briefly lost sight of the green SUV. He made up ground quickly but still couldn't be certain Beth's car was the one he saw entering. He had no choice but to cruise the aisles.

~

Navigating the airport rental process required more time than Beth had patience for. Frustrated and anxious, she returned to the lot exceeding speed limits when she could. At the entrance toll booth, she yanked the ticket and accelerated to row Q. She turned wide into the aisle and leaned forward off the seat back, peering nervously along both sides; there were so many more cars now.

Only a few empty spots. Disoriented, she slowed halfway along the row, finally coming to space thirty-two. She slammed the brakes, seeing a red Lexus backed in.

"Allie, no!" she cried out loud, pounding a fist on the console. "Don't do this!" Beth grabbed for her ticket to confirm and fearfully scanned ahead for the car. "Dammit!"

As she pulled forward slowly, her phone rang.

"Allie, thank God!"

In a hushed voice, Allie said. "I'm on row eighteen. The black Forerunner is here, searching for us. I'm in between a white pick-up and a minivan. Space twenty-six." She grew silent.

"Allie?"

"You should hurry," she whispered.

Beth took a panicked look around and pulled ahead.

~

Twenty minutes later, Beth and Allie exited La Guardia's perimeter and retraced north on Interstate 87. They drove three miles before Beth felt safe. She took the next cloverleaf and picked up 95, rerouting again through the city. They crept with traffic along the busy streetscape for half an hour. Beth's free left hand tapped her thigh ceaselessly. She inched through red lights and squeezed across jammed intersections, becoming more unnerved with each block. She monitored every sidewalk and scrutinized each car that came close; certain she saw the black SUV following behind more than once.

Traffic eased as they got to the Hudson River, and their speed picked up through the tunnel at Fort Lee. Both exhausted, they drove in silence, still glancing repeatedly in the mirrors. Allie's head rested against the passenger-side window; her eyes fixed on the fading city skyline. The New Jersey Turnpike opened up in front of them, and Beth tested the Subaru's pick-up. Washington, DC, was three and a half hours away.

Allie straightened against the seat and sighed. "I wish I hadn't gotten you into this, Beth, whatever this is."

"Don't be. It's okay, I'm sure. I'm just tired. We need to get you home." Minutes passed before Beth finally said, "Seeing Rick; all of it." She shook her head.

Allie stared through the window. "A lifetime apart," she murmured. "It's so sad."

Beth held a tight grip around the wheel, her attention ahead unwavering. "All of it was sad for a long time, and then it wasn't." She faltered and glanced at Allie. "Did you know a man named Tremaine?"

Allie turned to her. "Tre?"

"I guess you did."

"I only met him a couple of times. He's unique. And likes to be alone. He's truly a kind man."

"I knew him, too, when I was very young. I wish I could remember more. I'm glad he's still kind." Her voice broke. "I hear he's had a difficult life."

They drove in silence for miles. Beth stayed in the right lane, holding the speed limit. Most of the other cars and trucks did not. She caught herself in a vacant gaze and instantly shook her head, hoping to restore the lost focus.

Allie twisted slightly on the seat. "Are you okay?"

"No." Beth mumbled, massaging her temple. "Allie, Rick told me Tre's not well. He's old. He may be very sick." She paused. "Rick wanted me to know. I thought you should, too."

Allie nodded and lowered her head, clasping both hands across her lap. "I told Rick I wanted to see him again. I hope I can."

"I hope we both can."

Stillness returned. Beth drove the next hour fully reliant on adrenaline. Unannounced, she took the exit ramp for Route 195 north to Trenton, NJ. Allie looked over.

"I can't do the rest of this trip tonight," Beth said.

"I can drive."

"Not anymore, no insurance."

"Is that really important now?"

"No chances. It's okay, we could both use a break."

As they approached the toll cameras, Allie knew the drill; she held the book up, covering her face. Beth took one look behind into the darkness, relieved not to see any lights. Three miles farther down 195, they pulled into the rear lot of a Comfort Inn. Minutes later, both collapsed onto the queen beds in room 215, across the hall from the exit stairs.

Beth closed her eyes, taking a moment in silence to process it all. "Allie, someone knows you're on the road," she finally said. "I don't know how, but we may need to stay out of sight for a couple of days.

"I thought you said no one was behind us on the turnpike."

"Someone knows." Beth pulled both hands slowly across her face. "We stay quiet, right here. Maybe just a day. No contact. Agreed?"

"Okay." Allie fixated on the bright, stippled ceiling. "Beth, thank you for everything."

Beth didn't answer.

"I know you want to get me home," Allie went on, her voice weaker. "But I need to see Rick . . . first."

The comment jolted Beth and she rolled on her side for eye contact. Tears streamed down Allie's face, her hands clutched at the bedspread.

Beth turned away, helpless. "I'm sorry about Tre." She sighed.

"Try to sleep. We'll talk in the morning."

They lay in silence, motionless, peering vacantly to the ceiling. Beth slowly surrendered to sleep.

Allie reached for the phone, eased out of bed, and stepped quietly into the bathroom. She closed the door and leaned back against the vanity. A chill rushed her as she typed. She composed the message, read it, changed some words, and re-read it. She clutched at it, confused about what to tell Rick. Tears started again as she searched her image in the mirror for help. She wiped them and read the text again. Her hands trembled as she hesitantly deleted all of it.

Chapter 31

The Friday afternoon sun was breaking through clouds, casting long shadows down the tight alley as Rick squeezed the truck in between two recycling bins. Delia came through the rear door of the diner as he got out. They shared smiles.

"You get my text?" he asked.

"Just now. Busy day in there."

"Busy is always good."

"I'm getting old. Couple of slow days sprinkled in would be good, too."

"Listen, sorry to just show up. I reached out to your sister-in-law, Anna."

Delia picked up on the hesitation. "About Tre, or Allie, or you?"

Rick gazed off down the alley. "Maybe all of us," he said quietly. "Lotta questions spinning around."

Delia nodded.

"She has a good heart," Rick said. "I appreciated what she tried to do for Tre."

"It was something, you trusting her with your dear friend. Anna's a wise woman, with credentials. And she does care. Hers is a heart that has to help." She reached a hand to his arm. "Which shelter? Northeast?"

"Anna said she's closing up the new one. Adams Morgan."

Delia closed her eyes and dragged both hands across her

forehead. She finally straightened with a brighter expression. "All of it sucks, Richard. But we aren't alone. None of us, ever. You want company?"

Rick exhaled and released his shoulders. "I was hoping. Do you have time?"

"Anna let me know you were on your way. I'll grab my bag."

~

Twenty-five minutes later, they found a rare space a block away.

Rick glanced at Delia. "Thank you again, dear friend."

"You ready?"

Rick sat motionless. "I guess."

After hours, the entrance vestibule to the center always remained locked. Anna rested against the ajar door, ready with a warm welcome as they approached. She ushered them through a small lobby and into the waiting room. Individual chairs sat spaced along three of the walls: an adult and one teenage girl occupied two of them under the streetside windows. The middle-aged man focused on his phone. The girl looked down at nothing. The wall color was a pastel, earthen green above a neutral tile floor. Intricate tapestries hung opposite the glass. Each of the three table lamps shone softly; healthy plants filled two corners. Tranquil surroundings to provide calm for guests.

Anna led them into a small windowless conference room with only a sliver of glass panel in the door. She hugged Delia, shook Rick's hand, and dropped into one of the chairs. Her shoulders fell and she opened both eyes wide to reset.

She reached a hand across the table to Delia's arm. "It's good to see you, sister," she said.

Delia sighed. "How are you, Anna? You ever find the help you needed?"

Anna frowned. "It's never enough. The crisis remains, and roadblocks do, too. The city and federal government keep promising. We keep waiting."

She patted Delia's hand and turned a tired smile to Rick. "How are you holding up, my friend?"

"On which front?"

"They might not be that different."

Rick shrugged. "Thanks for taking the time, Anna."

"Of course. How's Tre doing? I think about him a lot. I was hoping he would have stayed with us."

"He's slipping, like you said he would."

Her expression softened with a slow nod. "It might not be too late," she said. "For some help. I know that's not what he wants. He told me, and I'm sure he's said the same to you. Some Vets don't after this long. The disconnect is too deep."

"No, it isn't what he wants. I've known him a long time, and when we talk about it, I can see the struggle in his mind. But his words are always the same."

"That's his fear, it's buried."

"Forty plus years of it."

Anna leaned in. "Rick, listen, anything I can do. Anytime. You know that." She bit her lips; her eyes fixed on his. "Is there any encouraging news about Allie?"

Rick glanced across the table to Delia, his lost expression inviting help.

"Unfortunately, nothing yet." She turned to Anna. "It's so hard waiting."

"Sometimes, it's all we can do, though, sis. And waiting sucks. All of it does." Anna exhaled as she pulled back. "Every year, in DC alone, close to a thousand kids, nine years old to twenty-one, go missing. That's who we're open for. Some find us, some find another refuge, but others find a more difficult journey. Nationwide, the number is five thousand. Most make it back—sadly some don't. All depends on where the escape takes them. If it lands them on the street, it's beyond difficult, and it's dangerous. With luck, they find a friend, someone, a place where they can be safe." Anna paused. "It's critical they find their way to us, though, or to others, for the help and time to think about the next step."

Anna stood and walked to the undercounter frig. She pulled out waters, set two on the table and leaned against the wall. "How can I help, Rick? You said you needed to talk."

Rick evaded, lowering his gaze to contemplate the water bottle. His trembling fingers pulled at the moist label.

Anna caught Delia's concern, observing them both for a few seconds. "Well, this is a good step. Trying to understand as much as you can."

Rick took a long drink.

Anna went on in a quieter voice, "Allie's likely blaming herself right now, wherever she is and regardless of the circumstances that made her run. That's going to take understanding and a lot of listening and support for her. Whatever the need is." She clasped her hands together. "There *is* something to hold onto though, and please don't take this the wrong way, Rick, but Allie is one of the fortunate ones, curious as that may sound. Her family has money, resources, notoriety, and lots of help in the search from the FBI. It's understating to say not every child has that. Allie won't be forgotten; too many are."

Rick nodded. "Yeah, it's something. All of that may be what she's running from."

"It might be," Anna said. "It's difficult to say what makes a child take the step. Every case is unique, but it's usually family problems. Sometimes a combination of things and the situation becomes desperate. Not money in Allie's case, but it could be the parenting; angry or absent, one or both. Bullying, emotional abuse about coming out, or pregnancy. The reasons are overwhelming. After so many years, sometimes I still wonder how kids survive." Anna folded her arms. "Did you notice anything different about her the last couple of weeks? Her mood, eating, conversations? Did she mention anything about school problems, or home?"

Rick gazed down at the table. "Truth is, Anna, I don't think she ever got over her mom dying. Living here in DC has been a challenge." He clenched both hands around the bottle. "But we only had short visits together. I didn't see anything."

"I understand, it's okay. Don't take that responsibility. Changes can be hard to notice, especially at her age. She's eighteen now, right?"

"A week ago."

Anna stepped to the table, hesitating. "Rick, I need to say this; girls will also leave because of physical abuse—that can mean sexual abuse, and too many of them are under eighteen." She drew a deep breath. "Pray that's not Allie's trauma. Those scars are deep, and they don't just fade away."

Anna lowered her head, rubbing both temples. After a moment, she paced again. "Whatever it is, though, it's *all* trauma. And I know you'll understand what that means, Rick. You've taken care of Tre, and you supported this young girl who needed someone as well. And now she's in trouble. Allie experienced something that made her run, and she's still facing it. It's the same battle, not unlike Tre's. Trauma, pain, fear, escape. A victim will try to protect themselves, and escape is one of the ways, in whatever form that takes over. Depression. Anxiety. Isolation. All of it can follow. You just hope that it all ends with healing."

Anna landed at the end of the table and sank into the chair.

"Wow, that was a lot. Forgive me, Rick. Long day. I'm usually a better listener."

He focused down in silence.

"If you're worried about being there for her, Rick, don't be. You'll do your best for Allie, as you have for Tre. That's all she needs from you."

"This doesn't feel like Tre," he said quietly.

Anna leaned toward him. "Delia said you went to see Beth."

Rick stiffened.

Her head tilted slightly. "It's important to understand that this could feel the same."

Delia's mouth fell open, instantly. Her brow wrinkled as she turned to Rick.

Peering at Anna, his jaw tensed. The words and image of Allie vanished for him. He squeezed his shaking hands together.

Anna quickly extended hers, but he pulled back.

"Rick," she said urgently. "I'm exhausted. And that awareness usually precedes a filter on my sometimes, brutal honesty approach in conversation. Please, forgive me. Mentioning Beth, I—"

"Anna," Rick said flatly. "It's okay."

He studied her weary expression. The compassion he had come to her for opposed years of painful experience, heartache, and struggle. From all of it, her earned knowledge and intuition had saved hundreds of lives and families, and she had trusted Rick with her truths. Below his sudden panic, he retained the belief she was trying to help, but his mind had been triggered, and he sensed the encroaching personal darkness. He knew it would take him.

Anna went on in a quiet voice, "Rick, with everything you experienced in the war, Beth was—"

"Anna! I did lose Beth, but I didn't feel this." He eyed each of them. "I was too drunk."

Delia collapsed back in her chair.

Anna lowered her head. "Rick, the pain was always there."

Without warning, he pushed up from the table, steadying himself. "No, it was all *forgotten*."

Delia reached for his arm, but he pulled away.

Rick's unsteady expression held on Anna. "Thank you," he finally managed. He slid the keys to Delia and left hurriedly through the door to the waiting room.

~

Minutes later, Rick stood transfixed on the sidewalk curb at the intersection of 16th and Euclid St NW, facing south, his mind mapping out the route and number of blocks to K Street. The late afternoon sun had fallen below the city rooftops, and the rush hour exodus was beginning; cars stacking at lights, crosswalks blocked, loud, intermittent horns sounding. Rick rubbed the back of his neck, assessing the crowded sidewalk stretching out before him. Finally, he jammed both hands into his pockets and plodded with the others down 16th Street. He tuned out the chattering voices around him and centered blankly ahead, hoping Adrian hadn't left early this day.

Chapter 32

Rick tensed when the elevator bell sounded on the third floor, immediately irritated about the stop. He appreciated having the cab to himself, hoping for an uninterrupted ride to Adrian's floor. The forty-five minute walk from Anna's had exhausted him, and he wiped at the perspiration on his forehead, the third time since entering the lobby minutes ago. The door opened, and a fortyish attorney joined him, uninterested in making eye contact. On twelve, he exited quickly, still seemingly unaware of Rick's presence against the back of the cab. Rick caught himself in the mirrored wall panels and shook his head. He pulled both hands through his hair a last time and moved into the large administrative space.

Mary's station was orderly, as always; a clear desk, two folders perfectly placed in the left corner, the desk light and computer both shut off. She was gone for the day. Surprised but relieved, Rick moved down the hall to the waiting area outside Adrian's office. Nancy peered up from her screen. Rick smiled and murmured 'hello', then shifted his attention to the opposite wall. A large, fully suited man filled the plush leather chair in the corner. He promptly looked up from his phone to survey Rick. Quickly uninterested, he touched his earpiece, glanced at Nancy, then returned his focus to the screen.

Nancy greeted Rick warmly. "Mr. Larson, good evening." Her forehead wrinkled as she studied the monitor. "I, umm, don't have you on Mr. Dumar's calendar. Is he expecting you? He's actually in a meeting right now." Nancy lowered her glasses; observing his damp shirt.

Rick's hand went immediately to the sweaty collar. He shrugged, slowing his breaths and checked over his shoulder for any interest from the man in the corner.

Nancy stood. "Can I get you something to drink, Mr. Larson?"

"A water would be great. Thank you."

As she stepped away from her desk, Rick moved casually toward Adrian's office doors. Abruptly, he pulled them open and barged in before the man could rise from his chair. Rick managed a few purposeful steps to the center of the room before being grabbed from behind by the senator's security aide. Michelle Baxter and Chris Evans occupied the corner couches facing the room. Adrian sat in the leather chair across from a low pedestal and glass tabletop.

Chris rose instantly. Michelle remained seated, shaking her head.

Adrian leapt to his feet, scowling, and gesturing to Michelle's security. "Hey! Hands off! It's okay."

The security aide held tight to Rick's arm, looking to the senator for direction.

Michelle's cynical voice trumpeted from the couch, "Is it really, Adrian? Is it really okay for just anyone to charge into your office and interrupt a private meeting? In the future, perhaps it would be better if we met on my home field."

She glared at him, then gestured to the aide. "Jim, thank you. Please wait for me outside."

Adrian moved to his friend as the door closed. "Rick, dammit. Look at you. What the—did you just walk here? What's going on? It's not a good time."

Nancy knocked lightly and came through the door. She hesitated, taking a brief scan of the room, then hurriedly handed Rick the water. She spun to leave, turning an embarrassed look of apology to her boss and the senator.

Adrian rested his hand on Rick's shoulder and spoke quietly, "Hey, brother, we were just going over some things about Allie. Can you and I talk later?"

Rick focused on Chris, then Michelle. "Shouldn't a conversation about Allie include her father? Where's Ben?"

"He's out of town, Mr. Larson," Michelle said bluntly. "But that's really none of your business."

Adrian tried again. "Rick, c'mon. Later?"

Rick held his stare on the senator. "Good timing, D. Allie's who I came to talk to you about as well. Allie, and the senator."

Chris scowled and approached Rick and Adrian. "Okay, enough of this bullshit. Jesus, Adrian! Your old 'Nam buddy needs to go. Do you want to call security, or should I?" Chris shook his head and pulled out his phone.

Adrian drew near, his jaw fixed. "That would be a career ending mistake, Mr. Evans."

"Not necessarily," Michelle said flatly.

Rick turned to her. "I was just talking about Allie, too, Senator. Earlier, with Anna Norris. She runs *Safe Promise.* We talked for a long time about runaways and what makes them leave. We talked about why families break apart."

Michelle nodded, fixing her gaze on Rick. "I know Anna and her work, Mr. Larson. She has saved countless lost souls. She's a national treasure—"

"Who reminded me why my daughter left," he said coldly. "Thankfully, Beth was saved from a rageful father, a man who hated himself and—"

"Touching, Mr. Larson. Truly." Michelle stood slowly. "Thank you for sharing, but we all know about your young daughter and the wife you abused. Married too young upon returning from war. A mortar round to the leg—a horrible injury, sadly leaving you incapable of being a father. And we know about your old Black friend on the island." Michelle folded her arms. "We know all of it. Yours has indeed been a challenging path. Your service is appreciated; I regret that it destroyed your life. Our discussion this evening, however, is about my stepdaughter, and to reiterate, none of this involves you."

"Anna is direct," Rick snapped. "She didn't hold back with the painful reminders. It wasn't an easy discussion. But the walk over gave me time to reflect. About Allie, and all she's shared with me about your lovely home." His jaw tensed. "And what might have pulled her away!"

Adrian eased in front of his friend, speaking softly. "Sergeant, hey. Been a while since I've seen this in you."

Rick's glare held. "Senator! The only thing I could come up with was you. Allie disappeared days after your last event. She always dreaded being alone with you."

"Rick!" Adrian barked. "That's enough!"

Rick boomed at Michelle. "What the hell happened that night, Senator?"

Michelle glowered at each of them and shook her head. "Mr. Larson, the question alone crosses a boundary to a part of the world that shouldn't concern you, Allie's world. Some may consider your pretense of caring about our daughter as noble and compassionate. I do not. Your association with her was a mistake, and not one made by me."

Michelle moved around the pedestal table, drawing closer to Rick. "I'm sure you've seen your fair share of restraining orders, Mr. Larson. Yes? Actually, I know you have; August 1973? Your lovely home state of New Jersey? Wasn't there an arrest as well? Some trouble stemming from self-prescribed alcohol during recovery. Was that it? Your wife and young daughter must have been terrified." Michelle tilted her head. "You were a dangerous person then, menacing to such a young girl. I can't assume you're any different now. So, I offer you this, *Sergeant*: time to forget you ever knew Allison Sheridan. Clear?"

Rick caught Chris' smug expression.

"Mr. Larson!" Michelle thundered. "Consider this your warning, or threat. Whichever will hold the most meaning for you. Just understand that you should crawl back to your side of the line; to your side of life and never return."

She turned expectantly to Adrian. He hesitated only a moment to glance at Rick, but the delay proved to be a mistake. The senator's security aide rushed through the door and advanced on Rick, grabbing his arm. Rick yanked free and Michelle gestured to her aide. He stiffened, then stepped back.

Michelle drew to within inches of Rick, her chin high. "You know, Allie has commented she's never seen you angry. That's curious to me, in light of our discussion here this evening. Did she speak the truth?"

Rick faltered.

"I didn't think so. The girl's a habitual liar." They locked stares for seconds until Michelle turned an impassioned nod to the aide. He closed on Rick again, pulling his jacket back to reveal the gun.

"Good-bye, Mr. Larson," Michelle's hateful eyes fix on his.

The aide took another step. Rick shot a look to Adrian, then spun and stormed across the room. Chris moved next to Michelle as the door slammed. He reached a hand to her arm, jutting his chin.

Michelle shook her head slowly and approached Adrian. She sighed, searching his lost expression. "You committed to law after the war, Adrian, embarking on the noble mission of veterans' disabilities. Wisely, though, you embraced your true calling: I've never known a more powerful force in the courtroom. However, it now seems that you are intending a return to your roots, perhaps to end your illustrious career on that same once virtuous note?" Michelle folded her arms. "Why you've maintained your loyalties to Richard Larson and Tremaine Wilson, never letting the cruel realities of life crash in around them, I'll never understand—"

"Always faithful," Adrian said quietly.

"Very quaint. However, the sentiment holds no meaning for me, and I will give the question no further reflection." She leaned in, her narrowed eyes inches away. "Ironic, isn't it Mr. Dumars? I was just going to explain to you the applicable statutes regarding threats to government officials. Or maybe you're already familiar with them. Threatening a senator is a felony, Adrian, punishable by enough years that your dear old friend would surely die in prison. In every way, Mr. Larson's presence here this evening, apparently condoned by you, constituted a threat to me, and I have a witness to corroborate."

"Senator—"

Michelle's hand flew up. "You had a chance, Adrian! Your choice was clear, and it leaves me with only one option. Richard Larson has become unhinged and a clear danger to others. We don't know what he did to Allie: it may be too late. Tomorrow morning, I'll be reaching out to the DA. Charges are appropriate and I'll make certain they are swift."

Rick arrived at the marina an hour later after retrieving his truck from Delia. He pulled to a stop four feet from the shed's overhead door, got out leaving the headlights on, and moved to the hoist chain. The door cooperated, rising with minimal objection. Rick switched on the weak overhead lights, moved to the bench seat and surveyed the disarray, the aim of his anger slowly shifting from Senator Baxter to the Metropolitan Police and FBI. Tomorrow was emergency shelter cooking, a make-up effort necessitated by two broken water lines in Trinity's kitchen the day before. Tre might be coming, even on a Saturday. Rick could never be sure, but he wouldn't chance his friend seeing the ruin of all he had created. Minutes later, CSN blared from the boombox. Schooner's tranquil recline filled the bench seat. Rick circled slowly, imagining his start. He bent over and picked up the first part, an eighteen-inch bronze porthole, and returned it to temporary safety on a pile of canvas cushions. Raising his gaze to the upper shelves where it belonged, he paused, hearing Sarah's approach from behind.

"Delia texted me a half hour ago." Her hesitant voice barely carried above the music.

Rick's shoulders slumped as he turned. Sarah stood in front of the truck's grille, flanked by the glaring headlights. He turned down the volume and drew closer, trying to find her expression in the blinding light.

"I came right over," she said. "I thought you might want some company?"

Rick halted feet away, answering with a silent stare, uncertain if the smile Sarah always shared was there in the shadows.

Sarah's voice cracked, "She also told me about this afternoon. I'm so sorry, Rick."

He took another step, shielding his eyes. "Sarah, are you okay?"

She clasped both hands in front of her chest. "I'm sad for you, Rick. My God, I don't even know you and I feel so much pain for you, for all of this. You went to see her for only good reasons, and—"

"And the scars I mentioned, yeah. The ones you can't see."

"I know," she mumbled, quickly lowering her head. "We all have some buried."

Rick sensed an unfamiliar strain. "Sarah?"

"My sister died young!" she blurted, squeezing her eyes shut.

"What?"

"An accident!" Sarah cried out, turning away. "And then the drugs that were supposed to help her through it . . . they didn't." She trembled. "Sadly, Kate added the alcohol."

Rick watched her, unable to move. Behind them, Schooner groaned as he lowered himself from the seat. He ambled over to Sarah, leaned against her leg, and cast a worried expression toward Rick.

Sarah leaned to rub his ears. Finally she straightened and faced Rick. "Guardian angels like Tre don't always get there in time." She bowed her head. "I didn't."

He moved close and took her hands.

"It's always the ones we can't see." Sarah pulled away and wandered past him, pausing in the center of the cavernous space. Holding herself with arms crossed, she slowly scanned the walls. "It's always the one's we can't see," she murmured.

They shared silence a while. Rick searched her eyes, hoping to hear himself offer a comforting voice, but the quiet remained. Sarah sighed after a moment and wiped the tears from her cheeks. Drawing a breath, she leaned over to pick up a small brass ship's bell. With unsteady arms, she held it out to Rick. "I could help. If you want."

Chapter 33

Tre's decline over the last year had been significant. Each week through the cold winter, he retreated further inside. Rick commonly observed it during the brief delivery visits, motivating him to find persuasions that would bring his friend ashore more often. Shelter cooking nights still survived as an occasional incentive.

But Tre hadn't left the marina to join the efforts at Trinity in years. He didn't recall the purpose, he didn't recall Fay, and he didn't remember the friends, some of whom had passed away long ago. After agreeing to accompany Rick back to the marina, he typically would then elect to stay behind, reclined in the boat, enjoying his comfortable spot low in the bow and sharing the floorboards with Schooner. Eventually, he might wander to the shed to work on the parts, or he might keep the Old Man company. Deliberation often held him positioned in the skiff for a few minutes or for an hour or more, all the while nursing a joint and fixating on the shed.

~

Rick tilted the small outboard, ignoring complaints from his stiff lower back, worsened by the overnight effort tending to the parts. He tossed a line around the piling and rotated on the bench seat. Tre and Schooner filled the small bow. Tre's only conversation as they traveled across the river that evening had involved Allie, asking repeatedly if Beth knew where she was. Each time, Rick told him she wasn't in Maine. Tre offered sad words of worry, then he forgot. Rick hunched forward, leaning in to rub Schooner's ears, aware of Tre's strained inhales.

He checked his watch. Soon he would need to head to Trinity. Rounding up troops to cook this evening at the shelter hadn't been easy for Fay. In response, she had promised a lighter production goal. Rick decided he had time to sit a while.

"Hey," he said. "I never thanked you."

Tre's forehead wrinkled. "Yeah, you did. Plenty of times. We're good, brother."

"I mean the other day."

Tre cocked his head. "Dude on the pier . . . up in your face?" He worked his jaw.

"Thought D's gift was retired."

"Pretty sure it is . . ."

Rick sighed, searching his friend's eyes. "That's good."

Schooner stretched closer against Tre's leg. His companion. Falling into contentment appeared so intuitive for the old Lab. Tre's faint smile appeared. He was present, and Schooner could help him stay there.

The scene comforted Rick and left him wavering. Adrian's necessary message had not been delivered. Rick rubbed the stubble across his chin, averting his eyes. Unprepared, he blurted, "Tre, Adrian thinks the timing's right for us to sell."

Tre lifted his gaze, slowly tilting his head.

Rick hurried the rest of the message. "He's worked hard on a deal for us. He says the contract's good."

Tre laid a hand on Schooner. "D's carried us a long time, hasn't he."

"Yeah, he has."

"He's a good man. Good soldier. A better friend." Tre leaned his head back. "He could've let me drift away."

"Both of us."

Tre's eyes closed. "Quiet ride to Parris Island that morning, wasn't it?" 'Til D started in with all that patriotic chatter and the singing."

Rick's eyebrows raised. "You on that bus this afternoon?"

Tre's half smile faded quickly. "Guess I am." A rough cough leaned him forward. Both shaky hands clutched at his knees. Seconds passed until he was able to nod. "D's a happy one. Big dude. Was gonna sing as much as he wanted on that ride. Took up one whole seat, you remember? Who was gonna bitch? The man was bigger than you. Never thought I'd see that."

"He sure pulled us in, didn't he, neither of us knowing what we were walking into. Some anxious times; different meaning for each of us."

"All about the Country for, D."

Rick explored the calm surface across the water. "And friendship."

"And honor."

"I never saw fear get a hold of him."

"The man was too busy singin'."

Rick chuckled. "You had a good coach."

"Yeah, I did."

Tre rubbed Schooner's head a while. The connection restored energy.

"Helluva thing, isn't it? The hiding and forgetting; seems like you and me been doin' that too long. Adrian had our backs, though, wasn't gonna let us fall. It's who the man is . . . and you had mine." His eyes held on Rick. "You and Schooner."

Tre pulled out a joint and lit it and shifted back against the life jackets padding the bow. He inhaled deeply and mumbled, "You two go ahead. I see it's time."

"It's the three of us, Tre. Together."

Tre wheezed suddenly and rushed another puff on the joint. "We'll see." His gaze drifted along the river. "It's something what we built here."

"A lot of work, and some good years."

"Was our life. When it's gone, what's left?"

"Money. That buys a new start."

Tre shook his head slowly. "Don't need money, and no new starts for me. Told you both. You and D, you two got this."

He squinted at Rick and offered the joint. "For the road?"

Rick accepted it as he had for decades but didn't smoke.

Tre reached to take it back, nodding. "Good for you, old man. Never wanna have to shoot you in that other arm."

"We'll find a place, Tre. It'll be warmer."

"Never minded the cold so much—Schooner'll like that, though." He drew another slow inhale. "I'm good here, with that old shed. Brought me a couple extra years. And you did, too. God's gift, a purpose. All I have left is that world in there." His eyes wandered again. "Thanks to you both for letting me see it."

"There's more, just not here."

Tre turned back. "What about, Beth?"

Rick scowled.

"Never like to answer that one, do ya?" Tre shook his head. "Definitely not too late, you know. Not 'til you die." He cradled Schooner's gray ears in both hands and leaned in. "Hard to lose someone close, someone important to you." He eyed Rick, his voice rough. "I do miss my brother. I miss Jonathan every day. Thought it was just him and me, then you snuck through that gate at the park. Been good having you both."

"I know you miss him."

"I kept looking, though, watching. Believing I would see him again. Try to find his face, but I can only see that little girl's . . . in the dream." His hands quivered. "Guess I'll see 'em when it's time. Same might be true about Allie." Tre turned to his friend.

"I don't know how to find her either, Tre." Rick hesitated. "You carved a box for Allie, didn't you?"

Tre's head lowered in thought. "Was just like the one you and I made."

"That was a good week. You did the work, I watched."

Without notice, Tre hunched forward, focusing on his open hands in a lost stare. Rick watched, cursing silently. The retreat. The painful memory. The trigger.

In slow, deliberate motions, Tre rubbed both hands, his confused eyes transfixed, holding tightly to something not a part of him. He moved the shaking fingers to his temples, massaging. His eyes squeezed shut; his only defense against the unknown.

Rick tried to find him. "I'm glad you came back with me this evening. Fay's gonna be happy to see you. Want me to wait?"

Tre hacked and had to spit over the side. Catching his breath, he muttered, "I'll be there."

Rick nodded to the untruth. Something unrecognizable in Tre's empty expression made him pause. His voice cracked, "See you in a bit? You remember the way, right?"

Tre lifted his chin. "After I fix up the shed—and look for Allie a little while. You check with, Beth?"

Rick wavered. "I did. Just like you asked. Allie wasn't there with her."

Tre drew a hand across his stubble, then leaned over to tighten his boot laces. "Maybe the shed . . . I'll watch for her. You and Schooner go on."

Rick couldn't pull his stare away.

Tre murmured. "You need to go."

Rick dropped his head, then rose slowly and lifted Schooner to the pier. He struggled out of the skiff, balanced a hand against the piling, and looked down at his friend, needing to ask again, "Remember the way?"

Tre's eyes closed as both hands returned to his temples. Rick's arms fell slack by his side. He stalled, catching a glimpse of the island, then turned and walked slowly down the pier into the fading afternoon shadows.

Chapter 34

Rick had been gone twenty minutes before Tre began his wander around the marina, Schooner close at his side, both appreciating the slow pace. Daylight was drifting away, and the path they took showed no purpose. They strolled as old friends, enjoying the residing peace. Soon, Tre came to a stop close to the shoreline by the north pier, looking at everything. He exhaled and leaned back against the Old Man, letting his hands rest against its rough skin. The crevices in the bark still held warmth from the sun's afternoon wash—Tre let his fingers explore. The tree stretched in the breeze and creaked, sharing its abiding voice. Schooner laid down beside him, happy to curl up in his worn spot between the mounds covering two large roots. Tre gazed upriver to the island, trying to make out the heroic flag waving above his bed, as it had each day and night. He stayed in the company of the Old Man a while, smoking, waiting for the contentment he always hoped would find him to come. As his refuge disappeared into the murkiness, he leaned over to scratch Schooner's ears. The old dog wheezed, deep in sleep.

Tre left him peacefully nestled and rambled across the lot to the shed. Lingering at the side door, he tried to recall the last visit. *Had it been days or months?* He entered slowly into complete darkness, finding his way confidently to the middle of the space. Reaching out, Tre lowered himself to the old Capri bench seat and leaned over to assess the wood box. In minutes, he had a small fire burning in the stone pit just feet away.

Shadows surrounded the low flames, and Tre drifted off, feeling the presence of their lives all around him. Rick's Constellation looming on stands, the endless shelving encircling him with ages of parts, all set in place with order, purpose, honor, and remembrance. Hundreds of feet of shelving, fifteen feet high, caretakers of a generation's stories from the lives of so many boats and people. Tre leaned his head back, hearkening to the soft voices around him retelling the testimony. Resolute voices he had always relied on to shield him. He re-lit the joint, slowly inviting the inhale. A rough cough followed instantly. Echoing, dark whispers in his mind grew louder, hiding the approaching steps from somewhere. Tre drew again, and the voices faded, departing for a deeper darkness as the blow from behind landed to his head.

Schooner's face hovered over him as Tre's eyes cracked open. He lay there, lost, staring across the sagging roof deck, as the last flickering lights struggled against deep shadows. He blinked, trying to focus, aware of an ominous fear advancing, the sensing of death all around. A fierce cough racked him, and he rolled quickly to his hands and knees, retching violently. Lifting his head, he teared up, already knowing the destruction that had befallen his sanctum. From his knees, Tre peered through the faint light at the emptied shelves, parts dumped into piles, others spread as trash across the cracked concrete slab. All but a few of the shelves had been overturned, collapsed onto discarded heirlooms. He braced against the seat to stand, struggling to draw in each breath. Another cough, and the sudden pain in the back of his head forced his eyes closed. He felt for the spot and pulled back his hand; blood spread across the fingers' worn skin. Tre shuffled toward the corner of the shed, carefully placing each step to avoid crushing the smaller parts.

Two opposing shelves stood intact, the only ones he had bolted to the building's steel frame. Pushing aside a heavy bronze winch and porthole teetering on the shelf's edge, he strained to reach for the back lip of the shelf. A last stretch, and he felt it; the small wooden box had survived. He pulled it out and clutched it to his chest, rocking slowly in a dance of relief. Minutes passed before he retraced his path through the piles strewn about, unable to look down again. He faltered at the bench seat, seeing the shattered picture frame. The photo of Allie was gone. His body slumped. His fingers tapped anxiously against the carved wood frame. For a long while, he stared blankly across the seat.

Schooner nudged his leg, and Tre flinched. He turned abruptly and lumbered through the overhead door opening, pausing once outside to lean forward. His body convulsed and the pain surged. He retched, then spat, again and again to clear his throat, soon forgetting about the blood. Gradually, the pain dulled, and he lost any fear of a stranger being close by; he could envision only what lay behind him—so much of his life destroyed and lost. Tre rested an assuring hand on Schooner's head as they started for the old Owens Cruiser sitting abandoned and isolated on stands far across the lot.

~

Three mostly depleted candles sat atop the dusty settee in the Owens' salon. Tre struck a match. The pungent sulfide, the faint flame, and the dancing light all returned a sense of the comfort he had understood living on the old boat for so many years before the island called. Tre would always light candles to burn against the darkness. Tonight, he placed them in a bed of gas-soaked rags. A deep sigh followed his glance around the cabin. He recovered three joints from the small galley cabinet and moved out through the confined hatchway to the aft deck and down the wooden ladder.

Easing himself to the ground, he labored, tucking the worn cotton fatigues into his combat boots and tightening the frayed laces. Finally, he pushed up with a wince and made his way to the gate. Schooner followed close beside, casting uncertain looks every few steps. Tre turned back to the Owens, mesmerized by the faint candlelight flickering through the dusty cabin windows. Unsteady, he lit one of the joints and drew the relief quickly into his lungs, fixating on the old boat and the coming death of another distant piece of his life. The rags ignited, and an ominous, orange glow slowly brightened the glass, gripping his entire body. The haunting eerie light he knew long ago had found him.

Tre spun and staggered several steps away, then halted. He rubbed both eyes and squinted down the tracks. The night was unusually warm, and a low fog suspended everywhere. The steel rails disappeared. He moved back to the entrance and struggled to pull the battered gate closed. He yanked on the rusty lock and chain before reaching through to touch Schooner's nose.

"Thank you, friend. You go on to the shed now, go on. You'll be okay there" He shot a last look at the Owens and raised the joint, murmuring, "Rick will understand."

Tre adjusted the worn boonie, gently pulling it lower across the back to cover the gash and dried blood. He watched Schooner amble to the shed door and disappear inside. Tre's first steps away from the marina down M Street, SE were slow and deliberate. He held his head low, letting the aimless thoughts wander until they found Allie. Deep into the fog came the unmistakable rumble of his truck's decaying muffler. Tre searched the darkness and soup swallowing the narrow road ahead. Motionless, he listened. Abruptly then, he turned across the tracks and quickened his pace. He found the path and vanished into the blackness of the hill's overgrowth. He had navigated every inch of the long, meager trail a thousand times and purpose guided his steps this night. He counted each one in a mumble until clearing the brush at the crest along the edge of Barney Circle.

Tre moved directly across Southeast Boulevard, pausing to consider the length of Kentucky Avenue before him. He walked often when ashore, usually guided by fear to places of solitude; M Street, SE, or the cemetery's solemn grounds. Familiar short routes with clear beginnings and returns. Never Kentucky Avenue, though; never the two-lane thoroughfare leading only in one direction—away from all he knew. He peered into the coming hours; the walk this evening would be longer, the timing of his homecoming uncertain. Tre drew a deep, gargled inhale and began his march, holding to the south side of the empty street. He maintained a steady pace, his gaze fixed only on the landing of each next step. Forcing the journey along Kentucky Avenue this late evening, he was grateful for the fog; it blurred everything around him not of his life—colorful, well-loved houses, noble trees, the church, the park, streetlights that were not harsh or bright. Even the sidewalk, with its character revealed in the strangely irregular surface. Thankfully, this night, all of it stood shadowed by the fog; this rich life tapestry sustained by those who slept along the tranquil street. For Tre, what he recognized and shared with this passage was the quiet, the stillness; only the things he needed most to overpower sad memories and the lost image of Allie.

Chapter 35

Minutes later, Tre's truck labored down M Street, SE, grumbling in first gear. Sight distance in the fog was terrible, and Rick held his speed at ten miles an hour, coasting down the last low slope. He slowed to a crawl at the path, as always, just to check. The explosion erupted ahead without warning, and Rick's right foot landed hard on the brake. His hands clenched at the wheel, and he stiffened back against the seat, straining to see down the road toward the marina. His heart raced, watching thick smoke rise quickly above a red and orange glow. He accelerated, blinded in the surreal veil of smoke and fog. Closing on the entrance, he clicked his high beams. The bright light flashed across the padlock and heavy chain wrapping the gateposts. Stunned, he slammed the brakes again. The truck slid on gravel, stopping just feet from the entrance.

Rick stumbled out of the truck and froze, fixating across the lot. Far from the shed and other boats, the Owens cruiser listed on its stands, engulfed in flames—Rick hoped it was far enough. Helpless, he watched the blaze grow, feasting on the sixty-year-old wood. He grabbed the rusty chain-link fence, shaking it, screaming for Tre. He frantically searched the property, desperate for any sign of his friend or Schooner. Rick yanked at the gate in vain, then returned to the truck. Clutch in, he raced the engine in low gear, eyeing the weakest section of fence, certain the lock and chain would not give way. He slammed the accelerator, the engine sputtered, and then the truck lurched forward, crashing through. Rick rolled over the scrub and pulled around the shed, stopping a hundred feet from the Owens. He got out and managed only a few steps toward the heat, terrified his friend had fallen asleep aboard. He moved closer, as near as the flames would allow, crying out for Tre again.

A determined noise from behind rose above the fire's sizzle and popping. Frantic scratching against metal. Rick spun and rushed to the shed's bay door and pulled furiously on the chain. The old door rose only a couple of feet before Schooner scrambled out. The dog circled, disoriented and frightened. He hovered close as Rick continued to fight the door. The opening grew, and light and smoke from the fire snuck in. Rick's eyes adjusted and grew wide as he scanned the walls, dazed at the sinister, growing shadows. His shoulders fell in disbelief, watching the ghostly light reveal another heartbreaking scene of destruction.

~

The first fire truck arrived ten minutes later. Rick wasn't sure why. In his panic, he hadn't called. Someone from across the river or in the neighborhood above. The chain and lock had proved no deterrent for the fire department and the crew worked efficiently, but the Owens was lost. Within seconds, a blanket of water sprayed, quickly reducing the roaring fire to thick smoke and smaller flames in search of remnants.

Detective Ward's sedan skidded to a stop in front of the marina office. The driver-side door flew open, and Ward hurried toward the truck. The firefighter operating controls motioned to his captain standing upwind of the boat, then gestured to the shed. Minutes later, the detective stood in the overhead door's large opening, waving away the last billow of funneling smoke. A few feet to one side, Rick leaned against the rusty angle jamb, arms folded, his immobilized look cast across the boat's smoldering shell.

Ward coughed and walked over. He glanced at the boat. "They said you thought someone might have been asleep in there."

"A friend," Rick said quietly.

"Same friend?" Ward waited a few seconds. "He wasn't. They got a look down below. No one there."

Rick turned his lost expression to the detective. "That's good."

"Tremaine?"

"He came ashore with me this evening."

Ward nodded. "We went through the office, too: it was so close to the fire. There's no one else here. What do you think started it?"

"I don't know. Twenty-five years ago, when the tug burned, it was kids."

"Yeah, could be." Ward lowered his head and kicked some gravel. Both hands soon went to his hips, and his gaze rose across the lot. "Sorry about the timing, but I need to tell you something."

Rick folded his arms.

"It's Baxter, she's coming after you."

Rick straightened slowly. "Last night?"

"Threatening a senator. You surprised?"

"Ambivalent."

"Well, don't be, she's filing charges." Ward rubbed his jaw. "Remember asking me before if you needed a lawyer? The answer today is, yes. This is real."

"Thought I had one."

Ward shook his head. "Adrian stepped in and tried to head it off, but not this time. I don't think his magic will fly. He works for her; pretty glaring conflict of interest. I'm sorry. Again." Ward sighed. "So, any idea where Sgt. Wilson might have gone?"

Rick's reply came in a weak voice. "None."

"Maybe the island?"

"No. The skiff's out there along the pier."

Ward turned and took a couple of steps into the shed. Much of the smoke had wafted out through holes in the roof. The emergency lights flashed, blues and reds chaotically bouncing off the walls. He stood motionless, shaking his head in disbelief, the wreckage slowly becoming visible before him. His brow furrowed. "What the hell? This is how we left it?"

Rick's eyes narrowed on the Owens; the hull's few remaining frames blackened and left smoking. "This wasn't you guys."

Chapter 36

It had happened for him rarely during the war, but when he could, Sgt. Tremaine Wilson would always stop briefly to listen. A radio picking up American Forces Vietnam Network. Someone's cassette sent from home. Sometimes he got lucky and caught a single by the Impressions. Those were escapes, always fleeting ones, though. But some escape was vital, in any form. So when he couldn't listen, he would sing—quietly to himself; inflection, emotion all mastered in his focused mind. Melody and rhythm, his cherished connection to home and something he sheltered deep inside. The bridge he needed to see his way back. But when that crossing finally ushered him home, the New Jersey that awaited appeared as another foreign land; different struggles, dangerous and hateful in their own way. Reentering those first years though, the bridge shepherded Tre once more, guiding him to a place he could hide, a place far from memories of war and the unfamiliar, intruding fears.

Rick had awakened Tre early in the evening on December 26, 1999. Curtis Mayfield had passed. Tre roamed across the lot to the Old Man. He sat bundled in blankets on a stained plastic chair, the bare canopy above singing along with a feisty breeze. Rick joined, and Tre offered the joint. He turned the boom box down but stayed with the song, spellbound, hitting the high notes, nonetheless. Tre sat forward in his chair to let his shoulders sway. For hours, he backed Curtis, and then Marvin Gaye, in his own soft, mellow voice, always beckoning to Rick. The music suspended above the dark water that night. Their stares followed its drift across the river. Tre had never once taken his eyes off the island.

~

Tre followed Kentucky Avenue eight blocks, heading northwest. At 3:00 a.m., he came to the intersection at Independence Avenue and continued west. He followed Independence ten more blocks to the Capitol, arriving forty-five minutes later. Slowing his pace, he navigated the longer walkway around the south end of the Capitol grounds. A police cruiser pulled out behind him and followed slowly, staying with Tre until he passed the Capitol reflecting pool and turned away, resuming his westward march. Tre halted on the curb along 3rd Street to let the lone panel van creep by. He crossed in eerie solitude and walked to the center of the National Mall's grass median. He stalled there, extending his arms and rotating in a full, slow circle, nodding appreciation to each of the monuments, concluding with a final address bestowed on the Capitol. He pulled out the last joint and stood motionless, peering down the length of the Mall toward the Washington Monument. His eyes drifted shut with the first inhale, and his journey began again, meandering down the lawn with slower steps, his heart rate rising.

The monument towered above him as he slowed his approach along the slight grade. He pulled on the joint and continued around the lights and the flags and down the western slope across 17th Street. He moved through the center of the World War II Memorial to the reflecting pool, stopping at its edge. The Lincoln Memorial stood shrouded in thin fog across the length of slender water. He lowered his weary head, listening for stories from the granite columns encircling the Memorial behind him. Awareness of his struggling breaths suddenly intruded, and he leaned over, bracing both hands against his knees. He wobbled, nearly collapsed, then shook his head, spurning the pounding in his chest and the garbled rumbling deep in his throat. He fought to inhale and managed to straighten, then found his bearings and faced to the northwest again.

The Vietnam Veterans Memorial reposed five hundred feet away, beyond the gardens, close to Constitution Avenue. Tre searched in the direction through the dark grove of trees, sensing its presence. His memory recalled the tapering black granite; he had been there once with Adrian. Once had been enough, the image permanently etched in his mind, like every shot he took in Asia. His soul meandered through the trees, envisioning the names. He had always been able to see things of importance. Tre's eyes closed as the anguished voices scattered through the darkness. He waited, anticipating the fear, but it didn't find a way into his mind. He inhaled quickly and deeply, hesitant to welcome the contentment that seemingly found him: the peaceful embrace finally there to shield his tormented spirit and mind from the forever lurking demons.

Tre returned his look to the reflecting pool's length, soft reflections of light mirrored across the still surface. In the gentle air's embrace, he retreated to the afternoon shared long ago with Rick, the Old Man, and the music. The melody came, and his tender voice floated across the water, sharing harmonies with Marvin Gaye. With little conscious thought, he marched again, moving west along the pool's stone edging toward the Lincoln Memorial. He coughed, but his steps and singing never faltered. The rhythmic sound of his boots on the concrete walk stirred him: memories came of a similar purpose he had held long ago.

An hour later, Sergeant Tremaine J. Wilson crossed Memorial

Bridge to the welcome of an awakening, sun-filled eastern sky. Early Sunday traffic raced past, some drivers turning a curious look. Tre adjusted his hat and wiped sweat from his forehead, not realizing how slowly his steps were coming now. Around the circle and continuing west on Memorial Avenue, he watched as rays of sunlight found the Women's Military Memorial on the east-facing hill. Arlington National Cemetery opened each day at 8:00 a.m. and Tre entered first through the Visitor's Center's doors. Minutes later he strode toward the entrance gate. Tre had visited the cemetery just once, long ago, but after salutes at the gate and a welcome from the guards, he moved on, confident in his path.

Roosevelt Drive extended out before him; the long uphill grade braced his resolve but steadily diminished his body. Tre slowed for a rest halfway up, silently regarding the endless grounds and gravestones, thousands of them, all brilliantly white in the new sun. Finally returning to the incline, his steps became efforts. He pushed hard, calling his voice to song again, trying to mask the intruding thunder from his weakening heart. When he reached the top, he veered onto Wilson, sweat soaking through his shirt and hat, thankful to suddenly see the tree he would never forget. It was the Old Man, strangely now, here in this place with him. A welcoming stone bench sat under the largest branch. He moved to it cautiously, stumbling once, unable to distract his eyes from the brilliant sun and the glistening Potomac River farther to the east. After some time, he slowly twisted his surrendered body on the bench to face the tree. "Hello, Old Man," he whispered, the quiet expression of a nickname for his childhood friend: affection earned simply by virtue of him being born three months earlier. Tre reached his hand to the tree's rough skin, seeing Rick standing beside him as he always was. "You cracked, but you never broke, my friend. Thank you."

Tre turned back, beholding once again the tapestry of honor spreading across the soft grades below him. Tears started down his cheeks. *So many voices.* Beyond, the river lay quiet and still. "Allie and Beth are coming home," he murmured. "I'm good now, Sergeant Larson . . . time to take care of them."

A sudden, rasping cough bent Tre over. His hands dropped to his legs, methodically rubbing across the damp fatigues. He struggled to inhale, leaning back against the strength of the Old Man. The sun promised warmth, and he rested a while, trying to restore just enough, closing his eyes at times, never acknowledging the few passersby close behind on Porter Drive. He lowered his vacant stare to the ground for only a short time, as another deep cough suddenly forced him to stand. He rose weakly, suddenly dizzy, his hands clutching at both knees. As his fragile lungs calmed, he pulled his shoulders back and stepped lightly past several headstones, stopping at the fifth one beyond the tree. He gently pulled off the boonie, came to attention and raised a salute, holding it, fixated on the name. Dull pain crept along his left arm as he reached into the coat pocket and pulled out the small wooden box, the memory carved so long ago with a friend in New Jersey. Coaxing it open, he squinted, welcoming the stories as his fingers lightly brushed his brother's Purple Heart. Gradually, Tre lowered himself to the ground, collapsing and reaching over to place the medal on the grass that had honored the memory of Jonathan for forty-three years. The Old Man's strong branches extended above them, pulling the two brothers close again. Tre blinked his weary eyes, gazing at their breadth, seeing so many long-ago lost visions return. He didn't recoil from them, he didn't tremble. He lay still, listening to the wind begin its tease through the smaller limbs. His hand crept to his heart, and he whispered, "I'm sorry." Then he summoned his brother's voice and slowly floated away.

Chapter 37

"Thank you for letting me know, Detective." Rick ended the call with a fading voice. He lowered the phone slowly to the table and turned from the window, his gaze lost quickly across the many faces filling the room. Delia approached with his breakfast plate but hesitated setting it down. She stood next to the chair across from him, studying the unfamiliar expression. Rick rose slowly, met her searching eyes, and quietly said, "It's Tre."

She sank into the chair, holding a knowing stare on him, and reached out to his arm.

"That was Ward."

"I know," she said softly, holding a hand to her heart. She shook her head, trembling. "When we met that first time about the kitchen, there weren't a lot of unnecessary words from either of you. None, in fact, from Tre. Only the man's sincere eyes, those eyes I knew were hiding something." Delia sighed. "Early on, I saw that immovable bond between the two of you. I sensed it," she whispered. "All you had in life was each other; that was his gift to you, Richard. And to Adrian." She lifted a shaking hand to her cheek. "I'll be here. You should go be with your friend."

—

The late afternoon's air was still. The sun's soft light fell content, resting across the face of the two descending walls. Rick approached the Vietnam Veterans Memorial from the south, following the concrete and stone path along Constitution Gardens. He slowed his pace as the full breadth of its tribute came into view, staring in amazement at the brilliance across the black granite and the deep shadow filling the apex. He stopped and took it all in for the first time. For decades he had lived less than seven miles away, but he had never found his way here, to be close to it. Inhaling deeply, he continued with slower steps along the walk until he reached the end of the east wall. He stood motionless, contemplating the length of the 246-foot sheer face, thousands of names blending into one, endless, disappearing into the bright sunlight's wash. Schooner panted slowly, resting with a lean against Rick's left leg. Rick knelt, extending his hand to the smooth black stone.

"Sergeant." The deep, unmistakable voice came from behind. Rick rose with effort and turned to his friend.

Adrian stood close, slowly shaking his head as he peered along the wall's face. "We were never going to be ready for this."

"No, we weren't."

They stood side by side for minutes. The sounds of their memories drowning out the bird calls overhead, the banter from passing tourists, the relentless drum of traffic.

Adrian finally broke the silence. "Sorry I missed the call. My week for greeting at church."

"I know what your Sundays are like. I'm glad you picked up the text."

"Tried you back."

"Phone died."

Adrian gazed at the clear blue sky. "It's okay, I knew what you meant."

Rick's text to his friend two hours earlier had been short. Two words. *It's Tre.* Rick knew Adrian would understand and also knew he would come as soon as he could. Rick had invited Schooner, prepared to wait as long as needed. Together in the early afternoon's warmth, they remained motionless, almost at attention, feeling the loss of their friend as they had for many years, but in an unfamiliar way. Finality, resolution and silence for Tre. Adrian put his arm around Rick and pulled him in.

"Detective Ward let me know," Rick said. "He called at 9:30, shortly after they found him. He was at Arlington, lying next to Jonathan's grave. A woman thought he was asleep."

Adrian's sad eyes followed the length of wall. "I was hoping your call wasn't about him. Be good news about Allie for God's sake; be about the sale, anything but Tre." Adrian nodded. "That's where he belongs: Arlington, with his brother."

"Not what the man wanted, D. He and I talked about it often. Strange, how present Tre was in those conversations. Something about death, the words would bring him back. He said it was the quiet he imagined; that he'd be able to forget. When it was time, he said he would welcome it, but not there, with so many voices."

"A lot of people still out there living thanks to him."

"His way of honoring a brother's death: a buried duty he felt and the way for him to welcome his peace. Isolated pursuits of the enemy; that's how he hoped to find it."

"The man was a hero."

"Yes, he was. But that's not what he wanted either. He loved his brother. He just wanted him back."

"You know Jonathan is saying thanks: you filled his shoes for a lot of years, Rick." Adrian's large chest expanded with a deep breath. "He walked the whole way, didn't he?"

"Seems that he did. Visitor's center clocked him in at 8:15 a.m.. There's security footage."

"What a lonely, damn march. My God. The man knew what he wanted, though. I'm glad he made it there to be with him. It's good he wasn't alone."

Rick removed his sunglasses and lowered his head. "He may not have been alone before that either, D."

Adrian turned to face him.

"Ward's not so sure," Rick went on. "But he thinks there may be more."

"What are you saying?"

"Tre came back with me yesterday. More and more, he's been needing some time and space when he does. This trip, he said he wanted to look for Allie. I went to cook. At some point, he must have ended up in the shed, like always. It's what works for us now; we talk late at night when he can. I came back at 11:15." Rick hesitated, glancing away. "I came back to a boat in flames. The shed was ransacked. Tre was gone. Ward showed up soon after Fire and Rescue."

"Because of Allie?"

Rick nodded. "He stayed a while. I didn't want to wake you. When the call came in this morning after they found him, Ward said his head was opened up."

"Oh, damn."

Rick set his jaw. "Impact from a blunt object. He could have fallen and landed on something, or someone could have hit him. With anything hard; a cleat, a porthole. Maybe a gun."

Adrian pulled back. "Hit him? A gun? No damn way! That peaceful man? What the hell is Bobby talking about?"

"D, it looked like a hurricane blew through the shed. Would Tre do that? And the boat?"

Adrian reached a hand to his shoulder. "We've both wondered for a long time, where Tre's head would be when he left us. Maybe we never spoke the words, but we gave it some thought. I did." He wavered. "How would we ever know?"

Rick offered no answer.

"How was he when you saw him earlier?"

"In and out. We talked a little. Then he got lost."

Adrian sighed. "How would we ever know?"

"Ward says we won't without an autopsy." Rick paused. "That what we want for him?"

"Hell no! Is Ward pushing for it?"

"Yes, but he's leaving it up to us, even though we aren't family."

"Bullshit, we aren't family!"

"Blood."

Adrian snapped, "I know what he means, but we sure as hell shared enough of that, too! He's trying for a link between Tre and Allie."

"Probably."

"You see anything?"

"They're both kindhearted. Neither deserves the path that found them."

"No, they don't."

"They spent a couple of afternoons together. A few hours here and there. Not a lot of time, but it meant something to both of them. The detective's in our court, D. He's trying to help."

Adrian pulled his fingers across both eyebrows. "I know."

"Earlier, Ward asked me to come by when I could to identify the body. I left as soon as he hung up. He made a point of meeting me at the coroner's office to apologize. Which he did several times. Said he felt responsible, because of our last conversation. I told him not to go there. I let him know we were never going to ask Tre to leave the island. It got an understanding smile from him, and another apology."

"Bobby Ward," Adrian said, shaking his head. "He is a good man. Somewhere inside, there's a damn good man."

Rick reached into his coat pocket and pulled out the small carved box. "Ward released Tre's personal items to me. There wasn't much." He handed the box to Adrian. "Tre was holding this in his hand, across Jonathan's grave. I thought you might want to have it."

Adrian dropped his head, raising a hand to his heart. After a moment, he cradled the box in both hands and turned it gently. "The one you two carved together. Wow, that was a long time ago. Tre carved. You sanded, as I recall the story." He opened the catch, lifting the top. The Purple Heart posthumously awarded to Jonathan Wilson in 1969 lay folded neatly in the bottom. Adrian stared until tears filled his eyes. Tenderly, he closed it and handed it back to Rick.

"I'm honored, Sergeant, but this is yours. You know Tre would only trust you with his brother."

"I'll give it a good home, D." Rick twisted to face him. "Ward needs to hear from us. About the autopsy."

Adrian's quiet answer came instantly. "Let the man rest in peace."

Rick nodded. "Let the man rest in peace."

Side by side again, their sadness returned to the wall. The experience, the shape, the energy, all of it inviting reflection and tribute. Adrian wiped both eyes and rested a hand on Rick's shoulder.

"Peace, brother. Peace be with you both."

Chapter 38

Rick had left the memorial an hour ago, starting east for home but soon meandering random streets instead. He found himself on 11th Street, SE, and crawled the truck past Sarah's front porch to glance in through the windows. The living room and porch lights shone, even though the vibrant sunset had more to offer for this day, its stunning array of colors filling the western sky. Rick hoped there would be no place to park, but Sunday's afternoon activities had apparently run long for some of the residents, and more than a few choices emerged. He pulled over and shut off the engine. After stalling, sitting motionless, he rested a reassuring hand on Schooner's head, then twisted to reflect on Tre's box behind the passenger seat. His hip barked, and he sat up, drew a breath, and took his time rotating out of the truck. After three noncommittal steps, he planted himself in front of the hood, leaned back against the grille, and drifted his reflections to the west.

"I knew you might not want to come in." Sarah's quiet voice filled in beside him. She took his hand. He sensed her peering but couldn't make himself turn.

"I'm so sorry about Tre," she said softly. "It's very, very sad. I was worried about you last night. Are you okay?"

Rick's voice cracked. "It was gonna happen someday; we all die."

Sarah's head fell to his shoulder. "I can just be here with you."

Rick fixated on the vibrant sunset, its broadening splashes of deep reds and purples slowly extending their reach overhead.

"Tre would have enjoyed this," he said. "Day's end with all its color. In Vietnam, he called it the bruised sky. Anywhere else in the world, it's a beautiful sight. During the war for him, it all depended. Sometimes it would bring him a sense of peace."

Sarah squeezed his hand. The dramatic scene held them captive in silence for minutes.

She finally pulled back and said softly, "You spoke about one shot Tre wanted back—"

"I shouldn't have mentioned that."

Sarah hesitated. "Maybe you needed to."

"Maybe." Rick faltered, holding his focus to the sky. "Tre and his spotter had been waiting since early morning, positioned on a ridge above the village. It was a high-value mission and just before dusk, the target showed. But Tre said the shot felt too far. He was at the end of his second tour. They hadn't slept. His eyes were burning. The spotter said it was clean. Nine hundred yards. It was too far. A young girl crossed behind in the sight as Tre fired . . . he saw her screams."

Sarah tensed. "Oh, my God. His shot?"

"The girl wasn't hurt, she scrambled away. That target was Tre's last confirmed kill. But it wasn't over for him." Rick's eyes closed. "Few years later, the night my wife pulled away with Beth, Tre heard the scream again. My best friend and only brother disappeared the next day. It took me a year and a half to find him on a street corner in Baltimore. His nightmares had started—the girl in the village always died in his dreams." Rick sighed. "The one shot he wanted back."

Rick twisted to her, his voice fading. "That was the day Sgt. Tremaine Wilson became my life's purpose . . . and it was a good one."

Sarah's hand raised to her mouth. "Rick, I can't imagine what it must have been like for him in the war, being alone in all of that."

"An unwanted, horrible skill inhabited my friend's very peaceful soul, for some reason I have never understood." Rick bowed his head. "It's what he did, better than most, but he hated his ability and that left him hating a part of himself. He's finally free of it, though. I just don't understand why it ended now. Allie would have liked to see him again. And maybe, Beth." Rick breathed in. "Tre would have enjoyed that, too. His time with them was short, but he connected. It's what he did with people; who he was, not who he became after his brother died. He found that again with Allie. He found himself again, just like he did with Beth." Rick straightened and rubbed his neck. "Tre really wanted me to find them, but—"

"Allie isn't gone because of you, Rick. You're important to her. If she is lost, that may be what brings her home; your heart and kindness, and Tre's. Your prayer, and everything you shared when she needed it."

Rick mumbled, "It's been a while, Sarah. Last time I prayed was that night driving to Baltimore."

She reached for his hand again. "I know you want to do more, but that might be all we have. And it may have to be enough."

Rick searched her expression briefly, then returned his gaze to the inspiring sky. Nothing had dimmed. The colorful expanse had only broadened.

"Tre's bruised sky," he whispered.

Sarah nodded. "It's humbling. Nature overwhelming us as she likes to do sometimes. Makes you wonder how it could not be something more."

"Tre did wonder. And often." Rick shook his head. "He

certainly would have enjoyed this." His voice faded. A moment later, he cleared his throat and stepped away from the grille. He fumbled to pull the keys out of his pocket.

Sarah reached for his hand. "Do you want to stay? Would you?"

"Schooner," came his answer. "Thank you, I should go. I have some things to clean up."

"I could help."

Rick leaned close and kissed her gently. "You have." He took his time moving around the front of the truck, finally stopping and looking back at her. "Sarah, I'm sorry about your sister."

Chapter 39

The chilly wind blew out of the east later that night, square across the port side of the old Trumpy and hard enough at times to make the bow and stern lines protest against the strain. Rick managed a comfortable position for his task. *MORNING STAR's* engine room was cold. Musty smells of old age from the hull's wood and a few seeping engine fittings pervaded the still air. A half hour ago, just after 11:00 p.m., Rick had fallen asleep on the frayed office couch. Twenty minutes later, the monitoring alarm had sounded on his remote. The Trumpy's emergency bilge pump.

Rick cupped his cold hands and blew as he assessed. So much for spring's arrival—he had been too eager. He crossed to the panel and flipped the space heater back on. The temperature in the cramped engine room steadily rose to forty-five degrees. Access for the bilge wasn't bad. He lifted the first floor board and sighed. The river could always find a pathway in; that was the nature of old wooden boats, but not on *MORNING STAR*. Rick contemplated the thin layer of dark water, weighing the options if he waited for daylight to trouble-shoot the other pumps—only a couple more hours and the emergency pump should be fine. His hands voted, already achy and stiff from the chill. He mumbled in disbelief at having to deal with low temperatures again in March. Focused and growing irritated, he didn't hear the approaching steps across the well-worn sole. He sensed a presence, though, and twisted to his right. Ben Sheridan stood between the two big diesels seven feet away.

"Kind of cold and late for an old man to be down in the engine room," Ben said.

Rick cleared his throat. "Wait 'til you get my bill this month."

"Need a hand?"

"That's Allie's greeting." Rick caught himself, immediately wanting the words back. *The damn cold.* He rubbed his hands and looked up at Ben.

"I know it is," he said weakly. "Can we talk?" Ben shuffled, casting distracted glances around the crowding mechanics.

Rick studied his face. "Gimme a minute." He returned all concentration to the task and reached into the cold water to confirm the depth. Assured, he struggled to his feet and followed Ben through the narrow door.

Ben switched on the small lamp sitting on the galley counter, its soft light barely revealing a man across the salon by the door. Rick noticed and turned to Ben, who promptly nodded in his direction. The man left silently through the door.

Rick stepped to the settee and settled on the end, still wiping the oily water off his hands, and checking for grease. He stretched out his leg, wincing.

"How's the arthritis?"

Rick frowned.

"Scrunched up in that cold bilge can't be good for it."

"Among other things. Just waiting for the warm weather. I hope this visit is good news."

Ben pivoted away.

Rick watched his pained expression drift around the boat.

"Just look at her." Ben said quietly. "This joinery, the paneling, the furniture." He shook his head. "Quite a pedigree, this family history of mine. Allie and I have always shared a deep devotion to her, and I swore we would never let *MORNING STAR* go. I promised to keep her just as she was sculpted in 1965, so we could hold onto that connection." Ben's voice cracked. "I treasure this boat, Rick, and I never doubted trusting her to you. Or my daughter." He drew a breath, running both hands through his hair.

"Do you know how many hotline tips we get each day? People hawking the reward?"

"I'm sure it's a lot." Rick took a moment. "That must be agonizing, Ben. Any of them credible?"

"How can you know?" Ben wandered again, slowing to brush his fingers along the varnished framed windows. "I have more people chasing them down and searching for her than the FBI." He paused. "There was one, a text from a burner phone. All it said was: 'She's safe.'"

"Just to you?"

"Michelle hasn't mentioned a thing. My instincts wanted to believe it."

"It's something, Ben. It's good. Believe it."

Ben stared through the window at reflections across the river. "There hasn't been anything else. I guess I have to."

"Yeah, I do, too."

Ben leaned back against the couch. "You know, Allie understood she had become a challenging, only child. She told me often. Of course it wasn't her fault."

"She told both of us, Ben. It was something I had always been impressed she could express."

Ben smiled. "Doesn't surprise me she told you. You've been here for her, Rick, and I never thanked you for that. You were the voice she needed. I wasn't around. Michelle wanted nothing to do with her, and that's being kind. That may have been what chased her away." He lowered his head. "Did I lose her?"

"It feels like it. I know that panic. Don't let it—"

"You went to Maine! My God, Rick! You saw your daughter . . . looking for mine." Ben looked away. "I can't imagine. Thank you for trying."

"Was following Tre's intuition. I wish he'd been right. But there was nothing there. For either of us." Rick pushed off on both knees and stood. "Allie will be home soon, Ben, and you two will be okay. It will take time, but you've got that. It's important to be there for her. Everything slips by, and reaching for it then is—"

"You know she'll come here," he blurted. "To you. It's where she feels safe. She won't come home. There's no trust for Michelle. Maybe less for me. I understand that now."

"If she doesn't come home to Georgetown, it won't be because of you. Believe me."

"If she doesn't, I need you to promise me something."

"Of course you'll be the first," Rick said.

Ben's lips flattened as he took a last slow look around the boat. "Allie's grandparents celebrated their sixtieth anniversary right here." With outstretched arms, he moved into the center of the salon. "Allie was eight. Her mother had died the year before." He rotated peacefully, taking it all in as if for the first time. "This boat kept us together: she mended some of it for us. This is what Allie will come back to."

A small gust suddenly blew against the hull and the Trumpy heeled slightly. They listened to the wind and the whistling, creaking conversation between the two.

"It will be soon," Rick said.

"Yeah, let's hope. I pray you're right." Ben's arms fell limp at his side. "It's late. I should go. Sorry my boat woke you up."

"Glad the baby monitor worked."

"Thanks for not letting her sink."

~

The man picked up in front of Ben and Rick as they stepped off the boarding walkway. He led them down the pier, staying thirty feet ahead. They walked side by side, saying little. The Land Rover sat idling in the darkness, no lights. A black SUV was positioned ten feet behind. Kate came around the front of the car, offering a sympathetic smile to Rick as she opened the door. Ben stalled, gazing across the marina yard. An eerie glow filled the overhead door opening; lights striving somewhere deep within. The blackened skeleton of the Owens sat alone in the shadows.

"I know what he meant to you, Rick. Allie cared for Tre, too. He appreciated all you did for him. I hope you know that."

"We helped each other for a long time." Rick's eyes landed on the shed, envisioning the crushing disarray spread out just inside.

"Ward told me," Ben said. "We can get you some help with all this."

"We'll see. The police need time to check it over. But thanks. Every day this hip tells me to move south. I may take you up on that offer."

"Rick, I'm going to the house in Massachusetts for a while. Tonight, before the weather. More than one reason, but mainly—I don't know, Allie may feel she needs to be there." Ben's voice faded. "It's a hope."

Rick nodded. "I think that's good, Ben."

"If it's okay, I'd like to have some people stay close. A few times a day, and some nights. Just a little company for you around here, in case my first intuition is the right one." He extended his hand.

Rick took it, shaking slowly. "I understand, Ben. Whatever you need."

~

Rick hadn't even tried to sleep. After Ben left, he spent a restless hour on the old couch in the office, fixated on the wood panel ceiling, following in step with Tre along his march through the city to Arlington. Shortly after midnight, the new day had called him to the water's edge. Rick leaned against the Old Man's rough skin in the quieting breeze, sharing the favorite spot with memories of his friend. Tre always loved to describe the sounds of the river. Something on the surface or below was perpetually moving, he would say, and with that would come the music of the water. Patiently, Tre would wait for the next new splash or gurgle along the rocks or simply the stillness. Silence was the sound he enjoyed most. For hours that night, Rick gratefully received the Old Man's embrace, listening for the voices of them both, envisioning how much Tre would have savored this evening; the calm, the quiet, the darkness.

Just after 3:00 a.m., Rick started across the dark lot toward the shed, thinking he might work for a while and restore some order in honor of his friend. Distraction. He wouldn't use a ladder, just the things he could reach along the shelves from the slab. Rick needed sleep, days of sleep, but he couldn't imagine closing his eyes right now. He walked slowly, allowing time for a change of heart. Schooner held close by his side as they approached the opening. The bright moon peeked from behind fast-moving clouds, casting a hazy wash of light across the failing metal panels. The shed's spent overhead lights had finally surrendered, with Tre, and the huge dark opening loomed above, a black hole in the middle of the old building's faintly illuminated skin. Rick wavered in front of the entrance, peering into the darkness left to shelter this enduring piece of Tre's life. Rick was only able to stare though; the motivation to move, not finding him, only a peaceful desire to look at it all and enter the past. Tired, Schooner hobbled straight to the bench seat and sprawled across, holding his attention on Rick momentarily before yielding to sleep.

The three flags above Rick's head hung motionless; the wind had finally calmed. The U.S. flag, POW/MIA, and Tre's self-designed pennant each appeared immovable in the still air, fixed against the building, seemingly as rigid as the rusty metal panels. The moon disappeared behind clouds as Rick looked to the centered black flag. The weak light above the door flickered. Twice it went out, then seconds later reappeared, casting again what faint light it could. The light disappeared a third time. Darkness took the flag away. Rick watched the tired old fixture. After a while, the bulb flickered back to life. He tilted his head slightly. *How could it not be something more?* "Goodnight, my brother," he said quietly. "Wasn't ready for you to go."

Schooner's eyes peeked as Rick walked to the old Capri bench seat to join him. He grabbed some branches from Tre's ever-ready pile, lit the fire, and eased himself down into the well-worn leather. The area around the bench was always reserved for important pieces of Tre's order. He would only surround himself with things that held deep meaning: his boombox earned a spot, a box of tapes next to it, Schooner's water bowl, an unopened bottle of Jack Daniels, and the cherished framed selfie Allie took of them. With all of this close, Tre had found some interludes of comfort and security; sitting for hours alone most times, with the huge door open to offer an exit for the smoke. He would sit and watch the passage of time, headphones on, leading him to an escape, brief glimpses of well-deserved contentment.

When the two of them shared time together, Rick would usually take the only chair across the pit from him. Tonight, he settled into Tre's spot on the worn bench seat, gazing through the opening as the moon reemerged and suspended peacefully above the river. Rick reached over to hit the play button, anxious to surrender into remembrances, anxious to hear Tre's voice in the music. *Heard it Through the Grapevine* came loudly through the speakers. Rick leaned back, sensing Tre's harmony floating lightly above. He opened the bottle of Jack Daniels and laid it down on the slab to empty. The bourbon flowed intently into the webbing of cracks across the concrete slab and soon disappeared. Rick reached a soft hand to rest on Tre's shattered picture frame and stared out across the world they had shared.

Chapter 40

An hour later, Rick stood motionless in the middle of the entrance drive, once more surveying the flattened section of fence collapsed across the wooden entrance sign. His tired eyes landed on the gate panels, lying twisted and torn from their top hinges. The fire department had seen no other choice. Rick sighed and called for Schooner. They crossed M Street, SE, and stepped tentatively, side by side, along the tracks, stopping at the path entrance. The day's first light would not show across the eastern horizon for another hour. Rick considered waiting, but Schooner dropped his nose and explored, quickly disappearing into the brush. Rick hesitated, then relented, trusting the old dog's vision in the dark. In the overlaying heaviness of vines and branches, the remembrance came to him instantly: the day long ago when he and Tre had hacked and pulled at the brush all the way up, creating their imagined and needed short-cut to civilization atop the hill. When Rick emerged minutes later, Schooner lay waiting. They followed Southeastern Boulevard a hundred yards to Pennsylvania Avenue and took a slow pace west along the quiet sidewalk.

Trinity Cathedral was dark, save for the few random solar lights along the property's brick walkways. Rick lifted the loose flagstone for the key and opened the kitchen door. Two ceiling lights remained on, providing sufficient light to navigate around the tables and equipment. The parish hall doors stood open, and Rick and Schooner moved down the large hall in darkness, crossing to the opposite side where a single door opened to the sanctuary corridor. Rick tried the first pair of doors, quietly coaxing the stubborn knob. Schooner entered tentatively, then ambled off to explore the aisles. Rick took the three steps leading to the altar. A lone candle shone in a wall-mounted lantern just left of the reredos. The carved wooden piece filled the altar's rear wall, rising full height to the coffered ceiling.

Rick reached into his pocket and pulled out Tre's small box. He opened it and the faint light found Jonathan Wilson's Purple Heart, the medal that had marshaled Rick and Tre on their journey long ago. In his other hand, Rick clasped Tre's Silver Star. Breathing deeply, he relaxed his hold and bowed his head to gently kiss the star. "For Valor, my friend," he whispered. Memories gripped him in honoring silence a moment. Finally, he placed the medal inside the box with his brother's. Closing it in goodbye, his fingers explored the texture of each side, recalling the nights in New Jersey and the pain in Tre's concentration as he chiseled and smoothed the resting place for this tribute to his brother. Unmoving, Rick cradled the box in both hands. He fixated on the reredos' exquisite carving, mesmerized by the candlelight's gentle wash across the recesses of the wood. Soon, he moved across the altar to a gold-plated pedestal positioned next to the communion rail, where he set the box down gently on a felt lined collection plate. Turning back to the center of the altar, he inhaled deeply, filling his lungs with the musty aroma of the altar's centuries old wood. An image of Tre and Fay in energetic discussion brought a deep sigh as he turned and crossed to the first pew. He lowered slowly and stretched out along the lumpy cushion to rest for just a while, clearing his mind in welcome to all of the memories.

Schooner licked his forehead again, and Rick stirred, his eyelids cracking slightly. The room was awakening from darkness. The large stained glass windows along the sanctuary's length had started their celebration of the first light. Highlights of deep color glowed across each recess. Rick's eyes crept open, startled by the faint image before him.

Allie stood close to the pew, her long hair pulled over one shoulder, both arms wrapped tightly around her middle. Beth held back several feet, her hands clasped at her waist, her legs and feet shuffling in small, restless movements. Rick imagined it all as a curious dream, and he too quickly pushed up to stand. Lightheaded, he reached for the end of the pew to balance. His disbelief faded as Allie threw her arms around his neck and let her face hide against his shoulder. Rick surrendered to the relief, then pulled back gently. Allie's moist eyes met his.

"I missed your words of wisdom," he said, hesitating. "How—"

"I remembered where you hid the key," Allie said nervously. "I didn't know where else to go. We went to the marina. I thought *MORNING STAR* would be safe, but the gate and fence were crushed. Are you okay, Rick?"

He shook his head slowly. "Where have you been?"

Allie looked at Beth.

Rick caught the expression and turned to his daughter. "You didn't tell me?"

Beth held a long, firm glare on him. "I don't know you," she said impassively. "The word father doesn't make you less of a stranger to me. Do you think I was going to hand over a frightened young girl?"

Rick's mind drifted to the pain, leaving him with blank looks back and forth between them. "Then—why are you here now?"

Allie reached for his arm and turned him.

"Beth told me about Tre." Her expression pleaded. "I wanted to see him. I need to."

Rick glanced at Beth, then reached for Allie's shoulders. "Allie, I'm sorry. Tre died." He struggled finding the next words. "Just yesterday . . . he's gone."

Allie's hands raised to her face as tears started down both cheeks. She slumped to the pew, casting a solemn stare through the dim light toward the altar. Beth shifted away, squeezing her eyes shut and dropping her head. Silence settled around them for a while.

"Tre was part of our family," Beth finally murmured. "But this isn't about us, Rick. There's more." She drew a deep breath and faced him. "We need a place to talk. All of us."

Rick watched her tremble, envisioning the struggle for control against exhaustion and sadness.

Beth's expression hardened. "When you're finished here, we'll be waiting outside."

Allie labored to stand, and they moved toward the aisle.

Rick hurried after them. "Beth, wait. I don't know how to say this, but—this isn't Maine, and I'm a person of interest in all of this. Keep Allie covered up."

Beth stepped close, scowling. "No shit, it's not Maine. We spent almost three days getting down here: hiding and driving in the dark. Somebody's been tailing us, Rick! Somebody's after her, and I don't think it's her parents." She spun away, taking Allie's hand. "Thanks for the heads up."

Chapter 41

Beth leaned back against her chair as Delia returned to Rick's corner table carrying three plates overflowing with eggs, sausage, waffles, and fruit. She made room to set them down, then straightened, taking a second for eye contact with each. Ignoring the tension, she leaned over to hug first Allie, then Beth, as she had done on each of her three previous trips to their table. She rested on this one, though, a hand on each of their shoulders.

"It's nice to have you both here and safe." She winked at Rick. "And a happy day for you, my friend."

Delia pulled back, focusing on Allie and shaking her head. "I can't believe you're here: you gave us quite a scare, young lady. Thank you, Beth, for everything. For being with her."

Beth managed a weak smile. Allie nodded and started to eat slowly.

"Hmm, not morning people, I see. I'll get some more coffee." Delia raised her eyebrows at Rick as she turned away.

"Delia is lovely," Beth said impassively. "I can imagine she's a big part of why this has been home for so long."

The time Delia spent in the kitchen making them breakfast had been enough for Allie to share her nightmare of the last two weeks. She struggled, though, her hands shaking immediately as she began, her head lowered. Beth filled in when Allie's voice cracked, recalling the man who followed her in Maine and the tail through Brooklyn. She studied her father's reaction, not knowing what to expect as Allie unfolded the frightening details. What she feared in him was the rage her mother had recounted: a haunted expression she could still imagine. Beth had no other expectations of what the anger would look like, but nothing resembling the story of her past appeared. Her father's manner presented an implausible calm, holding his attentive eyes on Allie, only occasionally and briefly glancing at Beth.

Rick dropped his gaze, reached for his fork and poked at the untouched eggs and sausage. "The police have been searching for Allie. The FBI is involved, and who knows how many people Ben Sheridan has out there. He's in pain, Beth, and you didn't let anyone know? Has Allie been with you the whole time?" His look of disapproval darted back and forth between them.

She turned away as Allie started, "Rick, I'm eighteen now. I get to make my own decisions."

He leaned back, shaking his head. "That's not the world you live in, Allie."

"I'm not going back to that house!"

Beth leaned forward on both elbows. "What she told me about family life, Rick, doesn't sound like such a safe place. Kind of hit some buttons for me."

Rick met her stare. "Like you said, Beth, this isn't about you, or us. It's about her. And *her* being missing gets a lot of attention. You let her stay because you hated me? I'll try to understand, but that didn't help anyone."

Beth scowled. "So, you've decided to try parenting after all."

Allie cut in, pleading. "Rick, Beth talked to me the next day. She said I needed to come back right away. She tried, but I begged her for some time, just to be away from it all. She didn't know everything that had happened." Allie pushed her plate aside and leaned in close to him, her hands clenched together. "But Rick, it's

Baxter. I can't go back. Not to her. Believe that. I won't."

"Allie, what about Ben? Why didn't you try to reach him?"

"No!" Allie jerked back. "Baxter will find out! Then she'll know. She's not good, and he can't stop her."

"It's not always going to be good, Allie, but running isn't the—"

Beth slammed her glass down. "Dammit! Sometimes it's the only answer!" She dropped her head instantly and stiffened. "This last week, judge me if you want—"

"It's not you, Beth, her family; they're anxious and frightened."

"Forgive my cynicism Rick, and for not having the faith in family that you apparently do, *now*. Congratulations. Ironically, it's good to see you care about something."

"Beth—"

"I hope Allie has gained some benefit from the time she spent with you. But again, cynicism clouds my thinking. I have no idea what that benefit might look like." Beth leaned back and crossed her arms, turning her impatience on Allie. "Maybe you can tell me—"

Allie thumped her fists, shaking the table. A glass teetered and fell, shattering on the floor. "Stop it!" she cried. "Both of you!"

Delia came through the kitchen door and approached, resting her hand on Rick's shoulder. "Everything okay?" She glanced around the table.

"No, it's not! Tre's dead!" Allie's voice faded. "He's dead." Her frightened look darted to Rick. "It had been two days since Evans . . . I didn't know what to do. I stood on the pier screaming, seeing you pull away. You couldn't hear me. Schooner didn't hear me." She trembled. "I was so cold out there."

Rick and Beth traded quick looks. He reached over and laid his hands on Allie's, holding them tightly.

"Allie, you're safe now—"

She yanked away and pulled a forearm across her face, wiping away the last tears in defiance. She drew a fast breath as her eyes narrowed on the center of the table. "I want to kill him."

Beth stared, unblinking. Allie sent both of them cold looks and abruptly pushed back from the table. Beth reached for her arm, but Allie jerked away and broke for the diner's service door into the alley. Rick shot up out of his chair to follow.

~

The alley door slammed back on its hinges. Rick stepped through and checked both directions. He spotted Allie running toward 8th Street. An instant later she cut the corner heading south and disappeared. Rick hobbled to the end of the alley and turned after her. Fifteen minutes later, he limped along a boxwood hedge in the small park a block away. Allie sat on a wooden bench in the corner, far from the old swings and slide. Rick approached slowly and stopped two feet in front of her, waiting for an okay. Allie slid over, and he joined her. Soon, her head was on his shoulder.

"I'm sorry I didn't hear you that night," he said quietly. "I'm sorry you were alone."

Allie's body rested limp against him, her vacant expression cast across the park.

Rick put his arm around her. "You're safe. It's time to get you home."

"I was serious, Rick. I'm not going back there."

"We have to call Ben, and he has to call the police. But he knows that."

"I know," she mumbled, straightening to lean back. "I miss Tre. I miss him for you." She laid her hand gently on his arm. "That first day he and I met, you brought him to the marina and introduced me as someone he needed to know. I won't ever forget that."

Rick leaned forward, resting both elbows on his knees. "He was an amazing friend, and a great man who got lost."

"He taught me to appreciate things, in just those few times we saw each other. About life and friendship. Not so much with what he said—he never talked that much—just being with him, and the way he would focus on you. When he did get started though, it was always about his best friend; you, and his brother." She shared a slight smile with Rick. "I loved his big, friendly eyes. He said he could see things others couldn't."

Rick nodded, scanning the patches of hopeful grass sprinkled across the park. "Tre was the one who knew how to find you, Allie. He saw where you were."

They heard the giggle and shifted to watch a mother follow her toddler to the swings.

Rick caught Allie's expression soften.

"You never saw what was in the bag," she said. "The gift he made me."

He turned to her. "No, I didn't."

"The most beautiful box. Tre carved it. So small and delicate. It was just like his, one he made for himself a long time ago. He said it was only for special things, and he showed me where he kept his in the shed. He said it would always be safe there. That night I ran, I left mine for him to find. Next to his on the shelf. The special thing was my mother's ring; I wore it every day since she died." Her head lowered. Both fists clenched in her lap. "I hit him hard, Rick. And I would again. The ring has Chris Evans' blood on it. I wanted it to be safe, next to Tre's." Her breath paused. "Until you both could help me clean it."

Rick rested a hand on her shoulder. "Tre would have made it look like new, and it's still safe, Allie. I promise Evans won't ever hurt you again."

The toddler's shriek startled them, capturing their attention again. Grinning in the seat, his chunky legs swayed with the motion. Rick envisioned Allie in the Old Man, her feet just above his head. Allie's lost gaze followed the steady arc of the swing. She inhaled deeply with each descending creak of the rusty chains; paced breaths Rick could hear.

Her words finally came in a low, distant voice, "No, he won't. Not if someone kills him first." She twisted to Rick, glaring with an unrecognizable force. "Tre also taught me how to hold a gun. I'm not going home."

~

Beth stood at the window, peering along 8th Street toward the park. Delia came up behind her and put an arm around her waist. Beth sighed, watching Rick and Allie cross the street. She envied their slow walk, the girl's connection with another father; the bond she never had experienced for herself. In all the stories Allie had shared with her about Rick, not once did she falter in expressing trust in him. Two lives touched in very different ways along this same man's lonely journey. Imaginings flashed through Beth's mind as she watched them approach, but she only witnessed the quiet resoluteness; Rick would protect this young woman. Whether intended or not, he was showing his daughter the kind of father he could have been.

Delia squeezed and Beth turned to her.

"It's been a horrible time for Allison Sheridan," Delia said.

"It's such a tragedy. It always is."

"Was hard for you, too, sweetie."

Beth's moist eyes drifted around the diner. "Allie wanted to see Tremaine so much. I did, too, in a way. But maybe it's better just having the warm stories of him to surprise me at times. My mom said he was a tender man who provided both of us a lot of comfort while Rick tore our lives apart. All these years, I could never comprehend the source of Tre's affection, but I do remember feeling his kindness in the midst of our nightmare. I hope I seemed grateful. It wasn't until Rick sat there on my patio and told me Tre was sick that I imagined seeing something; an understanding for the first time." Beth lowered her head. "Tre's horrifying tours of duty: he hid the anguish from us at home behind the tenderness—for as long as he could."

"A young man with an old soul," Delia said softly.

"Is that what I felt in his hugs?"

"Of course. Tre was there the night you both ran, facing that fear and rage destroying his best friend, and knowing his family had to escape."

Beth's voice cracked. "Years later, my mother shared Tre's last words as we pulled away: *He would always protect Rick and do anything to save him.*" She turned to the window. "Did Tre save him for Allie?"

Delia's shoulders fell. "You know I have pain in my heart for both of you."

Beth looked past her. "Allie needs the comfort. I hope she can get it."

"I'm not sure who that is now, hopefully her dad. Forget the senator. Richard was that someone for her these past two years." Delia hesitated. "I'm sure that sounds strange; it's not what you had from the man. I know who he was that long time ago: I heard, from him and from Tre when he'd talk. No child should have to go through that."

"The damn war," Beth mumbled, wondering if she would believe the words.

Delia wavered, watching her. "Your father needed help, Beth, but he couldn't push through the sadness. We all tried, but Richard wouldn't budge. Every ounce he had was going to his dear friend. End of story. So, *damn war* is right. The poor man still hears things from his time there. He won't say what and it's not often, far as I know, but when it happens—the rush of it all grips him again and he feels like he can't get there in time to help." Delia nodded knowingly. "It's what your father lived too many times in the war, and he still endures the panic."

"Is that our real demon to blame?"

"It takes people away. Some die, some still live, but they've gone away just the same." Delia reached for her hand. "But if you let him, maybe he's ready to find his way back."

Beth raised a hand to her mouth as Rick and Allie entered the alley.

Delia tilted to find her eyes. "And maybe he already did." She smiled. "Maybe Tre saved him for both of you."

~

Rick held the trash bag for Delia as she dropped the last empty water bottle in. She leaned across the front seat for a last look through the car.

"Wanna make it so nice for you both," she called out, pulling a couple of old French fries out from under the driver's seat.

Allie had crawled in back and was out, her head leaning against the side window.

Delia moved close to Beth and Rick. "Allie's already asleep," she said. "This is too much for her. You both need some rest." She held the keys out.

Beth scowled at Rick. "Is this absolutely necessary? I have the rental!"

"Let's play it safe. There are a lot of people desperate to find her. There may be a few looking for you, too. Rental or not, they may have your plates and know your car. I'm sorry you're involved, Beth."

"Save it! I can take care of myself. I want this shithead in jail, for Allie."

"Sarah said come whenever you're ready." Rick balked. "You'll like her, and you'll be safe there."

Beth's voice raised. "Doesn't all of this seem a little ironic to you: me hiding out at your girlfriend's place?"

Rick let the comment go. "It won't be long. If I had a better option—"

"Forget it," Beth snapped. She folded her arms and glared.

Delia let a few seconds pass before dangling the keys.

Beth shook her head and finally reached out. "Thank you, Delia. Thanks for both of us." She spun to Rick. "Tell me something, though, why aren't I taking her home? Why aren't *we* taking her home? They can get her to a doctor and call the police. It's pretty clear in my mind, that's the next rational step."

"You don't know Senator Baxter." Rick drew a deep breath. "The mid-term elections are next—"

"Elections!" Beth cried. "Are you kidding me?" She stepped closer to him "Fuck the mid-term elections! Did you really just say that?"

"She's not in Allie's corner, and that's significant. And Chris Evans, the guy who attacked her—"

"Raped her, Rick! My God, you should say the word. He tried to rape her!" She shook her head, her voice trailing off. "And maybe he did."

"Beth, he's after her, and not on behalf of the family. We don't know what might put her in danger, or both of you."

"Oh, please." Beth waved off the concern.

"We agreed on getting to her dad first. Quietly. I'm calling him as soon as you two are safe at Sarah's. Ben Sheridan should be the first to decide what happens next. You both need some rest. Take the offer and let me get ahold of him. You heard Allie; she's not going back. The wrong call, and I think she could be gone again."

"What?"

Rick stalled, checking the back seat. Allie slept soundly, but he stepped away from the car and waited for Beth to come near.

"In so many words," he whispered. "Allie said she wants Evans dead. A few minutes ago, she told me Tre showed her how to use a gun and—"

"Stop!" Beth's hand flew up. "I've heard too many of these stories! The shattered lives, the scars! Who should I hate more, Allie's attacker or the father who destroyed our family?" Beth seethed. "I don't blame, Allie. I would feel the same."

Delia moved close and reached a hand to her arm. "Beth, please."

Beth backed away. "As I mentioned to Delia, this is trauma, Rick! The word may shock you or make you nervous. That doesn't surprise me."

Beth stepped between them abruptly and got in the car. She twisted to check on Allie, then accelerated down the alley. She braked hard to a stop at 9th Street, clutched the wheel, and forced herself to look in the rear-view mirror. Rick stood centered on the broken pavement, staring after them. Beth squeezed her eyes shut, fighting off the imminent memory: watching her father disappear behind them into the dark as her mother sped away. Her head fell as tears streamed, just as they had that night long ago.

Chapter 42

They arrived at Sarah's at 3:00 p.m. and found a spot halfway down the block. Beth surveyed the street as she called over the seat to wake Allie. Out of the car quickly, they hurried along the sidewalk and slipped inside. The first-floor curtains were already closed. After exhausted introductions and pleasantries, such as they were, Sarah encouraged Allie to take the first-floor bedroom. Allie's silent smile was all the thanks she could summon. She crashed quickly, clothes on, lying across the bed, sound asleep again in seconds. Sarah pulled the door gently and offered Beth a room upstairs if she needed rest as well. Beth had a drink in mind, and Sarah happily volunteered to keep her company. Deciding on jackets and the screened-in porch, they eased the sliding door closed and settled into comfortable wicker chairs in the corner. Sarah opened the wine and poured Beth a full glass.

They sat in silence for minutes, absorbed in the late afternoon's softening light.

"Awkward," Beth finally said, gazing into her glass. "You're involved with a man I should know but never did."

Sarah leaned close and reached for Beth's hand.

"I feel like there's a lot you could probably share with me. About who he is."

Sarah held back until Beth looked up. "My dad died when I was twelve." She paused. "Whatever the reasons for a father being gone, it's never easy to understand, no matter how old we are."

"No, it isn't," Beth said softly. "I'm sorry."

"I am, too."

"How much of it has he told you?"

"A lot."

"The drinking?"

Sarah nodded. "I know there's more. I just don't know how much more."

"It would scare you to hear everything."

"A lot of what he told me is difficult to believe, but I do. I've seen it up close in my own family. I know it must have been horrible for you."

Beth stared into her glass. "It still is, and it *would* scare you, Sarah." Beth turned to her. "You and him, are you sure you want to do this?"

Sarah tilted her head. "I haven't seen that person in him."

Beth shifted to face her. "By all appearances, you're an accomplished woman, Sarah." Successful, likely intuitive—"

"That's very nice of you. But the generous attributes you imply have in no way precluded me from making bad decisions involving damaged men." She hoisted both hands in confession. "I'm not perfect, Beth, and I've *known* damaged men. My ex-husband became one of them."

"Sarah, I didn't mean to—"

Sarah brushed it off with a gesture. "It's fine. Thank goodness for choice." She sipped her wine. "The damage Rick inflicted, I believe he regrets it with his entire being. The tragedy humbled him, Beth, but his world was already gone. I think his heart's just been waiting."

"Waiting for what?"

"For you, of course."

Beth quivered and hurried another sip. Sensing Sarah's earnest look, she dropped her head a moment. Finally, in a quiet voice, she said, "Maybe he's been waiting for you."

Sarah sighed. "Maybe for both of us."

Beth raised a hand to her cheek. "Has he ever mentioned me?"

"Once." Sarah set her glass on the table. "It wasn't easy for him. He couldn't say much, and he didn't need to. I saw his affection for you, Beth, and I know he wanted it all back. He's always wanted you back."

~

At 7:20 p.m., Beth went back inside to check on Allie. She opened the bedroom door slowly with an invitation to join them in a few minutes for carryout. Beth switched on the light and froze, stunned to find the bed empty. She scanned the room, pushing aside her panic. She tried the closet, then hurried into the hall. She yanked open the door to a dark bathroom and slammed it shut just as quickly. Her heart raced as she called out to Allie in a cracking voice. She remained still only seconds to listen, then pulled out her phone, dialing as she moved through the other rooms on the first floor.

Sarah stood at the kitchen island assembling place settings. She heard Beth's next fearful shout for Allie and rushed to the living room. Beth stood by the front window dialing again.

"C'mon, Rick!" Beth said, anger and plea filling her expression. She met Sarah's stare across the room. "I think she's gone!"

"I'll look upstairs." Sarah rushed away.

Beth paced the room, clenching her phone, fixated on the screen. "Allie!" she screamed. She dialed again, twisting anxiously as Sarah came down the stairs shaking her head.

"The window?" Beth said.

"Bars outside. It had to be the front door. She must have known we wouldn't hear."

Beth bolted through the storm door and onto the porch, following a sudden image of Allie rocking peacefully in a chair. She scrambled down the steps to the sidewalk, frantically searching in both directions along the street, still holding the phone to her ear, trying for the fifth time.

Rick finally answered. "Are you okay?" he said quickly.

Beth shrieked, "Where the hell have you been? Why didn't you pick up?"

"Trying for a little sleep. Probably like you and Allie—"

"No, not like Allie! Allie's gone!"

The anger came fast. Rick knew she was already blaming him. For all of it. "What do you—"

"She's gone! I don't know where!"

"When?"

"Dammit, Rick! Sometime in the last half hour! She was asleep. We were getting food, and then she was gone!"

"Beth—"

"Where's her Goddam father, Rick? Tell me you called him. Tell me!"

Rick fumbled for words. "He's on his way. But weather has Logan delayed. Most of the northeast. It just missed us and—"

"I don't give a damn about the forecast!"

"Beth, if he can't find another option, he's driving. He gave me an address to meet him."

Beth's shoulders sagged as she leaned back against a parked car. She shook her head, letting it fall, instantly lost in the streetlight reflection across the damp pavement. "What the hell is all this," she muttered, restraining an urge to attack him again. "What is going—"

"Call me back! Five minutes."

The call ended abruptly, leaving Beth to stare blankly down the street again.

~

Rick sprung up and grabbed his boots. Schooner got only a minute outside to find his spot, while Rick rushed to fill the food bowl. He hurried Schooner back inside, grabbed his coat and was in the truck pulling out of the marina lot when Beth's call came in.

Tre's old truck had come off the assembly line fifty years before Bluetooth. The rumble from the rusted-through mufflers rendered the phone's speaker useless, in all but the lowest gears. Rick held the cell to his ear, trying to shift and steer with one hand. He hadn't heard or understood the details of how she knew, but Beth said Allie was heading for Northwest, DC. She had taken her backpack and likely met an Uber up the block, calling from the extra phone Karen offered as a loaner on her third day in Maine. Beth had enabled the tracking app immediately, convincing Allie it was for her own protection. Beth said Allie welcomed the caring and concern at the time. Rick caught only a few of her next words as he accelerated in a roar off the Southeast Boulevard ramp and onto Interstate 395. Beth whispered a hope Allie would forget about the caution.

Getting up to speed, the truck protested in each higher gear, leaving a trailing swirl of blue smoke. Rick heard nothing else. He cut off Beth and redialed, but the phone slipped from his hand during a lane change. For half a mile, he tried in vain to reach for it as it slid across the dirty floor mats. Frustrated, he checked his mirror and veered off onto the shoulder to retrieve it, redialing as he pulled back onto the highway without looking.

A tractor trailer's horn erupted close behind as Beth answered.

"What the hell is that?"

"Forget it," Rick shouted. "Start again. I'm only hearing every other word."

"She couldn't have left long ago. She's stopped in traffic on Independence Avenue!"

Rick frowned and swerved back across the right lane to exit off 395. He stayed with the overpass to a stoplight at Maine Avenue.

"What is she *doing*, Rick?" Beth screamed. "Why northwest? What's there?"

Rick stared at the long red light in silence until it finally changed. He slammed the pedal and pushed the truck hard through the gears, racing to make the next green signal two blocks away.

"Home," he finally said, as the RPMs settled in fourth. "For what that's worth." Thoughts of Allie left him quiet again, leaving only an echo across the cab from the truck's grumble.

"Rick? Did I lose you?"

"And law firms. Baker and Dumars." He spoke the words with his choice made, already mapping the route to Adrian's office in his mind. He would stay on Maine Avenue along the river to 17th, cross Constitution, then eight more blocks to 20th and K. Maybe five minutes if he was lucky and got the lights, and the truck didn't overheat.

Beth's shaking voice brought him back. "Where Chris Evans works? My God, Rick, Allie took her backpack. She has her dad's gun."

Chapter 43

The building edge along K Street NW presented as so many others in the city: plain facades and a similar number of stories, with mandated height restrictions at 130 feet. Most of the buildings stood as simple assemblies of glass and precast concrete, with ground-level service businesses fronting the ten-foot-wide sidewalk and generous square footage in the floors above— second homes to attorneys, accountants, and bankers. Block after block, relentless walls of the city that made Rick uncomfortable. Active and bustling during the day but often deserted by 8:00 p.m.; there was sparse nightlife to entice people to stay.

Rick was okay with that as he stood in front of 20858 K Street, NW, catching his breath and trying inconspicuously to look through the tall glass entrance doors. The substantial security desk sat twenty feet beyond; Curtis was in his seat. Activity at the firm slowed noticeably after 9:00 p.m., but across the twelve floors of attorneys, lights would inevitably burn in more than a couple of offices late into the night. Security was provided 24/7. Curtis always took the evening shift, his second work effort on most days, some easy time paying good money.

Meetings with Adrian usually occurred after hours, and Rick and Curtis had enjoyed many brief conversations over the years. Curtis would remember Rick, and he would open the doors for him. But Rick felt certain he had never met Allie, and Curtis always played by the rules, even for someone claiming to be a senator's stepdaughter.

If Allie came here with the goal of confronting Chris Evans, the garage would have been her only option. Maybe a chance to slip under the gate as an exhausted attorney exited, eyes focused on the cars along K Street and nothing else. Rick hoped his reasoning for coming to Adrian's office had been wrong and that Allie had finally relented and reached out to her father and was now safe somewhere waiting for him. But understanding her pain and all he had witnessed and heard from her since their return had panicked him and led him here to his friend's firm.

~

The substantial building's garage had three levels below grade, with partner-designated spaces along the aisles closest to the elevators on each floor. Allie crept down the concrete stairs, checking each level for Chris' black Tesla. She found it on the lowest level, shared with only two other cars parked far across the garage. Allie took a position behind one of the large columns and reached into her backpack. She pulled the Red Sox hat down lower on her forehead, put the sunglasses on, zipped up the hoodie and waited, leaning against the cold concrete and trying to control the shaking in her core.

At 9:15 p.m., the elevator doors opened. Chris walked out, head down, riveted to his phone. Allie filled her lungs and flattened against the column. Still trembling, she squeezed her eyes shut, with both hands buried deep inside the sweatshirt, and the gun gripped tightly in her right pocket. Finally able to exhale, she stepped clear and warily crossed the drive aisle to intercept as Chris approached his car. The Tesla beeped and he looked up. Allie faced him from the opposite side.

"Allie?" Chris said, tilting slightly to try and see the face under the brim.

She held her stare and pulled off the dark-rimmed glasses.

"Allie." Chris' mouth fell open. "You're safe." His declaration held no concern or relief.

Rick heard the low voices from the third level stair landing and hurried down the last set of steps. He crept to the doorway and snuck a look around the corner; Allie was retreating as Chris moved around the hood of the car.

"Stay away from me." Her first words came in a fragile voice.

Chris stopped. "Allie, it's okay." He took another step toward her. "We've all been trying to find you. Everyone is worried. Where have you been?"

Rick caught the tremble in her right pocket.

Allie flexed her arm and faltered. "I've told people about you, and what you did to me. You can't—"

"What are you talking about?" Chris took another step.

"I'm going to the police."

Chris stopped. "You've been through a lot. Let me call your mom. Does she—"

Allie's voice cracked. "My mom's dead you asshole. I'm going to the police."

Chris tilted his head, his narrowed eyes fixed on her. "Then why are you *here*?" He moved closer. "What would you tell them?"

"Exactly what happened that night."

"The night of the party?" A cynical smile grew as he slipped closer. "Nothing happened, Allie, that I'm aware of. You had way too much to drink. I do remember now; is that what you want to discuss with the police? The senator has mentioned her concern."

Rick peered from behind a column. Allie's hand moved slightly. Chris came closer as she started to pull the gun out.

Allie hissed, "You don't get away with this! You don't—"

"Allie!" Rick's shout froze her.

Chris turned quickly to find Rick hustling toward them. Unconcerned, he grabbed Allie roughly and yanked her next to him.

"You came looking for me?" He squeezed her arm until she winced. "What were you going to do?" He pressed in, the slits of his fierce eyes within inches.

Rick heard Allie's low growl as she twisted, fighting to pull free. He was only feet away when Chris wrenched her arm again.

"Where's the fucking ring, you little bitch!"

His hand dropped to her right pocket, but Rick grabbed his wrist. He pulled Chris back and slammed him against the car, clutching at his jacket. "You should be asking *me* that, shithead!"

Chris swung and connected, but Rick didn't let go. Rick blocked the second swing and slammed Chris' head against the passenger door window. Chris went limp, slipping down against the door.

"She's right, asshole. You don't get to do that to her." Rick lifted him and drove a knee hard just below the ribs. Chris groaned, slumping over.

Rick grabbed Allie's hand and hurried her across the garage. A quick shot echoed through the empty space as they reached the stair door. The bullet found Rick's left shoulder, and his knees buckled, as he stumbled back against the wall.

Chris crouched next to the open driver's side door, still pointing the gun. "A kidnapper, Larson! That's what you are. The police will believe it. I was trying to save her. Self-defense!" he screamed. "What choice did I have?"

Rick pushed Allie into the stairwell as another shot rang out, missing her head by inches. He collapsed to the concrete slab. From his knees, he found Allie's panicked eyes and pointed to her pocket.

"Gimme," he said. "C'mon!"

Allie slid the gun to him.

Rick turned to see Chris slam the car door shut in a rage. He steadied his hand to aim as the Tesla bolted forward, sideswiping a concrete column. Screeching tires followed the acceleration, resounding loudly throughout the garage. Chris slid around the first corner and disappeared up the exit ramp. Rick lowered the gun as Allie knelt beside him.

"Rick!"

He pulled his jacket back to assess. The bullet had missed bone, but the bleeding was heavy. He leaned back against the concrete stair wall.

"It's okay," he said hoarsely. "Went through." He adjusted against the wall and let his head rest back. "Damn."

"What do I do?" Allie reached both hands to his arms.

"I can make it to the truck. C'mon, help me up. I need to get this closed. Stop the bleeding. And we need to get you out of here."

"You need a doctor!"

Rick pulled off his hat and pressed it against the wound. He shook his head, his breaths short and loud. "Nope, no time. It's okay." He applied pressure and closed his eyes, fighting back the shock. "Delia can take care of it." He leaned forward, accepting Allie's help with his jacket.

Rick and Allie made it up the steps, pausing at the on grade exit door to check. They moved down the sidewalk as casually as Rick could manage. He held his head low, hiding his grimace, still pressing a hand to his shoulder. Allie guided him with a hand on his back. They walked in silence, finally turning on L Street, relieved to have empty sidewalks. The truck sat parked half a block down. Allie stepped ahead to open the door, but Rick paused at the bed to lean back. He scanned the street in both directions; only one couple leaving the Japanese restaurant across the street, hurrying south down the sidewalk, uninterested in the old man and young girl perched against the derelict Chevy.

Rick moved to the passenger door, braced himself, and groaned as he squeezed in, struggling to lift and rotate his legs. He grabbed his iced tea bottle and drained it in a couple of gulps. Allie slid in on the driver's side as Rick slammed the seat back. He opened the glove box and pulled out a roll of duct tape and gauze packets.

"I need to do this here."

Allie raised a shaking hand to his arm. "I can take you to a hospital."

"Don't think that's our safest option. Not with Chris and a gun."

"Why would he shoot at us?"

Rick shot her a frown and shook his head. "Let's answer that later." He winced and shifted in the seat. "Help me get my arm out."

"Rick, I can get us to an emergency clinic. We can wait in a corner and hide."

He managed to smile. "It's an idea, but not that simple. Gunshot wounds get you a conversation with the police. Here, grab the end of my sleeve. C'mon."

After intense minutes of clenched teeth and focus, Rick had effectively sandwiched gauze on each side of his shoulder and wrapped the area with duct tape. Allie gently helped pull the jacket back on. Rick took a long drink from the extra water bottle and leaned his head back.

"Is anyone coming down the sidewalk?" he mumbled.

"No, we're okay."

He nodded, and for minutes, they remained still. The pounding in his heart gradually calmed. Soon, his eyes crept open and he pulled forward, struggling to face her.

"You went there with a gun . . ."

Allie lowered her head, both hands clutching the steering wheel. "Beth used the word victim," she said quietly. "I heard her talking to Karen." Allie straightened, her blank stare drifting down the street.

Rick watched the tremble in her fingers.

Her voice cracked, "I won't be a victim."

"Allie, he won't hurt you again. Can you trust me?"

The trembling crept to her arms. "I do. But not home. I can't go back there, Rick. Please, not to her."

Rick reached for her hand. "It's going to be okay. Your dad's on his way back. He's in Massachusetts; he thought you might go back to the old house."

Allie's eyes widened slightly as she turned in the seat.

"He's a few hours away."

Rick's shoulder spasmed, and he squeezed both eyes shut, biting his lip. "But we need time with Delia," he murmured. "Just long enough for her to take care of this. Ben has a place for us to meet. It might not be safe at the marina."

Chapter 44

"I never believed Chris could handle this," Michelle said, her voice unusually soft. "Jesus, Adrian." She shook her head slowly, staring across the dark Potomac. "Chris is weak, distractible. I listened to Adrian, and that was a mistake."

Leah sat on one end of the large leather sofa, watching the flames dance in the fireplace. "It's worse." She wavered. "Chris made a—"

Michelle waved her hand, anticipating the rest. "Please, I know all about Mr. Evans' error in judgment. It's not his first. Strangely, perhaps, I thought this one would serve as motivation for him to handle things quietly. How ironic, my co-sponsoring the Protection from Predators bills in the past." Michelle turned to her. "A surprisingly difficult legislation to push through."

Leah stared, unblinking.

"I've wondered why you didn't bring this to me?" Michelle asked.

"We were trying to protect you."

"Considerate of you both, I suppose."

Leah's cell buzzed, and she glanced at the text from Chris. Offering no expression, she walked over and handed the phone to Michelle. "Like I said, it's worse."

Michelle read, raising her eyebrows. "So, Allie's back. And with guns. Sounds like a messy reunion. It also sounds like our wandering soul got lucky." She turned away, deliberating. "Chris shouldn't be far away. Please ask him to join us. Now."

Michelle paced, speaking in monotones as Leah texted. "I had hoped she wouldn't be back until after the elections. Surprisingly, the 'not knowing' sympathy has polled well in her absence. This, however, the messiness, the associations, this will not." She shook her head. "I truly wish the girl would have waited, if she was going to come back at all."

Leah checked her phone again. "He's on his way."

"Good. Curious, isn't it? How long has Allie been back? Larson obviously knew, and I'm not happy about that, nor will the police be."

"No, they won't."

Michelle sighed. "Regardless, and now while we have a minute, I see two choices. Prop Chris up as the hero or let him take the fall. I certainly wasn't prepared to make this decision yet, but I knew it was a possibility with him, and here we are."

"And the victim in all this?"

"The alleged victim? Allie?" Michelle moved to the bar and poured a glass of wine. "Jury's still out."

Michelle lifted the crystal, holding it close, fixating on the delicate etching. Chris had struggled before. She had heard the stories, but judiciously avoided the details; self-inflicted complications in his earlier life stemming from hurtful decisions and perilous missteps. Thankfully, his father had been able to right the young man's course. But having fallen again, this time on her watch, Michelle's first instincts echoed an urgency for separation. Distance was what she needed, perhaps letting all of this land on him. It wouldn't come without challenges, though; Adrian held Chris in high esteem. The young man had a presence. He was a star, much like she had been at that age, in line for greatness. She saw the possibilities, too. At times. Five, maybe eight more years in the practice working closely with her, and then a Senate run of his own. A future colleague groomed would return substantial benefits. Allies are important. And then the next step—that certainly was not out of the question for Mr. Evans. At least, it wasn't.

Michelle sipped her wine. "At this point, Leah, I'm not certain both of them can be saved. So, who to choose? The alleged victim or the predator? If I do let him take the fall—"

"As you should, he tried to rape a minor."

Michelle's head tilted slightly. "So, you're ready to convict?"

"He confessed. It may be cleaner for you after the dust settles."

"Perhaps."

Michelle's phone buzzed. "Ah, speak of the devil. That would be Mr. Evans, now." She crossed the room and opened the door, nodding to her security detail on the lowest step and motioning Chris inside.

"Well, you've had quite a night. My goodness. Come have a drink."

Chris ignored Leah's stare on his way to the couch. He collapsed into the cushions. Michelle approached with a scotch, and he immediately downed it.

Michelle's wry smile grew as she searched his lost expression. "Our precious Allie is back. Good news. Please tell me what happened."

Chris squirmed, deflected, averted his eyes, and went on in broken sentences for twenty minutes. The rambling replay grew tedious, and Michelle's impatience surfaced mid-sentence.

"Enough! I'm sure there's more, but does it really matter?" She studied his face. "Bottom line, I simply have to decide whether to believe any of this as truth and whether to trust you or not."

"Why wouldn't you?" he growled, standing and moving to the bar.

"What an interesting question to pose, when here we are, with your past, present, and future all colliding now in a monumental display of ineptitude!"

"Senator." Leah rose from the couch. "Chris will need to bring this to Adrian. Soon."

"Agreed." Michelle eyed the desk clock. "Clearly, it is too late now, but it will need to be told tomorrow morning, early."

"He'll wonder why I didn't call the police."

"Yes, he will, as would any reasonable mind, which Adrian has. But we all know the precise reason you didn't call, don't we, Chris? Allie will be accusing you of assault."

"Bullshit! Whatever Allie says is—"

"The truth?" Michelle sneered. "Stop! Enough denials. You and I both know why we're here this evening, and we also know the cause for Allie running! *We* know the truth, but Adrian will never need to. What we don't know, is why the girl came back when she did. And guns for God's sake!" Michelle spun and roamed the room, shaking her head.

Chris stood motionless, his face rigid.

Michelle's eyes lowered; her hands clenched in front. When she finally spoke, the anger had been released. "Well, perhaps it would be more productive for us to focus on the present, and this evening's debacle." She crossed back toward Chris, exploring his nervous eyes. "Two shots fired, correct? One hit him: the other a miss? So, we have evidence likely embedded in the concrete garage at Baker Dumars. One bullet, maybe two. Tell me, is the gun registered?"

Chris stared into his glass.

"I'll take that as a no, and we'll put it in the plus column for you—for the time being. But the gun stays here with me. Please leave it when we're finished." She waited for his attention. "Now then, regarding our communication with Mr. Dumars, there is really only one story to share with him in light of this evening's events. First. No, you didn't call Detective Ward. Your responsibility was to call me, which you did. I expressed to you my hesitation about involving the police, fearing that Allie might run again. It's been weeks, a nightmare for her, and I thought it best for her father and I to be the first to approach her. Ben has resources involved, and it was my decision, what I deemed best for the safety of Allie. Second, your gun will disappear. Your irresponsible and illegal ownership just happens to serve you well in this instance. So, you worked until 9:30, and then Allie appeared, surprising you in the garage. Dear Allie made a ruinous mistake. She returned to Larson, a man she had foolishly come to trust, instead of coming home, only to become trapped in his snare again and unable to escape. She fled Larson, coming to you for safety, coming to you first, trusting that you would help her get home. Larson followed with his gun. He found you both. There was a struggle. You did all you could, trying to defend her. In the clash, you overpowered an old man; very believable. His gun went off. Two shots were fired. All in the defense of our daughter. Larson was hit in the shoulder but still able to pull Allie away with him, using her as a shield. You chose caution and didn't pursue. You were afraid for Allie, and you called me."

Michelle wandered to the bar as she concluded and poured scotch into her empty wine glass. "Isn't this how you remember things unfolding, Chris?"

"Sure." His jaw clenched.

"Good. This is what you will convey to Adrian tomorrow morning. And when appropriate, I will corroborate. Now, finally, as to our uncertain future, yours *used* to be quite bright, Chris. A run for president someday? That was entirely believable and quite intriguing to me. Sadly, all of this puts a substantial wrinkle in those plans."

"Nothing changes!"

"Oh, I'm afraid things *have* changed. All of these shameless decisions you continue to make pose distractions that can diminish one's voice and influence, distractions I will not have following me. And the scrutiny my judgment will come under, about associations I chose, about you, Chris. All of it has the potential to cast a relentless, nagging doubt, regardless of whose story you believe. I can't have that, and I won't. *My* career is not ending this evening. Understood?"

He glared. "And you think mine is?"

"Quite possibly, yes! All of this is so fucking inexcusable!" Michelle's arms flared out as she closed on him. "Two options, counselor! Just two! The first involves your full confession. The pathetic truth. And some would argue that this is the only option you deserve."

"Senator—"

Michelle lifted a hand, spinning away to wander her precious surroundings.

After a moment composing herself, she said, "You know, in spite of everything, Chris, I still value your future more than I do Allison's, and I'm willing to offer an alternative story: a confession *of sorts*, a version of the truth. Allie as a young girl who fantasized about a powerful person such as yourself being attracted to her. Your concern and relationship with her, however, involved nothing of the kind, only support. Your word against Allie's, and we have leverage if needed: she did pull a gun on you." Michelle cocked her head. "You will begin the story. I, of course, will then be the one to finish it. I will express our thanks to you for all the help you've offered Allie over the years, and for trying to save our daughter this evening." Her hand rose in sweeping gesture. "I will speak of your courage: it was beyond anything we might have expected. It will be an ending that plays well, it will celebrate you. And when the inevitable legal and media discussions start, together we will handle the barrage and the tedious confrontation with Ben and his daughter. You can trust that I will protect you, Chris. For all of the challenges, I am still invested in you. There are stakes involved here that far outweigh the few years of therapy Allie may require. Someday she will come to realize the relative insignificance of your misstep, perhaps the same day on which she decides whether to vote for you or not." Michelle smirked. "Adrian is no longer needed: I will protect you. Just play your part."

She released a deep breath. "There. An alternative. Everything will be fine."

"What about the ring, and the blood," Chris snapped.

"The blood itself doesn't place you in her company. There are any number of viable explanations. So, remain calm, Chris. Your promising career will not meet its downfall this evening, not with this account of the circumstances." Michelle moved closer and extended both hands to his shoulders. "I believe this to be what's best for you, Chris, *and* history will tell, perhaps what's best for our country."

Chris pulled back, his narrowed eyes darting between them. "Too risky and too much wasted time." His mouth curled into a cynical smile. "Allie as collateral damage," he blurted.

Michelle stiffened, observing as Chris lifted his glass.

"It's how the story needs to end, Michelle. Tonight. Collateral damage. All of this would go away." He glowered at her. "You've said so yourself."

Her head tilted. "Whatever are you talking about, counselor? An odd, misplaced assertion. Be careful." She sipped her drink and turned aside, considering the words. "Collateral damage, though—as in, a tragic truth plays out this evening? One we've perhaps seen too often; war time trauma surfacing so many years later. An aging Veteran from a long-ago conflict, reclusive, estranged from his wife and daughter, a dear friend lost recently. Wounded hours earlier, the pain surfaced, and the trauma rushed in. That could trigger anything in him, couldn't it?" Michelle paused in reflection. "With that torment buried inside for so long, would it surprise you if he took his own life? And would he harm someone else? Is Allie in danger?" She spun, her chin high. "Collateral damage?"

Chris smirked. "Exactly."

"I see." Michelle studied his expression. "You've obviously given this some thought."

"You as well?"

"Not as much as you, apparently. And if you can go there in your mind, Chris, you must be able to speak the words. So, let me hear you say them."

Chris didn't falter. "Kidnapping, murder-suicide."

Michelle's slow nod began. "The tragic war hero; it *is* perfect."

"Larson needs to be the demon and the casualty. Allie needs to be the tragedy."

"In the wrong place at the wrong time. It's sad in so many ways."

"It all goes away. It's the insurance we need to get separation."

"*We*?"

"She hates you, Michelle. You know that. You would be relieved to have her out of your life."

"We do have our differences . . ." Michelle pulled a hand across her jaw. "And while that may be true—"

"You and I also know Allie never appreciated the advantage she had in life, all that people tried to do for her. Who knows if she ever would. And that's where the risk lies for us; she's unpredictable, at best. And God only knows what Ben will do with this." Chris eyed each of them. "It's only so much of a waste, if something did happen to her."

They stared in silence.

Michelle finally sighed. "Of course, Ben would be devastated, but he would only have himself to blame, having been the one to let her share in Larson's troubled existence. Am I understanding you?"

"It's clean, Michelle. Efficient for you. A simple, short month of consoling words from constituents and colleagues, and then the story disappears."

"This is a dark path you're traveling, Chris."

"Is it? We don't know that Larson hasn't already killed her."

"Interesting. No, we don't. And if that were to happen, well, much of our discussion here would have no relevance." She pulled her chin in, studying him.

"Allie endangered herself by running and then returning to him. *Her* choice not to come home."

"It's disappointing, and unexpected." Michelle stepped close and murmured, "You appear prepared to have her die for the decision."

"Aren't you?"

"I am prepared to groom a president, Mr. Evans. The decisions of others and consequences realized along that journey reside in the hands of fate; they are not of *my* doing." Michelle's face tightened, fixated on his defiant expression. "Look at me. Look at me! I would never advise either of you on what to do in a difficult situation like this. The scenarios are too painful to consider. You've started this landslide, though, Chris, and now you need to finish it. In whatever manner you deem best for all of us. Is that something I can count on you to arrange?"

Chris balked.

"Actually, that is not a question. Whatever path you elect needs to happen this evening, before your discussion with Adrian tomorrow. You shot Larson, Allie's dear old friend, so now you've wounded both of them. That could and likely will lead to any number of retaliations, none of which will support your ambitions. And by the time you meet with Adrian, who knows what news will be streaming, maybe nothing other than the same political and global chaos, or maybe something closer to home. That all depends on you."

He folded his arms, holding her stare.

"What I've shared with you, Chris, is what Mr. Dumars will hear from you tomorrow morning. The beginning: how it all started this evening. Our version of the story. It has to be the first news he gets for the day, so you have to be ready. And consider that Adrian may be difficult with this. He may or may not know something. Be prepared for either and keep it brief; there was a struggle, you overpowered an old man, his gun went off hitting him, and Allie's gone again. You called me, not the police."

Michelle's jaw tensed. "This is the future, counselor. The story's ending is up to you. I trust you to know what's best."

She twisted to Leah. "Thoughts?"

Leah faltered, unblinking.

"Very well." Michelle glanced at her watch. A half-smile emerged then faded as she turned to Chris. "There, I think we've talked enough."

He emptied his glass and growled, "I have to make a call." He sneered at Leah and hurried toward the door.

Michelle called after him, "Chris. The gun?"

Snatching his jacket from the settee, he shook his head and slammed the gun down on the small side table.

Michelle approached calmly and leaned close. "Make it tragic," she said quietly. "Make it tonight."

He swallowed hard and pulled away. "Understood."

~

Michelle leaned against the door frame. She took a moment to swirl her ice before crossing the room to Leah. "Now," she said, "I'd like your honest thoughts."

"Allie as collateral damage? That wasn't one of the options you laid out earlier. I'm not sure."

"It was an adjustment."

"Chris taking the fall, that's what I heard. You left the decision to him."

She deliberated. "Perhaps."

"Was all of that for my benefit then?"

"As you said earlier; probably cleaner after the dust settles."

"Trusting Chris, I see that as a significant risk. He assaulted a young girl. He should be done. Move on and let Allie live her life."

Michelle waved off the suggestion and strode away. "Fate will decide."

"Chris is enough. Too many things can go wrong. You can find another superstar."

"And I will, if that becomes necessary." Michelle stopped abruptly and pivoted, eyeing Leah. "Be careful, Leah; conscience has its place. This girl is drowning, and I can't help her. It's always a danger; will you be pulled under trying to save the person? That's not a risk I'm willing to take. I'm not going in after her. As mentioned, I've concluded Chris is of more value to me than Allison Sheridan."

"Then, you *are* prepared to let her die."

Michelle shrugged. "I'm casting off her father. Why not both of them?"

"That wasn't the question."

Michelle's chin lifted. "I'm always prepared to face the harsh realities of life, and for this evening, sadly, that may mean Allie is already dead. Or soon will be. We don't know Larson; the scenario Chris laid out is plausible. We won't know anything until morning."

Leah shook her head. "I don't like it. You wanted my thoughts. Larson may be in the emergency room for all we know."

"Unlikely. He broke into a place of business and assaulted an attorney. He would only have gone to the hospital if he was dying. Chris is not good with a gun. He carries it as an accessory, like a watch. I'm sure Larson is fine and only attending to Allie."

Michelle turned back to the mesmerizing flames. "Ben is in Massachusetts, and we know where Larson ran: a wounded animal crawling back into his hole. It's mystifying how they entangled Allie in their two very different lives. Very unexpected." Michelle shrugged and drew her attention back to Leah. "No matter, but we are still left with a last loose end: Allie may be trying to connect with her father. It doesn't change our timing; it would take hours for Ben to return. I suppose there's nothing to do but let fate have its way again." She deliberated a minute, then abruptly proceeded toward the door. "Come, you have a busy night ahead."

Leah followed.

Michelle slowed to a stop and faced her. "I have one last favor to ask you tonight." She handed Leah a thumb drive.

"What am I accepting?"

"More insurance. Chris will thank you." Michelle's expression hardened. "Perhaps, consider this a test as well," she said bluntly. "After all we've discussed this evening, I'm left with some questions as to your loyalties. Taking care of this for me is a way for you to allay those concerns." Michelle extended a firm hand to her shoulder. "We have much to accomplish together, Leah. Don't disappoint me."

Leah lowered her blank eyes and pocketed the drive. "Cameras?"

Michelle nodded. "My husband is very protective and very thorough, in most things. He was away on business the night Allie disappeared. He never made the association."

"I was wondering when—"

"He still trusts me, strangely. This is the original. Unedited, from the hall outside Allie's room. I let Chris believe it also included her bedroom. He needed to live in fear for a while. Regardless, it is not favorable footage for him. More importantly, nor is it for me. Dispose of this, please. No one ever sees it again. Do you understand? We have a country to protect." Michelle reached for the gun on the table and handed it to Leah. "This as well." She hurried opening the door. "And if the tragic were to happen tonight, sadly of course, your discretion will be rewarded."

Leah sat in her car, idling, considering the details of Senator Baxter's expectations over the next couple of hours. She watched lights go out in the office as she pulled around the circular drive. Waiting for the gate to open, she dialed Ron. He answered after the first ring.

"Things are changing," she said. "We need some help tonight. The girl's back. You were right."

"I know."

"It's unfortunate you lost them; it made things difficult. Have you heard from Chris?"

"Nothing. Should I have?"

"It doesn't matter. He fucked up and a fix is required. And

Baxter wants all of it cleaned up tonight."

"Seems ambitious."

"The girl is with Larson now. He's been shot."

"Chris?"

"Yes. Careless and stupid. Baxter wants Larson to take the fall. For all of it. Kidnapping and—well, the rest is a very ugly front page. Read between the lines."

"Direction only, please. So, the Sheridan kid? Am I understanding correctly?"

"In the senator's thinking, she is unessential. Her words. The other one, Tremaine, went off the rails. Why not Larson, too? Emotional trauma catches up with him, and Allie is the victim. I'm not so sure she needs to be, though."

"Sounds tragic on many levels. Also sounds like you have something else in mind."

Leah held silent a moment. "To be determined."

"Okay, what do you need?"

"To start, we need to find them. I need your eyes on the marina. Larson's hurt. They'll go somewhere to wait. Sheridan's on his way back, so we don't have long. I'm checking out the girlfriend's place. If they aren't at either, it's going to be a long night. You know what he drives, right?"

"If it still runs."

"Just watch. If they *are* there, no moves. Wait for me."

"If Chris contacts me, will I be getting the same?"

"He'll call," Leah barked. "But I'm handling this now! I just need your eyes. You understand?"

The long red light at Wisconsin and M Street finally changed, and Leah slammed the accelerator. "How soon can you get there?"

"I'm in my car."

"Just eyes, Ron."

Chapter 45

"If there's a spot, take it," Rick said. "You see the house?"

Allie didn't answer, her focus locked on maneuvering the old truck down the narrow street, trying not to clip any of the side mirrors on parked cars. It was late. Rick had hoped to arrive unannounced, but even idling slowly, the truck's rumble was out of place on the peaceful lane. Allie navigated the city well, but it had been a slow trip, as insisted upon by Rick. Slower speeds meant better reaction time for potholes. Bumps awakened the pain. With Rick distracting himself as spotter, they had managed to miss most of them.

After parking the truck, Allie mapped their path along the sidewalk, not wanting Rick to stumble. Once through Sarah's gate, he rested at the porch steps, catching his breath. Allie stood close, her steadying hand remaining against his back. The door opened as he reached for the stair railing.

Beth and Sarah came through, both halting when they saw Rick's blood-soaked jacket. Sarah hurried down the steps and reached out to him, immediately focused on his arm.

"My God, Rick . . ."

"It's fine, Sarah."

"I doubt that. Come inside! I need to take a look."

Rick shook his head and held his ground.

"Rick! You need a doctor. I'm calling 911."

"Delia's my doctor tonight. I'm okay. We're not staying. I just need the car."

Beth glanced at Rick as she stepped past to Allie. "You're alright?" she asked, holding Allie's shoulders with both hands.

Allie nodded.

Beth shook her head. "You scared the shit out of me." She wrapped her arm around and pulled Allie close, eyeing Rick's shoulder.

"You're hurt. How bad?"

"Let's talk later." A stabbing pain shot through Rick's chest, and he leaned against the railing, grimacing. "I just need the car."

Beth scowled, finally showing Delia's keys. "You said Allie's dad gave you an address: I'm going with you."

"No way."

"Then she stays with me. He can pick her up here."

"Beth, you don't understand—"

"Don't be so sure."

Rick sensed the fierce loyalty in her eyes, and tried to straighten. "Then she has two bodyguards for the rest of the night. We need to go. Marina first, so Delia can close this. She'll meet us—"

"We have her car!" Beth snapped. "You're making her walk?"

"She doesn't mind. It won't be the first time."

Beth shook her head.

Rick turned to Allie. "Then we get you to your dad. Okay?"

Beth brushed in front of him and led Allie to the sidewalk.

Rick watched them hurry across the street to Delia's car. Twisting back to Sarah, he flinched. "I'm sorry," he said in a weak voice. "Getting you involved and—"

"Don't be, I'm good. Lou's coming over." She stepped closer, taking his hand and helping him back down the walk.

Holding the car door, she balked. "Are you sure about this? You've been shot for God's sake."

Rick winced. "Yeah."

She squeezed his hand. "Rick, we have to call the police. Please."

"Sarah, I'll take care of Ward. Don't open your door."

Chapter 46

Rick watched the traffic light sixty feet away turn from yellow to red. Beth accelerated, ran it anyway, and barely cleared the intersection onto M Street, SE before the oncoming traffic closed in. Her decision got them a prolonged horn blast from a black Lexus. Allie and Rick sat in the back, her hand resting on his left arm, just below the bandage. The pain from the wound discovered all parts of his body, rushing to any jar or reflex. Rick held still and searched the river for distraction, tracing mixed reflections from the far shore as they dissolved somewhere toward the middle, long before reaching the banks of his lost home. The marina was less than a half mile away but seemed much farther and very distant to him now. In that moment next to Allie, he sensed that all he had shared with her and Tre; any spirit or meaning this place once held for them was gone. He couldn't see it. It had died with Tre.

Rick looked across the seat. Allie's forehead rested against the window. Darkness saturated the car, and he perceived only her motionless profile. He imagined the subject of her stare: eyes transfixed in one position, unable to focus on any of what hurried past outside.

Beth accelerated to thirty as they came upon the first gradual slope, one of several following the lonely road's descent to four feet above sea level. The lights on Pennsylvania Avenue disappeared, yielding to the utter blackness engulfing them now.

Rick strained to peer ahead, calling to mind every step along the road, every bump and hole, every abandoned building—all of it. He knew every inch, but he recognized nothing. M Street, SE, never seemed darker to him. His eyes might as well have been closed. He considered whether the darkness this evening was protection; it had always been comforting to him. Or was it cloaking his life's next demon?

Allie glared into the black and whispered. "What happened to the path, Rick?"

He missed the words over Beth's sudden, hard braking. A slow-moving raccoon made it safely across. Rick searched beyond the headlights' reach for the beacon farther up the road, the solitary, low-voltage floodlight that dimly illuminated the marina's entrance sign. Overgrown with ivy for years, though, it managed only splashes of weak light on a few of the wood letters. Rick watched intently, anxious to spot its familiar welcoming glow.

The grade fell off again and he pulled forward slightly against the pain, curious that no light had appeared. Abruptly, the car skidded, as Beth swerved late into the marina's gravel entrance. Across the lot, Delia rose quickly from the office steps as they coasted up. She hurried to the passenger-side door and helped Rick out.

"Richard Larson. What in God's name did you do now?" Delia opened his jacket gently for a quick look. "Oh, dear." She shook her head, adding a sympathetic scowl. "It wasn't two weeks ago you were lying on my kitchen floor with paramedics kneeling beside, checking out your heart. Nice to see you managing your stress, old man. So much for any concerns about A-Fib."

Delia turned to Allie and Beth. "Let's go. Help me get him inside."

Schooner rose to greet him with an energetic wag, as Rick took the old leather chair in the corner. With Beth's help, the coat came off quickly. The torn tee shirt tied off at the wound was soaked in blood. Allie leaned against the front wall, fixing her worried expression on Rick's shoulder.

Delia nodded assurances to her and moved to a wall cabinet and pulled out a leather first aid bag, caked in dust, with a rusted zipper half open. She approached Rick with a frown and pulled up a chair. Cutting away the rest of the shirt, she cocked her head surveying the wound.

"Well, friend, I can't say you dodged a bullet. But you did get lucky again this time. Now you've got a memory on each of these hairy arms. I'm thinking the last shot was probably better, though, this one took some blood away. How's your belly feeling?"

"I could use a drink."

Delia chuckled as she rooted through the contents in the bag. "Oh my, you sayin' that in front of Beth? This arm isn't gonna be the only thing bleeding soon." Delia winked at Beth and pulled out a stained bottle of peroxide, then pulled in close to clean away the blood.

Leaning in, she spoke quietly to Rick, "Wanna tell me what's happening here?"

Rick stole a look toward Allie and struggled to shift in his chair. "Can we do that later?"

Delia's lips flattened.

"I'm okay, Delia. Just close it up for me. Your fastest work. Please?"

Delia concentrated on the wound, grumbling. "Your fastest work? You're never in a hurry, Richard." She tilted for a better angle. "What's so different about today, hmm?"

Beth returned from the fridge and handed Rick a water bottle.

Delia gestured to her. "He's just kidding Beth; don't you believe him. Not a drop of the stuff since the last time he was shot, that one courtesy of Tre, saving his best friend from himself. So the story goes. You have my word." Delia dampened the cotton wipe again and started on the exit wound just above the shoulder blade.

Allie sat on the floor, arms wrapping her knees. Beth moved to stand next to her.

"Went through clean, Richard," Delia said. "That's good. You want me to stitch it?" She reached for the bag. "Let me see if everything I need is here."

Rick shook his head. "Just pull it closed and pack it for me."

"And wait for what?"

"Tomorrow."

"Won't take long. Gonna be a little harder tomorrow."

"Not now. I need to do something."

Delia leaned back, pulling in her chin with a wrinkled forehead as she eyed Beth and Allie for support. She turned back to him and said, "There is nothing in this bag for the pain, Richard."

He managed a half nod. "It's okay, I won't be long."

"You're an old man who's lost a lot of blood." Delia's brow creased. "Whatever it is, you sure?"

"Twenty minutes is all I need." Rick turned to Beth and Allie. "I need you both to stay here."

"I'll stay with them," Delia said quickly.

Beth stepped closer to Rick. "Stay here? Where the hell are you going? We're meeting Allie's father!"

Rick shook his head, unwilling to explain. "Call Detective Ward. Allie, your dad will be here soon."

Beth wavered, then pulled the gun out of her shoulder bag, glaring at Rick. "Delia," she said in a controlled voice. "You go ahead. You've already done more than anyone should have asked of you."

Delia reached a hand to Beth's shoulder. "No such thing, dear."

"Please, take your car." Beth set her gun on the table. "We'll be fine."

Delia folded her arms and scowled at Rick, "Twenty minutes, right?"

"Right." He gulped the last water, sucked in a breath, and pushed up out of the chair.

Delia caught the grimace and reached to steady him. "Hope you know what you're doing, friend." Shaking her head, she glanced at Beth and Allie. "I don't need the car, but I'll take Schooner. You okay, Allie?"

Beth answered first. "I've got her."

Allie stood, clenching her hands. "Rick, you said it might not be safe here."

He moved close, speaking in a low voice. "This is something I have to do, Allie; a couple of minutes. If you hear anything, you know where the keys are to *MORNING STAR*—hide there if you need to."

Rick hobbled to the closet and pulled out his river coat. Schooner noticed and scrambled to stand. "Not this time, friend. Rick moved to the door and paused, not looking back. "Thanks," he said quietly. The door groaned as he yanked it open. He walked out into the late night, took a quick scan around the property, and headed for the pier.

⁓

The Lyman runabout sat on rusty stands at the north end of the lot, anchoring a short row of long-ago abandoned boats. Just a month before, the pole light standing between the five boats and the line of yews still cast its soft yellow glow, assuring they would not be forgotten in the dark. After so many years, though, the light had finally expired.

Ron stood casually beside the transom of the old Lyman, one

hundred feet from the office. With no light, there wasn't a reason to seek the shadows, and Ron felt assured the weak beams creeping through the office windows would never reach him. He had just listened to Rick's slow fading progress across the gravel lot and watched the dark image of him turn the corner from the office. He had then heard the more careful steps along the creaking deck boards as Rick disappeared into the blackness halfway down the pier.

Ron considered following, curious about the purpose, but instead chose to wait. Leah had said, 'just eyes'. Not a sound for minutes, until the struggling start of a small outboard. The motor idled roughly, then evened out at higher rpms, traveling away somewhere into the blackness over the river. Ron monitored the fading sound of the engine while holding his watch on the small office windows. The door opened suddenly, and Delia emerged, taking an apprehensive look around. She hustled to her car, ensured that it was locked, and walked hurriedly across the lot toward the gate, passing not sixty feet away from the Lyman. Comfortable in the dark's shroud, Ron stood motionless. His phone suddenly vibrated. He declined without looking, his stare following Delia's anxious walk as she and Schooner disappeared into the darkness along M Street, SE. Ron glanced toward the office and lifted his phone to check the call.

Chapter 47

Just before midnight, Chris Evans swerved onto Wharf Street. Enraged, he accelerated down the short block to his town home, needing to brake hard with tires screeching as he swerved onto the concrete apron in front of his garage. He focused nervously through the side windows, tapping his fingers against the wheel as the door rose. Inside, he took his first look at the damaged fender, instantly scripting the necessary story he would share with others. Resigned, he set the alarm and hurried into the lower level. Taking the stairs to the kitchen, he dialed the burner phone again.

Ron answered in a hushed voice. "Sorry, couldn't talk."

"The Sheridan girl is back," Chris said.

"I know. I've had a conversation with Leah. It was only a matter of time. She told me about your evening."

"A poor decision on her part. Nevertheless, the Sheridan girl can't be here."

"I'm at the marina. I just saw her."

"She should have stayed away. She can't be here. Do you understand?" Chris deliberated. "This is from Baxter."

"Only direction, remember?" Ron paused. "Larson's daughter is still with her."

"That's unfortunate. They both should have stayed away. It doesn't change anything."

"You sure? Leah indicated that—"

"Fuck her. You and I have had this discussion already. I

accepted assurances that you would accomplish things Leah might be hesitant to deal with."

"Relax counselor. Understood. What about Larson?"

"Is he still walking?"

"Not quickly."

"That should make it easier, but don't underestimate him. If you've talked to Leah, you know what this is supposed to look like, right?"

"Sad story about an old Vet coming apart. Innocent people in the wrong place."

"Exactly. Text when you're done. The phone goes in the river." A long silence followed before Chris said, "One more thing. We don't talk again." The call ended as he slammed his phone on the table.

Chris walked to the bar and poured a full glass of bourbon. He wandered across the dark living room and eased into his favorite chair in front of the French doors. Dimmed pendant lights over the kitchen island cast the floor's only faint light. He let his head fall back and fixated on the procession of headlights across the bridge. Mesmerized, he parked the memory of Ron's call far away and made space for brief thoughts of Allie. She had left her door unlocked that night. Why was she doing this to him now? Chris sipped the bourbon and narrowed his eyes across the dark water. He wouldn't let her destroy him. If she was strong enough to run and then return, she would try. He smiled and raised his glass to good fortune; Larson's loyalty had made things easy for him.

Chris settled into the hushed solitude, making notes in his mind, considering every witness, and preparing for trial, just as his father had done for endless hours in their study. The drink calmed him. He would rehearse a bit longer; his opening statement needed to be strong. He would take the time he needed before reaching out to Adrian.

Chapter 48

The west wind had blown most of the day, pushing water down and out of the Potomac River and pulling tributary levels with it. Low tide arrived an hour earlier. Rick envisioned the Anacostia's shoreline as not presenting her best self, with shallow muddy flats and hazards now too close to the surface. He held the skiff offshore, closer to the middle of the channel. With the throttle wide open, the flat bottom slapped across the light chop. Each bounce brought spikes of pain shooting into Rick's shoulder. The entire left side of his body burned but he held the speed full on. Random lighting from apartment buildings across the river did nothing to define the undulating western bank Rick followed. He knew it by heart, but his mind was laboring, much as his body. He trained on the dark stretch of shoreline, searching for any distraction from the wound. Leaning slightly, he struggled to recognize anything through the extraordinary darkness, wondering how the land could disappear so completely into the river. For half of his life, time on this water at night had always held two comforting purposes: visiting Tre or coming back to the home they had created in this quiet, forgotten place. Both destinations always had held refuge for Rick; the return trips provided reconnection with the comforting boundaries of his life and brought him the only peace he had come to know along his weary journey. It always had been Tre who greeted him. Now, it was only the remnants of Tre's shelter waiting.

Rick lost himself briefly to the image, staring west, unaware of the small boat's increasingly errant path across the dark water. The flashing trestle lights appeared suddenly off the bow, racing toward him. Rick's eyes widened, trying to adjust. The large wooden cross members loomed high above, thirty feet away. He slammed the tiller arm over hard, and the bow came around; he could have reached a hand to the wooden structure. His wounded arm instinctively braced against the gunwale, and the pain bent him over. He jerked his hand back and tried to straighten as the boat veered away to the east. Lifting his head to see, Rick squeezed each blink to clear the tears. He coaxed more from the throttle, and the skiff danced the last hundred yards to the island's shore.

~

Rick stood motionless, leaning slightly to favor his left side. His vacant gaze drifted across the abandoned encampment. The rifle lay covered in its stand. Pockets of rain nestled in stretched out sections of the canopy. Fleeting memories blanketed him, but he spared them only seconds before returning to his purpose. He shuffled to the bank of coolers and opened the faded red one. He moved Tre's heavy sweaters to the side and grabbed the plastic bag, snagging a worn sweatshirt as he anxiously pulled back to confirm the ring was there. He squeezed the baggie tightly around the small diamond and concealed it in his side pocket. Repositioning the sweaters, he spotted the worn leather case resting flush against the cooler bottom and secured precisely by a carved driftwood wedge. The custom case was sized for a single handgun, a gun he believed would be there, a gun he often threatened to throw in the river. He had regarded the threat and action as necessary to expel recurring, unwanted flashbacks; but Tre was a hoarder and wouldn't consider it and never allowed Rick unaccompanied access to the faded red cooler. When the occasional banter came up, Tre advised that Rick should keep it with him at the office; Schooner was old and provided little protection. Rick refused without fail, and always for the same reasons. Tre would respect the boundary but also remind his friend that the gun would be well cared for and ready for him if ever needed.

Grimacing, Rick retrieved the case with his good arm and placed it on the cooler. He faltered opening the top. A Colt M1911 pistol lay on a bed of stained seat foam; the valued sidearm Adrian believed his friend should be able to keep—the magic Adrian had worked to make it happen. Rick stared, facing it for the first time in thirty-five years.

His phone buzzed, jarring the stillness. Rick read the message, and his anxious eyes rose instantly. He searched the darkness downriver toward the marina, then reached for the old binoculars hanging from a craggy branch propping the canopy. Lifting them with one hand, he strained to focus through the office's two small windows. The single-bulb lamp still shone. Rick spotted Allie sitting at his desk, but he couldn't find Beth. He clenched his teeth and forced his other hand to raise, steadying the casing. A man crossed in front of the window but the pain jabbed abruptly, forcing Rick to lower his arm.

He let the binoculars fall and spun, his panicked eyes landing on the rifle. He stumbled to it, yanked the cover away and lowered to the ground, letting the loud growl escape. Lying close, unaware, he reached for the rifle stock first. The *short, muffled crack* sounded in both ears, shattering his silence and slowly building to echoes in his mind. His breath halted instantly. Unable to move, he fixated on the trigger, helpless against the gripping swarm of demons. He dropped his head and squeezed his eyes closed. The phone buzzed again. Rick filled his lungs and reached for a piece of driftwood, swallowing the scream as he swung it desperately against the wound. The shadowy visions scattered. He collapsed over onto his back, staring at the black sky, his chest rising in erratic rhythm. Precious time slipped away as he listened for the past. Gradually, he clenched his fists and rolled back, his mind thankfully quiet.

He clutched the rifle to steady it, eyeing through the scope, hopeful the old sight could find enough light—hoping for the clear view he needed. Faint images appeared, drifting in and out of focus. He trained on the window, not having to wait before the man reappeared. Rick couldn't recognize the face. He instinctively readied his finger on the trigger, captive to the terrorizing images threatening Allie. The man jerked around as Beth lunged between them. Rick saw the gun rise and then the fierce swing across Beth's head; she fell instantly and vanished. Sweat ran across Rick's hand. He tried to balance the rifle, but the pain pulsed fiercely. He held the man in crosshairs, his finger twitching. The rifle's aim wandered. It was too far. Rick flinched, his mind swarmed with tragic flashes of what a failed shot would mean. He pulled back slowly, shaking his head in jerking motions, trying to clear it, hoping steadiness would find him. He looked into the sight once more. Beth was gone. Allie leaned forward, only partially visible.

Rick struggled to his feet. A wave of nausea rushed through him. He leaned over, heaving, his body desperate to expel the panic. He waited for the adrenaline to surge, then staggered to the cooler and retrieved the gun. Clutching it, he hurried to the boat. Blocking out the wound, he grabbed the starter cord with his right hand and pulled. The immediate burn emptied his lungs. He gasped for air quickly, then forced another pull. The motor caught and sputtered to life. He pushed off and headed the bow across the remnants of the light westerly. Rick opened up the throttle, stomping his foot on the floorboards, imploring the old skiff to push faster through the small chop. His fixation held on the light in the office window as he reached down to open the case.

Southeast Boulevard ran north-south along the crest of the hill overlooking M Street, SE, and the marina below. A half dozen cars typically sat parked on the west shoulder at night, illegally but usually tolerated as overflow parking for the full residential streets beyond the cemetery entrance. Ron's Four Runner was one of them, tucked into the last space fifty feet past the entrance to the path. Leah crept up behind and shut off the engine. She took time focusing on the mirrors and combed the dark street for any movement.

Thirty minutes before, she had heard what she needed from Ron: Allie and Rick were there at the marina. A minute later and the text would have been too late; Leah had grown impatient waiting. Having seen the truck at Sarah's house in Southeast, she entered through the gate and into the backyard, following the same path she had taken a week ago in her search for the box. Standing again in shadow behind the small shed, she stared intently through the sliding doors, locked on Sarah and Lou Cromwell at the kitchen island and waiting for any sign of Rick Larson or Allie. Leah had come prepared to wait only so long before forcing her way in for confirmation. It wasn't her first choice; it would present complications she hoped to avoid, but she intended to secure Allie this evening. How Michelle Baxter chose to deal with Rick Larson and Chris was no longer her concern. The low counter lighting did little to illuminate Leah's presence. She stood poised in the darkness not forty feet from the kitchen door, gun drawn, calculating her careful steps across the patio, when Ron's text vibrated with the short message. Leah exhaled and retraced quickly to her car. Driving to the marina, she had dialed Ron repeatedly, but each call dropped. She followed with urgent texts, 'eyes only', but received no response. Growing anxious, she centered on her options: *Collateral damage was never going to include the Sheridan girl.* Leah had quickly made her decision and swerved into the empty left lane, racing down Pennsylvania Avenue toward the marina.

~

Leah got out, closed her door gently, and surveilled the area once more. The quiet street stood empty. She started toward the path, slowing at Ron's car windows to peek inside. She approached the dark opening into the thicket, and paused to peer down the hill toward the marina. The sparse light from front porches and streetlights behind her disappeared not far into the path. Leah checked the small shoulder bag for her gun and stepped into the void.

Chapter 49

Rick shut down the motor as the skiff slid closer to the pier, the west wind carrying the last exhaust fumes and smoke away from the office. He coasted silently up to the transom of *MORNING STAR*. Relieved, he extended his good arm, letting his hand slide gently across the letters. Within seconds he had tied off on the port side. The office door was less than a hundred feet away. Rick stole down the pier and hesitated at the corner, his chest pounding as he listened. He searched the property for any sign of the man he had seen. He took two steps and leaned to peek in through the window. Beth sat slumped in a chair; Allie tended to her forehead. Rick blocked the jabbing across his shoulder, ducked the window, and stepped carefully around to the office entrance. With his back to the door, he examined the marina a last time, hunting for the threatening presence Detective Ward cautioned might appear. The same darkness he stared into had provided him with complete refuge for a very long time. This evening though, the stillness and deep blackness of shadows felt very different. Rick knew what occupied every corner of his property, but he felt the threat's presence, certain it had invaded and found a place to hide, a place he didn't recall. He believed what the dark river had revealed through the old rifle's scope: *Tre's eyes*, he sensed. But where was it? He scanned frantically but witnessed only the grim surroundings. Reaching for the knob, his beaten mind began to question the danger as illusion.

Rick opened the door slowly, the old gun ready. He entered with quiet steps, combing the cluttered office for the man, his eyes landing quickly on Beth's bleeding forehead. His face tensed. "Where is he?" he growled, deadbolting the door behind him.

"Looking for you."

"Your pistol—"

Beth shook her head.

Allie rushed to Rick, her voice breaking. "We didn't know where you were. We tried to get out the back to *MORNING STAR*, but he hit Beth so hard. I told him you were close—"

"Allie!" Beth forced herself to stand, holding the cloth to her head. "I'm okay."

Rick watched helplessly, anguished that he had endangered his daughter once again. He crossed the creaking floor to her.

In an instant, the office door burst open, splintering the tired wood and slamming back against the rusty hinges. Ron rushed through, flashing his gun across the room. Rick grabbed Allie and pulled her close to Beth, the three of them ducking as Ron fired one silenced shot into the wall above their heads. They froze, backed into the corner. Rick slowly faced him, holding Allie and Beth behind with his wounded arm. In the other, he held the Colt pistol, fighting to steady it on Ron's head.

Ron twisted his lips into a cruel smile. "Thanks for bringing that, Larson. I think I'll be able to make good use of it. So much cleaner to use your gun on Allie. Helps the story come together."

Rick's heart pounded. His arm weakened.

"Chris sends his condolences." Ron sneered. "He's officially closing the case on the disappearance and sad passing of Allison Sheridan tonight."

Rick grimaced, forcing himself to raise the gun. The instant pain erupted a fierce howl that echoed. Without warning, two quick thuds sounded. Rick didn't hear the shots. He only saw the vacant expression on Ron's face suddenly change; the eyes lost in disbelief. Ron's hand fell. The gun dropped to the floor as he collapsed forward into the office. Rick heard steps outside, approaching fast across the gravel. A stocky man slipped through the open door and crouched slightly; his gun ready. His eyes darted around the room as he knelt to check Ron. He straightened and moved quickly toward Allie as another man appeared in the doorway, holding his back to them and a watchful glare into the darkness.

The man stood close, his voice comforting. "Ms. Sheridan, are you okay?"

Allie stared at him, both arms limp by her side.

"We work for your father. He's not far away. We're going to take you to him."

Allie crept next to Rick. "I'm not going home!" Her fearful eyes raised to his.

"Not there," the man said. "Another place. He'll be waiting for you. We need to go right now."

Allie looked to Rick, tears starting.

"It's okay," he said. "Go with them. You'll be safe."

Allie wrapped both arms tenderly around Rick, holding him close. He stiffened from the pain but managed to lift his good arm to her back.

The man reached out, gently encouraging her. "Ms. Sheridan, we have to leave now." He glanced at Ron's body and pivoted to Rick. "We found the car. We're certain he was alone, but we're taking one last sweep." He eyed Rick's bleeding shoulder. "The police are on their way, an ambulance, too. Will you be alright?"

"Yeah."

"Mr. Larson, Ben asks that you please let him speak to the details. Tomorrow." He stepped aside for Allie. "Ms. Sheridan, if you would."

Allie hesitated, startled as the one at the door called, "Clear." Within seconds, they had disappeared across the dark lot.

Rick stepped to the open door, and stared after them. Lost for a long moment, he finally managed quiet words to his friend. "All is well, Tre. She's safe now."

Beth moved close behind Rick and put her hand on his back.

He shook his head. "Ben told me he would have people here—I never saw them." He turned to his daughter, his softened gaze falling to her forehead. "My God, I'm sorry. How is it?"

"I'm fine," Beth said. "I was moving."

Rick extended a gentle hand to her cut, seeing his wife's eyes looking back at him. "Who taught you that?"

"Life," she said softly. "That poor girl." She nodded, letting a relieved smile appear.

"You should never have been a part of this."

"Not the reunion I imagined. How's your shoulder?"

"Tre's a better shot."

She sighed. "Dear, Tre."

They held their stare a while, strangely familiar eyes searching for expressions of an unimagined beginning. Beth let her head fall gently to his shoulder. The sound of far-off sirens broke the dark silence.

"Time to get you to a hospital."

Rick exhaled deeply. "Soon. You first."

~

The shed's side door stood open, pulled back against the metal panels, and held in place by rusty wire wrapped around the knob. The yellow light over the door flickered. Minutes ago, Leah had slipped through the doorway as Rick came around the corner of the office. She had watched Ron appear out of the shadows and hurry across the lot to follow him inside. Incensed immediately with his decision to engage, she started after them but pulled up quickly as the muffled shots fired. She recoiled deeper into the doorway's small opening, staring from the darkness toward the office door. Ron lay lifeless. Soon, two men guided Allie across the lot and north on M Street, SE, toward *Sea Keepers*. Stunned, Leah waited, alert for any movement from Ron. The sound of strong engines broke her attention as two SUVs raced past the marina entrance. Sirens in the distance followed. She shook her head, refocusing on the office; Rick Larson filled the doorway, motionless, surveying the night. Leah retreated further into the shed, her vision slowly adjusting in the shadows. She made her way to the bench seat, the sirens drawing closer. Frantically, she reached into her bag and pulled out Chris' gun and the thumb drive, both tightly wrapped in a cotton rag. She laid them down on the shattered picture frame in the corner of the worn vinyl, then cautiously hurried around the disarray of parts toward the door. Within minutes, she stumbled across the tracks and escaped into the path's blackness again, seconds before the first two police cars braked and turned hard into the marina lot.

Chapter 50

Chris stood on the balcony casting a lost expression across the river. The glass of bourbon sat balanced on the corner railing post. He reached for it, as he had already done too many times that long evening, and raised his unsteady hand for a slow drink. His eyes closed and he swayed, immediately needing to catch his balance against the small wrought iron table. Forcing himself, he checked the burner phone again for messages. 4:15 a.m. and nothing from Ron. He pulled out his personal phone as well, only to be left staring at a blank screen. Lifting his glass again, he turned back to the Potomac. An hour earlier he had stared upriver in awe upon his city and the ever-present nighttime shimmer across its embracing waters. Now, he gazed blankly at the same water disappearing into darkness, imagining he saw the mouth of the Anacostia bend east at Buzzard Point, beginning its lonely meander to the north along the forsaken M Street, SE, past the dying marinas, into the unyielding blackness. The images filled his desperate mind and left him to contemplate why salvation along the river had not come for him this night.

Chris downed the last inch of bourbon and hurled the glass across the buffer of marsh. Returning to the decision he had made hours ago, he drew a deep breath and dialed Adrian's private line.

~

Two pre-dawn delivery trucks had already come and gone in

the dark alley behind 20858 K Street. The police cruiser pulled up and stopped under a shallow canopy. Detective Ward and Special Agent Parsons got out on the curb side. Rick struggled with his arm but finally got the driver's side rear door open. The blank metal service door to the building opened suddenly, and they were ushered in by two security officers. The patrol officer followed. They were led down the delivery entrance corridor to the freight elevator next to the electric room. Rick leaned against the back wall of the cab, favoring his right shoulder.

"How's it feeling?" Ward asked.

"Been a long time since I've been shot. Not my favorite thing."

"You should be at the hospital."

Rick nodded. "It's on the list."

"We're spending too much time together. You know that don't you?"

Rick managed to smile. "Been a busy night, but Allie's safe."

"Thanks to you."

"Thanks to her father."

The doors opened on the top floor, and they moved into another isolated corridor behind the building's core. Parsons took long strides, checking his watch twice as they hurried to the fifth door and entered along the rear wall of a small conference room. A young woman sat at the only table, working her laptop keys efficiently, looking back and forth between her screen and the large monitor on the wall. The image showed Adrian's adjoining corner office. She adjusted the brightness and tested the audio. Satisfied with the preparations, she stood and walked out the same door. A selection of beverages and pastries filled one end of the sidewall cabinet. The patrol officer casually considered the choices, nodding his appreciation. Ward leaned against the wall. Rick chose coffee and settled into one of the chairs.

Agent Parsons paced, watching Rick from across the table. "That was a nice present someone left you on the boat seat, Larson, but we need more. The gun is unregistered, and it's been wiped; we'll still try for prints, though. And forensics is all over the garage; we should get the bullets. The jump drive: it's something, but it doesn't put him in the room." Parsons stopped across from Rick, shaking his head. "Like I said, we need more, but we give this only a couple of minutes. If it's not going anywhere with Adrian, we continue the discussion with Mr. Evans downtown. Larson, I may want him to see you, but *do not* come in that room unless I signal for you." Parsons' brows closed. "Understood? Open the door and make an appearance. That's it. With any luck, we get something from the guy: a reaction, a comment. Something. He may think you're dead."

The arrest warrant for Chris had been issued at 3:00 a.m. The police arrived at his home in Chevy Chase a half hour later, only to learn from the au pair that his wife and children were in New England for the weekend. She had no idea where Chris was. The search continued to the firm's private condo in southwest, DC, without success. Detective Ward got the lead shortly after 5:00—the call from Adrian, but with no information as to the whereabouts of Chris Evans, only the requested meeting time.

Adrian opened the conference room door from his office. Seeing Rick, he released a deep sigh. Rick sat at the table, his right arm supported in a padded sling, compliments of the paramedics who arrived at the marina four hours ago. Adrian shook his head and took a chair across from him.

Rick leaned back and sipped his coffee, meeting his friend's eyes. "Just like old times, huh?"

"Shouldn't you be in some emergency room?"

"I keep hearing that."

Adrian frowned. "Sounds like you had a big night, brother."

"Small price," Rick said. "Allie's safe. That's the good part. What time are you meeting our friend?"

"He called me at 4:30. Started off rambling, but you could hear the scared voice on the other end. He got to my favorite part, where he said you took a shot at him but missed. Lucky it wasn't Tre he bumped into, right? Chris kept going on. Said all of it; accused you of kidnapping and trying to kill Allie. It was tough to listen to, and I let him know I wasn't doing this over the phone. I cut him off and told him to get his ass in here early. He said seven. That ended the call."

Adrian leaned back and frowned. "Then I tried to reach you for some truth. Dead phone, though. What a surprise. Bobby was my back- up. He filled me in. Damn, what a night, Rick."

Rick tilted his head to Detective Ward, still standing against the wall. "When do I get to start calling you Bobby?"

Ward glanced up from his phone and shook his head. "Let's give that some more time." He didn't hide the smile and turned to take a call.

Adrian pulled forward and rested his arms on the conference table. "I'm sorry, Rick. Dammit. Chris has always been ambitious, but how in the hell does that translate into all of this? Never could've imagined, I just missed it. You know I'd like this one back."

Rick leaned forward and extended his good arm, resting his hand on Adrian's. "He's not gonna hurt Allie again, or anyone else. It's good."

Detective Ward finished the call and stepped toward the table. "Okay, we're up. Evans is in the lobby. Remember Adrian, don't give him anything; you haven't heard a word. Hopefully, Evans hasn't either."

On the days Adrian Dumars came into his office, he rarely arrived before 10:00 a.m. He didn't often witness the dramatic early morning views. Waiting for Chris, though, he stood close to the glass corner, Rick's favorite spot, appreciating the layers of dark and pink clouds slowly moving east. Nancy knocked at 7:05. Adrian spun as the door pushed open. She held her hand on the knob, anxious to show in Chris and then leave.

Adrian positioned himself next to one of the couches in the corner. Chris strode to the center of the large office, his nervous look bouncing around the room.

Adrian frowned. "You look like hell. What was all that about last night? You wanna start again?"

Adrian settled into the couch. Chris crossed the floor and took a leather chair.

Adrian drummed his fingers along the back cushions. "So?"

Chris coughed and caught Adrian's stare but hunted for distraction instantly. Landing his gaze on the skyline, he rubbed the back of his neck with shaking hands and said, "I need you to help me get out in front of something, Adrian . . . it's not good. It's Larson. He kidnapped Allie. I knew he was involved."

Adrian offered nothing.

"I'm pretty sure he's had her this whole time."

"Watch it, Chris—"

"Adrian! They were here last night, late! Both of them in the garage. Allie found me just as I was leaving. She came to me, upset. She was panicked. Crying that she trusted me." He averted his eyes, talking faster. "She'd gotten away from Larson somehow, I don't know. There wasn't time to talk; he followed her there, too. Chasing her. He had a gun, and I tried to get Allie to the car. There were shots. Larson fired at us first and I tried to protect her. I think I hit him. He grabbed her and they were gone."

Adrian folded his arms. "You know who you're talking about, right? My best friend?"

Chris blurted, "It's not about your burned-out war buddy anymore, Adrian. This is about Allie!" He pushed out of the chair abruptly. "If it's a problem for you with Larson, I can take this to the police! I came to you first out of respect, for this firm and for our client."

"Chris, take it easy. Ward will be our first call, but why didn't you go to him last night?"

Chris rubbed both temples and lowered his head. "I shot a man, Adrian! And I lost Allie, too." He wavered. "It was late, I knew I needed to talk to the senator. I called her first. She was anxious and needed to stay on the call. She said she would handle things with the police." He flashed Adrian a quick look. "I'm surprised you haven't heard from her."

Adrian shook his head. "Not a word." He pushed off on both knees and rose slowly from the couch. Lifting his chin, he glared down at Chris. "So, what you're saying is, you shot my war buddy."

Chris erupted. His jaw clenched in a menacing scowl as he moved toward Adrian, pulling up inches away. "I had no choice, Goddammit! Self-defense! I said I was protecting Allie!"

Ward and Parsons turned from the conference room screen and exchanged nods.

Detective Ward looked at Rick, "That's why your friend makes the big bucks."

"Okay," Parsons said. "That's it. Let's go. He yanked the door open. Ward followed him through. The patrol officer came last, gun drawn.

Adrian headed toward the conference room door as the three

rushed Chris. Instantly, they had his upper body pinned across the large desk. Chris resisted, jerking his hands free and twisting to Ward, but Parsons slammed a forearm against his back, pushing him down again. They frisked him, found the gun in his back holster, and read him his rights. As Parsons reached for handcuffs, the conference room door flew open. Rick stood in full view. Chris instantly thrashed against the agent's strong grip, straining to turn his head, his eyes narrowing. Rick crossed the room, locking a fierce stare on him. Chris growled and fought to spin away. He made two steps toward Adrian before Ward grabbed him. Adrian moved in front of Rick; his large arm extended to block his friend's advance.

"You're fucking kidding me!" Chris' frantic look darted back and forth between them. "I don't believe this, Adrian! I trusted you! I should have known you'd buy his bullshit."

Ward and Parsons wrestled Chris back to the desk and cuffed him. The patrol officer grabbed his arm, pulling him forcefully toward the door. Rick stepped in front of them.

"Larson!" Parsons's voice boomed across the room.

Chris seethed, his face red and sweaty. Rick pushed in close, studying the same soulless eyes he had defied on the pier—the same darkness Tre must have seen.

"I said last night you don't get away with this, Evans."

"We'll see. I thought for sure you'd bleed out."

Rick pulled back a step, raising a hand to his shoulder. "This? Oh, please. Maybe next time, Chris. Marksmanship takes practice, or the will. Tre could've helped you work on that."

Adrian closed and reached for Rick's arm. "C'mon brother, it's done."

Rick stepped aside as the patrol officer pushed past. Chris' roared, "This won't go well for you, old man!"

Rick spun and took a step after him. "Old man?" he said

defiantly. "You talking to me, Schooner or the tree?"

Chris' face contorted. His curious gape held as the officer forced him through the door.

Chapter 51

Chris Evans' vacant expression showed through the rear window of the cruiser as Special Agent Parsons shook Detective Ward's hand.

"Nice work, Detective." Parsons hurriedly pulled open the car door. "See you at the station."

Ward took a call as he watched the cruiser accelerate down the alley. The Land Rover's idle rumbled. Kate stood next to the driver's door. Ben Sheridan leaned against the hood, arms folded, with Rick next to him and Adrian close by, teetering on the curb.

Rick said, "Allie may be ready to share what happened, Ben."

"I hope so."

"I know someone. She's amazing. She could help or help you find the right person. Only if you need a place to start."

"Thanks, Rick."

Detective Ward walked over, nodding his head in approval of the morning's work. Ben reached out to shake his hand.

"How's Allie doing?" Ward asked.

"Better. Resting, somewhere safe. Thank you, Detective, for everything."

"She has a difficult road ahead."

"Yes, she does. I know you need a statement from her, but we're starting with her doctors first, this afternoon. I assumed that would be fine."

"Of course. Let me know. Sooner is better, but we've got plenty to get us started."

Ben turned back to Rick and inhaled deeply, his face showing little color. Rick saw exhaustion, relief, and remnants of worry clouded across his eyes and expression.

Ben extended a hand to Rick's good shoulder. "I'm glad she has you."

"You made the right call, Ben. You knew."

He stumbled back a step. "We'll talk soon."

"Go be with your daughter; she needs you."

Ben nodded and shook Adrian's hand as Kate held his door. As they drove off, Adrian and Detective Ward moved close to Rick.

Watching down the alley, he said, "Think it's enough?"

Ward shrugged. "Hope so. We've got the ring now, thanks to you. We'll get DNA. And the drive still tells a pretty compelling story. With statements from the two of you, we should be fine."

Adrian said, "He has a lot of horsepower behind him, Bobby, so be careful and cross your T's. If I can do anything, just pick up the phone."

"Count on it. But we may have something else—Leah Benning. I know you've both had the pleasure. I heard from her, and she wants to talk. About Allie."

Adrian folded his arms. "She'll want a deal."

"We'll see." Ward checked his phone. "Should know soon enough. I need to get going." He paused, sharing a look with each of them. "I'm sorry about, Tre. I've never seen closer friends. Thank you all for your service."

Adrian and Rick glanced at each other, sharing the memory. Rick extended his hand. "You too, Detective. Adrian told me you were a good man, and he always speaks the truth. Thank you, Bobby."

Ward smiled. "I guess it's time." He winked at Adrian. "Mr.

Dumars, it's been a pleasure. I'll let you know what Leah has."

"Should be interesting. So, how about one last favor, Detective Ward?"

"Detective Ward?" he said, grinning. "I kind of like that. Name it."

Adrian put his arm around Rick. "This man could really use a ride to the hospital."

Ward chuckled and moved to open the car door. He gestured the offer to Rick. "About time. C'mon, Sergeant."

Chapter 52

Adrian and Rick stood alone at the end of Pier D. The sun hung suspended low above the Ward 6 neighborhood rooftops, high on the hill to the west. Familiar light crept through the old tugboat's broken windows. The late June's southerly breathed, and they watched faint reflections dance across the water toward them.

"Seems empty around here without *MORNING STAR*," Adrian said. "And Allie."

"They took her up north. She and her dad left yesterday."

Adrian nodded. "A new start."

"For all of us, right?"

"Yeah. Including our friend Evans. Did you hear?"

"Ben told me."

"He'll be gone for a good long while."

"I think that gave Allie some comfort." Rick sighed. "There's still a lot for her to work through, but it's a start. Thankfully, she's in good hands now."

"Ward still thinks Evans did the damage to Tre. He's not letting that go."

"Like you said, he's a good man."

"Ben mention anything to you about Baxter? Didn't really work out too well for our senator." Adrian clapped his hands. "I know she likes the spotlight; not so sure she's too pleased with where the current one is shining, though. I hear she is not a happy camper."

"Karma will bite you in the ass if you step on it. At least it's something. Hopefully her day in court is not far behind."

"That one's going to be a battle." Adrian turned to look across the marina property and down the shoreline. "You won't recognize this piece of history in five years." He paused. "For better or for worse."

Rick's gaze landed on the Old Man. The same roots maintained their defiant grasp along the tenuous shoreline edge, contesting with large rocks for connection to the river's bottom, the tangle reminding the waters of its enduring determination to survive. The rising breeze teased the branches to sway, but the Old Man resisted. Outwardly, he had decided long ago that growing tall was not as important as growing strong; his branches were all thick, though not as long as they might have been, with the tree having survived for so many years. More spirited rushes of wind would be needed to make him dance.

"We need to save the Old Man, D."

"I know, we promised Tre, and I'm doing my best. Maybe, though, this was just their time. Both of them."

"I don't know, brother, this one goes to your legacy. No pressure, but I think you got this."

"Glad there's no pressure." Adrian laid his hand on Rick's shoulder. "You and Tre had a good long run here."

"Was the three of us, D; wouldn't have happened without you."

"You gonna miss it?"

"I already do." Rick lowered his head. "I miss my friend. I'm glad I still have you. But I know what's coming; I'm gonna miss you, too. Seems our journey together has run its course."

"All things pass away, brother, but not everything at once." Adrian's head tilted from side to side as a grin returned. "Seems this is as good a time as any," he teased. "Thought I'd let you know, I'm calling it quits soon."

Rick's eyebrows raised.

"And that means lots of free time coming my way. You may see more of me than you want."

Rick nodded his approval. "That's not possible, D." Rick reached for his hand. "I'm happy for you, brother. You've done a lot of good for this world."

"Yeah, we'll see. It's a big step. But this isn't good-bye just yet; there's still plenty to do around here that needs your expertise before we back out of that gate for the last time. A few million knickknacks still there in what's left of that old shed. And the Constellation—and that old Lyman."

"Yeah, it's a lot."

"How's it going on the island?"

"Done. Like he was never there." Rick's voice cracked. "I have some things you might want to keep."

Schooner lay at Rick's feet, his belly warmed by the decking. For some time, Rick and Adrian stood close to each other, attentive to Tre's serene energy across the water.

Adrian finally reached down for the bag sitting next to him on the pier. "Brought us something." He pulled out a small flask and a bottle of iced tea, handing it to Rick. Then he reached in again and pulled out a round, brass urn.

Rick's voice cracked. "Hey, there he is." He bit his lip and had to look away.

Adrian watched his friend. "Allie wasn't ready for this, was she?"

"Nope," Rick said softly. "It's okay, though." He stared back at the urn, shaking his head slowly. "Thank you, my friend. Thanks for taking care of that."

"A little here, maybe some by the shed?"

"That's perfect." Rick glanced upriver. "And some for the island. South wind's blowing straight down." He faltered. "He'll enjoy the adventure. Sure beats the hell out of that worn out skiff."

Delia approached quietly, drawing near behind them.

"How about some for the Old Man, too?" she pronounced.

Adrian spun and beamed. "Hey, Delia! You just get here, young lady? Perfect timing: we were just talking about that old gentleman. Tre did love that tree, didn't he? Think it's only right they share that ground a while longer."

Rick tilted his head and looked past them to the willful cherry clinging to the river's edge, knowing it, too, may perish soon.

Delia reached out, playfully rubbing his healing shoulder. "Speaking of old men, how's it feeling, Richard?"

"Both of us have some scars, seems they come with the stories."

Adrian opened the bag and handed Delia a beer. "You know I'd never forget about you, my dear." He held up his flask. Rick tapped with his bottle of tea.

"Nice afternoon to be together," Delia said quietly.

Adrian moved across the pier and pulled the plastic bag open. They watched the dusting of ashes float lightly down, spreading across the water in a faint blanket.

Rick stepped to the edge next to him. "You sure you're good with me taking care of the rest?"

"Wasn't anyone more important to Tre than you, brother. He trusts you. Not even a question for me."

"I hope so."

For minutes, they watched upriver, content in silent witness to Tre's last journey to the island.

Adrian eventually broke the peace. "Ready to walk?" He turned to Rick. "See you back here in a month. Still lots to do, right?"

"Maybe sooner."

Delia held a hand on both of them, squinting into the day's last sunlight. "If you're working 'round here, put me down for the catering; you seniors gotta keep your strength up." She leaned over and unzipped her backpack, mumbling as she rummaged through the largest pocket. "Now, you two wait *just* a minute . . ." She pulled out two red napkins, both folded into precise triangles. Her eyes started to water as she handed one to each of them.

"Gift from, Fay," she said.

"Fay's still kickin'?" Adrian chuckled. "Well, good for her."

"Oh, she is indeed. But you never know for how long, so go on now and open."

Rick and Adrian traded quick looks, then pulled back the corners. The sun quickly found the medals' shiny gold and bronze. Shimmers winked up at them.

Delia extended a hand to each and said, "Fay was humbled to see these in the collection plate not long ago. Said she talked to the Big Guy, and received only thanks, His specialty. But apparently, He needs nothing more from those two fine men and wants you both to keep these safe for Him. Fay's very words." Delia's eyes twinkled. "But He does wanna hold onto that beautiful box."

Chapter 53

The house on Water's Edge Drive in Rockland, Maine, was the only place Sarah had been willing to consider. If Fate had called her to spend time away from DC and her daughter, the location needed to be special, and they found it. The house held a long history, wear that showed in places, but overall, it was well cared for, with each space comfortably furnished. Neighbors' homes stood generously spaced along the quiet road; a half dozen houses, two longtime residents, the others seasonal. Rick liked the privacy and the peace. The house faced north across the expansive water, only a quarter mile from Beth and Karen's spot farther out the peninsula to the east.

The owners offered the property for sale or as a rent-to-buy if desired, and although Sarah had her checkbook ready, she yielded to Rick's conservative vote to start with a rental contract. She was growing accustomed to his pace through life, appreciating the value of taking things slowly in the beginning, even at their age. Beth liked the baby-steps approach as well, which nevertheless was encouraging to Rick, as any steps with his daughter were welcome. Sarah's decision to move came as a surprise to Lou, but she acquiesced soon enough, picked out their room for visits with Noah and embraced the adventure for her mother. Schooner had closed the deal for them, walking out to the bluff on their first visit and planting himself decidedly in the grass, holding his nose up to the story-filled ocean breezes.

Rick and Sarah parked in the city lot and strolled down the sidewalk to *Morning's Buns*. They stopped at the corner, and Sarah reached both hands to his face, feeling the joy in his new energy.

She kissed him and said, "You spent your life taking care of a friend; now it's your turn. This is going to be a good day for you, Mr. Larson. Text me later?" She whirled and floated off down the sidewalk, waving back over her shoulder.

Rick returned the wave, savoring the view of her cheerful stroll, before moving through the gate and onto the patio. He sat in the same chair at the same round corner table, as he had each day for the past month, waiting for Beth to join him. Sometimes they sat together for an hour or more; sometimes five minutes was all she could spare. It didn't matter to Rick how long; he was thankful for each second. Opening up and sharing had come more easily with each morning visit, though occasionally, anxious thoughts would intrude on these times with his daughter. So much of it was unfamiliar to him. So much had been missed. He confessed to her about experiencing flashes of panic with not having enough time left. In response, Beth had gifted him with a vision of life lived in the embrace of contentment, in each moment, with no expectations for the future. Long ago, she had survived discovering this awareness. Now, the invitation was extended to her father, to join in the only journey she could take with him right now.

Beth hurried through the door carrying Rick's coffee, riveted to her phone. Rick could not recall her ever approaching with such urgency. A bad sign, he thought. He waited anxiously for her attention.

"The smaller oven just went out," she finally said, shaking her head, talking rapidly.

Rick relaxed. "Oh."

"We've been nursing it along; so much for that."

"Sorry." He pushed back Tre's boonie. "Good morning."

"Hey, if you can keep those big diesels running, this should be a piece of cake. Wanna take a look?"

"You trying to pull me out of retirement?"

A short chuckle came first. "Kidding," she said. "Listen, I have to call my supplier."

Beth turned, dialing as she headed to the door. She stopped after a few steps and spun back with a broadening smile. Rick didn't take his gaze off her. For a long moment, their fixed eyes witnessed the promise of a new story together.

Beth came back to the table and calmly leaned over to kiss her father on top of his hat. "See you tomorrow, Dad."

The words Rick had heard from her each day—thirty-five and counting—since he and Sarah had moved to Rockland; heartening words he had missed for too long.

Beth hurried to the door and held it for Allie, who balanced the tray holding his two blueberry muffins.

She presented them, offered the fist bump, and rested her hand on his shoulder. "How's it feeling today?"

"Every day's better."

"Always good news, old man." Allie winked and rubbed his back.

"Sounds like a busy morning. Can you still take the time?"

"I have all day." Allie grinned. "Don't have to be in California for another two weeks."

The late July breeze encouraged Rick and Allie as they ambled down the gangplank to the floating dock eight feet below. Schooner led the way, tentatively finding his confidence along the rocking boards. Fifty feet from the dock's end, the small Lyman Lapstrake rested gently against three bright blue fenders, nestled between two well-used work boats. Rick stopped to admire.

"Remember this old girl?"

Allie's forehead wrinkled. Rick enjoyed her study of the fresh white paint and glistening varnished wood, surprised though, with how long she took to assess the lovely craft. When Allie finally spun, he met her wide eyes with both palms turned up.

"Ta-da."

"No way!" She beamed. "Is this the same—"

"Told you she was on the list. Couldn't leave her there all alone." Rick pulled a crumpled brown paper lunch bag from his coat pocket and held it to Allie, inviting her to reach in.

"Can I look this time?" Allie laughed, slowly retrieving a boat key and float. Her mouth fell open. "Rick . . ."

"A present from Adrian and me." Rick reached into the bag and pulled out Allie's carved wooden box. "And from Tre."

Her eyes watered instantly as she took the box in both hands.

"Sarah kept it safe for you," Rick said.

"And Tre." Allie bit her lip and lowered her head. "I forgot," she murmured.

"No, you didn't; he'll never let you."

She ran her fingers over the carvings. "Thank you, Rick. For everything."

He rested a hand on her back, and gazed across the shimmering expanse of water. "There's an island, about a mile and a half out. Gentle breeze today. I thought that would be a nice place for our friend." He leaned in close. "Not as nice as the Anacostia, but in the neighborhood. He would like that."

Allie pressed against his shoulder and took a moment searching for the island. "Need a ride?" she finally teased, wiping her tears and holding up the key.

"You have room for all of us?"

They turned to Schooner. Having found his balance, the old Lab stood nobly, close to the dock's edge. He hovered over the Lyman's varnished gunwale, panting deeply, wagging his tail, watching every move Rick and Allie made, and waiting for the invitation.

THE END

Acknowledgements

I want to express my deepest appreciation to my friends and family, for only through your encouragement and generosity did this story find its way to the page. Thanks to my parents for their excitement and belief that this was possible—Jack, my eager boatyard adventurer, and Noma, my earliest beta reader. To Heather, my loving partner, for always inspiring me to stay focused on the important things, and for those twelfth-hour words of wisdom during edits; "Time to have the baby!" To my amazing sons, Ben and Nate, for always cheering me on.

Thank you Ellie Storck, Sarah Corley, Annabel Tierney, and my sister, Nancy Selden, for your generous reading and essential notes and comments. To Barbara Morrison, my heartfelt gratitude for being my editor and always just a phone call away. Through your insights and editorial wisdom, you made this story better. A special thanks to all of the team at Apprentice House Press for believing in this book. Kevin Atticks, Chase Lawson, Leo Arcelay-Christiano, and Cecelia Durborow, I am grateful for your kind invitation and guidance.

About the Author

Dave Strang began his writing journey with children's books and short stories, fortunate to be guided in his early endeavors by authors Peter Taylor and James Alan McPherson. *Eyes of the River* is his second novel and first published work. A story inspired many years ago when Dave and his father, a WWII veteran, first ventured into an aging marina along Washington, DC's Anacostia River and entered the *shed*. A treasure of boat parts, memories and the seeds of a story accompanied them home that day.

Dave lives with his wife in Annapolis, MD, where they raised two sons and several rescue labs, surrounded still by the collection of nautical gems discovered that spring afternoon with his fellow boat lover.

Apprentice House is the country's only campus-based, student-staffed book publishing company. Directed by professors and industry professionals, it is a nonprofit activity of the Communication Department at Loyola University Maryland.

Using state-of-the-art technology and an experiential learning model of education, Apprentice House publishes books in untraditional ways. This dual responsibility as publishers and educators creates an unprecedented collaborative environment among faculty and students, while teaching tomorrow's editors, designers, and marketers.

Eclectic and provocative, Apprentice House titles intend to entertain as well as spark dialogue on a variety of topics. Financial contributions to sustain the press's work are welcomed. Contributions are tax deductible to the fullest extent allowed by the IRS.

To learn more about Apprentice House books or to obtain submission guidelines, please visit www.apprenticehouse.com.

Apprentice House Press
Communication Department
Loyola University Maryland
4501 N. Charles Street
Baltimore, MD 21210
Ph: 410-617-5265
info@apprenticehouse.com • www.apprenticehouse.com

www.ingramcontent.com/pod-product-compliance
Lightning Source LLC
LaVergne TN
LVHW010558100826
845148LV00014B/2761

* 9 7 8 1 6 2 7 2 0 6 7 5 4 *